PLAY ME

ADRIANA LOCKE

UMBRELLA
PUBLISHING INC.

Published by Umbrella Publishing, Inc.

Paperback ISBN: 978-1-960355-38-6
Special Edition Paperback ISBN: 978-1-960355-39-3

Cover Design by Sarah Hansen, Okay Creations
Photography by Michelle Lancaster, @lanefotograf

BOOKS BY ADRIANA LOCKE

My Amazon Store

Signed Copies

Brewer Family Series

The Proposal | The Arrangement | The Invitation | The Merger |
The Situation

Carmichael Family Series

Flirt | Fling | Fluke | Flaunt | Flame

Landry Family Series

Sway | Swing | Switch | Swear | Swink | Sweet

Landry Family Security Series

Pulse

Gibson Boys Series

Crank | Craft | Cross | Crave | Crazy

The Mason Family Series

Restraint | The Relationship Pact | Reputation | Reckless |
Relentless | Resolution

The Peachwood Falls Series

Tempt | Truly

The Exception Series

The Exception | The Perception

Dogwood Lane Series

Tumble | Tangle | Trouble

CAST OF CHARACTERS

Gray Adler
Astrid Lawsen
Gianna Bardot
Audrey Van
Renn Brewer
Brooks Dempsey
Hartley Adler

PLAYLIST

Why Won't You Love Me - 5 Seconds of Summer
Complicated - Olivia O'Brien
Enemies - The Score
Breaking Me - Topic, A7S
Truth Hurts - Lizzo
Jack & Diane - John Mellencamp

🎶 Full playlist on Spotify 🎶

SYNOPSIS

He's supposed to be playing rugby—not playing *me*.

I didn't think it was possible to hate someone. Like utterly despise another human. Then **I was hired to babysit the Royals' newest star** and found out just how wrong I was.

My job should've been easy. Keep the hotshot on time and out of trouble. But that's hard to do when I dream of smothering him with his jersey.

Every day delivers a new reason to detest Gray Adler. His truck is the size of a whale, and he uses the horn like a weapon. *And, no, that's not a euphemism.* He can't manage a sentence without being rude. And the universe, in its cruelest joke, gave that tattooed, walking red flag the body of a Greek god.

Just when I finally get used to hating him, things take a turn.

A **scalding-hot, mind-blowing** *I can't do this with a man I work with* sort of turn.

Suddenly, those rough hands make my skin sizzle. His sinful smirks fade into grins just for me. And our banter shifts into something much more profound than it should.

But Gray Adler is hiding something. And when those secrets collide with my vulnerable heart, I ask myself an important question.

Is he finally telling me the truth, or am I still getting played?

CHAPTER
ONE

ASTRID

"Can you still track me?"

"That doesn't make me sound creepy at all," I say, watching dollar bills flow from my bank account into my gas tank. My compact car may not be flashy, but what it lacks in style, it makes up for in gas mileage. *Thank God.* "But, yes, I can see where you are unless you removed yourself from our friend circle in the app. Why?"

Gianna sighs. "Because I'm about to meet a guy in front of a defunct carpet store, and all I can think about is a scene in a horror movie where the killer asks the girl to help him load a rug. You can guess how that ends."

"I'd rather not." I release the trigger, let the residual drips of gas fall into my tank—*gotta get every penny's worth in this economy*—and return the dispenser to the pump.

The late morning is unseasonably warm for spring. Birds perch along the power lines, forming neat little rows overhead. The sky is cloudless, allowing the sun's bright rays to heat my face as I duck back into my car.

"Okay," I say, giving my friend all my attention once I'm settled in my seat. "Do you know this guy you're meeting?"

"Nope. Met him on Social last night."

"And why are you meeting him?"

She groans. "To buy a urinal."

"As one does."

"Don't be a smart-ass, Astrid."

I laugh. "I just wish this surprised me a little more. That's all."

I start the engine and wait for my phone to reconnect to Bluetooth.

Gianna and I have been friends since we were kids. A classmate put gum in her hair in first grade, so I dumped my juice on his crotch and made it look like he peed his pants. Turns out that juice on your pants is a much bigger travesty than gum in your hair in elementary school.

It also creates the best friendships, even if her dreamy Pisces tendencies occasionally drive my goal-oriented brain bananas.

"Finding a urinal has been on my bucket list for a long time," she says. "You'd be surprised how hard they are to find. And they're not cheap."

"At least tell me it's a new one." My response is met with silence. I rest my head against the seat and take a long breath. "Let me get this straight. You're meeting a stranger in an abandoned parking lot to buy a used urinal you found on the black market?"

"Don't say it like that."

"Why? Because it sounds utterly ridiculous?" I sigh, fastening my seat belt. "I love your love for art, but I really need you to implement more stranger-danger protocols—like not meeting strange men in strange places for strange items." I glance at the clock. "If you can wait an hour, I can go with you. I just have to take care of a few returns for my boss's wife, and then I can get away for a little while."

"Can't. I'm meeting him in fifteen minutes."

Oh, for the love of Pete.

I stare out my windshield and wonder if this is what parenting feels like. You watch someone you love toddle into the world, hoping they don't kill themselves. Over a urinal.

It's amazing humans still exist, especially ones like Gianna Bardot. That she's survived for the past twenty-seven years amazes me.

I grab my phone and find the app our friend group uses to share our locations.

"You're logged in," I say, watching her designated car emoji travel south out of the city. "I'm watching you now."

"Good. Okay. If you don't hear from me in twenty minutes, I've probably been stuffed in the back of a van. Literally, not figuratively, unfortunately."

I snort, glancing in the rearview mirror as a large black truck pulls in behind me. The engine rumbles, creating a low vibration that I feel in my bones. I narrow my eyes to see who's sitting in the driver's seat, but the window tint's too dark.

"What are you doing for dinner?" Gianna asks, pulling my attention back to our conversation.

I drop my phone in the cup holder. "No clue. I just finished breakfast."

"Just now? I've been up working since six thirty."

"I didn't say I just woke up." I've already done a load of laundry, loaded the dishwasher, and cleaned out two closets today. "Not only have I finished my chores and completed nearly all my tasks for Renn and Blakely for the day but I've also spent a couple of hours looking for a new side hustle."

"Your last side hustle just ended. Can't you take a few weeks off and relax for once?"

I wish. "No. If I have time on my hands, I need to pay down this debt faster. The interest is killing me."

Gianna sighs. "That means you don't read enough. If you read more books, you wouldn't have time to worry about your debt."

"That's a responsible take on things." I laugh. "Besides, I can't sit still long enough to read a book for fun."

"Audiobooks were made for a reason, Astrid."

"So were books about personal safety, but you ignore those."

She laughs. "Sometimes you have to risk things for art."

Her joy over this urinal and the sense of adventure she feels about the process brings a smile to my face.

If there were one thing, one habit, that I would adopt from someone else, it's Gianna's *passion*. She throws herself into random art pieces, recipes, and side quests she unearths as a wildly successful advice columnist. It's something I could never do. The lack of structure makes me itchy, and I feel the overwhelming need to put it all on a calendar … and take the fun out of it.

"Want to meet at Stupey's for overpriced sandwiches?" Gianna asks. "My treat since you bought last time. I think Audrey's going to be around this weekend. The three of us haven't been all together for two whole weeks."

"Sure." I glance back at the truck again. It's still behind me despite nearly every other pump available. *Weird.* I consider pointing out how aware I am of my surroundings and suggesting that Gianna do the same. But she's too fixated on the urinal to listen now. "I'll drop it in the chat, and we'll work it out."

"Sounds like a plan."

My boss's name flashes across my infotainment center. At the same time, the black truck revs its engine. *Is he revving that thing at me?*

"Hey, Renn's calling me," I say, glaring at the truck. "Text me when you secure the toilet and you're on your way home."

"Urinal, Astrid. *Ur-in-al.*"

I laugh. "Bye."

"Bye, friend."

I tap the button to accept Renn's call, push in the brake, and then move my hand to the gear shifter. But as soon as I touch the knob, the truck revs again—and that stops me in my tracks. *He's definitely revving his engine at me.*

"Hey, Renn," I say, watching the behemoth behind me. Irritation snakes its way down my spine. "What's up?"

"It's been a hell of a morning. I didn't catch you in the middle of anything, did I?"

"Nothing much. Just waiting out some guy who's overcompensating for something by having an extra-large truck."

Renn pauses. "Waiting him out? For what?"

"He pulled in right behind me even though every other pump but one is open. I'm at the gas station, by the way. And because I haven't rushed to get out of his way, he's revving his engine at me."

"*Oh.*"

"What can I do for you?"

"Don't get arrested? That would be great."

The engine roars again—louder this time.

"Can you hear that?" I ask, my fingers gripping the steering wheel.

"Yeah, I can. Are you able to leave?"

"Sure, I could. And I would if he hadn't tried to bully me." I roll my window down and hold my hand out, palm-side up. "Now, I'm going to sit here until he leaves."

"*Astrid.*"

A large, thick forearm sticks out of the driver's side window, mimicking my gesture. *Fucker.*

"Why did you say you called?" I ask, annoyance stinging my cheeks.

Renn sighs as if he doesn't know what to say. It's like a part of him wants to continue persuading me to leave, but the rest of him knows it's pointless—and that side is right. I'll gladly back down from a skirmish if I'm wrong. I'll even apologize. *But in this case?* I'm not. So I won't.

"I have a proposition to discuss with you," he says.

"That sounds vaguely interesting."

"Will you move?" a voice shouts from the truck.

I mute Renn. *"Yeah. When I'm ready!"* I yell back before unmuting my boss. "Do you want to discuss it now or later?"

"Do you think you can swing by my office this afternoon?" Renn asks.

"Some of us have things to do today!" he shouts again.

I hit mute and then stick my head out the window. "Then pick another pump!" I settle back in my seat and huff before unmuting Renn again. "Sure. I have a couple of errands to run for Blakely, and then I'll be free."

"That works."

A horn blasts out of nowhere, the sound echoing thanks to the awning covering the gas station. I jump, anger prickling my scalp, and unbuckle myself. *He did not just do that.* "I'll see you then."

"What's going on?" Renn asks.

"I gotta go."

"Astrid, what's happening?"

I pop the handle, and my door swings open. "This asshole just honked at me."

"Let it go."

"Thanks for the advice, Elsa," I say, my finger hovering over the button to end the call. "I'll let you know when I'm on my way. Talk soon."

I drop my fingertip against the red button, then fling my legs out of the car, slamming the door behind me. I storm toward the truck, my anger singeing the edges of my restraint.

My tennis shoes pound against the asphalt with more force than is probably necessary, but I can't help it. If there's one thing I hate more than anything, it's men who audaciously think that their penis gives them a free pass to act like a chump. It's like they believe that their five-incher has magical powers. In my twenty-eight years of life, I've never met a woman who claims a penis gave her more than a headache and, on the rare occasion, a semi-satisfying orgasm.

Heat billows from the front of the truck, blasting me as I march by. The top of the tires are waist-high, and I can't fathom why anyone driving in the city needs tires this big. It's obnoxious … kind of like the driver.

"Do you have a problem?" I yell over the sound coming from beneath the hood. The scent of gasoline and grease fills the air, stinging my nostrils. It crosses my mind for one quick, fleeting moment that this may not be significantly different from Gianna's meetup for the urinal.

I'll just have to be a hypocrite today.

I round the side mirror jutting out and come face-to-face with my nemesis. He stares down at me from his perch in the cab of the truck with a sardonic expression that sends my temper soaring.

He arches a thick brow, pinning me to the spot with deep, walnut-colored eyes. "Yeah, I do have a problem. You're blocking the pump."

"There are literally …" I peel my gaze from his and quickly count the vacant pumps. *All of them are open.* Every. Last. One. "You have nine different options. Pick another one."

"I want this one."

"You can't always get what you want."

His lips twitch. "True, because I'd also like to take that stick out of your ass, but that's probably off the table, too, huh?"

I gasp, startled by his crudeness. Surprise siphons the blood from my face. Words wedge themselves in my throat from the shock of the moment.

"You're a fucking asshole."

"I've been called worse," he says with a nonchalant shrug. "Will you move now?"

"I would've happily moved out of your way if you'd asked nicely. But you didn't," I say, pointing a finger at him. "Instead, you rolled up here in this ridiculous truck and revved your engine at me like some kind of threat."

He makes the cockiest face—quirked brow, subtle smirk—like I'm acting irrational, and he thinks it's funny.

"Then you honked your horn at me, which is unacceptable anywhere except maybe to avoid a collision." I'm fighting to stay calm. "You are rude and disrespectful, and I have a personal rule that I don't acquiesce to men who try to bully me."

"Wow." He grins, displaying a set of dimples. "Bully you? *Okay*. You realize that you were sitting in your little car, taking up real estate while you had social hour, right?"

"Not that it's any of your business, but I was talking to my boss."

The lively twinkle in his eye is like throwing fuel on my simmering fury. "Do it in the office, sweetheart. Not here."

"*Sweetheart*?" I bark, my eyes widening. "You will *never* get the pleasure of knowing me well enough to call me sweetheart."

"Thank God for small favors." The chuckle he only half-heartedly tries to suppress proves otherwise. "Know what I find interesting?" he asks, rolling his tongue along his bottom lip. "I find it interesting that you claim to be some kind of manners police when you're the one blocking the damn pump."

My hands go to my hips as I bite back the first thought that comes to mind because, unfortunately, I know he's *technically* right. It *is* bad manners to block a pump. But they say the devil is in the details, and I try to avoid the devil at all costs.

I take a breath, then wear the biggest, most facetious smile I can manage. "I'll leave when you ask nicely, *sweetheart*."

He rests one massive forearm along the window and gives me the most blasé look ever. I pointedly ignore his pouty bottom lip and the perfect amount of scruff peppering a rock-hard jawline. Instead, I remember his insolence.

"I should sit here all day just because you're a jerk," I say, unblinking.

He turns off his truck without breaking eye contact. "Fine by me. I have time today."

Before I can think of something quick-witted to say—*didn't he just say he has somewhere to be?*— an older sedan pulls up to the pump beside us, nearly clipping the bollards protecting the equipment. A small, older lady gets out, oblivious to the standoff happening feet from her, and waddles around the back of the car in her Velcro-strapped shoes. She fiddles with the pump, groaning as she tries to lift the nozzle from the machine. Whiffs of grandma perfume float in the air, and I suddenly crave snickerdoodles.

I fold my arms over my chest, unable to argue with this guy in front of somebody's grandma.

He sighs. "Move," he says more softly this time, bringing my attention to him once again.

I take a step back as the truck door swings open. He doesn't bother with the step rail but instead hops down with a natural ease. He doesn't bother to look my way either.

He's taller than average, which surprises me. Broad shoulders fill out a plain black T-shirt, and thick thighs stretch the denim covering them. Dark hair is cut close to his head. He carries himself with a confidence that's universally accepted as attractive—and it's such a shame.

Why waste a package like this on a guy with such a bad attitude?

"Are you doing okay over here?" he asks the woman like he wasn't just being awful to me five seconds ago. "These pumps can get a little tricky."

"Yes, they can." She sighs, clutching her pocketbook in her free hand. "I have a heck of a time wrangling these things. My arthritis is something awful. My John used to pump my gas for me, but he's been gone for twenty-three years now. Feels like yesterday sometimes."

"I'm not John, but I'd be happy to pump your gas for you today."

Oh, please.

I shuffle a bit closer so I can hear more clearly.

She coos, clearly smitten with him and his thoughtfulness. And, although she's getting played by Truck Boy, I can't blame her. He must seem genuinely sweet from her perspective. There's no way for her to know he's a fox in sheep's clothing.

"You don't mind?" she asks. "I don't want to take up too much of your time."

He glances at me out of the corner of his eye, his dimple shining in his cheek. "Not at all, ma'am. I'm going to be here a while anyway."

I glare at him.

"Oh, you're such a good boy. So many young men don't want to bother with an old woman like me." She loops her arm through his elbow, and they slowly move to the driver's side. "When you get to be my age, you feel like you don't belong in the world anymore. You can barely work the new gadgets, and everyone's so impatient with you. It's terrible."

"I'm sorry you feel that way," he says as he opens her car door.

I stand beside his truck and watch them, trying to make sense of this encounter. He flipped from prick to prince in five seconds flat. My mind spins in bewilderment.

"Wait just a second," the lady says, dropping into her seat with a huff. "I forgot to put my card in to pay."

"It's on me today," he says.

I roll my eyes so hard it hurts.

He comes back to the pump, his gaze leveling with mine. A smug grin is all it takes to send me back into a free fall. But, before I can get a word out, he steps to the left and out of sight.

My first instinct is to stand my ground and wait for him to finish. If I move, he wins. But with each second that passes without him in my line of sight, I think more clearly. And a glance around reminds me that I'm standing at a gas station, arguing with a stranger over a pump.

It's like a bucket of cold water being tossed on my head.

So what if he wants to be a child about this? I have errands to run ... and I'm getting off schedule.

"If you want to play games, Truck Boy, you'll have to find someone else to play with you," I say.

I throw my hair over my shoulder in a final act of defiance and march my way back to my car.

Take a deep breath, Astrid. Get out of fight or flight. It's over.

I fill my lungs again and slowly exhale.

At least my asshole quota has been met for the day, and it can only get better from here.

Thank God for that.

CHAPTER
TWO

ASTRID

The early afternoon is bright, flooding my boss's expansive office with light. Trophies from various rugby championships glimmer on the shelves behind his mahogany desk. His Most Valuable Player awards shine from their spot above a wet bar filled with pricey liquors and crystal drinkware that I've never seen him use. Plants dot the space, giving the gray walls and rich woods a pop of vibrance. The room screams serenity, wealth, and success.

It's almost rude.

"There you are," Renn says, leaning back in his oversized desk chair. The slight Australian accent he picked up during his overseas career still catches me off guard even after all these years. "Glad to see you didn't wind up in the county jail this afternoon."

"I'm not going to lie. It was a close call."

Memories of my encounter with Truck Boy trigger the muscles in my shoulders to tense again. *Just when I'd started to relax, too.*

If grudge-holding were a professional sport, I'd have an

office like Renn's. Tiaras would sit on my shelves, and scepters would hang over my wine rack filled with expensive reds and glass bottles of Coke. It might not scream serenity and wealth, but it would demonstrate my professional level of grudgery. I'm not exactly proud of that, but I've grown to accept it.

"Grab a seat," Renn says, motioning to the leather chair facing him.

I pull my clipboard out of my bag before I sit and get situated.

Most of the work I do for Renn or his family members is done virtually. If I need to pop into their homes or offices for something, they're usually away. I have to say, though, seeing Renn in person never fails to stagger me a bit. He's *that* handsome.

Perfect symmetry. Full lips. He has a regal air about him but also an approachability that makes him impossible not to love. Everyone loves Renn Brewer.

"I have a proposition for you," he says, running a hand through his tobacco-colored locks.

On the surface, his statement is routine. It's a typical exchange between a boss and his employee. But I've worked with Renn long enough to hear the emphasis on certain syllables and the touch of hesitance in the words. That only means one thing: this isn't going to be an innocuous proposal.

I lift a brow. "Usually, you just text those to me."

He smiles—but not the kind that floods me with the warm and fuzzies. This one tightens my stomach. This smile is a cherry-red flag.

"Just say it," I say.

"I acquired a new scrum half from Denver."

He nods as if he's mentally applauding himself. This acquisition means nothing to me ... *so why is he telling me about it?*

"Congratulations," I say, my tone filled with suspicion.

"Thanks. It was practically a steal. This guy was the best player in the league."

Was? I don't want to ask why he said that in the past tense.

The more I know about the player and his backstory, the worse off I'll be. But the way my boss is watching me makes it awkward *not* to ask.

"Why would you want someone on a downhill slope?" I ask with the enthusiasm of a sleeping sloth.

He leans forward. "Because I don't believe it's a death spiral. He might be a shadow of the player he used to be, but he's still great—just not as fit or focused as he once was. There's so much untapped potential, so much room for greatness, and I think we can get him to come back around with a little guidance."

What's with this we *shit?* I stare at him. Street signs may not be guiding us to our destination, but I can see the path as clear as a bell. Renn must've taken more hits to the head than we realized if he thinks I'm going to go along with this.

"That's where you come in," he says.

Ugh. I knew it. I look at the ceiling and exhale harshly.

"He needs someone to match his … temperament," Renn says carefully.

"Meaning?"

"Meaning that he needs an assistant—someone who will stand up to him. Who won't back down from a challenge. Someone I can trust to help him get on the right track."

"I don't know how to do that," I deadpan.

"Of course you do."

Technically, I do know how to do that. And technically, I can do it. But that doesn't mean I want to—and Renn knows it.

I've had enough experience with the sports world to know that athletes are a lot of work—too much work for what it's worth. I've met other personal assistants to players through Renn, and their stories are wild. These guys seem to be cut from the same cloth. They're overconfident and dismissive. Hard-headed as hell. Most of them can't, or won't, follow directions, and very few of them appreciate the work other people are putting forth to help make them great. I don't want any part of that.

I'm fortunate to have worked with Renn. He's a unicorn. I'd like to keep it that way.

"There's a reason I don't have kids, Renn. *I don't like them.* They're little fun suckers, and this feels very fun sucky, but with a very large male."

He coughs back a chuckle. "Remind me. When was the last time you had fun?"

I glare at him even though he has a point. It's not like personal assisting his player would put a crimp in my lifestyle. I don't *have* a lifestyle beyond egg sandwiches for breakfast, working hard throughout the day, and watching trash television at night while I promise myself that I'll do better tomorrow. But none of that is relevant in this conversation.

"I'm only asking that you do for him what you did for me when I was playing," he says.

"So I should plan on answering calls from his father about why he's in the emergency room with contusions on his head and a prostitute in his hotel room who refuses to leave?"

"That wasn't like it sounds, and you know it."

I watch him carefully. He's avoiding my gaze and grabbing at the collar of his shirt—two telltale signs that he's hiding something. "What are you not saying?"

"There may be rumors of gambling problems and a fetish for sex workers."

"Renn!"

He holds his hands out in front of him. "For what it's worth, I don't believe them. And I want you to think about it like this— I'm going to pay you to help someone turn their life around."

"That would be great if I cared." I shrug, pausing to give him a moment to remember who he's talking to. *"But I don't.* I don't care whether he turns his life around, if he gives his money away, or if he gets his dick wet at the rabbit ranch or bunny basket or whatever it's called."

Renn presses his lips together and tries not to laugh.

"You realize what you're doing to me, don't you?" I ask.

"You're asking me to babysit a grown-ass man. If I wanted to do that, I would've worked for your youngest brother."

"Just through the rest of rugby season, and we're already halfway done. Then we'll reassess."

I slide my pen from my clipboard and throw it at him. He chuckles, moving his head an inch to the right and easily dodging the projectile. The device sails right by, landing next to a lamp.

I don't always *love Renn Brewer.*

My lips pucker in annoyance at the position Renn has put me in. Athletes are generally my least favorite humans. And the thought of having to deal with the arrogance, moodiness, and demands of a rugby hero—because they all think they're one— makes my skin crawl.

But what can I really do?

I had twenty dollars to my name when I met Renn's sister, Bianca. Hours before our impromptu meeting at the dry cleaner's where I worked, my then-boyfriend had thrown me out of his apartment over a busty brunette with bright blue eyes. I had no money and nowhere to go besides asking my friends if I could couch surf—something my pride *couldn't* do. Bianca came in as I was preparing to ask my boss if I could stay in the back of the building until I could get on my feet.

While another employee located Bianca's garments, we started talking. And through a series of fortunate events, I was able to offer her tips on getting wine out of her coat, told her who to call to locate missing luggage from an airline, and I fixed her Social account from automatically cross-posting her content to another platform.

Before she left, she gave me her card. Two days later, I was officially Renn's and her personal assistant, and introduced to a world I didn't know existed. She changed my life, and I'll never forget that.

"What will it take?" Renn asks.

"What do you mean—*what will it take?*"

"I'm willing to do whatever it takes to get you on board."

"What if I say there's no way to do that?"

He smirks. "Then I'll just have to wear you down."

I groan, knowing that's exactly what he'll do … and that he'll eventually succeed. Because even though this is a no-good, awful, terrible idea, my loyalty is to Renn. If he needs me to corral one of his minions, I can't say no.

My gaze shifts from Renn to the floor-to-ceiling windows on my left, displaying a near-panoramic view of Nashville. Although I've seen it countless times from this vantage point, it never ceases to steal my breath. The mix of modern skyscrapers and iconic landmarks is beautiful. The lazy Cumberland River winding through the city and the pockets of green forests breaking up the concrete jungle create a living art exhibit. I could watch the cars crawling below for hours.

And to see it all from this perch in the sky, in one of the swankiest offices in the city? It's more than I ever imagined for myself.

"I'll double your pay," he says flatly.

My jaw drops. "What?"

"I'll double it unless that's not enough. Name your price."

"Whoa, slow down," I say, laughing in disbelief. "You're starting to talk out of your ass."

"I'm desperate."

"Clearly."

I can't keep my head from spinning. *He'll double my pay?*

The Brewers pay me very well, but the cost of living is nearly unbearable, and interest rates suck. By the time I pay for the basics—shelter, food, and gas—and pay for my student loans, medical bills, and boatloads of credit card debt, there's not a lot left to save. Nothing at all, really. I've managed to dig myself into a hole that's neck-deep, and my shovel is broken.

However, if my pay were doubled, depending on how long that lasted, I could shuffle that to my debt. That would be amazing. It would also keep me from having to scramble to find another side hustle. I'd have options. *It would be a gift from above.*

I gather myself and clear my throat. "Start over. Who is this guy, and what would this entail?"

Relief washes across Renn's features.

"I haven't said yes," I warn him. "I'm just fact-finding."

"Of course you are." He smirks, settling back in his seat again. "His name is Gray Adler. He's twenty-nine, and we're getting him from Denver. Not married, no kids. He's originally from Sugar Creek—about an hour from here. I've met him a few times over the years, and he's a great guy."

"Cool. Why don't you babysit him then?"

"I have a franchise to run, if you weren't aware."

Despite the overwhelming sense of uneasiness rippling low in my stomach, I concede. Everything is an opportunity if you choose to see it that way, and this is no different. After this morning's squabble at the gas station, maybe this is my repayment for not throttling that guy.

"Give me a pen," I say, rolling my eyes.

Renn smiles cautiously, dropping a black fine tip onto my palm.

"Does the team dietitian have his individualized meal plan ready?" I ask, falling back into the groove I once maneuvered like the back of my hand. I take a fresh legal pad out of my bag and fasten it to my clipboard.

"It should be done today."

"Do we have a report from strength and conditioning?"

"He's reporting to the S&C coaches on Monday."

I scribble a few notes, trying to recall what I know about the rugby world thanks to Renn's time on the pitch. A lot of the guys work part-time jobs in the offseason or work on a skill. That way, they have something to fall back on when they retire or leave the game.

"Is he full-time rugby, or does he have a side hustle? College classes? Anything like that?" I ask.

"I'm not sure. He has several endorsements, so I doubt he has something going on the side. But you never know."

"Does he have housing set up?"

Renn leans forward, nodding. "Yes. We're paying for an apartment a few blocks away from the facilities. It was a part of his contract. It was also a part of his agreement that we'd supply him with an assistant."

I glance up at Renn, holding his gaze.

"Gray is contractually obligated to work with you," he says. "I'll be honest. I pushed for that, not him. I wound up adding a little money to his deal for him to agree to this."

"Oh, so he's not going to want me around. Great. That makes this even better."

He shakes his head. "No, it's not like that. I'm just saying that it was my idea. Gray is a nice guy. I'm sure you won't have any problems with him."

I call bullshit on that one.

"He just got into town last night," Renn says. "It was a mid-season transfer, so he can't officially practice or play until the end of the week. League rules. That'll give you two enough time to get him settled and acclimated to things here before he hits the ground running."

"Yay."

Renn gives me a soft smile that deflates a bit of my sarcasm. "So you'll do it?"

I sink back into my chair and wish I could turn him down.

Renn loves nothing more than his family and the Tennessee Royals. This is his non-human baby, the love of his sports life. He brings in the best of the best. Players and coaches, medical, legal, and media departments—they're all the brightest in their field. If Renn trusts me enough to bring me on board in this capacity, to be lumped in with the rest of his hand-selected staff? That's an honor and a big flex.

And he is *doubling my pay.*

"Fine." I shrug. "I'm in. I want it on the record that I don't want to be in, but I'll do it for you."

"Thanks, Astrid. This is really important to me, and there's no one else I trust more for this."

"Maybe I should be less reliable," I say as Renn picks up his phone. "I'm really a victim of my own success."

Renn says something to his executive assistant, then puts the receiver back into the cradle.

"When do I get started with Gray?" I ask.

A knock raps twice against the door behind me. The sound is not a gentle rapping. It's loud. Aggressive. *Foreshadowing.*

"That's him," Renn says to me before looking over my shoulder. "Come in."

I turn around, my stomach tightening at the anticipation of meeting Gray. It would've been nice to have a few minutes to get a plan together—to figure out how to charm him into cooperating with me. Because something tells me that this isn't going to go as smoothly as Renn hopes, regardless of whether Gray signed a contract that included the stipulation or not.

I paste a smile on my face and poise myself to say hello. But that goodwill gesture melts as my gaze lands on a set of broody, and familiar, deep brown eyes.

"What are you doing here?" I ask, gripping the armrests like I'm trying to strangle them.

"Astrid, this is Gray Adler. He's the newest member of the Tennessee Royals," Renn says. "Gray, it's good to see you. This is Astrid Lawsen. She'll be your personal assistant for the rest of the season."

A slow smirk settles against his lips.

Oh, hell no.

CHAPTER
THREE

There's no fucking way.

My gaze sweeps over Miss Manners, the hothead from the gas station, sitting across from my new boss.

"Gray, come on in and grab a seat," Mr. Brewer says as I shut the door behind me.

Astrid's shock swiftly darkens, staring daggers at me as I sit in the chair next to her. Mr. Brewer looks between us, picking up on the fact that something is amiss … and potentially volatile. I'm sure he's wondering how that's possible since I just got to Nashville. It usually takes me at least a week to make enemies.

His gaze settles on me. I shrug in response.

The world's a shit show, sir. Welcome to mine.

I sit calmly, running my hands down my thighs, and don't look at Astrid. That's partially because this isn't the appropriate venue to fight with her, and I have a feeling that's what it'll be. She's not one to back down, and frankly, neither am I.

My mind tries to process this strange turn of events, but there's no time. Our boss jumps into the thick of it before I can get my thoughts together.

"I take it you two have met," he says.

"You could say that." Astrid shifts in her chair, putting as much space between us as she can. I find that oddly amusing.

"Is she always like this?" I ask, jamming my thumb in her direction.

Astrid flinches, whipping her freckled face to me. Her disdain for me is apparent, and she's ready to claw at me again. But before she can go for the kill, Mr. Brewer steps in.

"Let me guess," he says. "The gas station?"

"How did you know that?" As soon as the words leave my mouth, the answer dawns on me. *"Not that it's any of your damn business, but I was talking to my boss."* I blow out a breath. "You know what? Never mind."

I don't know why I'm surprised that this is happening. It's par for the course. When things start to go right for me, they quickly fall apart. This one disintegrated faster than usual, but hey—at least my life's consistent.

Mr. Brewer kicks back in his chair and chews on the end of a pen. I can't tell whether he's entertained by this or stumped. That makes two of us.

The room grows quiet as the three of us assess the situation. His face stays blank as he watches Astrid and me like he's trying to read a play on the pitch. Astrid crosses her arms over her chest, making her displeasure with my presence apparent. I fold my hands on my lap and look straight ahead.

Every muscle in my body aches from riding in the truck all night, and my head has pounded like a damn drum since Astrid's little fit this morning. *Who the hell acts like that to a random stranger?* She's lucky it was me and not a short-fused asshole. She's even luckier that the old lady showed up. Otherwise, one of us would probably be in orange right about now.

"I can't believe I'm saying this," Astrid says, wincing, "but is there any way I can work for Tate instead?"

They share a grin, and I have no clue what it's about. All I know is Tate, whoever he is, is screwed. Better him than me.

"No, you can't go to work for my brother," Mr. Brewer says. "Good try, though."

Astrid frowns and, for the first time since I met her, we're on the same page.

"Are you ready to get to work, Gray?" he asks me.

I clear my throat, shifting in my seat. "Absolutely. I'm honored to have the opportunity to play for you and the Royals, sir."

"That's great to hear. And you can call me Renn."

I nod, unsure if I can call him by his first name. It feels wrong. He's the owner of this club. *A legend.*

"Do you have any questions or concerns?" Renn asks me.

"No, not really. Aside from this … situation," I say, gesturing between Astrid and me. *Surely, he can tell this isn't a good fit.* "This isn't what I expected, if you know what I mean."

Astrid holds up an index finger. "I know what he means. I didn't expect this either when I tentatively agreed to your proposition."

"I know you two got off on the wrong foot," Renn says. "But I'm sure you can figure it out. We have a lot of work to do. Understood?"

Sure, I understand that we need to get to work. That's what I'm here for. But I don't know how he thinks Astrid and I can figure this out. There's no being logical with this woman. *I've tried.* She's pushed me to the point with her bullshit that I don't want to try to get along with her. It's a waste of energy.

Can't you just give me a college kid in a button-down shirt who'll go through the motions and stay out of my way?

"You signed a contract stating you'd receive a personal assistant for the duration of your time in Nashville," he says, lifting a brow.

Astrid stills, holding her breath.

"I know what I signed." I look at *my assistant* over my shoulder and wonder for a split second whether she's going to shout at Renn and me, or if she's going to get up and leave the room. Much to my surprise, she remains quiet and seated. "But nowhere in that contract did it say that I had to work with anyone I found … combative."

"While I take offense to the adjective, I concur," Astrid says, breaking her blissful silence. "In *my* employment contract, it doesn't say a word about working with assholes." She looks over her shoulder at me. "I meant that offensively."

I smirk just to piss her off. "You're going to have to try harder if you want to offend me."

"Challenge accepted."

Her green eyes blaze, and the gold flecks scattered about in her irises catch the light. With pretty eyes, big tits, and a juicy ass, Astrid could be a knockout if she weren't such a shrew.

"Astrid, you don't have an employment contract," Renn says, smiling at her. It's clear he likes her and has some level of respect for the redhead. He's a better man than me. "But now I'm thinking about making you sign one."

"Hey, that's a bargaining chip," she says. "Let's negotiate."

"And your contract, Gray, specifically states that I get to choose your assistant." Renn looks at me with far less kindness and ignores Astrid's suggestion. "Call your agent if you want to argue about it."

I stretch my neck, working it from side to side in a futile attempt to relieve the stress in my shoulders.

This whole situation is unnecessary—I didn't want an assistant to start with, and the fact that we're wasting time with it pokes at me. *I'm tired. I'm hungry. I want a little peace and quiet after driving almost twenty hours from Denver with my life in boxes. Is that too much to ask?*

"You're both professionals." Renn pushes away from his desk and stands. "I'm going to grab a drink from the café downstairs." He looks pointedly at Astrid. "Have this handled when I get back."

Fuck. We sit like scolded children as he moves past us and exits the room.

"That went well," I mutter, running a hand down my face.

"You're like a bad penny," she grumbles. "You just keep showing up."

"Some people say it's a part of my charm."

She snorts. "Charm is not one of the first thousand words that comes to mind when I think of you."

"You're probably not used to it. I would imagine not many charming people choose to spend their time with you."

Astrid stands abruptly, knocking the clipboard on her lap to the floor. Instead of picking it up, she marches to the windows and stands with her back to me. I'm not sure if giving me a magnificent view of her ass is supposed to be a *fuck you* or not, but it's one I can work with.

Hell, maybe it's a peace offering. God knows I've accepted less.

"So how do you suggest we get ourselves out of this?" she asks. "Because I'm not putting up with your bullshit for the next couple of months."

"*My* bullshit? Because if I remember correctly, and I do, you were the one who marched back to my truck like some gas pump princess to scream at me."

She glares at me over her shoulder. "Scream at you? I did no such thing."

"What word makes you feel better about it, then? Berate? Yell? Shout?"

"Oh, look at you," she mocks me. "Such an extensive vocabulary. Let me get you a cookie."

"Oh, look at you," I mock her right back. *God, I hate this woman.* "Deflecting from the point I just made."

She pivots on her heel to face me with her lips pressed in a thin, tight line.

I've never met someone this argumentative, and I've met some absolute fuckheads in my life. But never has someone just plucked me out from the crowd and stormed into my space with such determination to pick a fight. Over everything.

What the fuck is her problem?

I rest my elbows on my knees and fold my hands together. "I'm contractually obligated to work with you. So you get to be the hero, which I'm sure you love to be, and bow out of this. Problem solved."

Astrid bristles, standing taller. I've hit a nerve. I can see it in her eyes.

"Contract or not, I was tasked with keeping you in line," she says. "Renn hand-picked me for this challenge. It's not any easier for me to extricate myself from this than it is for you."

I lean back, absorbing her words. *Tasked with keeping me in line?*

The sentence slices right through me. Suddenly, a lot of shit makes sense.

My heart beats harder as I unpack this situation. It felt a bit off since Renn offered to give me a giant bonus in exchange for accepting an assistant, but I brushed it off as a quirk of an owner. Weirder things have happened.

But that's not what it is. It's not a quirk.

Renn Brewer doesn't think I need an assistant. He thinks I need a fucking babysitter.

Fucking hell.

I run a hand over my head and grit my teeth, trying to bite back the feelings rushing to the surface. This trade was supposed to be a fresh start. Renn sold it as a way for me to slide into a program with a great group of guys and build on a solid foundation. I took it as a solution to a problem and a way to get closer to my roots. But, in reality, he was placating me. He'd heard the stories and bought into the stupid rumors just like everyone else.

Wow.

Astrid nestles a hand on the curve of her hip. "I'm established here. People have expectations of me. *Renn* has expectations of me. To be blunt about it, I can't have my success tied to yours, considering your reputation and all."

Whatever issues she had with me before I arrived in Renn's office are now exacerbated by his commentary. There's no beating this, no matter what I do. She's already decided who I am. *They've* already decided who I am. The only thing I can control is getting my bonus, finishing this contract, and figuring it out from there.

If I didn't need the cash, I'd tell Renn and his nasty little stooge to get fucked.

"I hate to break the news to you," I say, licking my bottom lip. "But I'm sure this won't be the first time you've been a disappointment."

Her green eyes darken. "I hate you."

"Feeling is *so* mutual, sweetheart."

She growls in the air, her fists balling up at her sides.

Despite my desire to walk out of here, burning everything down behind me, I can't. The ink is dry on my contract, and promises have been made. Money has been spent. I'm stuck. I'm stuck here, and I'm stuck with *her*.

She turns her back on me again and faces the window.

I stretch my legs in front of me, rolling my head around my neck. There must be a solution to this—one that will let me keep my bonus close and Miss Manners far away from me. *But what is it?*

Think, Adler.

She's made it clear that she wants no part of me, but she also won't disappoint Renn. I want absolutely no part of her. And if I push back too hard, Renn won't just be disappointed in me—not that I care about that—but he'll find me in breach of my contract. No matter what, that can't happen.

I lick my lips as a plan comes to my mind.

If I can't refuse her help and she won't quit, all I can do is frustrate her so much that she avoids me. Odds are she'll do that, anyway. She can't risk her precious reputation getting tainted by mine. I might have to cover for her if asked and sing her praises so Renn thinks she's been a world-class babysitter. Although that makes me want to puke, I can do it. I've done worse for much, much less.

There's really no other choice.

"All right," I say, resolved to my fate. "You do what you need to do, but I'm telling Renn I'm good with this."

She stiffens before facing me with a slack jaw. "Why would you do that?"

"Because I have a lot of money on the line, and I'm not risking it to appease you."

"So you expect me to tell Renn no?"

I smirk. "Just stomp to his desk and give him a lecture on how his actions are inconveniencing you. Call him a bully. It helps when you point your finger." I demonstrate the way she pointed it at me earlier today. "That really drives your point home."

Her lips part, fury undoubtedly on the tip of her tongue. But before she can spew her vitriol my way, the door opens. Renn comes in with a glass in his hand. He looks at Astrid, then at me. The tension is thick enough to cut with a hot knife, but if Renn senses it, he does a great job of hiding it.

"Are things handled?" he asks.

"Yeah," I say, shrugging casually. "We talked it out, and we're on the same page. We're gonna make a great team."

"Glad to hear it," he says.

He turns away from us to close the door, and I think he chuckles under his breath. Astrid uses the opportunity to glare at me with such force that, if looks could kill, I'd already be ten feet under with daisies growing on top of me.

I wink at her, just to watch the steam rise from her head. Maybe she'll lose her cool and throw one of her fits. That just might make this morning worth it.

Renn takes his seat. Astrid walks between me and Renn's desk, with her back to him, to get to her chair. As she passes me, her eyes narrow to slits.

"This isn't funny," she whispers angrily.

"You can always tell him you refuse," I whisper back, grinning. "Be the bad guy. You're so good at it."

Renn sets his drink down and pulls a computer in front of him. "Now that we have that settled, let's get down to business. Astrid, do you have any more questions for me or Gray? Or are you good to go?"

I turn to her, expecting to see her trying not to explode. But that's not what's happening. She's … calm. *Too calm.* She's the calmest she's been since I met her.

The way she breathes is unnerving. It reminds me of an animal before it attacks. Her chin lifts, and a slow, mischievous smile curls her lips.

My heart begins to pound. A knot forms in my stomach, pulling tighter by the minute. I stay silent, waiting for her to make a move. She's quick on her feet, as I learned this morning. *But that smile?* That I don't trust.

Astrid picks up the clipboard that fell earlier. "No, I think I have all that I need." She flips a page with a cheerfulness that's downright unsettling. "I'll email the performance team and get a copy of Gray's meal plan, and I'll follow up with S&C about his training regimen on Monday. I doubt that the communications team has any media lined up for him, but I'll shoot them an email, too, and be sure."

What?

"That sounds great." Renn nods in approval. "This is exactly what I was hoping for. I'm glad we had this chat."

Astrid turns to me, her eyes twinkling with mirth. She brushes a loose tendril of crimson hair off her delicate shoulder. "I'll meet you downstairs in the performance center on Monday morning. I do have a commitment first thing, so let's shoot for ten o'clock. The whole staff should be there by then. We can do a tour, I'll introduce you to the team, and we can go over how I can make your transition to the Royals a success."

You will, huh?

She sits in some misplaced triumph, like she's just bested me.

Like she's going to be the one calling the shots between us. Her smile says she expects me to be thrown off my axis and capitulate to her or, at the very least, make an ass out of myself by pushing back. It's too bad that I can do this so much better than she can.

I crack a grin of my own. "That sounds perfect. I can't wait."

"Do you need anything from me right now, Gray?" she asks, sweetness dripping from each word.

"Not that I can think of, Astrid," I say, holding her gaze tightly. "You've really gone above and beyond today."

Renn stands. "Then I think that's it for us. Thanks for coming in, Gray. We're excited that you're a Royal. I expect great things from you."

I rip my attention from Astrid. *I very much doubt that you think that now that I know the truth.* "I won't disappoint you, Mr. Brewer. I mean, Renn." I get to my feet and shake his hand. Then I turn to *my assistant*. "I'll see *you* on Monday."

"Oh, I'll be looking forward to it."

Renn answers a call on his cell phone as I turn away. I glance over my shoulder to ensure he's occupied and then lean toward Astrid. "Stay out of my way, and things will be fine," I say just loud enough for her to hear.

She laughs as I walk away. "Gray?"

I pause with my hand on the doorknob.

"Make sure you get some protein and stay hydrated," she says, smiling devilishly. "It's going to be a big week."

You have no idea.

I toss her a wink and walk out the door.

Let the games begin.

CHAPTER
FOUR

ASTRID

I hum along to the radio as I wait for my opponent to make his final move.

Playing a quick game of chess before I get out of my car and go into my house is one of my small joys in life. I started doing it years ago when I was in my last relationship, mostly because I didn't want to go in and deal with … that. But I've come to enjoy the peace, and the way it feels like I'm in a protected bubble away from the world.

It's a habit that I have no interest in giving up.

"Just make it," I say, humming happily and watching my phone screen. "End your pain, sucker."

My opponent wastes entirely too much time choosing his next move. Finally, he slides right into the trap I set six moves back. And I win.

"Check …" I make my final move, wait for him to accept defeat, and then log off the app. "Mate."

I reach for the door handle to go inside, but my phone buzzes with an incoming text. Audrey's name is printed on the screen above her message.

. . .

Audrey: Sorry for the delayed response. My
reception was awful on the beach. I know, I
know. Poor me.   Dinner tomorrow night
sounds great! I fly back in the morning and land
around noon.

Me: Stupey's at seven. Does that work for
everyone?

Gianna: I'll be there.

Audrey: Me, too! Love you guys!

Me: xoxo

Gianna: M

I close the app but reopen it when it buzzes again, figuring
Audrey must have forgotten something. I'm surprised to see
Renn's name on the screen.

Renn: Just wanted to thank you for being the
bigger person today. I know you didn't hit it off
with Gray, and I appreciate you setting your
sword down to get the job done.

Laughter topples from my lips at the memory of Gray's face
when I shifted tactics. *He* thought he had *me*. He wanted to make
me look bad in front of Renn and control the situation. But, by
his reaction, he didn't expect me to play along—or to play the
game better than him.

If he thinks we can be a "great team," I'll make him regret it.

"Stay out of my way, and things will be fine."

The memory makes me chuckle. I'm going to be so deep into his business that he'll wish he'd have taken my advice and found a way out of this while there was time.

Me: I still have the sword, but I promise to make you proud. 😉

Renn: I knew I could count on you.

Me: Always. Have a good night.

Renn: You, too.

I gather my things from the passenger's seat, slip my phone into my bag, and head inside.

I need a glass of wine and a bubble bath. It's time to get to work figuring out how to get a step ahead of Gray fucking Adler.

CHAPTER
FIVE

"You look cute." Audrey leans up, pulling me into a quick hug. The scent of vanilla envelops me right along with her. "That shirt is great on you. Where did you get it?"

I set my purse next to Gianna's on the empty chair to my right. "Gianna. I wouldn't have picked this out on my own, but I kind of like it. It's doing great things for my cleavage."

The pale-yellow top is cut lower than I usually wear and is a bit tighter than I'd choose for myself. But I haven't worn it yet, and Gianna pays attention to this sort of thing. The last thing I'd ever want to do is to hurt her feelings.

"I bought it for myself, but the fabric made me itchy," Gianna says. "It looks great on you, Astrid. Your cleavage is hot."

"Thanks." I smile at my friends. "Did you guys get here early or what? I'm twelve minutes early myself, and you already have drinks."

"Yeah. We carpooled, and traffic was light. We got you a glass of sangria," Gianna says, pointing at a drink in front of me.

My friends know me so well. "Thank you."

Stupey's is busy but not crowded, especially for a Saturday

night. The cozy eatery transitions from a bougie sandwich shop during the day to sandwiches and a rotating menu of dinners at night. It's one of those places where you feel at home as soon as you walk in the door.

I take a sip of my drink and watch my friends look at photos on Audrey's phone. Gianna's trademark navy blue nails shine under the light hanging above our table, while a delicate pink ribbon hangs down Audrey's long blond hair. You wouldn't necessarily think the two of them, opposites in so many ways, would be such good friends. Add me and my clipboard to the mix, and none of it should make sense. But it does.

Gianna keeps things spicy. Audrey keeps us grounded. I balance them, encouraging Audrey to spread her wings, but keeping Gianna from overextending hers. I try, anyway.

"What are you two looking at?" I ask, leaning over to get a peek.

Audrey turns her phone to show me her screen. Her cheeks are as pink as the ribbon in her hair. "We're looking at *this*."

"I know you're shocked," Gianna says, hiding a grin.

Staring back at me is Audrey's kryptonite—a blond-haired, blue-eyed mixed martial arts expert. *Her brother's best friend*. It's a small inconvenience that he doesn't know she exists. This doesn't stop her from trying, and I respect her game. She attends as many of her brother's fights as she can, positioning herself in as many places as her crush will likely be. So far, no luck.

"I actually ran into him a couple of nights ago," she says, pushing her hair off her shoulder. She threatens to cut it at least once a month, but chickens out at the last minute every time. "A bunch of the guys went to a dive bar after the fights, and Andrew was nice enough to let his little sister tag along."

Gianna giggles. "I'm sorry. The thought of our sweet little Audrey at an MMA fight still cracks me up."

Audrey fires her the meanest look she can manage, which isn't more than a wrinkle of her nose.

"Did you actually talk to him?" I ask.

She smiles from ear to ear. "I did. I mean, we just said hello. But it's a start, right?"

"Absolutely," I say, smiling back at her.

Kim, our favorite server, comes by and drops off this weekend's dinner menu.

"Oh!" Audrey says, digging into her purse. "I brought you guys something from Boston." She retrieves two small squares and hands Gianna one and me the other. "I saw the star earrings at a little touristy shop by the beach and knew you had to have them, Astrid."

"I love these," I say, touched by her thoughtfulness. "Thanks, Aud."

I run my thumb over the small pink stars with a slight shimmer that will look great in my collection. My grandmother started it for me when I was a baby. Despite my name having no connection to stars, Grandma thought it did and said that stars reminded her of me. I wear a pair of star earrings almost every day. They make me feel closer to her.

Often, I wonder what she would think about the life I'm creating for myself. *Would she be proud of me? Disappointed? What were her hopes and dreams for her only grandchild?* I'll never know, and that's precisely why not having those answers shouldn't bother me.

Yet it does.

"Yours aren't earrings, Gianna," Audrey says, "but I loved this little pin. The pencil reminds me of your journals and all the writing you do for the column." She grins. "I hope you love it and don't think it's silly."

"Are you kidding me?" Gianna inspects her gift. "I love it. It's perfect." She looks up and winces. "But now I feel rude."

"Why?" I ask.

"Because Aud brought me a gift, and I have a shirt in my purse that I brought for her to hem."

I laugh, taking another drink of my sangria while Audrey

convinces Gianna she's not rude. Even if it were, Audrey would never tell Gianna that. She's too sweet.

The faint music drifting through the dining area shifts from a piano interlude to a soft opera. I know absolutely nothing about operas or music in general, for that matter. But every time I listen to this genre, I can't help but wonder what they're singing about. *Are they falling in love? Heartbroken? Are they ready to commit murder?* They could be singing about orgies and cocaine for all I know. It sounds lovely and romantic, regardless.

"Are you ladies ready to order?" Kim asks, pausing at our table.

"We can be," I say, handing my friends menus from the stack at the end of the table. "It's not like we haven't tried everything at one point or another."

"There's no rush," Kim says.

"I'm probably getting the salmon," Audrey says. She closes her menu seconds after opening it. "Yeah, I'm boring. I'll take the salmon for the fourth time in a row."

Kim laughs. "You're lucky that's a menu staple."

I scan the offerings, ruling out everything with peanuts. "I love the pad Thai, just not a possible trip to the emergency room after."

The only item this week that looks totally safe is the lemon chicken with rice. And while my reactions are thankfully mild to most triggers, I don't feel like living on the wild side tonight. I'd like to start the new week without hives or swollen lips.

Especially considering what the upcoming week will bring.

My stomach twists into a tight knot at the thought of Gray Adler. He's taken up more of my mental real estate than I care to admit since he walked out of Renn's office yesterday. Thinking of him immediately puts me in a bad mood, and I promised myself I wouldn't think about him tonight. So I push the bastard out of my head and focus on ordering.

"Lemon chicken with rice, please," I say.

"Ooh, I'll have that, too. I loved that the last time you ordered it." Gianna takes our menus and hands them to Kim. "Thank you."

"Thank *you*. I'll put this order in. Let me know if you need anything else," Kim says before walking away.

"How's the urinal?" I ask Gianna as soon as Kim is out of earshot.

"Urinal?" Audrey asks. "Do I even want to know?"

Gianna rolls her eyes. "I bought a—"

"Used," I interject.

"Urinal—"

"From a guy on Social," I add.

Gianna gives me a look. "For an art project. And it's great, thanks for asking."

Audrey and I exchange a grin. While this might be the grossest thing our friend has purchased, it's not the weirdest. Gianna once bought a box of old, used lottery tickets to use as wallpaper for bird houses. She keeps things interesting.

"You guys are never going to guess the question we had come in for my segment *Just Between Friends*," Gianna says, steepling her fingers in front of her like a villain. "The stuff we get in every week for this column is *batshit crazy*, you guys. I don't know why it draws in the kind of questions it does, but it never fails to entertain. Sometimes, though, we get one that's just …" Her eyes go wide, and she flinches. "It's wild out there, folks."

"What was the question?" I ask.

She leans forward. "This guy wrote in and said that he wants to slather his cock in avocado and bang his girlfriend. But he's worried she'll think he's weird and that she might get an infection."

"*Oh my God*," I say, covering my mouth with my hand.

"That's so gross." Audrey looks slightly horrified.

"Food play is a total thing." Gianna giggles at Audrey's reaction. "You have so much to learn, Auddie."

Audrey reaches for her drink, an Arnold Palmer, and takes a long sip.

These discussions always freak her out a little. Audrey has only ever had two boyfriends and no hookups in her twenty-seven years. She's a good girl, a rule follower—a PhD in philosophy. I'm not sure if she's ever uttered a curse word in her life. She's had sex, but I'm sure she's never had *good sex*. From what I can tell, missionary is the limit of her experience. And while there's nothing to be embarrassed about when it comes to sexual experience, she's self-conscious about it.

"Are you going to respond to Mr. Avocado?" I ask.

"Hell, no." Gianna laughs. "I feel like I'd have to have a therapist and gynecologist weigh in, and I don't want to have those discussions."

"I get that, but I'm kind of curious," I say, grinning. "I think avocados have both antibacterial and anti-inflammatory properties. While I'm not saying I'd be inclined to let a guy make guacamole in bed—"

"*Stop it*," Audrey says.

"—I do wonder if it could theoretically be a holistic treatment," I say.

Gianna's laughter turns into a mischievous chuckle. "I have to admit that now I'm kind of curious, too. Hey, maybe *you should* write this column, Astrid. Give us a peek into your dark, demented mind."

"Um, no. Thanks, though. My mind would bore the crap out of you."

"I have a feeling that's not true," Gianna says, biting her lip to keep from smiling too wide.

Ignoring her, I reach for my sangria.

"Sometimes I worry about the two of you." Audrey sighs.

"Information is good to have," I tell her instead. "And when you've been in a dry spell as long as I have been, you have a heightened sense of curiosity."

Audrey groans. "You wanna talk about dry spells? Let's talk about dry spells."

"I keep telling you two that I can lead you to the oasis." Gianna winks, far too entertained for anyone's good. "There's a party on a houseboat next weekend. You'll receive a colored wristband upon boarding, representing your interests." She looks at Audrey. "Fetishes, kinks—that kind of thing. Not sewing or making cupcakes. Although making guac might count …"

I snort.

Audrey rolls her eyes. "I gathered. I'm inexperienced, not incapable of understanding context clues."

"Just making sure," Gianna says, bumping her shoulder playfully.

"Are you going?" Audrey asks her.

Gianna shrugs. "We'll see. If you guys want to go, I'll happily be your tour guide."

"I don't think I'll be buying a ticket to that tour, but thank you for the invitation," I say.

"I think you'd love it, Astrid," Gianna says.

Audrey makes a face at me, expressing her disagreement.

"Don't get me wrong," I say. "I'm all for meeting a man and hooking up. But I need there to be more than a colored bracelet involved."

"Yeah, we know," Gianna groans. "You'd have so much fun if you could just relax and trust me."

"Trusting you isn't the problem." *You two women are really the only people I trust at all.* "I'll live vicariously through your wild tales. That's enough for me."

I hope.

Audrey shifts in her seat. "How was your week, Astrid? Anything exciting happen to you while I was gone?"

I grab my glass and take a long slug of my sangria. The alcohol heats my cheeks, sending a welcome warmth through my veins. I wait for it to hit the bundles of stress in my body before I even consider discussing yesterday. I'll have to handle it carefully, or things will fly off the rails before I know what's happening. Audrey will take this situation with Gray and turn it into an impending love story fit for the big screen. Gianna will concoct all the ways Gray and I could dispel our growing hatred for one another, and she'll remind me that, in her opinion, hate sex is the best sex.

This thing with Gray is the farthest thing from either of those things as it can get.

"My week was fine until yesterday," I say, feeling the tension in my jaw again.

"What happened yesterday?" Audrey asks.

"Renn called me into his office and asked me to take on another project."

Gianna's dark brows pull together. "He did? You didn't mention that to me."

"It happened after I talked to you." I heave a breath, pushing the air past the tightness in my lungs. "I'm not happy, to put it mildly."

"What's going on?" Gianna asks. "It's rare that you're annoyed by Renn. Or did he finally assign you to Tate?"

I snort. "I *begged* to work with Tate. Let that sink in."

Audrey's eyes widen, and Gianna makes a face in surprise. *Yeah. It's that bad.* They know how opposed I've been in the past to working with Renn's baby brother. My admission isn't lost on them.

I shrug, feeling the weight of the world on my shoulders. "I've just been assigned a giant man-child with a horrible personality to 'assist'," I say, using my fingers for air quotes, "for the rest of the rugby season."

Gianna fights a grin. "You're assisting a rugby player?"

I fire her a look, knowing damn good and well where she's going with this—right to the gutter.

"What's his name?" she asks coyly.

"Gray Adler." I sigh dramatically, crossing my arms over my

chest as Gianna leans over Audrey's shoulder to see her phone again. "You're going to see all kinds of headlines that say he's an asshole and—"

"*Oh my God.*" Gianna's jaw hangs to the table as she faces me. "He's hot as fuck, Astrid."

I groan, glancing around to ensure no one can hear her. "Lower your voice. This is a public place."

"We were just talking about avocado dicks," Gianna deadpans. "I'm pretty sure the line was crossed back there, not here."

"Even his name is hot." Audrey continues to swipe across her screen. "Have you seen him with his shirt off?"

Gianna moans. "I can think of many, *many* ways I could assist that man. Holy shit."

Despite knowing this would happen, it still irritates me. I don't want them focusing on his looks. I'm sure women do that every day and give him a pass because he has a sexy smirk and a body chiseled from marble. I want my friends to be on my side—to hate him because I do.

"He's a top-tier jerk," I say.

"Of course, he's an asshole," Gianna says, waving a hand through the air. "He's a professional athlete. They're supposed to be all testosterone-fueled, sweaty, alpha males." She peers at Audrey's phone again and gasps. "Look at his legs. *And he has a thigh tattoo.*" She pauses to whimper. "I never want to hear you complain about work again. Ever."

"But you—"

"*Ever,*" Gianna says, holding up a finger. "I don't know why God loves you more than me, but put in a good word for me, will you?"

"We want weekly recaps of everything that happens while you work with him." Audrey glances up for the first time. When her eyes meet mine, she turns off her phone, and her gaze softens. "Because I want to know every mean thing he does to you so I can be mad, too."

Thanks, Audrey.

I smile at her as Kim sets our plates in front of us. She checks our drinks, we thank her, and then she disappears again.

"For the record," Gianna says, picking up her fork. "If he hit on me, I'd turn him down and hurt his feelings with dramatic flair just for you." She looks up at me and winks. "But he *is* hot. If you get a Bring Your Friend to Work day, I call dibs."

"Can we talk about something else?" I groan, rolling my eyes. "Please?"

"Let me use this to segue from rugby booty to pirates' booty." Gianna giggles. "I saw this thing online about this island where men dress up as pirates and … hold on. Let me pull up the article. You have to see this for yourselves."

I lean back, my shoulders relaxing, and breathe a sigh of relief. Audrey catches my eye and offers me a sweet smile.

Although I didn't want to talk about him at all, I knew that I'd have to, and I'm glad it's over without me having to get too in the weeds about it. I'm tired of replaying my interactions with Gray and dissecting every word, gesture, and look we exchanged. And God knows I'm tired of worrying about what the next couple of months will entail.

This is a new predicament for me because I generally avoid men like him. *Moody, spiteful, arrogant men.* That's why being forced to work with him is very discombobulating. I don't understand how I got here or why this is happening to me. *Who did I piss off in my last life?*

I can only do my job to the best of my ability, enjoy that raise in salary, and let the chips fall where they may.

I only hope that isn't at my feet in a million little pieces.

"So they were pretending to be pirates?" Audrey asks.

"Role-playing pirates." Gianna shrugs, looking at me for help. "You want to take this one, or should I?"

I laugh, grateful for Audrey's naivete. "I'll take this one."

It's the perfect silly thing to take my mind off the real-life pirate trying to plunder my happiness.

CHAPTER
SIX

Gray

"I gotta get some blinds," I mutter, shielding my eyes from the sunlight piercing the thin curtains in the bedroom.

My body protests the movement, screaming and aching in places that shouldn't hurt from driving and sleeping. Fog clouds my head. A sound emanates from my stomach with a reminder that I haven't eaten much since I left Denver on Thursday, and it's now … *Sunday*?

I swipe at the bedside table until my hand lands on my phone. *Sunday at noon. Shit.*

"How the hell is it noon already?" I grab the edge of the only blanket I could find without really looking too hard and rip it off the one leg it covers. "I gotta get my ass up."

Groaning, I roll out of bed and slip on a pair of shorts.

The apartment's warm and stuffy as I stumble into the living room, still in a haze. Everything I own is shoved in boxes that are stacked in a fucked-up game of Jenga in the corner. I've avoided dealing with it. Unpacking and putting it all away feels like a bad omen. If my contract doesn't get extended past this year, I'll just be loading it all up in a couple of months.

I don't want to jinx it. Because even if Renn thinks I'm a fuckup, there are too many upsides to playing for the Royals. I can't screw this up.

"I gotta get some food," I say, yawning. But before I can make it to the kitchen, my phone buzzes in my hand.

Hartley: Are you alive?

The corners of my lips curl toward the ceiling at my younger brother's name displayed at the top of the screen.

Me: I think so.

Hartley: Then call me.

He doesn't wait for that to happen, probably because he doesn't trust that I'll do it. Instead, my device lights up with an incoming call.

"You didn't give me time," I joke, entering the kitchen. I tap the speakerphone button and carry the phone in front of me.

"I could have given you a year, and I'd still be waiting on the phone to ring."

"Yeah, you're probably right."

He snorts. "So how was the trip?"

"Long," I say, opening the refrigerator. Empty shelves stare back at me, so I close it. "Rained so hard in Kansas City that I stopped for an hour. Then I sat behind an overturned semi for far too fucking long. Otherwise, it was uneventful."

"Better to have an uneventful trip than a trip full of problems."

A door slams in the background, followed by the crunching of gravel, probably in the shape of my brother's favorite worn-out cowboy boots. The sound evokes the scent of dirt and the sensation of sunshine on my face. I can almost hear the flag in front of his house, the one we grew up in, whipping in the wind.

My chest pulls tight at the thought of a place that holds so many great memories for me. Sitting down with family for Sunday dinners after church. Running through the fields with my brother on warm summer days. Splashing in the creek that Mom forbade us to play in, building forts in the woods, and pestering Dad's workers for a taste of their tobacco. The one time we managed to get some from a ranch hand named Earl, we hurled our guts out behind the barn. I still can't smell mint without wanting to puke.

The trade from Denver to Nashville, within an hour of Sugar Creek, felt like an opportunity to try to find that again. The irony is not lost on me that I'm running toward the very thing from which I bolted. Simplicity. Peace. Being surrounded by people who know who you are and not what the media says you've become.

"What's going on with you?" I ask, rubbing my sternum.

"Same old stuff. Just got home from church. I had to duck out of there during the last hymn, so I didn't get roped into the monthly birthday potluck after the service."

"Since when do you turn down home-cooked food?" I laugh as my stomach growls. "Or do you have a woman helping you take care of that these days?"

"I usually stay for it, but I have two ewes in labor. I left Bobby in the barn to keep an eye on them this morning, but he has somewhere to be by four o'clock. I told him I'd be back in plenty of time for him to get cleaned up and get out of there."

I lean against the side of the couch and smile knowingly. The chances of Hartley having a woman at the ranch are about one in however many women are in Sugar County. And that *one* hasn't been around in years, but he won't move on. Just in case.

That's the thing about Hartley—he's a good man. He inherited Mom's patience and Dad's aptitude, and he does nothing without going all in. He's loved Mira St. James since he was five years old. By the looks of it, I doubt that'll ever change.

"Things back there okay?" I ask.

"Well, you could answer that question yourself if you'd stop by. If you need directions, let me know."

I grin, but his point is not lost on me. "Very funny."

He chuckles. "It's been a while since you graced us with your presence. A lot of people back here would love to see ya."

"Of course, they would."

"I mean, they'd probably be ready for you to leave within five minutes, but they'd like to see you nonetheless."

Our laughter blends together, reminding me of days gone by. Back when life was simple and good. Before everything got so damn complicated.

"Saw Brooks the other day," Hartley says. "He came by to say hi."

My brows tug together as my stomach growls again. "Brooks Dempsey?"

"How many Brooks do you know?" Hartley laughs. "And how many Brooks do you know who would be in Sugar County?"

"Isn't he training in Vegas?"

"Yeah, but he's injured. Tore his rotator cuff. He's hoping to be back in the gym in six months, but he's probably looking at a year from the sound of it. It'll be longer than that before he can fight again."

Heat colors my cheeks as I realize just how out of touch I am. Brooks was my best friend when I was a kid, and well into my twenties. Between his fighting career and my rugby schedule, we'd meet up for weekends a few times a year to catch up. But at some point, my phone stopped ringing. Or maybe his did. Either way, I haven't talked to him in ... *months?* I don't even know.

I haven't really talked to anyone lately except Hartley.

"I should give him a call," I say, my voice gruff.

"He'd probably like that." Hartley blows out a breath. "So are you getting settled in? Got everything ya need?"

My gaze drifts around the empty kitchen and into the living room. There's a table, a sofa, and a decent-sized television. The place is bigger than the one I had in Denver, too.

"I can't complain. They hooked me up with a furnished apartment, so that helps. I just need to go through my stuff and find a grocery store. I think I had a protein bar and a banana on Friday morning, a couple of shitty sandwiches yesterday afternoon … and that's it. I'm dying."

"Doesn't the team have a cafeteria or something?"

"Something like that," I say, running a hand over my head. My stomach tightens as I let my brain drift to the Royals … and her.

I've managed to avoid the thought of Astrid for most of the weekend, despite the leading role she played in a nightmare last night. She was chasing me around a gas station with her fucking clipboard. Other than that, she's been a persona non grata in my life. Knowing that's about to change makes me want to go back to bed.

"Then why are you complaining?" Hartley asks. "Just go there and grab some food."

"Tomorrow is my first day at the facility."

He laughs. "Don't sound so excited."

I run a hand down my face. *"Make sure you get some protein and stay hydrated. It's going to be a big week."*

That's one way to put it. A hell week is probably more like it.

"Listen to this shit," I say, leaning against the kitchen counter. "The Royals insisted on giving me a personal assistant."

"Fancy."

"Yeah, I wish." My body tenses as I acquiesce to my new reality. I might as well think about it now and try to get used to it. After all, there doesn't seem to be a way out of it. Not easily, anyway. "She's essentially a fucking babysitter."

The line grows quiet, and I'm sure Hartley's trying to figure out what to say. I save him the trouble.

"She's fucking miserable," I say, my jaw pulsing as Astrid's little smirk shoves its way through my mind. "She's a know-it-all with delusions of grandeur. I don't know if everyone in her life rolls over for her or what, but she's obviously not used to not getting her way."

Hartley hums. "I bet that goes over really well with you, doesn't it?"

"If you're imagining us squared up, you're spot-on."

"What's her problem?"

"Fuck if I know." I shrug helplessly. "She has a superiority complex that I can't get around. Her mind is made up about me —and her conclusions aren't great." *No thanks to Renn, it seems.* "She's determined to lord over me for the next couple of months, so she doesn't lose her Employee of the Month title or whatever the hell is going on. And I'm not about to back down and lose the bonus I got for agreeing to this mess."

My mouth hardens as her admission rattles through my head. *"I was tasked with keeping you in line."*

That's the line I can't forget—the one I can't let go.

"Got any advice for me?" I ask, reading an alert that pops across the screen.

Reminder: Payment due in 3 days

I clear my throat and dismiss the message. By the time I tune back into Hartley's voice, his tone has changed.

"Hey, Gray, I'm sorry but I gotta go. I need to check this ewe. Bobby already took off, so it's just me here."

"Yeah, go. Don't let me keep you."

"Let me know if you can grab some free time. I'd love to see you."

I run a hand down my face. "Yeah. For sure. Let me get my feet on the ground and I'll be there."

"Good deal. Talk to you later."

"See ya."

"Bye, Gray."

The call ends abruptly as he rushes off to tend to his animals, and I'm left standing in my empty apartment.

There's a hollowness in the middle of my chest that has nothing to do with hunger pains. I hate acknowledging its presence, not because of the sensation. *Because of what it represents.*

My life is lonely but admitting that—even to myself—makes me feel like a little bitch. How can I possibly complain about anything when I'm doing exactly what I want? I'm alive and healthy. I'm getting paid very well to play a fucking game for a living. Things could be so much worse.

Maybe I'll never quite have it all. But maybe I don't deserve it, either.

I force a swallow and place a hand on my rumbling stomach. Before I can decide whether to grab a shower or order a sandwich to be delivered, my phone buzzes again. I glance down, expecting to see a picture of a baby animal in Hartley's barn. Instead, I'm accosted by a series of texts hitting the screen in rapid succession.

Unknown: An email has been sent to the address on file with a list of people, phone numbers, addresses, and other pertinent information you need going forward. Please review ASAP.

Unknown: We'll go over this week's schedule in full tomorrow. Here's a breakdown for your convenience.

Unknown: Monday:

Unknown: 10:00 a.m.: meet me at the training facility for a tour and introductions

Unknown: 11:00 a.m.: appointment with strength coaches

Unknown: 12:30 – 1:30 p.m.: lunch with the other backs in the café (I've reviewed and approved your nutrition plan with the dietitian. A copy is in your email.)

"The fuck?" I swipe through the rest of the texts as they come through. My jaw is on the floor.

Unknown: 2:15 p.m.: meet with the equipment department regarding your uniform, etc.

Unknown: 3:15 p.m.: Communications wants to meet with you to sign tip-in sheets for an upcoming media event (more on that in the email). There's a chance you'll need to take these home. The turnaround is quick, so prioritize this

Unknown: 4:45 p.m.: I was able to get a quick strength session scheduled for you

Unknown: Dinner will be boxed for you to take home. I'll show you tomorrow where to find it.

Unknown: Use your discretion for cardio

"Use my discretion for cardio?" I ask, chuckling in disbelief. "Well, damn. Thanks, Astrid, for trusting me to decide whether I need cardio or not." *Ding! Ding! Ding!* Her texts pour in for each day of the week, each with a laundry list of shit for me to do. "Who does this woman think she is?"

By the time I get to Thursday, I'm heated.

If she thinks this is going to fly, she's out of her damn mind. There's no reason in hell that she needs to hold my hand through this process like I've never done it before. It's not just unhelpful. *It's damaging.* I need to meet my new team on my own terms—

and I need to do it without her as a bridge between us. *What's it going to look like when I come in with a fucking chaperone?*

"I didn't come here to have my nuts removed," I say. "If that's what Renn thinks he's gonna do, he can suck my cock."

A doorbell rings through the apartment. The sound jolts me—I had no idea I had a doorbell—and adds to the tension overwhelming me. *Now isn't the time.*

I contemplate grabbing a shirt, but the bell rings again. So I march to the door and yank it open, ready to tell someone to fuck off. Before I can utter a word, I spot a kid who can't be any older than sixteen standing on the doormat with both hands full of grocery bags.

"I think you're at the wrong place, kid," I say, squeezing my phone in my hand so hard I think it might shatter.

"Are you Gray Adler?"

"Yeah."

He smiles. "Good. I got halfway up the sidewalk and forgot your name and apartment number."

The kid clearly isn't into rugby. "I didn't order any groceries."

"Well, they're yours."

"Not possible," I say, starting to shut the door.

He shoves his shoe in the doorway so the door can't entirely shut and sighs as if this is killing him. "Look, I'm a man who doesn't like to do things twice. So either take these bags or tell me where to put them, and then I'll check my phone for information. They're cutting off the blood supply to my fingers."

"Then take them back to your car. Otherwise, you'll have to pick them back up. That's doing things twice."

He wiggles his nose to reposition the black-framed glasses on his face. "Do you think I made up your name, chose a random apartment in the city, and thought, 'Let me go buy groceries for this person I just made up and take it to this random apartment' where someone with that name actually lives? On what planet is that possible?" He tilts his head, lifting a brow like I'm goofy. "Be real."

There's nothing I can say to that. *And his fingers do look a little blue.*

"Here," I say, holding my hands in front of me. "Give me the bags so you can figure out where to take this shit."

He slips the bags onto my forearms, over the phone in my right hand, and then digs his phone out of his pocket. It only takes him a few seconds to locate the information.

"Do you know an Astrid?" he asks, looking up at me.

My jaw sets.

Of course, it's from Astrid.

I glance briefly into the bags. It's all things I'd typically eat: milk, meat, eggs. There's fruit, oatmeal, and some peanut butter. The fact that it's all things I like makes me even madder.

She probably knows I'm starving, so she sent me poisoned food. Pretty brilliant.

"Astrid?" the kid asks again. "Do you know her or not?"

"Unfortunately." I consider sending him back with the bags and refusing the delivery, but the look in his eye tells me he has no interest in hauling this shit back to his car. As much as I don't want anything from Satan's daughter, it's not this boy's fault—and there's no sense in bringing another victim into her madness. "Follow me and let me get you some cash."

"It's paid for."

"I meant for you."

He lights up. "Hey, that'd be great. Thanks, man."

I head to the kitchen and set the bags and phone down on the countertop. Then I find my wallet in the bedroom and pull out a couple of twenties.

"Here you go," I say, coming into the living room and handing him the money. "For your troubles."

He tries to hand one back to me. "There are two."

"There are two because I gave you two."

His eyes are as big as saucers behind his glasses. "No joke?"

"No joke."

"You're the best." He nods appreciatively. "Thanks. I thought you were gonna be a dick. Good save."

What? He doesn't wait for a response before turning on his heel and hightailing it out of my apartment.

I wait until the door closes before I exhale.

My stomach wails, begging for food, but my brain can't let this go. I told her to stay out of my way and things would be fine—and I know damn good and well she doesn't want to be doing this. So either she doesn't understand plain English, or she's doing this to be a pain in the ass.

The woman has a firm grasp on the English language.

I grab my phone and unlock the screen, saving her name with a witch emoji. Then I tap out a response.

> Me: Show Renn your receipt like a good little girl and then stop it.

> Astrid 🧹: Are you upset? I'll send tissues next time.

> Me: There won't be a next time.

> Astrid 🧹: Oh, that's where you're wrong, sweetheart. I'm doing my job, just like you said you wanted. If that's not true, you can always give Renn a call. 🙂

My fingers pound against the keys.

> Me: You really don't want to play this game with me.

> Astrid 🧹: We agree. I don't. I really don't want to do ANYTHING with you.

I pace the apartment, trying to dispel some of the energy building inside me. It's like she's throwing it in my face that Renn thinks I'm *this* incapable. This inept.

This is not how I saw this going. Even when I was walking out of Renn's office and she acted like a suck-up, I thought it was because he was sitting there. I didn't think she'd keep the ruse going once he wasn't around.

My eyes slide up the text chain again until they hit on a particular line. *If you didn't want this, you should have done something about it.*

"You're playing right into her hand, Adler," I say aloud. "She's winding you up, and you're letting her."

I take a long, deep breath and blow it out. My chest shakes as my lungs deflate, but I feel myself finding a balance again.

"She can poke at me all she wants because she's doing the boss's bidding. But I need to figure out how I can even the playing field. Because if one of us is going to quit, it's not going to be me." I glance around the apartment, thinking, until my gaze settles on the mound of boxes in the corner. "Bingo."

Grinning, I type out another message.

> Me: I'm going to need you to come over Tuesday evening.

> Astrid 🐿️ : Over where?

> Me: My apartment.

> Astrid 🐿️ : Why would I do that?

> Me: Because you're my assistant, and I need assistance.

I wait, but no response comes. "Didn't like that, did you?"

Me: I have about thirty boxes I need unpacked.

Still no response.

The idea of having her here is about as attractive as fighting a wounded badger, but if I'm going to get her to either remove herself or keep a distance, then I have no choice. I have to make this so unbearable that she can't stand it.

Astrid 🧎: Don't choke on anything. That would be a tragedy.

Me: Have a good day, sweetheart.

I chuckle, knowing that pissed her off, and power down my phone. She's going to fire back at me, and I'm not giving her the pleasure of getting a read receipt. And I don't know how to turn that feature off, either.

Satisfied, I take in the bags of groceries on the counter. There's a chance they're laced with arsenic—and I wouldn't put it past her to go that far—but the toxicology report on my cadaver would point directly at her, and she's too bright not to know that. Besides, she's only doing this to brownnose Renn, and the food is already here.

I may as well reap the benefits of it.

"She's doing her job, and I need to focus on mine," I say, heading to the kitchen. "That'll be easier with a full stomach."

I busy myself with putting the cold items away and thinking about how I'll handle Astrid tomorrow. No matter what happens, I can't let her think she's going to call all the shots. That would be an epic failure on so many levels. But something tells me that she's not going to want to show up here on Tuesday, and that might just be enough to get her to back off.

I hope.

CHAPTER
SEVEN

Gray saunters through the archway into the Royals performance center, one hand in a pocket and the other running along the top of his head. With a bag slung over his right shoulder and a pair of sunglasses hooked in the front of his crisp white T-shirt, he's fresh and relaxed. *Unrushed.*

A wedge of irritation lodges itself in my throat, and I fight the urge to release a mouthful of expletives. He could've at least had the decency to show up breathless or in a half jog—something to imply that he cares that he's wasted my time. We do have a job to do, after all.

I push away from the table I've inhabited for the last half hour with more force than necessary.

"You're late," I say, irked that this doesn't seem to bother him.

"It was ten minutes. It's not that serious."

Excuse me?

"There are two things you should know about me." I snap my clipboard off the table. "One is that I operate under the premise that if you're not ten minutes early, you're late. And being late conveys a lack of consideration for other people's time." I lift a brow. "In short, it's rude."

"I could've left an hour ago, and it wouldn't have made any difference. I was stopped behind an accident three miles from here." He lifts a brow. "Besides, don't act like you've never been late before."

Sure, I have. But I've also apologized for it.

Ignoring him, I proceed. "The other thing you should know is that I don't do excuses. We can't communicate or problem-solve if you give me a bunch of bullshit when you fuck up. Got it?"

"Then it looks like we're not going to solve many problems, doesn't it?"

He holds my gaze like a vise. They're like looking into pools of the cheap chocolate you get at Easter. On the surface, it's dazzling. But once you settle into it, you realize it's highly unsatisfying and will only give you a stomachache.

A woman from the media department walks by, opens her mouth like she's about to say something, but reads the room and waves instead. Before she slips into the staff entry to The Royal Café, she does a quick, not-so-subtle perusal of Gray. I roll my eyes at her little grin.

The lobby of the performance center is one of my favorite places in the Royals facilities. When Renn bought the team a couple of years ago, he completely remodeled every square inch of the building. Nothing was overlooked or untouched. However, the best transformation occurred here, in the entrance hall, where both players and staff are welcomed every day. The glass ceiling gives it a bright, solarium-like vibe. The team colors of purple and gold lend a sense of regalness to the space. Several plants dot the area thanks to Renn's plant-loving sister-in-law, and screens highlighting team facts have been deftly positioned on the walls.

It's exciting and inspiring—unless you're here to be a babysitter.

"I don't know how things were done at the other teams you've played for," I say. "But here you're expected to be on time."

"I'll do my best."

His cool aloofness—and complete disregard for the seriousness of the day—irritates me. I don't know how anyone walks into their first day of work with the casualness of a beach day. And I *really* don't know how I'm supposed to manage this. Sure, I expected a level of incorrigibility, but I expected it aimed *at me*. I didn't think he'd fly a fuck-you flag to his team on day one.

May God help me.

"All right. Let's get on with it since we only have forty-five minutes before you meet with the strength coaches," I say, glancing at the time on my phone as I turn toward The Royal Café. It took me forever to organize his first day and fit as much as possible into his schedule. He won't appreciate it, I'm sure, but it makes me feel accomplished … and it's good for the team, which means it's good for Renn. That's what matters to me.

"There's no rush."

I stop so suddenly that my sneakers squeak against the floor. "There's no rush?"

"Yeah, there's no rush." He shrugs, the corner of his lips lifting. "I moved the strength assessment to this afternoon."

A flush stings my cheeks. I clutch my clipboard, trying to process his statement. "I'm sorry," I say, trying to shake the apparent cobwebs clouding my head. "You did *what?*"

"I had a workout at four forty-five, anyway. I just moved the assessment in that slot."

"You can't just do that."

"I can." He leans forward, that ridiculous dimple dotting his cheek. *"And I did."*

My heart pounds as I struggle to keep from losing my absolute shit.

"While we're at it, I shot an email to the nutritionist who created my diet plan," he says, grinning with an air of arrogance.

"We're modifying it. So if you're going to send groceries my way again, you better make sure you check that out before you screw it up."

He can't be serious.

"You need to stop," I say, the words a thinly veiled warning.

"I need to stop what, exactly?"

"You need to stop screwing with the plan. I spent a lot of time putting that together for you and—"

"Oh, like you care." He scoffs. "You didn't put that together for me. At best, you put it together to save your ass. At worst, you did it to piss me off."

I start to fire back a retort but pause when a group of players leave the café and head toward the wellness center. Thankfully, they don't notice us on the other side of the lobby. I'm not in the mood to deal with multiple athletes at once. I'm trying desperately not to kill this one.

"You're right about one thing," I say, leading him toward the café. "I don't care whether you succeed or fail. But I care if *I* do, and that's dependent on whether I wrangle you or not."

He bristles at my side, but I ignore it.

"This is where you'll get your food, drinks, and snacks," I say as we enter the cafeteria, fitted as a café. "Obviously, it's all free. This section is only for players, and the rest of the staff use another area."

Gray takes it all in.

"There's a buffet for breakfast and lunch," I tell him. "You'll have snacks with your name on them in that cooler midmorning and midafternoon. They customize them to meet your nutritional needs depending on the day's activities. I also opted you into dinner service. So if you didn't override that in your flagrant dismissal of my efforts, you can pick up a boxed dinner before you leave the facilities in the evening." I sigh. "Any questions?"

"Nope. Renn will give you an A+."

I nod at one of the chefs as we exit the room, biting back the *fuck you* that I want to lodge at Gray. "The elevators are over there," I say as we move through the lobby again. "Or you can use the staircase to go up. You can read, so follow the signs. As you may recall from yesterday, the administration offices are located on the upper levels. We can go up there in a bit, but let's start down here."

He doesn't respond, so I head down the corridor toward the player wing.

Silence looms between us like a gaping chasm that neither of us wants to, or can, cross. We might be shoulder to shoulder as we move through the building, but we couldn't be farther apart. At least the silence gives me a moment to pull myself back together.

Screens are positioned along the walls, hosting muted videos of great plays and victorious moments in the Royals history. I can't help but grin at the way the players jump on each other in celebration of a special moment. I've never experienced that.

I've always wondered what it would be like to be on a team. The closest I ever got to being a part of one was when Gianna played volleyball in middle school, and I went to all of her games. My dad couldn't afford it, choosing to spend his money on vodka and lottery tickets, so I pretended I wasn't a sports girl. In reality, it's all I ever really wanted to be.

What I was after probably wasn't a team, but a sense of belonging. I'd come home from school and turn on the television, losing myself in sitcoms. The laughter gave our home a sense of levity, and when I sat down with their fictional families for dinner, my canned ravioli tasted a little better. I chased that feeling for a long time—until I was old enough to realize it didn't exist in the real world. It's called fiction for a reason.

"To the left is the wellness center," I say, pointing at a sign. "You'll get Wednesday's scheduled massage in there."

He arches a brow. *Tell me you at least scanned my email.*

"The cold plunges, hot tubs, saunas—all that stuff is a part of the center. You can access that anytime." I lead him farther down the hallway. "The strength and conditioning rooms are to your right. We'll tackle that in a minute. But this door is the locker room." We stop in front of the bold purple door. "Go in first and make sure it's empty."

He smirks, licking his lips. "Scared of what you might see?"

"It's called being respectful, asshole. I know that's a novel idea in your world."

"You are just a ray of fucking sunshine. Do you know that?" He pokes his head into the room. "All clear. Not a dick in sight."

"Maybe from your vantage point."

He gives me a mocking, smug grin. "Aw, are you working on getting a sense of humor?"

"Shut up and move."

I step in behind him, rechecking the time. I have to be on the other side of town in two hours and can't get off track because Gray was late—and there's still so much to cover. I need to hand him off to someone else as soon as possible.

"From here, you can access the wellness center, weight room, and the pitch," I say, pointing at different doors. "The showers are through that archway, and I'm sure you can figure out which locker is yours."

He moves across the room to a gold locker denoted with his name and number on a shiny metal plate above it. I'm not sure whether he's in awe of the locker room or nervous about being in it, but I can't help but notice his stiffened shoulders and tense back. He switches his bag from one hand to the other as he pulls the door open.

"I laminated and taped your practice and game schedule to the inside wall," I say. "I also included a list of coaches and weekly meeting times. Those could change, of course. You'll obviously attend the group meetings for backs, but I added the group times for forward, too." *Which I thought was an added touch.*

He sets his bag down and surveys the contents that I carefully curated over the weekend. Balls, resistance bands, and a first-aid kit. Deodorant. Backup mouthpiece, just in case. His training jersey and shorts hang from a hook with a towel folded neatly below it.

"When did you do this?" he asks without turning around.

There's an edge to his voice that puts *me* on edge.

"Before you got here," I say, stopping myself from pointing out that I was rushing around this morning even though he wasn't.

Gray turns slowly to me.

Uneasiness blooms in my stomach as his eyes find mine. My spine stiffens as I brace myself in anticipation of his reaction. I don't know how in the world he could get mad about this, but something tells me that's the case.

"The correct response would be *thank you*," I say.

"I told you to back off."

"*This is my job.*" My hands go to my hips in defiance. "What part of that is difficult for you to understand? What's not registering? I mean, God knows I'm not doing this out of the kindness of my heart."

"That would be hard to do, considering I don't think you have one."

My jaw falls open before I can lock it in place. *What a bastard.*

I force a swallow as his words seep into my psyche. Nothing he's said to me so far has bothered me. I slept like a baby all weekend. But this quip hits differently.

I tell myself it's because he's so ungrateful for the opportunity being given to him. I'm just shocked that someone can have everything laid out for them like this and still be unappreciative. The idea that this spoiled asshole could have the power to hurt my feelings is implausible.

I'm beyond that.

"Again, if you don't like it, you should've done something about it," I say, glaring right back and ignoring the swipe at me. I won't back down from him. I'll hold my ground. "Because I don't want to be here. This isn't my idea of a good time either."

"You've crossed a line, Astrid."

"*Okay*," I say, mocking him.

"You don't call the shots here." His features darken. "I mean it. The groceries were one thing. The fucking schedule was another. *But this?* This is my locker room with *my team*." He glances over his shoulder, the vein in the side of his neck throbbing. "I know you and Renn seem to think I'm incompetent, but I think I can manage getting my locker together."

I throw my hands in the air. "It's deodorant and a first-aid kit, for Pete's sake. It's not like I'm giving you a box of condoms and a sandwich."

"Right. I might've been able to use those."

I groan, huffing a breath to keep myself from choking on my frustration.

He stalks across the room, filling the air with the warm scent of his cologne, yet a sudden chill hangs between us. He's glowering at me.

Out of all the things I thought he'd get upset about, putting together his locker wasn't it. I also didn't expect him to be so … mad.

"Guess the articles I read online about you were true," I say with a shrug.

"The locker room is off-limits to you," he says, his eyes blazing. "I'm not joking."

"Unfortunately, that's not your decision."

He runs a thick palm over his head in evident frustration.

"If you don't like it, take it up with Renn," I say, my hands gripping my hips even tighter. "Because he's under the impression you need me, and just because you're a *complete fucking dick*, I'm going all in. I'm going to go the extra mile just to piss you off."

His nostrils flare. "You'll regret that."

"Yeah, probably not. Because you'll be out of here in a few months, and I won't."

A door behind me opens, and voices fill the locker room. I rip my gaze from Gray's.

"Did we interrupt something?" a guy everyone calls Breaker asks.

Gray's stare burns a hole in the side of my face. I don't acknowledge it.

"No, you didn't," I say, giving Breaker and Jory Plath a smile. I've met Jory a couple of times. Calling him one of my favorite players would be a lie, considering that I don't like any of them. But he's one of the least grating. "I was just giving Gray a tour. Guys, this is your new scrum half, Gray Adler." I look at him over my shoulder. *Fucker.* "This is Breaker and Jory Plath."

"We know who the hell he is," Jory says, laughing. "Gray, it's good to fuckin' meet ya, my man." He extends a hand to him. "It's nice to have ya here. Welcome to Nashville."

"It's good to be here," Gray says, shaking his hand before reaching for Breaker's. "Nicest facility I've ever seen, that's for damn sure."

"Fuck, yeah," Jory says. "This facility has all the perks. They treat us like gods here."

Breaker chuckles, side-eyeing me. "Looks like Adler got a perk of his own."

A perk? My blood boils.

Jory shoves Breaker's shoulder, knocking him off-balance. Gray starts to speak, but I jump in before he can get anything out. I certainly don't want him piling on me in front of other people. This is embarrassing enough.

"Oh, Breaker, that's where you've fucked up," I say, smiling sweetly. "I'm no one's perk. But if you ever demean me or reduce me to *a perk* again, I won't be your perk. But I will be your fucking problem." I let my gaze linger on his before ripping it away.

Jory winces. I don't give Gray the time of day. If he can rearrange his schedule, he can find his way around the complex.

"Have a good day, boys," I say, walking out the door and not looking back.

CHAPTER
EIGHT

"Shift it wide!" Coach Farrell shouts from across the pitch, watching the backs unit work on attacks for this week's game. "When that happens, I want you to use the overlap." He claps twice, motioning for them to regroup. "Let's run through that again."

A breeze ripples across the stadium, bringing with it the scent of freshly cut grass and sweat. It delivers a hit of nostalgia, of being young and playing in the spring, not far from here, with my parents in the stands. Brooks would be beside me, and girls would be yelling at us from the bleachers. After the game, we'd go home with a large Piper's Pizza and Brooks in tow. Mom would always let him come over, as long as Hartley and I still completed our barn chores before bed.

I tuck my hands into the pockets of my hoodie and take in the energy and activity around me. Each unit runs through its job-specific tasks, honing ways to create opportunities during Saturday's match. The rhythm of the game—the movements, the patterns—restores a beat to my life that's been missing over the past few days.

"So what do you think, Adler?" Coach Farrell smiles. "Are you ready to get out there, or are you enjoying your break?"

"Hell, no, I'm not enjoying it. Not sure I've ever gone six days straight without being on the pitch since I was a kid."

He clamps a hand on my shoulder and chuckles. "Spoken like a true rugger."

I shrug, smiling at him.

"Can't play you this weekend since you're not eligible until Thursday," he says, gesturing to Jory to wind the guys down. "I'll have you out here for Thursday's practice, though. We'll throw you right into the fire."

"Looking forward to it, Coach."

He steps in front of me, looking me in the eyes. His intensity makes my heart pound, but I don't look away.

"We have a great team here," Coach says. "It's a great group of men. I believe you can find a home here and make a significant contribution to the team's success if you put your head down and bring your best. This can be the start of something special, if you want it bad enough."

I lift my chin and boldly meet his gaze. "You can count on it."

He stares at me for a moment, then two, as if he's weighing the truth of my statement. *As if he's not sure whether he believes me.* I stare right back, choosing not to clear up any misconceptions.

I see the questions in his eyes. The rumors he's heard and the conversations that have been had behind my back sit on the tip of his tongue, poised to launch my way. I don't blame him for being curious, and I sure as hell don't blame him for being concerned. I haven't played with my heart for two years—and anyone with eyeballs can tell.

But when I left Denver, I promised myself that I'd leave all the baggage that I could behind. I owe it to myself, and Caroline, to start fresh and make the most of this opportunity. For both of us.

If I open the door to questions and start trying to explain myself, then I may as well have stayed in Colorado. Because one inquiry will beget another. And all of the shit I tried to leave in Denver will be firmly lodged in my life here. I can't do that. I can't survive it.

I love this game, and now, more than ever, *I need it*—but I keep that to myself, too.

Satisfied with whatever he sees in my reaction, he pats my shoulder again and joins the forward coach at the touchline.

"So what do you think?" Jory Plath rubs a towel emblazoned with the Royals logo across his heated face as he approaches me. "Think you can work with this?"

He flashes me a wide, toothy smile that matches his personality. He's easygoing, as far as I could tell yesterday, and welcomed me to the team with no hesitation. Tall, with a body built for the strength and agility of a top winger, he'd be imposing if it wasn't for that damn grin.

"Abso-fucking-lutely," I say, bumping his outstretched knuckle with mine.

Practice is adjourned on the pitch below, and players head to the locker room in small groups. Jory and I follow everyone toward the purple double doors.

"Have you been added to the group chat yet?" Jory asks, running the towel over his head.

"Group chat?"

"Yeah, the team chat on text messages. It's currently called The Unemployed because Chase got pissed at Nico and Ridge for posting memes all the time. He told us we were gonna be unemployed if we didn't take shit seriously, then he changed the group name and left it."

I chuckle. *This is gonna be fun.* "Nope. I didn't know there was a team chat, but it sounds like a good time."

"I'll add you," he says, flipping off one of our hookers as we pass him. "The forwards come in early on Sundays for recovery." He looks at me and grins. "Whatever the fuck you do, don't get here before noon. Those motherfuckers come in, arguing about whose bruises are worse. They hog the saunas—and they're gross. I've never heard a group fart as much as those fucks. Don't stand behind any of them during yoga. You'll thank me later."

He gags, his face twisting into a horrified grimace.

I laugh, returning Nico's nod as he jogs by. "This is all good information."

"It's the least I can do since you're gonna be leading us to a championship this year."

I look at him out of the corner of my eye to see if he's joking or poking around for a reaction. Much to my surprise, there's no humor or nosiness in his expression. *Huh.*

It takes a second to absorb the words he stated so matter-of-factly. *"Since you're gonna be leading us to a championship this year."* His confidence in me brings a genuine smile to my lips.

"Have you been to Nashville before?" Jory asks, tossing the towel over his shoulder.

"Oh, yeah," I say, clearing my throat. "I grew up about an hour from here in a little place called Sugar Creek. What about you?"

"I'm from the Bay Area. Played in Chicago after college, then spent a couple of years in Hartford before I got the call to come here when Renn Brewer took over." He laughs. "I about pissed my pants when I got that call."

"You and me both. I told my agent that I was getting pranked when I got word about the trade."

"How'd you like playing in Denver?"

There's a loaded question. I scratch the top of my head, trying to separate playing in Denver from my time living in Denver—two vastly different yet interconnected experiences. It's hard, nearly impossible, really, to separate them since one affected the other so much.

"It's a great program," I say fairly. And leave it at that.

We pause at a gate that separates the player facilities from the practice pitch to allow a large group of our teammates to go first. I spot Breaker entering the locker room ahead of us. With a bald head the size of a bowling ball and the shoulders the width of a barn, he's hard to miss in any crowd. Everyone seems to like him, and he has a good rapport with the Royals staff. And I want to like him too … I just can't.

"I'll get you added to the chat," Jory says as we step inside the clubhouse. "See you tomorrow."

"Yeah. See you tomorrow. Thanks for the heads-up about yoga."

He laughs, heading across the room.

The air's heavy with sweat and body wash. Rock music plays from a speaker propped up on a shelf above a bench. I head to my locker to get my bag and a box of tip sheets that need to be signed, but end up stopping every few feet to chat with someone new.

Each conversation is smooth and painless—much easier than I anticipated. I can't help but get caught up in Chase's retelling of a play from last week's game, and I chat with Ridge about game play for a full twenty minutes. We share the theory that the game is best played primarily off instinct, and it was a relief to know that I connect with someone here on that level.

By the time Ridge and I are finished, the room has thinned out. I pull my locker open and take out my bag. The back of my hand brushes across the first-aid kit Astrid left me dangling on a hook. The contact—the reminder of yesterday—claws at my insides as our conversation replays through my head.

"The correct response would be thank you."

"I told you to back off."

My gaze drifts to the laminated schedule that fell to the bottom of my locker this morning, and I pick it up. It's heavy in my palm—much heavier than a plastic-coated paper should be.

"This is my job. What part of that is difficult for you to understand? What's not registering? I mean, God knows I'm not doing this out of the kindness of my heart."

"That would be hard to do, considering I don't think you have one."

The flash of emotion through her green eyes lived with me all night. No matter how hard I try, I can't quite get it out of my mind. It was so quick, barely noticeable, and too fast to identify. But it was present—a burst of something other than ice-queen vibes. Although I shouldn't wonder what it was all about or what part of our sparring triggered it, I do.

I tell myself that I'm only curious because this is the first time she's shown a human side. And I write off the heat creeping up my neck as leftover fury from her being in my space. But there's a wobble in my stomach, a dead weight in my sternum, that has me shifting uncomfortably.

"It doesn't matter what that was all about," I mutter, glancing at the date on the schedule. "That's her problem. You have bigger fish to fry, Adler."

I set my bag on the chair in front of me and dig out my phone.

> Me: Hey, I haven't seen my bonus hit my bank account yet. Is that still happening this week?

I start to slip my phone back in my bag, but my agent surprises me with a quick response for once.

> Chuck: I'm 99 percent sure. Let me check on it and get back with you.

> Me: I'd appreciate it. I have bills due.

> Chuck: Understood.

I force a swallow, the pressure of the moment rising so high inside me that I worry it might spill over—and I don't know what that would look like. "No, Chuck, I don't think you do."

"Hey, Adler," Ridge says, distracting me. He's standing

across the room with a bag over his shoulder. "A few of us get here an hour early on Wednesdays for extra recovery treatments. You're welcome to join us, man."

"Yeah. Thanks," I say, thankful for the redirection. "I'll be here. It'll be good to get back into a routine again."

"Wednesdays are heavy lifting days. I only survive if I go into it prepped."

I laugh. "Sounds about right."

"He knows what Wednesdays are," Breaker says, coming out of the showers. His slick grin immediately puts me on edge. "Brewer gave him a fine piece of ass to help him prep. You should see this bitch, Ridge. She's a fucking dime."

"Whoa, Break," Ridge says, holding out a hand.

An eerie calm settles over me, erasing any thoughts outside of what's happening in this room. His words were lodged at me like an arrow. *Is he waiting to see if I'll bleed?*

My hands dangle at my sides as the air surrounding us impregnates with a static charge. Breaker squares his shoulders to mine, standing tall as if to confirm my suspicions. He's trying to get a reaction out of me. *Why?* I'm not sure. *Is he implying that I'm getting unfair treatment by having an assistant? Is he insinuating that I'm fucking Astrid? Or is he just being a dick?*

This blowhard has a problem, and we're going to solve it right fucking now.

My jaw flexes as I stare Breaker down. He's a big piece of shit —easily three or four inches taller than me and about one hundred pounds heavier. And, by the looks of it, just smart enough to get himself killed.

"You have a decision to make," I say to him, my voice stone-cold.

He smirks. "Is that so?"

"*Fuck*," Ridge says, sighing. "Let's not do this, guys."

"Shut the fuck up and keep your teeth, or run your mouth and don't," I say to Breaker.

He laughs, projecting the sound louder and more obnoxiously than necessary.

I smirk back. *"You better think this through,"* I warn, taunting him.

In the back of my mind, I know I should get my shit and get the hell out of here. Fighting a teammate before I'm even officially on the squad would ruin everything—and maybe even get me tossed out of the league altogether. But his insinuations can't go unchecked. I can't let that shit begin to take hold here.

"Let's take a breath," Ridge says. "Let's think this through."

Breaker takes a step toward me.

"I will knock you the fuck out before you get your hands up," I say calmly. "Take another step …"

His confidence wobbles, likely because he didn't count on me to still be standing here. But that's all I need to know to understand that he doesn't want any part of this. *Of me.* That's both a disappointment and a relief.

Finally, Breaker's lips twist into an amused, cocky grin. "Calm the fuck down. I was just messing around."

"Good choice." I close my locker, my heart hammering like a drum. I keep an eye on Breaker in case he's the kind of guy to throw a sucker punch when my back is turned. "See you both tomorrow."

"See you tomorrow," Ridge says.

Breaker doesn't say anything, but I expected that.

I make my way through the facility, not making eye contact with anyone. It's one foot in front of the other until I'm inside my truck.

My jaw aches from grinding my teeth together, and my breaths are still haggard from the adrenaline coursing through my veins like a roller coaster. The enormity of what nearly happened hits me in the center of my chest. *I just about fucked all the way up.*

I grip the steering wheel until my knuckles turn white.

But the thought of letting Breaker run his mouth is too much to let go. And allowing him to belittle Astrid behind her back feels like fucking up too. I'm no knight in shining armor—not that she needs one, the woman can handle herself—but it would be hard to look at her and know I let this go without saying a word. Dignity isn't disposable.

"Dammit," I say, smacking my palm against the armrest.

I glance down as my phone lights up with a text. Astrid's name flashes on the screen. *I've summoned the beast.*

My chest tightens as I read her words, reminding me that she'll be at my house in an hour. It's the last thing I want to do tonight, but I can't call it off. Because, after today, I need her gone more than ever.

Me: Okay.

Then I start my truck and leave the parking lot and the locker room behind me.

CHAPTER
NINE

"There's this guy ..." Gianna sighs on the other end of the phone. "Don't laugh."

I don't.

The sun hovers ahead, just above the horizon. Stately buildings standing tall on either side of the road frame the sunset like a picture frame. It looks like I could drive straight into the vivid oranges and pinks if I keep my foot on the accelerator. Considering my destination and the day I've had, testing that theory doesn't sound like a bad plan.

"How many is that? Twenty-eight?" I ask, trying to remember how many times Gianna has started a sentence with that phrase since Audrey and I started counting a year ago. "No. Audrey said you used *'There's this guy ...'* on Sunday when you went out for drinks without me."

"Don't start. You were invited and chose to stay home."

"So that's twenty-nine." I ignore her comment about me bowing out of drinks because I had a headache. I *did* have a headache, and his name was Gray Adler. *It's just that particular headache is of the seven-days-a-week variety.* "Anyway, what about him?"

I take a right onto Pinecrest, saying goodbye to the gorgeous sunset. I can't help but acknowledge how metaphoric the moment really is. I'm leaving the light behind and descending into darkness.

A thought nags me in the forefront of my mind, telling me to turn the car around and go home. To save myself. Nothing good will come out of this evening with Gray because his whole point is to make me miserable. As much as I hate to admit it, his plan is already working, and I'm not even there yet.

Although he doesn't know it, he got an assist in the form of my ex-boyfriend Trace this afternoon.

"An email came in a few weeks ago from this guy who said he'd been fucking his employee's wife," Gianna says.

"*What*? His employee's wife?" *The things Gianna gets into …* "Like, the guy works for him and he's banging his girl?"

"Yeah. Just like that. According to him—and who knows if he's telling the truth, but that's neither here nor there—he didn't know it. He met her while he was getting his tires rotated."

"Is that a euphemism?"

She giggles. "No. They were at an actual mechanic shop."

I slow down for a red light and try to piece together where this story is headed. It's much more entertaining than thinking about Trace's crap. "So how did he find out she was … who she was?"

"His employee got an award, and they had a company dinner to celebrate him. He walked in with her on his arm."

"Bet that was awkward." I proceed forward, making a right at a fancy bar called The Swill, and quickly enter a residential area. Apartment buildings are interspersed with small homes that have tidy front lawns and flowers hanging off the porch. My window is rolled up, but if it weren't, I bet I could smell cookies baking somewhere. *If this is where Renn houses his employees, I should negotiate housing in my nonexistent employment contract. Damn.* "Did he tell the guy he was banging his wife or what?"

She smacks her lips together. "I hate this color on me. I got three new lipsticks, and I'm trying each of them. Why haven't you ever told me coral isn't my color?"

"Gianna, can you focus?" I sigh, knowing that if she goes off track too far, I'll never get her back—and I kind of want to know the end of this story. "I'm almost to Gray's."

"Shit. I just dropped my earrings. Can you hold on a sec?"

I roll my eyes. "Sure."

I reduce my speed, coming to a crawl, as I survey the scene in front of me. Gray's apartment is on my left, and even if I wasn't sure which was his, I'd recognize that ridiculous truck.

My body tightens, pulling so hard that I wince as I park along the curb. I've been nauseous since I got the mail this afternoon. This isn't helping.

Everything inside me screams not to go inside with a volume so loud that it's deafening. I need to go home and deal with the letter I received this afternoon while I'm still clear-minded, not walk into Gray's for another pointless battle. That's especially true since, as much as I don't want to admit it, my feelings are still hurt from yesterday.

"That would be hard to do, considering I don't think you have one."

I fight the lump in my throat and turn my attention back to Gianna.

"Sorry about that," she says. "To answer your question, no, he didn't say a word to the guy about banging his wife, and that's why he was writing into the column. He wanted to know if he should say something or let her handle it since it was her marriage and he was a semi-innocent bystander. Sort of."

The lilt to her voice gives her away. I sigh, knowing there's more to the story than what she's shared. "What are you not telling me?"

"I may have asked him to meet me for dinner tomorrow night."

"What? Why would you do that?" I stop myself. *Well, she did meet a stranger in an empty parking lot for a urinal, so is this really that surprising?* I sigh yet again. "You don't even know this guy."

"I like the way he emails, okay? But the dinner isn't confirmed, so don't panic yet." She giggles. "Okay, that's my news. Update me on your life, please."

I grip the steering wheel like I'm trying to disintegrate it and glance at the envelope on the passenger's seat. Bile coats the back of my throat. Even though my instincts say to keep this to myself and handle it on my own, I know that's unhealthy. I need to lean on my friends in hard situations.

Here we go … My damp palms slide down my thighs.

"Oh, I have a dandy update for you," I say. "Guess what I got in the mail today."

"No clue."

I take a deep, shaky breath. "I got a letter from an attorney stating that I owe *almost twenty thousand dollars* because Trace, who kicked me out, keep in mind, didn't pay his rent." I twirl the earrings that Audrey brought me from Boston. "Then when he did leave, he left it a disaster. Broken dishwasher, ruined carpets. Apparently, he trashed the entire place."

"How is that your problem?"

Good question. I breathe deeply to try to put out the fire burning my chest. Trace was such a bad decision, and I can't escape him. It's been years since I've seen or communicated with him at all, and he's still throwing wrenches in my life. I'd cry if I weren't so numb.

"Because I paid the rent a number of times, and the trash pickup was in my name, so that somehow makes me legally liable for the rest of it. Sounds unbelievable to me, but I'll have to get an attorney, I think." I groan, sinking into my seat. "I don't know what to do."

"Don't pay it. That's illegal."

I shrug. "Let us pray. But I don't want to talk about it, and I need to go anyway. I have more immediate headaches at hand."

"Okay, I have to go, too. I'm having dinner with my sister. She's in town for a couple of days."

"That's right. Have fun with Lucia and tell her I said hi."

"Will do. Bye, friend."

"Bye."

The silence wraps around me, sucking the air out of my lungs. It's going to be torture sharing space with Gray—especially when I'm already on edge. But if I don't deal with this asshole, I won't have the money to deal with the other one.

Twenty thousand dollars? My stomach churns, and I shove the thought out of my mind.

"Go on," I mutter, turning the car off and grabbing my bag. "Get this over with."

I get out, locking up behind me, and start up the long sidewalk to the four apartments on this block. They're more like townhomes from this angle, each with a garage and a small porch. A child plays with a puppy on one side of Gray's home. On the other, an older man sits on a porch swing, smoking a cigar. He waves like we're old friends, and I can't help but smile at him in return.

Gray's front stoop is the only one with no welcome mat or flowerpot. *Seems fitting.*

Blood thunders in my ears as I raise my fist to knock. I lift my chin, hiding any vulnerability that might be streaked across my features, and rap against the door. I might be anxious, but he can never know that.

After a few seconds, the door swings open, and I drag in a quick breath. *Of course, he's shirtless.*

I don't allow my gaze to drop from his eyes. "Where are the boxes?"

He steps aside, face blank, and motions for me to enter. "In the corner."

"Great."

I march by him as if he's not standing in a pair of shorts and bare feet, and with his hair damp from the shower. I'd bet he dressed, or undressed, perhaps, like this just to see if it would bother me. He'll just have to try harder if he wants a reaction out of me. I'm laser-focused on the boxes and not on his body. *I wonder if* that *bothers* him.

His apartment is cool but smells warm, like body wash and cinnamon. It's cozier than I expected. A few nice touches—a plant, a couple of pictures, and a candle—and this place could pass as a real home.

The door slamming makes me jump. This is a lot of stimuli to process at once.

I drop my bag onto the sofa and straighten my shirt, gathering my composure. "Are there any boxes you don't want me to open?"

"Nah."

I roll my eyes with my back to him, trying to create a plan. The mere sight of the boxes so haphazardly tossed into the corner of the room melts my brain. He's just lived like this for days. *How?*

He really is an animal.

"So just sort through them and put the stuff wherever I want to put it?" I ask.

"Yup."

"Fine."

"Great."

I huff, grabbing one box on top of the stack and hauling it to the floor. Gray sits at the kitchen island with a permanent marker in his hand, signing papers for the media department. Neither of us speaks or even looks at the other.

My chest cinches like a belt is strapped around it, as if it's bracing me for the moment the brittle air between us shatters. An invisible pressure makes it difficult to breathe.

The top of the first box is already open. I peer inside … and try not to gasp. A myriad of items are crammed inside like a toddler was given the task. A skillet is wedged between a bathroom towel and a book. Bottles of supplements are strewn across the bottom. *Are all the boxes like this?* I open another one and find a bottle of shampoo hanging out with a coffee maker.

For a moment, all I can do is stare. This mess prickles every bit of my organizational-loving heart. Gray doesn't need an assistant. The guy needs a mother.

I take a long, deep breath. *Think of it as an opportunity to set something right in the world so you don't crash out—even if that something is just Gray's socks.* Not sure where to start, I pull a smaller box from beneath a pair of shorts that seem to have been casually tossed on the stack like the star on a strange version of a Christmas tree. It's lighter and rattles slightly. I open it carefully.

"Hey," I say, pulling out the contents. "This is cool."

A chessboard that appears to be handmade with a dark wood and teal-hued resin catches the light above me. A drawer is made into the bottom to hold the chess pieces. It's heavy and solid and beautiful—and, thankfully, undamaged.

I glance up and catch Gray watching me. It's only now that I realize I've been talking out loud.

"Oh, I wasn't talking to you," I say flippantly. "I was just admiring your board."

He lifts a brow as if this surprises him. "Do you play?"

I place the board gently on the sofa.

"I love chess," I say, grabbing another box and peering inside. "But I play mostly in my driveway."

"In your driveway?"

"Some people sit in the driveway and listen to music," I say, moving a few towels out of my view. "I sit in mine and play chess."

"Why don't you just play it in the house like everyone else on earth?"

It's all kitchen stuff. "Because the habit started when I was avoiding going in the house." I lift the hefty package, swallowing my groan, and carry it to the kitchen.

"Do you need my help?" he asks, setting his marker down.

"Nope."

"Your face is turning red."

I grimace, placing the load on the counter. "Kind of you to notice."

He dips his chin and picks the marker back up. I think he mutters something under his breath, and it's probably for the best that I can't hear it.

I busy myself by finding a spot for his four seasonings, a trivet, and six kitchen towels that should be laundered before they're used. A cutting board, I think, made of marble, weighs nearly as much as I do. *Odd thing for him to have, but whatever.* He has a can opener, two knives, and one measuring cup, and I leave them on the counter. Then I find another box of kitchen supplies and haul them into the room, too. It's such a nice distraction from the situation with Trace.

This is not as bad as I imagined. Twenty minutes have passed, and not only have I made progress, but Gray and I haven't killed each other. It's a small victory I'm too happy to take. I appreciate the opportunity to create order somewhere since I can't seem to do it in my own life. This also feeds a morbid curiosity about how he lives. It's like running a background report on him without visiting a sketchy website for the information and risking getting a virus. *And seeing photos I can't unsee ...*

I find a few canned goods, but there's no pantry in the kitchen. The logical place to put them is on the top shelf above the spices and protein powders, but I can't quite reach. So I line up the cans so they'll be easily accessible and then hop onto the counter.

"What are you doing?" Gray asks as if it's killing him to watch me.

My knees dig into the countertops, and I balance myself. "What's it look like I'm doing?"

"Looks like you're trying to break an arm."

"Don't worry." I grimace, trying to move around in the narrow space. "If that happens, I'll drive myself to the hospital."

He groans, huffing behind me. "Why don't you just ask for help?"

"Because I don't need it." I place the cans perfectly equidistant from each other in the middle of the shelf. "You think I'm joking. I broke my arm in the third grade by jumping out of a swing on the playground. My dad was half in a bottle of vodka when I got home from school." I add a final can of green beans to the lineup. "I couldn't take the pain by dinner, so I walked to the hospital."

I pause to appreciate the perfection of the cabinet before hopping off the counter with a little more coordination than I knew I had in me. *Score!* Gray's eyes follow me to the living room, and they're hot on my back as I open another box.

My body temperature rises as I play my broken arm story back through my mind and wish I hadn't shared that with him. He doesn't need to know anything about me, and God knows he doesn't deserve to have that kind of access to my life. Men like him are gatherers and hunters. They gather information, then hunt you down with it.

I glance inside the next box and shove it away. I don't want to ask him for help, but there's no way around this one. "You're going to have to deal with this one. It goes to the kitchen."

"Too heavy for you?"

I look up and sigh. "No, it's too peanutty for me. I'd rather not go into anaphylaxis here and have to call the paramedics while gasping for air." I pause. "Not that I couldn't do it."

"Of course you could," he deadpans, hopping off the chair. This time, I don't think fast enough to keep myself from getting an eyeful.

Ho-ly shit.

Gray's body wasn't built. *It was crafted.* Forged. His chest is barreled, and his abdomen is stonelike. His legs are just short of tree trunks—thick thighs and strong calves. Scars and bruises accent his skin as much as the dark ink that embraces his left upper leg.

He's a machine that moves with an oddly refined grace.

Even the devil was once an angel.

I gulp and refocus on the box, contemplating whether to move it myself. But Gray is at my side before I can get the courage to go through with it.

"Where do you want it?" he asks.

"That should go in the spice cabinet above the coffee maker." I hold my breath as he reaches in front of me and grasps the jar. Whiffs of his body wash caress me almost criminally. It lingers in the air long after he's walked away, and I mentally berate myself for noticing it. "Open a few drawers while you're in there and let me know what you think."

"Searching for external validation?"

"Some of us didn't have our needs met as children." An unwelcome blush colors my cheeks, betraying my instructions to be cool. I make a face like I'm being a smart-ass, so he doesn't weaponize that against me later either. "Anyway, I don't care whether you like it or not. You can move stuff around if you hate it."

"I'm sure I will."

Fucker. I turn to the rest of the boxes and make a production out of sorting through them.

His clothes are crammed into two boxes, mostly T-shirts, shorts, and joggers. A couple of pairs of jeans. There are a few hoodies and a heavy coat, but aside from boxer briefs and socks, that's about it. I'm not sure what I expected, but it strikes me as odd. *Doesn't he own a pair of pants or a dress shirt? A belt? A tie?*

A phone rings and I turn to see if it's mine, but before I can even reach for my bag, he's answering his.

"Hello," he says, his voice low. He licks his lips while he listens. "Are you kidding me? I thought it would be in my account this week."

I fold his shirts, thinking he should really use fabric softener, and try not to listen.

"I can't wait two weeks," he says, his voice full of gravel that rakes across my skin. "You'll have to figure it the fuck out." He stares at the cabinets while he listens to whoever's on the other side of the call. "Yeah, that's not gonna work. I don't care how you phrase it."

Standing with the stack of shirts in my hands, I carry them to his bedroom. Gray's voice carries through the apartment like a roll of thunder. It's so distracting that I can't even snoop around his room. Instead, I stand at his dresser, one hand gripping the top edge, and listen. *Who is he talking to?*

"That's not my problem," he says. "Call me back and tell me when I'll have the money. I need at least half of it by the end of the week."

The sound of what I assume is a phone hitting a countertop makes me grimace.

I unload the shirts into a drawer as quickly as I can and then return to the living room. My steps are hesitant, and I move as quietly as possible. His conversation doesn't seem to have gone well, and I'm not sure what his mood will be like now.

He's standing at the fridge when I enter, his back muscles flexing and his spine stiff. *He's pissed* … and I have no idea what to do. I'm not asking him what's going on because it's none of my business, but Renn also said there were whispers about Gray having a gambling problem. If this involves the mob or an underground betting ring, I'm better off not knowing anything. I've watched enough movies to know that.

You can't be tortured for information you don't have.

Gray doesn't acknowledge me, which is for the best. I grab a new box and get back to work. The faster I complete this, the sooner I can get out of here.

I open the top and reach inside, my fingers hitting something smooth and cool. A picture frame. It's the first personal item he's had so far, and my curiosity is piqued.

The frame is placed on a blanket that appears to have been carefully wrapped around the picture at one point. It's sturdy with the weight of a quality piece as I remove it from the box. I sit back on my knees and take in the image staring back at me.

A stunning blonde is bent over, laughing. Her eyes are lit up, and the wind is rippling her hair. She's probably in her mid-twenties, if I were guessing, and holds a rugby ball.

Who is she?

She looks nothing like Gray, so unless one of them was adopted, I'm guessing it's not his sister. The moment feels intimate, and the look in her eyes gives adoration. *She has to be his girlfriend.*

The thought makes me pause. The idea of grumpy Gray with his bad attitude having a girlfriend who is so … happy—carefree, even—is wild. *Was he ever happy like that? Is he still with her? Or did they break up, and that's why he's a dick now?*

I chew my bottom lip and glance around the room. I could put the frame on the kitchen island or tack it to a wall. But if she's an ex, he might not want to be reminded of her every day. *Only one way to find out …*

"Where do you want me to put this?" I ask, holding up the picture.

He turns, his lips parted to speak, but as soon as his attention lands on my hand, his mouth slams shut.

"I could put it out here somewhere," I say. "Or in your room."

"Put that down."

I ignore the chill in his voice. "Okay. Where?"

He slams the refrigerator door closed.

I avert my eyes from his and lay the picture back inside the box, then I carefully get to my feet.

My defense mechanisms kick in, shooting adrenaline into my veins. I'm hyperaware of his proximity, the sound of his movements in the kitchen, and the rapidness of my breath. I'm not sure what I've done to piss him off, only that I have.

"If you don't want me going through your things—"

"This isn't about that, Astrid."

"That's what it seems like, Gray."

He holds my gaze from across the room. His scrutiny makes me squirm, mainly because we're in his personal space and not a neutral one, which changes the dynamics. But I won't be walked over just because he asked me to be here.

"Leave," he says flatly.

"What the hell did I do—"

"*Leave.*" His icy tone chills me to the bone. "Please."

What is happening?

He wasn't exactly welcoming when I arrived, but he most certainly wasn't like this. But this isn't the first time he's flip-flopped on me. He did it yesterday, too.

Maybe this is his pattern. He's lukewarm, then ice-cold. *Is that why Renn didn't trust him to navigate the team on his own?* He's unpredictable. Hard to deal with. Insubordinate. How Renn believes he's a "nice guy" is beyond me. He usually reads people so much better than this.

My throat squeezes, but I swallow through it.

"We need to get a couple of things straight," I say, facing him and crossing my arms over my chest. "You're not going to waste my time or play games with my head, by literally turning around and being a complete dickhead out of nowhere."

He runs a hand down his face and groans.

"I don't know what set you off in the locker room yesterday, or if it was your call or the picture today, but neither of them has anything to do with me," I say, my voice rising. "I don't understand."

"You wouldn't understand if I told you."

His dismissive tone is flat and clipped. He's shelving what I'm saying without ever hearing it. *Like I'm heartless.*

I stand taller, ripping my bag off the sofa, then I pin him to his spot with a dirty look. I hold tight to my anger. If it starts to slip, a vulnerable ache will take its spot in my chest, and my bruises will start to show. And I don't show those to anyone.

"Believe it or not, I'm not a heartless bitch," I say, spitting the words at him.

"Astrid …"

I pause with my hand on the doorknob. "Or maybe I am."

If he says anything else, I don't know what I'll do. *Explode? Cry? God, I'm not going to let him see me cry.*

"Astrid—"

I yank the door open and close it between us before he has the chance to say something more.

CHAPTER
TEN

Gray

"I don't know why I agreed to this," I grumble, squinting in the early morning sunlight as I step out of my truck. "At least it's recovery work and not weights first thing."

Early morning workouts are usually my jam. Something is invigorating about the air before it's filled with exhaust and bull-shit. I think better, breathe better, perform better. But I got out of my routine and haven't been able to find it again. I haven't been eating right, my mind has been cloudy, and I can't remember the last time I had a good night's sleep.

And I feel it everywhere. Especially today, since I barely closed my eyes last night.

I toss my bag over my shoulder and close the door, locking it behind me.

Astrid's face and those fucking green eyes have flashed through my mind a hundred times since she stormed out of the apartment. Anger. Confusion. *Pain?*

It's reminiscent of the same look she had when she left the locker room. It's slightly different from the usual pissed-off vibe she wears around me. Typically, her dirty looks are believable.

Pure loathing, which I understand. I don't like her either. But before her exit from the facility and again before she left my apartment, it wasn't just her being mad. Whatever was swimming around those gold flecks has eaten away at me. It's kept me up. It's gnawed at my gut.

"Fuck," I mutter, tucking my chin to my chest against the chill. I slide a hand in my pocket, only to feel it buzz. Again. And again. And again. "These assholes."

I don't have to look to see who it is because I already did that … when Nico and Ridge started sending memes to the team chat at five thirty this morning. As annoying as it was, some of them *were* funny. None, however, was as hilarious as Chase's reaction since someone added him back to the chat against his will.

I'm about to silence the whole damn thing when the vibration changes, and it begins to ring.

My brows pull together as I yank it from my pocket. Chuck's name is displayed across the top of the screen.

"Good morning, Chuck," I say carefully. *Why is he calling so early in the day?*

"Probably not."

I stop just a few steps from the front door. My heart skips a beat, then two. I swear I can hear my ribs cracking with the heaviness of the moment squatting on my chest. "Why is that?"

He sighs. "What the fuck did you do, Adler?"

Huh? I nod, acknowledging a couple of guys as they arrive at the facility.

"I hope you have answers because I sure as hell don't." Chuck is clearly ready to throttle me. "I got the cancellation notice about fifteen minutes ago. Care to explain?"

My fingers grow cold, a chill creeping through each digit as if my body pulls all my blood to my center to keep my vital organs working. I stand in place with my gaze fixed on the gate to the pitch. "I don't know what you're talking about."

"Dammit, Adler."

I blow out a breath, trying desperately not to lose my shit. "What cancellation?"

"Your bonus."

My bonus? "Wait—what?" I pace toward the gate, sure I misunderstood him. Or, at the very least, I'm overthinking this. "What happened? Did they cancel a payment? It'll be another week or something?"

"No. They canceled it altogether. I have a call in to Brewer to see what the fuck happened, but that's all I know. Are you telling me *you* don't know?"

"*No, I don't fucking know,*" I say, running a hand over the top of my head. "It's gotta be a mistake. Why would they do that?"

"Again, I have a call in, and I'll let you know when I know something. So you haven't gotten into any trouble there?"

"No," I snap.

He blows out a breath as if he's over the day already. "Then go on about your morning, and I'll let you know as soon as I hear something. If you haven't done something to expressly void your contract, then I'll fight back on this, obviously."

"I'd fucking hope so."

"All right. Talk to you soon."

The line goes dead.

I squeeze the phone so hard that something crunches. I'm not sure if it's the device or my bones—and I don't really care which one might be broken. *I'm so fucking pissed.*

Ideas, situations, and probabilities spin around in my head, trying to land on the reason this is happening. Surely, it's a mistake. It must be. Because if it's not … I'm fucked.

A cold sweat trickles down my back despite the cool temperature. *Why is Renn doing this? What's the point?* I jerk the collar of my hoodie away from my neck, clawing at the fabric to make room to breathe. When I turn around, Jory is holding the door open and watching me.

"Are you okay?" he asks with genuine concern written on his face.

"Yeah. No. I don't know." I exhale and shrug, frustration setting up residence in my shoulders. "You good?"

He motions for me to enter the lobby ahead of him. "Better than you, by the looks of it."

"At this point, it wouldn't take much."

The building is quiet with just a few bodies shuffling around this early. The first rays of the sun beam in, illuminating the space with a promise of a bright day. It would be inspiring if my day hadn't just taken a nosedive into the fiery pits of hell.

"I'm gonna grab a protein shake before we head back," Jory says. "Want one?"

"I ..." My gaze shifts to movement at the elevator bank. Renn is stepping out, his attention focused on his phone. "I'm good. Thanks."

"See ya back there," Jory says.

My feet move toward Renn before my brain makes the decision. I clutch the strap of my bag at my shoulder and remind myself to stay calm. *It's probably just a mistake.*

"Good morning," I say, struggling to keep from clenching my teeth.

Renn's head snaps up. There's no smile, no offer of a handshake.

Fuck. "Hey, I just got a call from Chuck ..." I'm not sure how to explain my question, or what words to use to get the point across.

"Yeah. Why don't you come up to my office?"

"Sure."

We stand shoulder to shoulder in the elevator as Renn types away on his phone. His nonchalance about this, like taking thousands of dollars out of my hands is no big deal, makes me want to punch something. Because the longer the ride to the top floor takes, the more panicked I become. He knew what I wanted to talk about without me saying it.

Something is very, very wrong.

He leads me past cubicles and staff members having breakfast at their desks. He's cordial to everyone who speaks to him—but few do. It's clear he's focused on business. *What is happening?*

"Come in and shut the door," he says, walking into his office and rounding the corner of his desk.

I shut it softly and drop my bag beside the same chair I sat in the last time I was here.

"Have a seat." Renn sits behind the stately desk and rocks back in the leather chair. He waits until I get comfortable before speaking. "I invited you up here because I don't discuss financials in front of players, and I assume that's what you were talking with Chuck about this morning."

"Yeah. With all due respect, what the fuck?"

"Hey, the contract conditions were very clear, and you and I went over them together."

I nod, bewildered. "I agree."

"You broke the contract, and I'm not in the business of paying out that kind of money for no reason. So the bonus is recalled."

I grip the armrests, holding myself steady. *"You broke the contract." What?*

I'm speechless. Disoriented. I replay the sentence again, like I can roll it over repeatedly, and it'll eventually be polished and make sense.

"Do I just let this season play out and deal with it at the end?" he asks. "Or do I assign you someone new and hope you can manage to work with them in a respectful manner? These are questions I'm pondering this morning."

"Whoa, wait a second." I sit up, finding a break in the fog. "Why would you assign me someone new? Where's Astrid?"

"She quit."

Static infiltrates my brain, making every thought fuzzy.

There's a tug-of-war inside my head. *She quit. Why do I have to give up my bonus?* But also … *why did she walk away?*

"Any other questions?" Renn asks. When my gaze shifts to

him, it's met with a pointed stare that feels a lot like I'm to blame for this.

"I guess the first thing I want to understand is why I lose my bonus if she's the one who quit."

"She quit with cause."

I lift a brow as a hot brick burns a hole in my stomach.

"Astrid feels uncomfortable working with you, and I refuse to ask her to continue doing something that makes her feel that way."

I flinch, struggling to repair the apparent disconnect between my brain and my ears. I hear what he's saying, but I sure as fuck don't understand it.

A cold chill snakes lazily down my spine as the memory of how she looked at me last night comes back to me.

Renn leans forward, resting his forearms on his desk. "I don't know what happened between the two of you, but I will tell you this. Astrid Lawsen is one of the smartest, most capable, and most respectable women I know. It takes a lot to rattle her, Gray. It takes a lot to get under the shield she carries around every day. It's unfortunate that the first person to do that was you."

I lean forward and bury my head in my hands.

Renn knows Astrid, so he must know that she's not a female you have to walk on eggshells around. She's not exactly a doormat waiting to be trampled. *She does the trampling.* Sure, things between us may not have been a walk in the park, but she gave as good as she got. *And she just quits?*

And I get fucked?

I lift my head, suppressing a groan.

Renn sits back again, this time crossing one ankle over his other knee. He peers at me with a look that I can't quite name, and it makes me fidget in my seat. He and Astrid are close, so I get that he'd listen to her … *but I need that damn bonus.* There are no other options.

I blow out a hasty breath. "Can we talk about this?"

"There's nothing to talk about."

"She hated me before she even knew who I was." I have one shot at convincing him to hear me out. If I don't take it now, I'll never get it again. "How do you know she didn't quit just to screw me over? Wouldn't it be more logical to give me an assistant who doesn't dislike me from the jump?"

"No."

"*No?*" I scoot to the edge of my seat, imploring him to listen. "Why her? I mean, I don't understand why you think I need a babysitter to begin with, but *why her*? Why not someone else?" I groan, slapping my knees as I sit back. "You can't just do this. You can't fuck me over like this."

Renn shoves away from his desk and stands.

"I brought you here because you're a highly skilled player," he says, his jaw ticking. "But I also brought you here to keep you from ruining your life."

I flinch at his words.

"Do you think I pay my players what I do without investigating them first?" he asks. "We have the highest payroll in the league—by far. Do you think I just sign those checks without knowing who I'm writing them to?"

This can't be right. "No, but—"

"No one is fucking you over, Adler."

I laugh in disbelief. "Oh really?"

"Yeah. Really." He rolls the cuffs of his shirtsleeves up his forearms. "You think everyone is against you, but it's really you against yourself. Face the facts."

"I didn't realize you were a philosopher on the side."

He pins me in my seat with a sharp look. "Look around. I'm doing just fine for myself. It would behoove you to shut your mouth and take notes."

If it were anyone else in the world saying those things, we'd brawl.

"I see me in you," he says. "I've not been exactly where you are right now, but I can imagine it."

"You can imagine it?" I lift a brow, not sure what he knows.

Doubtful that Renn Brewer could ever understand my shit. "I find that hard to believe."

Renn finishes his sleeve and adjusts it to his liking before he looks at me again. Once he does, I know the truth. He's done his research.

He knows.

The room closes in, the walls rapidly encroaching. My heart kicks into overdrive, rushing blood through my veins at warp speed. I haven't discussed this at length with anyone—not Brooks, not Hartley. *No one.* I'm not prepared to talk to Renn about it, and I sure as fuck don't want to talk about it now.

Everything feels urgent, and I'm desperate with no direction. My life is slipping through my fingers, and I'm watching it happen. No matter how tightly I curl them, I can't stop the grains from falling to the floor.

"A few years ago, my father did some very unscrupulous things to my family," he says, his temple throbbing. "He's now living the rest of his life in a cage—that's how bad it was."

I still.

"So I've been through some shit, my friend," he says. "And I've battled a lot of demons. A lot of guilt. I've maneuvered a lot of blame." He takes a breath, and it feels like the room does, too. "Do you know what I've learned?"

I subtly shake my head.

"Every loss doesn't mean someone fumbled." He tosses that into the room with the casualness of a weather report. He plants both hands on his desk and levels his attention on me. "I brought you here to try to save you—to give you an opportunity to save yourself. If you don't want to do that, that's on you. But you won't take Astrid down, too."

I rest my elbows on my knees and hang my head.

His words slice me like a thousand papercuts. Maybe it wouldn't have been so bad if I was prepared—but I wasn't. I wasn't ready to have things brought to the surface and shoved in my face.

I didn't want to look in this mirror.

As hard as it is to hear, knowing that Renn has some idea of what I'm going through does marginally ease the burden. Just enough to breathe. That small opening reduces the fog in my head and lets me think clearly.

And the first thought that comes through the haze is Astrid. *She's uncomfortable working with me.* Renn's statement echoes throughout my body, winding through my veins like venom. The words are deliberate. She doesn't just dislike working with me, and she doesn't just hate me. She's *uncomfortable* with me.

Flashes of our interaction in the locker room come rolling back. The words *I* chose. The way I chose to deliver them. The impact they might've had …

"But you won't take Astrid down, too."

Those thoughts are followed by the memory of her standing in my living room, holding that fucking picture, and the fury and embarrassment I felt—and that I let get to me. That I let spill over to Astrid.

Sure, she's a savage who has poked me as many times as I've needled her. But she's really an innocent bystander in all of this, and she doesn't deserve my bullshit. *That look in her eyes?* It *was* pain.

I'm no better than Breaker.

Fuck.

I sit up, fortified by the clarity in the truth, and clear my throat. "I said a few things more … *harshly* than Astrid deserved, and I can man up to that."

Renn nods.

"Is there any chance she'll work with me again?"

"There's zero chance I'm asking her to do that."

Fair. "What if I talk to her?" That feels a lot like walking into a lion's den right about now, but there's no alternative. And I probably have it coming.

His lips twist as he thinks. Finally, he shrugs. "You have until midnight. I can reinstate the bonus before the end of the day. Otherwise, it's over."

"Okay."

"But if you do get her to agree to this, and you *ever* push her to this point again …" His look is cold. *Lethal.* "Don't do it. Let's leave it at that."

"Understood."

"Now get out of here," he says, shooing me toward the door. "You've wasted enough of my day."

I get up, grab my bag, and rush to the door. Before I open it, though, I turn to him. "Renn?"

He looks up from his computer.

"Thanks," I say, swallowing hard. "For all that."

"Pay me back by bringing a title to Nashville. Now go."

"Yes, sir."

I step into the hallway, yanking my phone out of my pocket before Renn's door is even closed. Astrid's name is in my recent text log, and I click on it.

Me: Can we talk?

CHAPTER
ELEVEN

ASTRID

"I think you need a hobby," Audrey says, poking at her salmon with a fork. "You need something to think about besides work."

"Unless we're going back to berry picking and cave dwelling, I have to think about work," I say. "That's what happens when no one teaches you financial responsibility, and you're up to your eyeballs in debt by the time you're a full adult."

Audrey rests her fork on the edge of her plate and looks at me with the sweetest blue eyes. "In your defense, you were surviving. And you were just a baby. Let's give little Astrid some grace."

"I'd rather we had given little Astrid a personal economics class," I mutter.

Stupey's is packed for a Wednesday night. We waited thirty minutes for a table, which has never happened on a weeknight. Kim saw us waiting and snuck us two sangrias and an Arnold Palmer. Apparently, a food vlogger gave them a glowing review on Sunday, and they've been smashed ever since.

Social media ruins everything—almost as quickly as men.

"You don't need a hobby, Astrid," Gianna says, lifting her lipstick-stained glass. "You just need to get fucked."

"There are children around," Audrey whispers with cheeks to match her cardigan.

I take my third glass of sangria and sit back, considering Gianna's advice for once. I usually assume she's saying things for shock value—and that might be true. But I can't deny that I need to work some of this tension out of my body, and *what better way to do that than to have it screwed out of me?*

It's better than the fucking I'm taking from everyone else in my life. Hell, I'm still getting reamed by a man who cheated on me, kicked me out of his house, and made me get a round of antibiotics as a party favor. *It never ends.* Between my bills, legal threats, and losing my extra pay over Gray's bullshit, I'm bent over a barrel, and there's nothing I can do about it … and I hate it.

Might as well be bent over something else and get something out of it.

I yawn, the sangria giving me the first taste of relaxation I've felt since I got that damn letter. Stress management is typically one of my strengths—mostly because I keep everything in my life in tidy little clusters. But I'm one wrong word from crashing all the way out.

"Do you know what, Gianna?" I say. "You might be right."

Audrey shakes her head. "*No.* Don't take Gianna's advice."

"And why not?" Gianna asks, feigning offense.

"Well, for one, your answer is always sex. Sex doesn't cure everything."

Gianna gasps. "I beg your finest pardon? Don't go spreading misinformation like that. Isn't that against your doctor's creed or something?"

"I believe you mean the Hippocratic oath, and no, philosophy PhDs don't take an oath. We're not dealing with life-and-death situations."

"I agree with Audrey that sex doesn't cure *everything*." The sharp edges of my frustration soften, allowing me to actually inflate my lungs all the way. "But neither do multivitamins, and I take them every morning."

Gianna beams. "That's my girl!"

"Let's talk this through," Audrey says, ignoring Gianna's celebration. "You're angry with one man. You don't need to bring another into the mix."

"Or she could take it out on that one." Gianna looks between us and shrugs. "I'm agreeing with you, Aud. It would be irresponsible to bring another poor, innocent man into this mess. The most effective thing would be to fuck the brains out of the man you're pissed at in the first place."

I sigh, narrowing my eyes at her. "I wouldn't fuck Gray Adler if he were the last man on earth and it was my duty to repopulate the planet."

"Let me point out that you immediately jumped to Gray and not Trace." Gianna grins.

As if he were summoned from the depths of Hades, my phone buzzes with the four-thousandth text I've received from Gray today.

Gray: I would really like to talk with you.

Audrey lifts a brow. "Is that him again?"

I nod, wishing I had turned my phone off. He hasn't said much in his million messages—just that he wants to talk in various iterations. But each time I see his name on my screen, I want to talk to him *less*.

I let Renn down, and I'm angry with Gray for putting me in that position. I've taken pride in never failing the Brewers in any task they've given me over the years. Not one. Hell, I've gone above and beyond, even helping Tate on a few occasions, and that's equivalent to taking a grenade to the face. That man is a walking disaster. But I've never failed … *until now.*

A rush of emotions burns the bridge of my nose, but I battle them back—like I should've with Gray. I let my feelings call the shots, and that's so weak of me. *Worse?* It cost me a raise that I desperately need.

I woke up in a panic this morning after a sleepless night filled with nightmares and sweats. I kept dreaming that I was in a deep pit and a group of men stood at the top, throwing credit cards and rental agreements at me. Each piece of paper and plastic cut my skin and left me bawling in a heap of tears and blood … and no one came to help me. So once I was awake and certain that no one was hurling anything at me, I called two law offices and inquired about retaining their services. It turns out that I'm either selling feet pics or auctioning off a kidney. The buyer would have to pay the hospital bills for my organ removal, though.

"Have you responded to Gray at all?" Gianna asks, crunching on a crouton.

"No. I have nothing to say."

"Seems like you have a lot to say," Audrey says. "Maybe you should just tell him how he made you feel—"

"*Ew.*" I wrinkle my nose. "Why would I do that?"

Audrey grins. "It might surprise you. I bet you'd feel a lot better."

"I told you what would make you feel better," Gianna says, grinning, too.

I glance from Audrey to Gianna and then back at Audrey. *Have they lost their minds?* "You two give the worst advice."

Gray: Could you just hear me out, sweetheart?

"No, he did not." I gasp, staring at the phone.

"What?" Gianna asks.

I barely hear her question, my mind choosing to focus on the perceived threat and not my harmless best friend. I can't believe my eyes, and I must reread it five times before it sinks in. *The fucker called me sweetheart.*

My fingers hit the keyboard and flurry away.

Me: Eat shit and die.

His response is immediate.

Gray: FINALLY.

"That bastard," I say, my jaw skimming the table. *I've been played.* "I took the bait."

"Well, he *is* one attractive lure," Gianna mumbles to Audrey.

I stare at the screen in disbelief. Heat paints my face as I battle back waves of humiliation. I don't know what to do now. My friends chatter beside me, giving their opinions on how I should react, but I don't make out their words. The voice screaming inside my head is much louder than theirs.

Gray: I'm not trying to make you
uncomfortable, and if my texts make you feel
that way, please tell me and I'll stop.

Me: THEY DO.

But I stop short of hitting Send.

The glasses of sangria I've consumed feel like ten in my stomach. They slosh around, splashing against the bottom of my esophagus and burning it. *Making it uncomfortable.*

Out of the twenty-two words he sent, that's the one that stands out.

"I can't work with him, Renn. His personality is all over the place, and it makes me uncomfortable."

"That's all I need to hear."

My conversation with Renn didn't last long—it was far shorter than I anticipated. He called to ask how it was going with Gray, and I didn't even really get to fully explain the situation. As soon as I told him I was uncomfortable and didn't want to work with him anymore, the call ended.

It can't be a coincidence that Gray used that term.

I erase my response and type out a new one.

Me: They annoy me.

Then I hit Send.

"Since you're all feisty tonight," Gianna says, "this might be a good time to bring this up, Astrid."

I look at her over the top of my phone, lifting a brow.

"We were brainstorming at work on Monday, and looking through old magazines for inspiration," she says. "We came across this column where they took a question and then had a few different people answer it. I thought you might find it fun—and it pays. Not a ton, but a couple of hundred dollars."

"A couple of hundred dollars for my response to a ridiculous question posed by a random person on the internet?" I ask. "That's it? No catch?"

"That's it. No catch."

"I'm in," I say, as my phone vibrates in my hand. *Guess I'll use that to start a legal fund.*

"Great! Give me a few days to get everything together, and then I'll give you more info."

Gray: We're better than this.

Me: Speak for yourself.

Gray: You are the only woman in the world who would argue with someone who's trying to say nice things about them.

Me: Your point?

Gray: This is not going how I imagined.

Me: Great. Lose my number.

I turn my phone to silent and place it face down on the table.

Focus—and not on him. "I need to find another form of income," I say, accepting another glass of sangria from Kim. "Thank you."

"Of course. Do you ladies need anything else?" she asks.

"If you want to bring me the check, that should be about it," Audrey says.

Kim winds her way through the maze of chairs and dirty tables.

"You need another form of income." Audrey loops us back to my statement. "What kind of a thing are you looking for?"

"Something that pays heart surgeon dollars for administrative assistant tasks," I say, blowing out a breath. "I'm in the same financial boat that I was in pre-Gray as long as the Trace thing doesn't cost me the only arm that I have left. But I don't have twenty thousand dollars to pay *his* bills, not to mention the attorney fees I'll incur to fight it. It just never stops. My financial boat is full of holes."

Audrey pats my hand. "I'll jump in your boat and help you bail water. Just let me know what kind of a pail to bring with me."

Gianna groans. "Why do you always have to be so good and make me look so bad?"

I giggle.

"Bring a pail and join us," Audrey says. "I didn't say you couldn't come."

"No, but you said it first. You're just so … *good.*"

Audrey and I laugh at the look of disgust on Gianna's face. As if being good is somehow a terrible thing. Slowly, Gianna gives in and laughs, too.

"It's a good thing I love you," she says.

"I love you, too," Audrey tells her. "And I'll make you good before it's over. Wait and see."

Kim stops again and hands Audrey the check. She glances at the paper and gives Kim her credit card. As Kim steps away, something across the room catches my eye.

I'm not sure if it's the plain black T-shirt that feels familiar or the width of his back. But when Gray turns around, putting his baseball hat on his head, his gaze collides with mine with the force of a Mack truck.

"Shit," I hiss, heat creeping up my neck.

"What's wrong?" Gianna asks. "Are you okay?"

"Did you eat a peanut?" Audrey reaches for my purse. "Where's your EpiPen?"

I peek up through my lashes to find a pair of thick thighs moving toward our table. *This is going to take more than an EpiPen, guys.*

His cologne reaches us before he does, caressing us into a false sense of ease. Gianna picks up on his proximity first, naturally. A slow, sexy smile kisses her lips as she sets her sights on Gray.

What are the odds that he's here? Why does the universe hate me?

Audrey flashes me a look, and I nod. Her face washes in horror.

I take a deep breath and then lift my chin. His eyes are still glued to me—a hot, sticky sort of glue that traps my attention and holds it tight. He comes to a stop beside Audrey, slipping his hands in his pockets.

My heartbeat quickens.

"Stalking is illegal in Tennessee," I deadpan.

"Maybe I was here first," he says.

Gianna sits back. "*Oh.*"

"Yeah," I say without breaking eye contact with my nemesis. "Gianna and Audrey, this is Gray Adler. He was just leaving."

"It's nice to meet you, ladies."

I roll my eyes. My friends don't say a word.

"Astrid, can we talk for a minute?" Gray asks.

"I'm pretty sure she's told you numerous times that she doesn't want to talk to you." Gianna stares him down.

Gray's lips twitch.

"You need to go," Gianna says. "I have a taser, and I will use it."

"Before you taser me …" He gives her a look like she's ridiculous. "Let me say one thing."

"Make it fast," Audrey says. "Gianna is quick with that thing."

He fights a chuckle, and it makes me want to kick him in the shins.

"Astrid, I'm sorry."

Huh? My eyes widen, and my heart skips a beat. As if the words alone weren't enough to confuse the hell out of me, his tone—soft, clear, and even—confuses me even more. *And in front of an audience?* He almost sounds like he means it.

"You can go now," Gianna says.

"Yes. But the apology was very—ouch!" Audrey says, earning an elbow to the ribs from Gianna.

Gray doesn't move a muscle. He watches me without the fire I usually see in his eyes. His brows are tugged together, and there are lines around his mouth. No arrogance, no snipe sitting on his tongue. I don't know what to do with that.

"We can talk in front of your friends if that makes you more comfortable," Gray offers.

Gianna and Audrey turn to me like they're watching a ping-pong match and wait for direction. If I tell them to get him out of here, they would without question. Audrey might even pinch him for me.

It must be the sangria clouding my vision—and my brain—because Gray kind of looks sorry. That or the stress of the past twenty-four hours has worn me down altogether because I *almost* want to hear him out. If I did give him five seconds to make his point, it might keep him from blowing up my phone. That would allow me to forget he exists and focus on the other asshole in my life causing problems.

"Why are you here?" I ask him.

"At Stupey's? Because Jory told me their pad Thai was killer. I had no idea you were here, if that's what you're thinking."

"Of course, that's what she's thinking," Gianna says. "You've pestered her all day."

He starts to respond but stops himself. That's probably smart. I might be slightly argumentative when pushed, but Gianna will rip his throat out of his body and use it as a straw.

Kim hands Audrey her card while side-eyeing Gray. "That's it, ladies. Need anything else?"

"We're good," I say. "Thanks, Kim."

"Good night, guys," she says, waving to the table and giving Gray a quick ogle as she flees.

"Good night," Audrey calls after her.

Gianna turns to me. "What do you want us to do?"

I look around at the dining area. It's still pretty full, and it appears a few people are waiting for a table. I can't, with a good conscience, take up space when Kim could be making tips from a new party.

"Did you tip her on the card?" I ask Audrey.

"Of course."

I grab my purse. "Let's go. Gray, you can follow us and talk while we walk, if you must."

I get to my feet and follow my friends through the restaurant. My instincts tell me that Gray is behind me, but I don't look. The hairs on the back of my neck wouldn't be standing up if he weren't.

My body tingles with anticipation even though there's no way to know what he's going to say. I'm sure he isn't thrilled that I quit, but I don't know if he's angry about it. But if I know one thing about him, it's that he can switch from hot to cold in two seconds flat.

A man holds the door open for us, and we step into the cool spring evening. We form a small circle on the sidewalk around a giant ball of tension. Audrey tugs her cardigan closer to her body, nibbling the inside of her cheek nervously.

Gray stands to my side, looming over me in his sneakers. He seems bigger out here than he has in our past interactions. There's scruff on his face, his lips look dry, and I want to remind him to add Celtic salt to his water for hydration, but I don't. He's not my problem anymore.

"You guys can go," I say, pulling my friends into a hug.

"Are you sure?" Gianna asks. "We'll wait for you. Want us to wait in the car in case we need to dig a very, very large hole tonight?"

Gray sighs in exasperation.

I smile at her. "I'm good. Promise."

"Call me when you get home," Audrey says. "Before you play driveway chess. I want to know you made it."

"I will."

They turn together and make their way to the parking lot.

The sidewalk feels much emptier without my friends. A

couple of strolls down the other side of the road, but our side is vacant. The only sound aside from the occasional car is the soft hum of the music from inside Stupey's.

I'm alone with Gray, only this time, I don't want to run. For the first time, I want to hear what he has to say. *A man who's sorry and admitting it?* Color me intrigued.

Taking a deep breath, I turn to him. His gaze meets mine immediately.

"Talk."

CHAPTER
TWELVE

GRAY

"I'm sorry," I say.

It's the second time I've uttered those words to Astrid, and it's the second time those words don't seem to matter.

My head's a fucking mess. I swear I'm hearing every second that passes. *Tick, tock. Tick, tock.* It's one beat closer to the end of the day—and the end of my window of opportunity to save this contract.

She gazes down the street with her arms wrapped around her stomach, and I'm honestly surprised she's still standing here. That gives me an opening, probably the only one I'll ever get, to convince her that I'm not the total asshole she thinks I am. *Even if I question that myself right now.*

"I was out of line." I run a hand roughly over my head. "And I apologize."

She drags her attention to me as if it's the last thing she wants to do. When her eyes meet mine, there's a coolness in them that slams into me. This isn't just an angry woman—God knows I've seen my share of those—but this woman *is* hurt.

Fuck me.

"You don't like me," I say, squaring my shoulders to hers. "I can live with that. I don't really like you either."

She narrows her eyes, but not quite like she wants to kill me. Or maybe just not as brutally as she usually does.

"But this ... *thing* between us," I say, forging ahead, "it's gotten out of hand. I regret behaving the way that I have, and it was wrong. There was no reason it needed to get so personal, and I never meant to make you uncomfortable."

Her chest rises and falls. She pulls back slightly, her posture stiffening. Her gaze flicks toward the ground.

"Renn said—"

"I can imagine what he said," she says, her voice rising along with her gaze. "And it was predicated on what I told him, which might've been taken out of context. Or allowed to be unexplained. Either way, you might make me feel a lot of ways, and it's just ... complicated." She hoists her purse onto her shoulder and shifts her weight. "I don't know why we're having this conversation. Did Renn make you do this? Then fine, I—"

"No, he didn't make me apologize to you." My jaw tenses. "I think he'd be happier if I never spoke to you again."

"Then why are you?"

That's a good fucking question.

I twist my head side to side to release some pressure gathering in the back of my neck. Her question is straightforward, and the answer was simple when I pleaded with her to talk to me today. I need her on board so I can satisfy my financial agreements. But now with the sun setting at her back and the gold flecks missing from her eyes, I'm not sure that's the whole reason.

"I want to call a truce," I say.

She scoffs, shaking her head like it's a ridiculous suggestion.

"Let's just start all over," I say, my voice as soft as I can make it. "Clean slate."

"Why would I do that?"

"Because I know Renn is important to you, and I'm making assumptions, but isn't it eating you alive that you—"

"Oh no." *The gold flecks are back.* She points a finger at me. "Don't you act like you know anything about me."

"You literally told me that you never let Renn down, so that's not speculation."

She groans, unable to argue with me because I'm right.

"Just give this another chance," I say. "Please."

She moves by me, and I think she's going to walk away. I reach for her, but drop my hand just as quickly as I raised it.

If I touch her, she'll undoubtedly break my nose.

Her hair whips through the air as she spins on her heel, facing me again, and the flush in her cheeks causes her freckles to shine. I've never been this close to her, or examined her this closely, which is why I notice the tiny stars that dot her ears. It's the only jewelry she wears aside from a tiny, thin cross around her neck. *Even scowling, she's beautiful. What an unfair joke from the universe.*

"I would love nothing more than to be able to deal with you," she says. "It would solve a few of the problems ruining my life right now. You see, I'm stuck in this place of financial versus mental solvency because I can't do both simultaneously. Apparently, I burned someone at the stake in my last life because it really feels like I'm being punished for something."

She's talking so fast, so animatedly, that it's hard to keep up. It's also hard not to grin. But I don't dare. I can't risk that.

"I just need something to be easy," she says, her voice growing louder. "I just need one thing to go right, and the more men I allow into my life, the more things get fucked up. And I *just. Need. A. Fucking. Break.*"

She huffs, her whole body moving with the sound.

I take a step back for good measure.

"So tell me, Gray," she says, moving toward me. "What can I do for you to make your life easier?"

She doesn't mean that. If her pursed lips weren't my first clue, the balled fists would give her away. It's a total trap.

"Let's—"

"Do not tell me to calm down," she warns.

"I wouldn't think of it." *Again, because the words were on the tip of my tongue.* I toss up a prayer of gratitude for avoiding that trigger.

Two couples take a wide berth around us to enter Stupey's. They give Astrid a look like she's a circus act, and that pisses me off. I glare at them, silently telling them to mind their own damn business. I know they've gotten the picture when they shuffle quickly into the restaurant without a second look.

Then I turn to Astrid. She appears to be two seconds from tilting her head to the sky and screaming.

"Why don't we take a walk?" I suggest carefully, like I'm coaxing a rabid dog. "We're blocking the door."

To my surprise, she stays beside me as I head away from Stupey's.

I take a moment to reconfigure what I want to say to her, because she's flipped the script on me. Now I don't know how to express the things I want to say and achieve the results I need. I'm also not totally sure what results I'm after, either.

Her words echo through my head, tugging on my brain. *"I just need one little thing to go right, and the more men I allow into my life, the more things get fucked up. And I just. Need. A. Fucking. Break."*

What's that supposed to mean?

The row of buildings comes to an end. An offshoot of the sidewalk leads into a large green space filled with blooming southern magnolia trees, and their lemony scent reminds me of long days at the ranch, hiding in the tree lines from Dad so I wouldn't have to help with chores.

I reach out and take a flower as we move by, feeling the glossy petals and fuzzy undersides against my fingers. I'm not sure how to break the ice with Astrid, and I'm afraid that the wrong approach will not just break the ice but also shatter my chances of fixing this situation. And I have to find a solution. *I have to.*

"I'm not heartless," she says after we've walked a fair way down the path. When I glance over my shoulder at her, she's staring straight ahead. But at least she's regained her composure. "And I'm not a total bitch, either."

That's a curious start, but it's a step forward.

"Well, I try my hardest …" I take a deep breath. *If I'm really trying to make headway here, I gotta be honest.* "No, that's a lie. I haven't tried very hard not to be a dick. I haven't tried at all, really."

"I'm glad to hear that because if you had, you'd be a complete failure."

I consider her words as we turn around and head back toward the restaurant. I play them repeatedly, trying to locate the part tickling the back of my brain. She thinks I'm an asshole, which isn't unexpected. Or a surprising revelation. And she wants me to know she's not a bitch.

But why is it important to her for me to know that?

I spy her out of the corner of my eye. When she doesn't think I'm watching, she almost looks like another person. Her lips are soft and parted instead of being pressed together. She moves more gently, less restrained. Her lashes appear longer, and her body is softened. The armor is gone, and a feminine vulnerability takes its place.

It's the first time I've seen her as a woman and not a wench. And that fucks with me.

"Fine," she says as the shield locks in again. "I'll admit that I haven't necessarily been the easiest to work with either."

"Look at you. You admitted it, and you're still alive."

She glares at me, making me laugh.

I pause beneath the magnolia trees and wait for her to stop, too. She takes a few steps before she halts, slowly turning to me.

Stupey's isn't far ahead and, once we reach there, my chance will be over. *Negotiate, Adler. That's what's needed here.*

Compromise. My least favorite word.

Astrid studies me from just out of arm's reach, her arms wrapped tightly around her middle. This is a habit of hers that I haven't thought much about until now. *Is she trying to protect herself with this posture? Is she making herself smaller?* I lick my bottom lip, trying to slow the questions storming through my brain.

She's so … *defensive.* She's too defensive for this to be solely about me.

"I'm tired of fighting with you," she says evenly. "I can't do it right now, which is probably what I was trying to communicate to Renn. Battling with you is too much on top of everything else." She frowns. "You aren't my biggest problem anymore, if that tells you anything."

I quirk a brow but don't comment. If I don't speak, I can't fuck this up … and I think we might be going in the right direction. But I don't want to get my hopes up yet.

"If we can set some ground rules, we *might* be able to make this work," she says carefully.

Easy, Adler. Go easy. I offer her the flower in my hand. She eyes it with suspicion before relenting. Her fingers take it from mine without touching me.

"But first," she says, bringing the flower to her nose, "what's in this for you?"

I shove a hand in my pocket and kick a rock down the sidewalk. "Honestly? I lost my bonus, and the only way to get it back is to get *you* back."

"Right. I see."

She drops the flower to her side. Her expression is blank, and I can't quite decipher that. I also can't spend time thinking about it.

"Either way, I owe you an apology," I say earnestly. "I guess needing the cash is the vehicle to do that. Otherwise …" I take a deep breath and set my pride aside for just a second. "I'm not sure I would've bothered."

"You would've just let me believe you're an ass?"

I shrug. "Probably."

She twists the flower between her fingers as she gazes at the horizon behind me. She's somber and pensive, and I wonder just how delicate she might be behind all that piss and vinegar.

Slowly, she brings her attention back to me. She's still pensive. But this time, she's also resolved.

"At least you're honest, I guess," she says.

"I'm trying to be." I go out on a limb and take a chance. "Can I ask what your conditions are?"

She brings the flower to her nose and takes a deep breath. Her lashes flutter closed as she pulls the petals away. Then she looks at me calmly and clearly. "You play rugby and leave the rest to me. I won't tell you how to do your job, and you won't tell me how to do mine."

"Done."

She blinks as if she's surprised. "Okay. You'll also have to cooperate with me. Answer my calls and provide me with the necessary information. And when I set up a schedule or make an appointment for you, you do it. You *don't* reschedule everything or fail to show up."

"So you want to be in control?"

"I have to be."

The words carry on the breeze rippling through the trees. But they don't get carried off fast enough for me t0 miss the heaviness in them. *The honesty.*

Her gaze doesn't break from mine.

My mouth goes dry as I mull her admission over in my mind. *"I have to be."* As I consider other things she's said about not having her needs met and hating bullies … it all starts to make sense. It begins to paint a picture that's much different from the one I held until now. But I have to put that aside for the time being.

"Can we call a truce?" I ask again. "Just until the season is over, then you can resume all hatred."

The corner of her lip curls toward the sky. "I still don't like you."

I chuckle. "Good, because I still don't like you either."

"Great."

"Great."

"A truce it is," she says, studying me. "But the first time you turn around and bite my head off for no good reason, I'll have Gianna taser you."

Relief washes away the thousand-pound boulder that's been sitting on my shoulders all day. I can finally breathe again. *Thank God.*

She takes a long, deep breath and blows it out slowly. Finally, she nods. "Okay. Deal." She pulls out her phone. "I need to let Renn know before he hires someone else to take my place."

Astrid taps away on her screen, then pauses, then taps again. She laughs and rolls her eyes. All the while, I'm waiting for some indication that it's official and I'm getting paid.

"Dammit," she says, looking up at me.

My heart drops. "What?"

"We have to FaceTime him."

"Who?"

"Renn. Who else would I be talking about?" She holds her phone up and stands next to me. "I don't think he believes I'm doing this willingly."

The call connects, and Renn's face appears on the screen.

"Well, if this isn't a sight," he says.

"Hey," I say, hoping it doesn't sound as curt to him as it does in my head.

"So Astrid tells me you're working together again. Is that right?"

I nod. "That's right. We've aired our grievances, and we're really on the same page this time."

"You're good with this, too, Astrid?" Renn asks.

She glances at me. "Yeah. I apologize for the drama. I feel goofy about that."

"Not a problem, Astrid. It's a bit of a problem for Gray, but not you." Renn grins at me. "Behave, Adler."

"Yes, sir," I say.

"Good night," Renn says, and then he's gone.

I heave a breath, relief washing over me in waves. I'm not entirely sure how I managed to pull this off. However, the important thing is that I did, and it's done—and money should be hitting my account soon.

Astrid seems relieved, too.

"I'll call you tomorrow and find a good time to get together," she says.

"For what?"

She grins with a little mischievous smile. "So I can get your life together, Adler. Your ass is mine now."

My stomach tightens, but not out of frustration. "You think so?"

"Oh, I know so ... sweetheart."

With a smile that dances through my veins, she turns and leaves me standing beneath the magnolia trees.

CHAPTER
THIRTEEN

I lower the speed of my walking pad and slow my pace to cool down after a five-mile almost-jog.

The bright sun and clear sky give me a dose of optimism and vitamin D. The guest bedroom that serves as my home office is just big enough for my standing desk, bookshelves, and a small sideboard that holds my printer and office supplies. It would feel bigger if I could strip the nineties wallpaper and paint the walls a lighter color. But when I proposed that to my landlord, I was met with a scowl and a hard no.

Forgive me for wanting to increase your property value. Oof.

I pull up the calendar I started for Gray last night and scroll through the entries. He operates so differently from Renn that it took me a while to determine the best way to organize his schedule. I could essentially make a list of the things Renn needed to do or address each day, and I could be reasonably confident that he would check them all off by the following morning. *But Gray?* I'm not sure what approach will work best for him. The only thing I'm relatively certain about is that it won't be easy.

"He might be a shadow of the player he used to be, but he's still

great—just not as fit or focused as he once was. There's so much untapped potential, so much room for greatness, and I think we can get him to come back around with a little guidance."

Until last night, I was worried about Renn's judgment. Nothing about Gray told me that he was anything other than an angry, entitled asshole who was ungrateful, undisciplined, and unwilling to be guided anywhere, let alone to greatness. I was convinced the rumors were correct. After all, I'm a proponent of believing someone when they show you who they are.

But what if the sincerity in his voice yesterday, the hint of vulnerability in his eyes, is showing me a piece of his truth, too? What does that mean?

"That means he's going to make my job ten times harder," I say, changing the color I chose for his tasks from a bloodred to a slightly more subdued blue.

I glance at the time on my computer and then switch off my walking pad. My legs burn from the intensity of the last hour. I went a little too long and a little too hard, but I needed something to displace the energy that met me when my eyes opened this morning.

My to-do list is still ripe for the picking, but I know what I must do before I can get balls deep into Gray's life.

I have to decide whether to call Trace.

The idea of hearing his voice makes my stomach tighten so hard that I want to hurl. I've sent him a text and an email to the last personal and work email addresses that I had from before we broke up. Unsurprisingly, he hasn't responded. Now I'm not sure what to do.

Not calling him would be the easiest way to move forward.

Memories from our relationship barrel their way through my mind, elbowing through the barriers I set up to keep them out. My heart races immediately, and sweat dampens my armpits and behind my knees. I tell myself it's from the last hour of walking, but that's not true. It's a trauma response ... one I haven't quite worked through yet.

I can't let that keep me from advocating for myself.

I pick up my phone and hop off the pad, feeling the baby hairs on the back of my neck cling to my skin. I press each number with determination and grind my teeth, hating how defenseless I am when dealing with Trace. He knew too much about me. He had too much access to my fears and pain—and he used them like a sharpened axe and hacked his way through my heart. *Leaving me shattered in every way.*

The line rings once, then twice. I shift the phone between my hands, practicing what I'm going to say, reminding myself to be calm and confident. He holds nothing over me anymore—no truths, secrets, or power. *Nothing.*

My heart lurches at the sound of his recorded voice instructing me to leave a message. I sag against my bookshelf in relief that he didn't answer and hang up before the beep.

"Look at you," I say to the empty room. "You're all bold and brave in public, but a big baby in private."

I clutch the phone to my chest and take a deep breath. Before I can overthink things or get stuck in a bad place, I pull up the tab with the attorney's information that Audrey sent this morning and place a call. As it rings, I wonder what my friends would say if they could see me now—sweaty and anxious over calling my ex-boyfriend. This certainly isn't the Astrid they know.

"Good morning," a cheerful voice says, answering the phone. "Thank you for calling Dixon Legal Group. This is Wanda. How may I assist you?"

"Hi, Wanda. My name is Astrid Lawsen," I say, clearing my throat. "I was referred to you by my friend Audrey Van."

"What can we do for you, Ms. Lawsen?"

"I received a letter from an attorney a couple of days ago regarding unpaid rent, utilities, and damages to an apartment that I lived in with a former boyfriend. They're threatening to sue me, but the rental agreement was never in my name, and I moved out of there years ago. I'm not sure what I should do."

"Okay, Ms. Lawsen. I can get you in for a free consultation with Dennis Dixon next Thursday at two thirty. Does that work for you?"

The word *free* is music to my ears. "That works. Absolutely."

"Let me get a bit of information from you."

"Sure."

I answer a few basic questions and agree to email her office the letter I received. It's the most painless thing I've done in a while. I end the call and feel a sense of relief, but also of being supported—of not fighting this alone—and I'm not sure which feeling is better.

I tap out a text to the group chat to let Audrey know I made the call.

Me: I got an appointment, Aud. You're the best.

Audrey: Yay! I met Dennis Dixon at a fundraiser last year, and he was super sharp. If he'll take you on, he'll do a great job.

Me: Well, I didn't talk to him. I do that next week. But his assistant was a doll.

Gianna: A doll? Are you talking about me again? 😉 Kidding. Glad you got an appointment, Astrid. Check your email. I sent you the question for the column.

Audrey: So I don't get to know the question? Rude.

Gianna: The question is essentially this … A woman wrote that she's in a relationship with her guy and she loves him, but she also loves other men flirting with her. She wants to know if it's cheating or if it means she doesn't love her guy to the depths of her soul.

Me: I'm getting paid to answer this? 😅

Audrey: Oooh. That's a tough one. I'd need more context before I could form an opinion.

I wander out to the living room and flop down on the sofa. My friends go back and forth on their first instincts about how they'd form their replies. I don't chime in. Instead, I consider it quietly.

There are so many ways to think about this. I don't know that it's cheating, exactly, but it's undoubtedly not an indication of a strong relationship. *Or is it? Is she just being honest?*

Audrey: What are you thinking, Astrid?

Me: I don't know. Now that I have the pressure of answering it to the person instead of just spewing my thoughts, it's not as easy as I imagined.

Gianna: You have a few weeks until it's due, honey bun. Let me know if you have any questions.

Audrey: Let me know if you need to brainstorm. It's one of my favorite pastimes.

Gianna: Mine is giving head.

Audrey: GIANNA BARDOT.

I laugh, imagining Audrey's face as she reads Gianna's message.

Gianna: I gotta go. Love you guys.

Audrey: Love you. Be good.

Gianna: Don't take away all of my fun.

Me: xo

I open my email and find Gianna's message. The question is there, in full, along with the due date and a legal blurb about terms and payment. It's straightforward enough.

A bubble of excitement swells in my stomach, growing larger with each passing second. My mind races with possibilities about how to approach this topic. There are so many angles to take, so many ways to look at it, that it gets my creative juices flowing. I remember feeling this way when I sat down with a pen and paper when I was a kid—for a while, anyway.

"What the hell do you have?" Dad sneers, ripping the small note-book out of my hands. His breath is hot and smells faintly like rubbing alcohol as he leans over me. "A journal? Where'd you get this?"

My stomach drops as I relive the moment. That notebook was my refuge, the only safe space in my life where I could … *be.* There was no right or wrong, no judgment or attempt at rewriting history. In a house that was supposed to be a home, those spiral-bound pieces of paper I bought at the discount store with money Gianna's mom gave me for folding some laundry were my soft spot. I was in control and could live without fear.

That was over the day Dad found my diary.

My father flips through the pages as spit gathers in the corners of his cracked lips. "Look at you wastin' your time with this bullshit." He glares at me with bloodshot eyes. "You're just like your goddamn mother. There's a sink full of dishes and laundry on the fuckin' floor, and you're in here cryin' around."

He becomes a haze behind the tears fogging my vision. My heart and soul—my biggest vulnerabilities and darkest fears—are on those pages, and he's wielding them in front of my twelve-year-old face like a knife. I feel my heart splinter with every page he turns and every word he reads.

I'm going to be sick. "Can I have that back?" But as soon as the words leave my mouth, I know I messed up.

His lip curls as he looks at me over his shoulder. "Nah. I think I'll keep this. And I think you'll clean this house top to bottom tonight, or I might have to tape these pages on the windows so everyone who comes by can read them."

I shiver, hopping to my feet and heading back to my computer. "No," I say to myself. "You're not allowing the bitter actions of a drunk to derail you. You're leaving all of that back there where it belongs."

Gray's schedule is still pulled up, so I go over it again.

His to-do items are blue, his rugby schedule is in yellow, and his personal items are in green. It's robust and mostly complete. Looking at it reminds me of who I am—a woman who is competent, confident, and who has fought for every crumb she has ever been given. I'm a survivor of everything the world has thrown my way.

I attach the calendar link to an email with steadier hands and forward it to Gray. Then I open my text app.

> Me: I emailed you a link to your calendar. I'll be adding to it regularly, so please check it at least every night for updates to the following day.

His response comes back immediately.

> Gray: Will do.

"Will do?" I flinch in surprise. "That was easy. Is he fucking with me or what?"

I tap out another message to test the waters.

> Me: We need to find a time to sit down and go over things that would take too long to text.

> Gray: Sunday is my only free day.

I laugh in disbelief. "Well, okay, then, Gray. You're just cooperating now?"

Me: How about we meet somewhere around four o'clock?

Gray: Sure. Want to just come over here?

Me: Not really.

Gray: Stupey's, then?

I mosey around the house and consider where I want to meet Gray. Stupey's would work, but it could be loud, and it would undoubtedly be distracting. Alternatively, I have no interest in inviting Gray here. That's … too much.

Maybe his house would be the best answer. *Oof.*

I grimace while typing out my reply.

Me: I'll come there.

Gray: Don't worry. I know you rolled your eyes. I don't think you WANT to come here.

I can't help it. I laugh at the cheeky bastard.

Me: Sunday at four.

Gray: Great.

Me: Great.

I'm not sure what to say now. I should put the phone down and get back to work. Instead, I hold the device in my hand and stare at the screen as if I expect another text to come through, even though I don't.

Still, a couple of minutes go by, and my phone dings again.

Gray: Thank you.

I grin, typing out my response.

Me: You're welcome.

Then I turn my phone off and focus on an email I need to send to Blakely.

CHAPTER
FOURTEEN

GRAY

"What the fuck?" I laugh, tucking my towel around my waist.

My phone is propped up against a bottle of lotion with a video from the team chat playing on the screen. Nico and Ridge are together, presumably at one of their homes. Nico is wearing an Easter bunny outfit minus the head. Ridge dons a beekeeper's veil and gloves. They each have a hula hoop, one pink and one purple, and are cracking each other up in a contest that involves hopscotch, a swimming pool, and a unicorn raft.

Jory: Have you been drinking?

Sebastian: You can do better than that, Nico.
Are you even trying?

Breaker: Try it again. Backward.

Nico: Am I trying? Fuck off. This is hard.

>Me: I think the bunny tail is throwing off your balance.

Nico: THAT IS THE ENERGY I NEED, ADLER.

Chase: I'm putting in a trade request.

Ridge: You can come over, Chase. We'll let you try. Don't be sad.

Nico: I'll even let you be the bunny!

"Chase is going to kill them," I say, chuckling. I grab my phone and head for the kitchen.

The group chat has turned out to be one of my favorite parts of the Royals team so far. And, unfortunately for Chase, it wouldn't be nearly as fun without Nico and Ridge. Although he complains about their shenanigans and pitches a fit about their goofiness, I noticed during practice and at the game yesterday that he respects the two of them more than he does most of the others.

The living room is filled with sunlight as I pass through it. A light breeze sweeps through the apartment from the windows I opened after my Sunday morning run. For the first time in a very long time, I feel almost … settled. *And, God, it feels good.*

I take a bottle of water from the refrigerator and unscrew the lid. Before I can take a drink, my phone rings. I look down and smile.

"Hey," I say, pushing the speakerphone button and setting the phone on the counter.

"How the hell are you?" Brooks Dempsey asks from the other end of the line.

A rush of familiarity settles between us. There's no awkward pause, no stilted conversation. My body sags in relief.

"I'm good," I say, taking a quick sip of water. "I contemplated coming down to Sugar Creek this morning for church but decided against it when the alarm went off."

"That's where I'm coming from now. I ran into Hartley while getting my ass reamed by Violet Crowder about not attending Sunday School, and he said he talked to you this week. I figured I'd see if I still had your number since you never call me anymore, you fucking asshole."

Thankfully, the lightness in his tone doesn't match the statement, just like his words don't match someone fresh from church. Still, I feel like an asshole. A guilty one, at that.

"I'm just fucking with you, Adler. It's not like I've called you either."

I exhale. "What's up with that? What have you been doing? Hart said you tore up your shoulder or something."

"Yeah, tore my rotator cuff. I was going full speed with this new guy the coach brought in to train with us. He blocked an overhand right, and it ripped my shoulder to shreds."

"When did that happen?"

"Six weeks ago. Doc says I'm out six months before I can even train again."

"That sucks," I say, knowing how hard it must be for Brooks to stay out of the gym. I screw the cap back on my water before I knock it over. "So what are you doing now? Hanging out back home?"

"For a while." A door opens and closes in the background. "I haven't been back here in a long time, and I figured I might as well use my downtime to visit Mom and everybody. You know?"

I nod even though he can't see me.

A part of me can't help but wonder if we feel similarly. We both left home to do something fun and wound up getting caught in the drama of it all. Brooks in Vegas, working to stay focused while living in a sparkling city known for sin. And me in Denver, white-knuckling life in a city that harbors the worst memories of my life.

Does Brooks feel detached from reality? Does he regret many of the choices he's made? Does he have a sense of loneliness spreading deep in his soul that he can't figure out how to ease?

Or … maybe I'm just weak.

"I get that," I say, securing the towel around my waist. "I haven't visited Sugar Creek in a long time."

"You'd better get your ass back here now. No excuses."

I laugh.

"Patsy's is still going strong," he says, laughing, too. "She got rid of the dollar shots on Monday nights, and hardly anyone line dances on the weekends anymore. But the place still smells like cheap cigarettes and piss, so it'll still feel like home."

Memories from nights at Patsy's Bar and Grill come back to me like clips from movie reels. Late nights at the booth below the mounted deer head, sipping beers and making plans. The time Brooks and I decided to hold a dart tournament that resulted in an emergency room visit for an out-of-state hunter who vowed never to return. Patsy's bright pink lips, the burgers she served only on the weekend from a grill that probably hasn't been cleaned since the seventies, and the table in the back by the dance floor with names carved in it spanning decades.

"Do you remember my eighteenth birthday?" I ask.

He barks another laugh. "Roughly. It's still a haze."

"How in the hell did we get away with that?" I lean against the counter and think back to one of the craziest experiences of my life. "How did you convince Patsy to let us in, because you know damn good and well that she knew we weren't twenty-one."

"True. But do you know what she *did* know?"

It's the tease in his voice that has me grimacing.

"She knew I packed a hard eight inches."

"*Fucking hell,*" I say, chuckling. "Don't tell me you screwed Patsy. She was in her sixties back then."

"Damn right, I did. Remember that little apron she wore when she made hamburgers?"

I laugh in a mixture of disbelief and absolute belief, shaking my head. I'm not certain if he's telling me the truth or just messing with me. But if he really did fuck Patsy, I won't be surprised. "Stop it."

"I only banged her out once," he says, egging me on. "She sucked me off once after that—"

"Dammit, Brooks. Stop."

"—but it did get me a free pass into the bar as long as I didn't abuse it."

"Abuse the privilege or her pussy?"

"Both." He cackles. "I'll admit to you that I've done a few things that I look back at and can't believe I did them. Patsy is one."

I open my water again and take a long, cold drink. "How did I not know about this?"

"You were at rugby camp, I think. I was left to my own devices." He sighs. "So enough about me and my sexcapades. How is it going with you?"

How's it going with me? Instead of answering, I chug the rest of the water.

There was a time in my life when I told Brooks everything. Hell, if he wasn't involved in whatever I was doing, he got pictures of it later. But the idea of spilling my guts to him—spewing the bullshit in my brain all over him—feels weird. And feeling weird makes it even stranger.

"It was my first week," I say, starting slowly. "So you know, there were a lot of things to figure out. Systems, processes. That sort of thing."

"But it went well?"

I nod. "Yeah, it went fine. My teammates are great." *Except Breaker.* "The staff is the best of the best. And the culture here is results-driven. It's a total championship mindset, which is nice."

"Hartley said you play your first game with them next weekend?"

"No. Next weekend is a bye week. I'm not sure whether we're practicing on Friday or not because a few guys said that they usually take a three-day weekend just to let their bodies heal up and rest."

"Well, damn. I was going to come up and watch you."

I place the empty glass bottle into the sink and try to ignore the warmth rising in my chest. No one has come to watch me play since Caroline. I've learned not to look in the stands. I don't scan the crowd before we play. I don't listen for my name anymore. The idea of walking onto the pitch and knowing Brooks was there would mean a lot to me.

"That would've been great," I say, glancing at the clock. "I think I'm going to drive down Friday or Saturday. Will you be around?"

"Hell, yeah. Let's do it."

"I'll let you know for sure by midweek," I say.

"Sounds like a plan."

I clear my throat as my heartbeat picks up. "Okay, I gotta get off here. I have a meeting with my assistant in a couple of hours, and I need to get a few things sorted."

"Hart mentioned you had an assistant. How's that going?"

A grin tugs at the corner of my lips. "Oh, it's going."

"A truce it is. But the first time you turn around and bite my head off for no good reason, I'll have Gianna taser you."

Brooks waits for an explanation, but there's not one that comes to mind that accurately depicts Astrid Lawsen. She's frustrating and a giant pain in my ass, but she's also surprisingly great at her job. I can't lie. My schedule is packed and a little overdone, but I've been more prepared the past couple of days than I've been in my life. Every morning when I wake up and have my coffee and reach for my supplements, I think about how nice it is just to have it all at my fingertips.

That would be easy enough to explain.

The other parts of her? Not so much.

I don't want to be curious about her—I want to dislike her and forget her—but Astrid is a porcupine. She's sharp and dangerous on the outside to protect what I suspect is a delicate and vulnerable inside.

And that's too complicated to get into with Brooks.

"I'll get with you next week," I say, heading toward my bedroom.

"All right, my man. I'll talk to you then."

"Bye."

"Later."

The line disconnects, and I turn off my screen. Before I can toss it on my bed, it rings again in my hand. I look down at the name and my stomach sinks.

I take a deep breath. "Hey."

"Sorry to call on a Sunday."

"No worries, Joe. What's up?"

Papers shuffle. His breathing's labored, which makes me wonder how much longer he can do this before he drops dead.

"Did you get confirmation on the money?" he asks. "Because you're already late making the payment."

"I sent you a text about it on Friday."

"You know I don't text, kid. Don't waste my time with that shit."

I roll my eyes. "My agent worked some magic, and the money will be in my account on Tuesday morning. I'll transfer it to you as soon as it hits."

"Good. Because they're going to want their chunk by the first and, right now, I don't have enough to give them."

I sit on the edge of my bed and sigh. My stomach sours as I deal with the mix of emotions that erupt every time Joe and I have this conversation. They come so fast, one after another—

grief, guilt, and anger. More guilt. More anger. So much resentment for so many things.

But resentment's the worst … because despite all the money that I've made, it's why my checking account barely has a five-figure balance. And all I own is my truck.

"You'll have it," I say in a monotone voice that sounds hollow, even to me.

"Call me when you send it."

"Okay."

The call ends as abruptly as it began.

I stare at the wall, letting myself feel what my mind is processing. The therapist I saw for a while in Denver suggested it. If you allow yourself to feel things, your body doesn't have a chance to get emotionally constipated. She thought my migraines were my body trying to expel the emotional shit backing up inside me.

That sounded like horseshit. But when I started just letting myself get angry or upset, the intensity of those things did lessen over time. Maybe that's a small win in all of this. I have to just live with it.

"I have to be."

I rest my elbows on my knees and let Astrid's words slip into my brain. It's a curious choice of words. Those nine letters feel heavier than the entire English language as I roll them around my mind.

Since Wednesday, I've pondered that sentence often. I've paired it with the things she's told me and the way she holds her body. Her behavior at the gas station. The flashes of gold in her eyes.

"Some of us didn't have our needs met as children."

I might be a dick because I'm tired of trying to convince people that I'm not. *What if she's a control freak because she's given up relying on people for help?*

My eyes widen, and I sit up, wincing like I've been punched in the gut.

I open my phone, noting the witch emoji beside her name. I click the info button, and her picture enlarges on my screen.

She's in a car with her hair pulled back away from her face. Her cheeks are a faint pink, like she's been laughing. A smile parts her lips and touches the corners of her eyes. I've never seen her like this before.

And I know why.

Because I'm ruining her, too.

CHAPTER
FIFTEEN

Astrid

I straighten my shirt—a sapphire-blue top I put entirely too much thought into when getting dressed this afternoon. I'm not the type of girl who obsesses over what she wears. I throw on something appropriate for the occasion and go about my day. But every T-shirt felt too casual, and every button-up too stuffy, and this is definitely not a sundress type of situation. I need to look professional, yet cordial … and I have no idea if I pulled that off.

"I probably should've called Audrey for advice," I mumble, gathering my bag and phone before heaving a breath and then climbing out of my car.

Gray's neighborhood is abuzz with kids on bicycles and adults on porches, watching the children play. The warm air is perfumed by thick shrubs hosting soft pink peonies in front of the apartments to my left. A screen door to my right is propped open, and eighties music floats on the breeze.

My fingers tap a quick text to my friends.

Me: I'm at Gray's. Pray for me.

Audrey: You don't need prayers. You got this!

Gianna: You don't need prayers. You need condoms. 😏

Audrey: GIANNA.

Gianna: No Bardot this time? 😜

Me: One of you is helpful and one of you is not. I'll let you think about that.

I slide my phone into my purse and exhale slowly.

This wouldn't be so terrible if I knew what to expect. My text exchanges with Gray have gone well since our truce, and he's been amenable to my suggestions with quick replies. As far as I know, he hasn't missed an appointment or practice either. But I can't help but wonder if they haven't gone a little too well. I'm afraid to hope this can work out because when your hope goes up, it's just a harder fall back to the ground.

I press the doorbell and say a quick prayer of my own since I can't count on my friends to do it for me.

You've agreed to a truce. Don't go in there assuming the worst. I frown. *Don't give him the benefit of the doubt, either. Aim for a nice neutrality.*

Energy flickers in my chest, but I'm not certain if it's from anticipation or dread. My thoughts run amok as I consider how he's going to react to seeing me in person again. It's our first time together since the Magnolia Peace Accord, and my first time at his apartment since Picture Gate. I don't know whether I'm walking into an ambush or preparing for a picnic.

It's impossible to steady my erratic pulse as Gray opens the door.

He peers down at me with his dark eyes, studying me

intently as if seeing me for the first time. A white cotton shirt hugs his torso, and a pair of black sweatpants kiss his thighs. I don't know him well enough to know if he shaves routinely or not, but it's evident that he hasn't met with a razor since I last saw him—and I hate that he looks even better with the scruff.

"Hi," he says. There's no warmth, but his tone is also void of a chill. *Is that a win?* I don't know. "Want to come in?"

"Sure."

"Great."

"Great," I say, stepping through the doorway.

The apartment looks about the same as it did the last time I was here, except a little more lived-in. A patchwork quilt is draped over the back of the sofa like the one my grandma had when I was a kid. A set of dumbbells sits in the middle of the living room floor, and his chessboard has been placed in the middle of the coffee table. The boxes, however, are gone. And the picture that caused our last tiff is nowhere in sight.

"You expected to find boxes, didn't you?" he asks as he closes the door.

"Yeah. You had practice on Thursday and Friday and were with the team at the game yesterday. I didn't figure you got up on your one day off and unpacked."

"Were you going to finish it for me?"

I drop my bag onto the sofa and then meet his gaze.

My first reaction is to bristle at his question. Instinctively, my hackles rise, and I mentally prepare a defense. My brain tells me he's judging me—insinuating that I didn't finish my job and he's deciding my worth. But something makes me pause. I'm not sure if it's his relaxed posture or the slight tilt of his head, but I don't fire back. Instead, I wait.

A lick of humor tickles his lips as he presses them together. "Hey, I'm kidding, you know."

A slow breath releases from my lungs. *No, I didn't know.*

"I did a couple of boxes each night," he says. "There wasn't too much left. Besides, despite what you and Renn might think, I'm capable of basic tasks."

He turns his back and heads toward the kitchen, and I lean against the sofa and watch him move farther away from me. With each step he takes, my shoulders soften, and I breathe a little easier. I relax a little more.

This is uncharted territory, as we're usually arguing by now. The thing that throws me for a loop, though, is his admission that he was joking. Or maybe it's the idea that he was joking with me in the first place. That hasn't happened before … *has it?*

"Renn doesn't think you're incapable of basic tasks," I say, as he grabs two glass bottles from the fridge. Staying focused on the work aspect of things is an arena I understand. So I keep us planted there.

"That's not really my takeaway from being assigned a babysitter."

"Did you ever consider that he just wanted to support you?"

Gray hands me a bottle, unscrews his lid, and takes a long drink. His eyes never leave mine.

"If Renn thought you were incapable, he wouldn't have traded for you," I say in defense of my boss. "He obviously thinks you're talented and can contribute to the team. Otherwise, he would've left you in Denver."

Gray takes a seat on the sofa. He props his bare feet up on the coffee table next to the chessboard. "You always take up for Renn, don't you?"

"I generally side with people who are right, and Renn is almost always right."

"What if he was wrong?"

I shrug and sit as far away from him as I can on his one piece of furniture.

His question seems straightforward, but I can't help but wonder if it's not. If it's to be taken on the surface, that's one thing. But if it's theoretical, that's something else completely. *Is he suggesting Renn is wrong about* him?

"To be honest," I say, slipping off my shoes and tucking my feet beneath me, "Renn has never been wrong. If he was, I'd probably just stay out of it."

"Why are you so loyal to him?"

Are you not? I start to ask that, but change my mind. Because if the answer is no, then that puts me in a pickle. I can't really be loyal to Renn and know that Gray is not. But I can't work for Gray and keep stuff from Renn.

It seems I'm reminded every time I'm here that it's better not to know everything.

"Why are you asking so many questions?" I ask and then take a sip of water.

He sits up and places his bottle on the floor beside him. His attention switches from me to the chessboard. He takes a white pawn and advances it two spaces. "Why do you take offense to me asking questions?"

"I don't." *Not exactly, anyway.* I put my feet on the floor. Then I lean forward and move a black pawn two squares, mirroring his move. "I'm just not sure why it matters."

He moves a knight. "Maybe it doesn't."

"Good. Then we can avoid that going forward." I move a knight to defend my pawn and ignore the smirk on his face. "Are you getting used to the calendar? I know it can be confusing at first, but I swear it'll make both of our lives easier once you get the hang of it."

"I find it a pain in the ass, honestly. It makes me feel like I'm on probation or something."

I laugh. "Does that make me your probation officer?"

"You're definitely more like a warden." He chuckles, grinning at me. "I can actually see you as a warden. You'd have the convicts shaking in their prison flip-flops."

"Oh, hell, no. I'd be terrified. I'm not cut out for prison life in any form."

He snorts. "Come on, Astrid. You can't tell me that having

control over hundreds of people at one time doesn't turn you on at least a little bit."

"Well, when you put it like that …"

He moves his bishop, pinning my knight to my king. "On a serious note, I do like how you've color-coded things. It's efficient."

Everything works better when it's color-coded.

"Thanks." I grin, advancing a pawn so he needs to decide whether to capture my knight or retreat. "I took longer than you'd imagine choosing those colors."

He studies the board, weighing his move. His lashes are so long, so dark from this angle that they look fake. "That's really not hard to believe."

I lean back into the sofa again and glance around the room. It's a decent size—probably a quarter bigger than mine. A window on the opposite wall allows a good amount of light in, definitely enough to grow a plant or two. If he had a few things on the walls and maybe a chair or reading lamp, this place could be downright cute.

He retreats. "Do you have a calendar like that for your life?"

"Of course, I do." I move another knight forward. "I have a personal one, a work one, Renn's, Blakely's, and now I have yours. But, believe it or not, I kinda love it. I was always the kid who scored high on organizational skills in high school. It feeds my soul."

"Calendars feed your soul?"

I nod.

His dimples shine in his cheeks. "You need a hobby."

"You are not the first person to tell me that recently."

He laughs as he castles his king.

The sound of his laughter catches me off guard. It's the first time I've heard it, aside from the occasional chuckle at my expense. It's in stark contrast to the argumentative, taciturn man I usually encounter. Wrapping my head around the fact that Gray is both men is difficult.

"Speaking of hobbies," I say, moving a bishop. "Do you do anything during the offseason that I should know about? Classes? Jobs? Endorsements? I just want to make sure to cover everything, and I know a lot of guys have side hustles after the season is over."

Gray leans back, resting against the cushions and watches me. No scowl. No glares. No tight lips or clenched fists.

The tension that's usually biting the air around us is nowhere to be found. In its place is a quiet understanding. *A truce.* It's oddly relaxing to sit peacefully with Gray and have full-sentence conversations without snapping at each other. I appreciate it but I also don't quite trust it. Because, if I trusted it, I think I might like it.

"Do I take classes?" he asks. "Nope. I should probably consider what I'm going to do after I retire from rugby, but I keep putting that off. Side jobs? Not right now. Endorsements? Yes. Actually, I have a few emails from a sports drink company that I just signed a deal with requesting deliverables—which I think are just videos they want me to take myself. Maybe I could forward those to you, and you could handle them?"

I grab my clipboard from my bag and unfasten my pen from the top. "If you could get that to me tonight, I can reach out to them tomorrow morning." I write a note to myself at the top of the page. "Any other deals I should know about?"

He shakes his head. "I mean, I do have more. There's one with a burger franchise that my agent hates that I took, and another with a sportswear company. But both of those are at the end of their terms, and I don't owe them anything unless we negotiate an extension."

"Keep me in the loop."

"Yes, boss."

My eyes lift to his to find them waiting on me.

I sink back against the sofa, mirroring his posture. His grin pulls at mine. I don't want to slip and give him anything that breaks the strictly professional agreement we've created because we're finally on semi-solid ground. Yet the longer I look at him, the harder it is not to smile back.

"There you go. That wasn't so hard, was it?" he asks, winking at me.

My cheeks flush.

He gets up and grabs his water bottle, then heads back to the kitchen. The silence isn't awkward—just noticeable. I scramble to fill it with something. Anything.

"Do you want me to look into some side hustles for you?" I ask, reaching for my drink. "I know a guy who helps athletes set up camps and programs. I think he takes twenty percent of the proceeds, but it's still profitable."

"Are you hungry?"

I blink twice, staring at the television ahead of me. *Am I hungry?* "What?"

"A snack. Want one?"

He really is like trying to corral a toddler. "No. I'm good. Thanks, though."

"No problem."

I stand and then make my way to the kitchen, where I find Gray at the counter, peeling an orange.

"Any thoughts on me reaching out to the guy about the camps?" I ask again.

"Let's keep that in mind, but it's not something I want to do right now." He pops a piece of fruit into his mouth. "I don't know where I'll be this offseason. If I'm around here, I think I'll probably head home and spend some time with my brother."

I climb onto a barstool while he peels another orange across from me. I pretend to make notes on my clipboard when I'm really trying to imagine Gray with his family and what *home* means to him. It's hard to envision and impossible to guess which version of him they get, or if there are more versions of this man I haven't uncovered yet.

He offers me a slice of the fruit. "There were no peanuts involved in the cutting of this orange."

I laugh and take the proffered piece, surprised but also touched that he remembered. Even Gianna sometimes forgets about my allergy.

Our fingertips brush against each other as I take the section. His heavy, calloused pads sliding against mine sends a charge shooting through my veins. Despite the intensity, it's a quiet shock—one that's personal and intimate. I hold my breath a moment longer than necessary and soak in the lingering heat of the contact burrowing into my memory.

As my heart starts to pound, my brain takes over.

You're not a robot. He's a good-looking man, and it's been a fortnight since you've had physical contact with the male species. Relax.

He clears his throat and grabs a towel from the drawer I piled them in the other night. Then he swipes up the juice that's been dripping onto the countertop from the piece of fruit in my hand. That I didn't notice was happening.

"I'm sorry," I say, leaning back and refusing to look at him just in case he can read minds. "I didn't realize it was dripping."

"It's no big deal."

I quickly eat the orange slice, then drag my clipboard in front of me again, becoming engrossed in my notes. "What about groceries? Do you want to make a list of the things you like or want me to have delivered?"

"Nah." He tosses the towel next to the sink. "You did a good job on it this week, even if I was afraid that you poisoned me."

"I thought about it." I hide a smile, going over the list of questions I wrote down before I left home. "Do you have any doctors or specialists that you see regularly that are not with the team?"

"Nope. Well, I do see a therapist from time to time."

I cross that question off the list. "Well, that would be at the Royals facility, so I don't need to make a separate entry for them."

He hesitates, causing me to look up.

"I meant a mental health expert," he says, licking a drop of juice from his bottom lip. His eyes are the clearest, most unguarded they've been since I've known him. "But I'll handle those appointments. I kind of just make them when I need them."

Oh.

We watch each other carefully, both of us searching the other's gaze. I think he's gauging my response to his admission. I'm just hoping this isn't what will make him switch into *cold Gray mode* again.

I clutch my pen, listening to each breath that fills my lungs. Gray doesn't look away or frown. He stands in front of me and lets me see … *him.* It's almost as if he's reassuring me that he's holding true to his promise to make this work between us, and that he wants me to know it. That he's giving me this one super-personal bit of information as a token of faith.

"Does that surprise you?" he asks, his voice gravelly.

I place my pen on the clipboard and take a breath. "Honestly? Yeah. It does. I mean, a lot of people, men specifically, it seems, have a hard time talking about mental health." I give him a half grin. "But I think it's great you have someone to talk to, and I appreciate you telling me that."

He holds a slice of orange in the air, and I put my palm out.

"You're probably thinking that if I'd see my therapist more, I'd be less of a dickhead, huh?" he asks, grinning.

I laugh as the tightness in my chest releases. "They're a therapist, not a magician."

Gray pops another slice of fruit into his mouth, and his jaw moves as he chews. He eats slowly. Intentionally. It's as if he's unbothered with me in his space and is living his best confident, alpha life.

I shiver. "That's all the questions that I had for you." I climb off the stool, my skin tingling from the thoughts splashing around in my head—thoughts that have absolutely no business being in my brain. "I better get going."

"Did you get everything you needed from me?"

Oh, the comments Gianna would make right now. I eat the piece of orange in one bite and then pick up my bag. "I expected to leave here with a couple of answers and a giant headache. So unless you do your famous one-eighty on me, I'll leave with the answers and no headache. And I'm not mad about that."

His chuckle is low and deep. He leads me to the door and pulls it open.

"What's that all about?" I ask.

"It's hard for me to think that you're not mad about something," he says, leaning against the doorframe.

I laugh, stopping beside him. "I'm not out of here yet. You still have time to piss me off."

Fresh air flows into the house, picking up notes of Gray's cologne and swirling them around me. The way he looks my way—curiously, but also without the hatred I'm used to—stirs a soft sense of vulnerability inside me. A warmth climbs up my neck and colors my cheeks, and I know he notices. *How could he not?*

He starts to speak but stops himself and then starts again. "This coming week is a bye week."

I nod, my tongue too thick to allow words to form.

"I'm probably going to head back to Sugar Creek for the weekend."

Where's that water when I need it? "Okay. Do you need me to make your reservations at a hotel or something?"

He smiles. Not a grin and not a smirk. An ear-to-ear *smile* that is unlike any I've seen from him yet.

"There's not a hotel in Sugar Creek," he says with another chuckle. "I'll stay with my brother at the ranch."

The ranch? I shake my head and hold up a finger, suddenly sparked back to life.

"Whoa. Hold up a second," I say. "Your brother has a ranch?"

"Yup. I grew up there. It's been in our family for over one hundred years."

I laugh freely, imagining Gray with a cowboy hat and boots. It's so different from this Gray—the sweatpants-and-T-shirt-wearing athlete in front of me. It's nearly impossible to see. "*You were a cowboy?*"

He snorts. "Hardly. I got out of as much of that as I could. Thank God that Hartley, my brother, loved that shit. It saved me hours of work."

"Gray the cowboy," I tease as I step onto his small porch. His eyes twinkle with mischief. "Did you have stirrups and the whole bit?"

"Bye, Astrid."

"What about holsters like in the old movies?" I say, wrinkling my nose.

His dimples sink deep into his cheeks as he shakes his head and starts to close the door.

"Are there pictures?" I ask, giggling and moving so I can see him as the door closes. "Give me one good yeehaw!"

I hear him groan as the lock clicks in place.

Gray as a cowboy. I laugh all the way to the car.

CHAPTER
SIXTEEN

ASTRID

"What's that look about?" Renn asks me, laughing.

I survey the scene around us and try to decide where to start. First, the air stinks like grass, mud, and water thanks to what can only be described as a deluge overnight. Puddles form on the edges of the pitch, and I'm certain the guys are intentionally getting as muddy as possible.

Children. All of them.

Then there are the things I heard shouted from player to player, things that I would take my earrings out to fight over if someone said them to me. Yet they all share a laugh and prepare to scrum again. *I think.* I can't quite tell if this is a free-for-all or if strategy is involved.

"I'll never understand rugby," I say, furrowing a brow as another scrum begins. "It's like football, soccer, and cheerleading had a baby with big thighs."

Renn's laughter grows louder at my analysis. "I don't know how the hell you got cheerleading in the mix."

"What is happening right now?" I ask, watching them scurry around.

"Right now, they're trying to work the ball to the back of the scrum to Ridge. Then—*there*. He has it now. See? Ridge is number eight."

I nod.

"Okay, Ridge will either pick up the ball and go, or Gray will take it. Like that," Renn narrates. "Gray can either snipe and run it himself if he sees a gap around the scrum or pass it to the fly-half or a forward."

Gray picks up the ball, then turns and lunges as if he's going to run to the right. As soon as everyone shifts that direction, he makes a quick change to the left and explodes forward. He makes it a few yards before he's tackled and lands on his side.

Renn smiles.

"I take it that went well," I say.

Renn's head subtly rocks back and forth as he turns to me. "He's the best in the game … when he wants to be."

The two of us stand on a balcony just outside a conference room on the executive level. It's Renn's personal observatory. He loves rugby too much not to want to be involved in every tier of the game. But he's told me more than once that if he gets involved with practices and games, it undermines the coaching staff and the ultimate goal of winning.

As the guys prepare to scrum again, my mind flirts with what Renn just said. *"Gray is the best in the game when he wants to be."* I can't fathom why he wouldn't want to be the best. But something tells me that Renn knows the answer.

"How has it been going with Gray?" Renn asks, watching the scrum unfold.

I sigh. "I thought I was here to help you get Blakely's birthday party organized."

"You are, and you did. I feel much better about the party after our chat today. But I also want to check in and see how things are working out between the two of you."

I watch Gray move about like he has endless energy. He's one of the smaller guys out there, but he's by far the quickest. He seems to know where the ball is going before it gets there, and his teammates appear to follow his gestures and commands without a second thought.

"They're going better," I say, my eyes glued to Gray and the way his body moves. There's mud all over him, and it's … hot. "We met in person on Sunday and managed an entire hour face-to-face without drawing blood."

Renn chuckles. "That's progress."

"Can I ask you something?"

"Sure."

A whistle blows below, and the activity comes to a stop. They all gather in a circle before breaking. Gray turns toward us with a towel in his hand. He's talking to Jory when he looks up … and his gaze crashes into mine.

I want to look away, embarrassed at being caught watching him, but a blush settles over my cheeks as a grin splits his. His attention flicks to Renn, then back to me. I return his small smile before he looks away and follows Jory to the locker room.

"You wanted to ask me something?" Renn motions for me to follow him inside the empty conference room. "Hang on just a second."

He walks to the other end of the room and quietly takes a call.

I slowly gather my things and the various samples and catalogs I brought with me and shove them in my bag. Renn was adorable as he picked out every detail for Blakely's birthday. He wanted a say in everything down to the napkins. By the time he gets off his call, I'm finished.

"Sorry," Renn says. "Back to your question."

"What made you want to take a risk on Gray?"

"What do you mean?"

"I mean that he's obviously a wild card. He's only the best when he wants to be. So what makes you think you can make him want to be great?"

Renn plucks his blazer off the back of a chair and shrugs it over his wide shoulders. His brows pull together, and he slips his phone into his pocket. Finally, he turns to me. "Everyone deserves a second chance."

I hoist my bag onto my shoulder and wait for the rest of the explanation, but it never comes. Instead, Renn leads me into the hallway toward the elevators. I follow him because it's all I can do.

We step inside the lift, and he presses the button to take us to the lobby.

"You know what?" Renn says, watching the numbers lower as we descend. His eyes darken. "I take that back. Not everyone deserves a second chance."

I know he's thinking about his father. The only time Renn looks like he could murder someone with his bare hands is when his dad is the topic of conversation. But it's justified. I'm nothing to Reid Brewer, and I want to kill the man myself for hurting his family the way that he did.

The doors part, and Renn waits for me to exit first.

"I'm meeting Tate down here in a few minutes." Renn smirks. "Want to hang around and wait with me?"

"Ha!" I back away from him slowly. "Good luck. I'll email you tonight with an update on the party plans. Let me know if you think of anything else."

"Thanks, Astrid."

"You're very welcome."

"I'll tell Tate that you said hi."

I glare at him, making him chuckle, then I turn around. I pull my bag tighter to my side and make my way through the lobby. My brain is in overdrive, picking apart my conversation with Renn. The one thing that stands out to me is that he thinks Gray deserves a second chance. *Why?*

It's not that Renn wants to give Gray another chance. It's why Gray needs it that bothers me. Because the way Renn said it didn't sound like Gray needed another chance at winning or competing. It was as if he needed another chance at … something else. And I can't figure out what that some-thing else is.

I push open the doors and step outside, heading for the parking lot.

"Okay, I need to get some of these things sourced for Blake-ly's surprise party," I say, voice messaging myself a note in my phone for later. "Send Renn an update on that. I need to confirm with Brewer Air that they'll have a jet for Renn to use for his trip to Vegas next week. And I—"

"Hey!"

I glance over my shoulder and see Gray coming toward me from the player facilities. I slide my phone into my pocket and try not to stare.

"Trying to get some cardio in today or what?" he says with a grin.

A person could see those dimples from outer space. I stop and wait for him to catch up, and he breaks into a slow jog. His hair is damp, and it catches the sunlight, making him look like he has a halo. The closer he gets, the more I notice a slight purple tint to the area beneath his right eye.

"What do you mean?" I ask as he joins me on the sidewalk, and we walk shoulder to shoulder toward our cars. "I got my cardio in before I left my house this morning."

"You're practically running out of here."

"Maybe I was trying to get away from you," I say, fighting the smile tugging at my lips.

He rolls his eyes. "Whatever. What are you doing here today, anyway?"

"Renn needed my help with a few things." My heart warms as I remember him obsessing over whether we should have light or dark pink balloons at Blakely's party, and how he wanted to touch the linen samples for the tablecloths before he made his decision. *And now I'm lugging them back to the store. Oof.* "What happened to your eye?"

"An elbow. I think it was Breaker's, but I can't be sure."

"You should've elbowed him back in the earhole just in case."

He laughs. "Earhole?"

"Isn't that what it's called?" I laugh, too. "I mean, it's a hole in your ear. *Earhole.*"

"We don't call your nostrils noseholes."

"But we do call the hole in your bottom an asshole, so your point is not valid."

He shakes his head. "You're such a weirdo."

"Thank you," I say, lifting my chin in pride.

My car is a row up from his behemoth and about five spots closer to the facility. I wanted to rev my engine as I passed his truck on my way in today, but I couldn't figure out how and didn't want to tear up my transmission. Again.

I open the back door and set my bag on the seat. "If you get time today, can you check your email? A woman from Wayside will be sending you a document to sign electronically. They won't even talk to me about your endorsement without having your approval on file."

"Yeah, I'll check it as soon as I get home."

"Thanks." I reach for the door to close it when I hear my phone ringing in my bag. "Hang on a second."

"Sure."

I dig the device out from under the linen samples and answer the unknown number. "Hello?"

"Hello, is this Ms. Lawsen?" a cheery female asks.

"Yes."

"Great. Hi, Ms. Lawsen. This is Wanda from Dixon Legal Group. How are you this afternoon?"

I glance at Gray. He's leaning against the back of my car and messing with his phone. And hopefully not eavesdropping on me … like I do him.

"I'm great," I say, walking a few paces away from Gray. "How are you?"

"Wonderful, thank you for asking. I'm calling because I need to reschedule your consultation with Mr. Dixon. An emergency has popped up, and he'll be unavailable until June first."

My jaw hangs open. "June first? That's weeks from now."

"I know, and I apologize. But unfortunately, there's nothing I can do about it. If two thirty still works, I can slot you in that day. Otherwise, I have a four o'clock that afternoon, and an eight fifteen that morning. We have a few slots the week after that, too."

I rub my forehead as my head begins to pound. *Fuck.* "I, um, I guess two thirty will have to work. You're sure there's no availability before then? Because the letter said I have to respond within two weeks from the postmark or they'll just file against me in civil court." *I think. Maybe it was in criminal court. Shit. Am I going to be a felon over this?*

"I'm sure. But I have you in for June first with Mr. Dixon at two thirty. You'll get an automated reminder via text the morning before your appointment. Can I do anything else for you?"

Yeah, just have him look at the damn letter and tell me what to do. "No, that's it."

"Great. We'll see you then. Have a great rest of your day."

"You, too." I sigh, squeezing my temples with my free hand.

Gray's eyes bore holes into the side of my face, but I don't acknowledge it. I know he overheard half of the conversation, but I don't know if I should explain what it was about. It's really none of his business, and maybe he won't bother to ask. It would be like him not to care.

I peek at him out of the corner of my eye.

"Are you all right over there?" he asks.

"Yeah. I'm fine."

He grins. "Just an everyday call about getting taken to court, right?"

I sigh, dropping my hands to my sides in frustration. "Do you know what? I still hate you."

He only laughs in response.

I pace a small circle and try not to rip my hair out. I can't take this. I can't have this lording over my head like the ghost from hellationship's past. *How hard is it to look at a letter and figure out how to legally shut it down?*

"Can I point something out to you?" he asks.

"No."

He chuckles again. "I forgot how feisty you can be."

"That was your first mistake."

"I'm going to point it out anyway," he says. "I told you that I have a therapist. That's very personal to me, but I told you."

My feet stop moving and I look at him. He's right. He did tell me that. But I didn't ask him to, and I didn't expect him to. And I didn't ask him about the picture aside from where he wanted it placed. So no bones.

"I didn't ask," I say.

"No, you didn't, and I doubt that you would've."

I cross my arms over my chest. "What's that supposed to mean?"

"It means that you …" He shakes his head and shoves off my car. "You know what? Never mind."

He adjusts his bag on his shoulder and starts to walk away, but the idea of leaving it like this between us again—irritated and awkward—only makes me feel worse. It's another problem that I'd almost resolved unwinding.

"Wait," I say, glancing around to ensure no one is within earshot of us. "I'm sorry."

He turns slowly. I don't have to see his smirk to know he's smirking. I can tell by the cockiness with which he moves.

"It's only fair that I apologize." I throw my pride and cares to the wind. "You were the bigger man last time. I can suck it up this round."

His eyes darken, and he stops himself from speaking by biting his bottom lip.

I move right along. "I received a letter telling me that I'll be sued for twenty thousand dollars over rent and damage to an apartment that I haven't lived in for years. Why haven't I lived there, you ask? Because my boyfriend, whose name was on the lease, kicked me out so he could move another woman in." A quick breath fills my lungs. "Audrey knew an attorney who was going to give me a free consult, but he just canceled. So it looks like I'm selling feet pictures or a kidney because I'm not farting in jars."

He chokes back a laugh.

"I'm at my wits' end," I say, frazzled.

Gray clears his throat and runs a hand across his mouth, dragging a finger along his bottom lip. "First of all, that doesn't make sense. How can you be on the hook?"

"They say because I paid the landlord a couple of times and the trash service was in my name while I lived there. Apparently, that makes me somehow responsible for back rent and damages that Trace and his very young, very beautiful personal trainer girlfriend left when they moved out."

Gray sets his bag on my trunk.

I groan, pushing on my eyeballs to keep them from tearing up. The pressure of this scenario is hitting a boiling point, and I don't know how much more I can take. I can't think too much about it or I'll break down. I don't have the infrastructure for support like Gianna or Audrey have with their families. It's just me over here. At times like this, that reality hits me hard ... like an ice pick to the heart.

"I apologize," I say, dropping my hands in frustration. "I shouldn't have dumped all that on your lap. Ignore me."

He gives me a pointed look. "You need an attorney. That's what you're saying?"

I shrug helplessly. I don't want to talk to him about this, but it's kind of too late now.

"I think so," I say. "At the least, I need someone to tell me what my options are. I obviously don't have twenty thousand dollars." I groan, the sound of that number making my stomach threaten to reject my lunch all over the asphalt. "And a part of me is petty, too, because why should I have to bail him out of his problems when he caused *me* so many problems? You know?"

Gray pulls his phone out of his pocket and taps around on the screen, then he brings the device to his ear. His jaw flexes as he waits for someone to answer. I don't know whether to get in the car, to shrivel in embarrassment, or wait for him to finish before exiting stage right from this overly dramatic and humbling scene.

"Hey, Joe. It's Gray." He nods, listening. "Yeah. I had it transferred to you around lunchtime. Did you get it?" He paces a crack in the concrete. "Let me know if not because I received confirmation. We should be good."

I open my driver's side door and toss my phone into the passenger's seat. I try to remember where I put the list of attorneys that I didn't call last week. There were three or four left. Maybe I can get an appointment with one of them. *I could put it all on a credit card or try to make payments.* The thought makes me want to weep.

Tears gather in the corners of my eyes, and I refuse to blink so they don't spill down my cheeks.

"One more thing. You don't happen to have any consulting slots open in the next few days, do you?" Gray asks.

What? I twirl around, seeing him through my unshed tears. "What are you doing?" The words are thick through the emotion lodged in my throat.

"It's for a friend of mine," he says, winking at me. "She's getting fucked by an ex and needs legal advice so she doesn't get extorted."

I stand frozen in place, unable to believe what I'm hearing.

"Friday at three?" Gray asks, looking at me with lifted brows. "Hang on, Joe." He drops the phone to his side. His features are sober. "Listen, I've known Joe for my whole life. He can look at your papers on Friday at three, if that works for you. He won't charge you, either. No pressure either way."

"Gray, you didn't have to do this."

He grins. "The correct response is thank you."

My cheeks heat as I remember saying those words to him. "Thank you. Three o'clock on Friday is wonderful."

I stand, stupefied, as he winds up his call. I'm not sure what to say or what to think about it. I can only hope he's not joking around about this because I might break down if so. *After I get Gianna's taser.*

He puts his phone away. "You got yourself an appointment."

"I don't know what to say." I laugh in shock. "Where is Joe? How do I get to his office?"

"Joe is in Sugar Creek."

"Your hometown?"

"Yeah." Gray clears his throat. "I was going back there to visit my brother this weekend, anyway. So if you want to hitch a ride, that'd be fine with me. We can make a pact not to talk, or you can wear earbuds, if you want."

No words appear on my tongue. It's like my brain stopped working, and I can't comprehend basic English. Because there is no way Gray just offered me help like this. It's not possible.

"I mean, you can drive yourself, too—"

"You just blindsided me. I'm sorry. Just give me a second." I take a long, deep breath and exhale slowly. "You didn't have to do this, Gray."

"You've already said that." He smirks. "And as far as you riding with me, I'm going anyway. It's not like I'm making a trip just for you. Don't think you're special or anything."

"Well, when you put it like that, fine," I say, struggling not to smile at him.

"Great."

"Great."

He tosses his bag over his shoulder and walks toward his truck. "I'd say I'll text you with details, but God knows you'll be texting me orders every day until then. I'll just hit reply."

I watch him until he reaches his truck. *How is this possible?*

My mind can barely break down what just happened as I

climb into my car. I close the door and then rest my head against the seat, closing my eyes. *And breathe.* Gray's truck starts up in the distance, loud and obnoxious as always.

This makes no sense. *Does Gray pity me? Is he thankful for my help? Are we going to arrive in Sugar Creek and find out that Joe is a drunkard with a magic eight ball?*

The thought makes me laugh, and my stress eases. Finally.

I start the car and buckle up, then I reach for the gear shifter. But I make a last-minute change of plans and grab my phone instead. Gray's name is at the top of my text chain with a cowboy by his name.

Me: I hate you a smidgen less.

Gray 🤠: Don't. You're buying my lunch while we're there, and I eat. A lot.

Me: Never mind. I hate you the same.

Gray 🤠: Thank God.

"Asshole," I say, grinning as I leave the facility.

CHAPTER
SEVENTEEN

Astrid

I need help.

My best friend and I have been in a serious rela-tionship for almost three years. We moved in together a year ago and have talked about getting married and starting a family. We're both ready to take the next step. But here's the problem—he's not talked to me in two weeks because he found out that I'm a flirt. (His friends witnessed some of my antics at a bar. Good times.)

I admit it, okay? I love to flirt. I love other men flirting with me. Dare I say that I need the attention? I don't do it in front of my boyfriend, and I have zero intention of letting it lead into anything more than a few innuendos and winks while I'm out with my *friends or on a work trip. I say it's a harmless way of bolstering my confidence. He says it's cheating.*

So ... am I the villain?

For the thirtieth time, I read through the question Gianna sent me to answer for the column. For the thirtieth time, I'm stupefied.

When I agreed to submit a response to an anonymous question, I expected it to be easy. After all, one of my not-so-finest qualities is that I can be judgmental. But as I sit with the question, I find that it's not easy at all.

I tuck my legs beneath me and curl up into the corner of my couch.

My first instinct was to tell the woman that if she values her relationship, she'll stop flirting. But I got halfway through that response and decided I didn't really agree with what I was writing. Flirting in and of itself isn't a bad thing. Then I started a reply that if her man can't trust her not to actually cheat, then she needs to run. It didn't take long until I realized that wasn't a good answer, either.

It's so hard when you're asked to be judgmental on the spot.

"Come in," I shout, closing my computer when a knock comes from the entryway.

"It's me!" Audrey's voice rings through my apartment before her pretty face appears around the corner. "Hey!"

I smile at her. "Hey. How was work?"

"We're not talking about it." She winces. "It was one of those days. But there was one bit of sunshine today."

"Really? Tell me."

The door clicks open again, and the telltale sign of Gianna's heels clicks against the linoleum floor. "Have I ever mentioned that I loathe street parking?"

Audrey looks at me and grins. "Only every time you do it."

"I wasn't born to be a parallel parker." Gianna sweeps through the room with main-character energy and collapses into a rocking chair that I picked up at a consignment store around Christmastime. "I need one of those cars that do it for you."

"They make those?" I wrinkle my nose. "I think you imagined that."

Gianna shakes her head. "No, they do. I have no idea what they're called, but I was boinking a dude from Franklin who drove one. It's a cool feature."

"Boinking." Audrey giggles. "Where do you come up with these terms?"

"Fine. *Fucking*. Is that better?" Gianna sticks her tongue out at Audrey. "Anyway, I'm here. Can someone fill me in on why we were summoned here on a rainy Thursday night? I canceled a nail appointment for this, I'll have you know."

All eyes are on me. I'm the one who called the emergency meeting, and I'm embarrassed about it.

Going with Gray to Sugar Creek tomorrow is no big deal. I've told myself this a thousand times. It's a free ride because he was going there anyway. But despite how many times I say it, whether it's just repeating it in my head or speaking it aloud, my body refuses to believe that I'm not about to run a marathon with lions.

The adrenaline and anxiety are real.

I uncoil my legs and plant them on the floor. My insides squirm with the anticipation of telling my friends about my trip tomorrow, and I wish I could get away with not telling them at all. They're going to overreact and probably make my nervousness worse before they make it better.

Why am I nervous to begin with?

And what am I going to wear?

God, I'm a mess. And I *hate* being messy.

I just need a moment to pull myself together.

"Before I get into why I asked you to come over, can you finish your sunshine story, Aud?" I ask.

She beams. "Yes. Okay. So Andrew called me last night about Mom and Dad's anniversary. We're throwing them a little get-together with their friends. It's going to be so cute. Anyway, while we were chatting, he might've mentioned that a few of the guys he hangs out with rented a little house on the Cape for a weekend coming up." She scoots to the edge of her seat, her eyes twinkling. "And guess who got an invite?" She squeals, tapping her feet against the floor. "If I could do a cartwheel, I would."

Gianna and I exchange a grin.

"I'm guessing your crush will be there?" I say.

"Yeah. It took a bit of finessing to find out if he was going without straight-up asking Andrew, but I managed."

"This might be it, Audrey," Gianna says, pointing at her. "This is your chance to put some moves on your man."

Audrey flushes. "I don't have any moves. How can I be your friend and not have moves?"

"Because you won't let me teach you," Gianna says. "How much time do we have? I can make you a little vixen, but I'll need a few weeks."

I fire a look at Gianna, warning her to tread lightly. We don't want to make Audrey freak out. She's waited too long for this. "You don't need moves, Aud. Guys love girls like you. You're sweet and pretty."

"You're fresh meat," Gianna deadpans.

Audrey curls her nose. "Nice visual."

"Did you bring my shirt, by any chance?" Gianna asks. "If you did, I don't want to forget it."

"It's in my car," Audrey says. "And don't try to hem it yourself next time, please. You just make it harder for me in the end."

Gianna shrugs.

"Your turn, Astrid," Audrey says, settling in for story time. "What's going on? Is this about the Trace thing? You met with the attorney today, didn't you?"

I toss a lock of hair over my shoulder and try to appear as cool as I can … when I'm really toeing the edge of a cliff.

"So Dixon's office called me earlier this week and canceled," I say, my voice nice and controlled. *Good, good. Keep it up.* "They couldn't reschedule me until June."

Audrey's face falls. "I'm sorry. That stinks so bad. I can look around for someone else. Don't panic."

"She's not panicking," Gianna says slowly, leaning forward with a smug grin on her face. "Why aren't you panicking, Astrid?"

"She's not panicking because she knows we'll help her, right, Astrid?" Audrey asks.

I bite my lip and dodge Gianna's gaze.

"No, Auddie," Gianna says. "Think about it. Astrid has her life planned to the hour. You're telling me that this fell through and she's all breezy about it. You know her better than that."

Damn you, Gianna.

Audrey cocks her head to the side. "You might be right."

I sigh and shift in my seat. Might as well go in headfirst … ish. "I don't need you to find me another name, Audrey, because I actually found someone who will give me a free consultation tomorrow afternoon."

"Great," Audrey says, grinning. "That's such great news."

"His name is Joe." I tuck a strand of hair behind my ear. "I have an appointment with him tomorrow afternoon."

"Stop touching your hair," Gianna says, eyeing me so closely that nothing is going to get by her. "And stop repeating yourself. Get to the point that you clearly don't want to make but feel like you have to share."

I groan, putting my hands on my lap. The longer I wait to lay it out there, the more suspicious they're going to be. It's time to rip the Band-Aid off. "Here's the thing." I pause. "Gray set it up for me."

Gianna laughs, falling back in her chair. She has a victorious smile on her face that leaves me perplexed. *Why does she look like she just won?*

"Darn it," Audrey says, stomping her foot. "I don't have twenty bucks in cash on me. Can I pay you the next time I see you?"

"That's fine." Gianna snickers, looking at me. "We bet twenty bucks on whether you'd cave to that good-looking motherfucker by the end of the month or not. I won."

"*What?*" I ask, my mouth hanging open.

Audrey sighs, frowning. "I thought you'd hold out at least a month. You're usually so much harder than this."

"I think the problem is that *he's* hard, if you know what I'm saying," Gianna says out of the side of her mouth.

"I didn't cave to anyone," I protest, looking between them. "You don't understand."

"What, exactly, do we not understand?" Gianna asks. "Your so-called mortal enemy set you up with an attorney to help you out of a bind. It seems pretty straightforward to me."

No, no, no. "It's not like that."

"That's not mortal-enemy shit," Gianna says.

I want to disagree with her, but I'm not sure how to approach it. It doesn't appear to be *enemy shit*, but we're not necessarily mortal enemies anymore. He's not my favorite person, and I'm sure I'm not his either. But we've managed to find a middle ground that I don't hate. I wish I did hate it because gosh, it was easier, but I don't.

"It's not a big deal," I insist despite the chaos inside me saying differently. "He was standing by me in the parking lot when the call from Dixon's office came in, and Gray overheard it. That's it."

"And then he gave you directions to the attorney's office?" Gianna asks. Her red lips are pressed together in a self-satisfied grin. "Need me to ride with you tomorrow?"

I glare at her and get to my feet, unable to sit still any longer.

"I could go," Audrey says. "I can cancel my meetings tomorrow. We can take a girls' trip. It'll be fun."

Gianna sighs. "She doesn't need us to go, Auddie." Gianna slowly brings her face to mine. "She's going with Gray."

Sometimes, I really dislike Gianna.

The world wobbles, then comes to a slow crawl. I move across the room to a nonworking fireplace with fake logs to put some distance between us.

Gianna holds up her hands. "Hey, don't be pissed at me because I can read the damn room."

"Okay." Audrey nods. "I see where this is going."

"It's not going anywhere." My face heats as I look between them. "We called a truce, and he's helping me like I help him. That's all."

Gianna smirks. "I like the reciprocation aspect of your relationship. You'll appreciate that in the later stages."

My stomach tightens, and I shoo those thoughts away. *I'm not going there.*

"I'm assuming you two are getting along much better now," Audrey says softly. "Is that true?"

"Yes. But it's a working relationship built on very thin ice. I need the two of you not to take this in the ways you're taking it."

"Wait until you see how you're going to be taking it," Gianna mutters. I glare at her, and she laughs. "I'm kidding. I'll stop."

Audrey glances at Gianna before returning her attention to me. "Tell us what you need. We're here for you."

Thank God for Audrey.

I blow out a shaky breath because I don't know what I need. I don't even know why I called them. It was a silly decision that I made in a moment of panic because I'm overwhelmed with stress, and I broke.

Everyone breaks sometimes.

Gianna stands, kicking off her heels. "What are you wearing?"

My shoulders soften. "I don't know."

She motions for Audrey and me to follow her into my bedroom. Once we're in there, she flips on the light and wastes no time flinging open my closet doors.

"Oh, you look hot as hell in this." Gianna pulls a lacy black camisole off a hanger.

I shake my head. "That's the wrong vibe. I'm meeting an attorney, for Pete's sake."

Audrey sits beside me on my bed.

"We're going to be in a truck for over an hour each way," I say. "He mentioned that he wanted to stop and see his brother, so I think we might be doing that. I'm not sure. And his brother lives on a ranch so—"

"*Stop it,*" Gianna hisses. "A ranch? You're freaking kidding me right now."

Audrey moans. "If Gray puts on Wranglers and cowboy boots, I might faint."

"Don't faint," Gianna says, laughing. "That's the moment when you ride that man like it's your damn job."

I cover my face with my hands. *This isn't helping. At all.*

Vivid images of Gray on a ranch with sweat dripping down his chest invade my mind, and there's no pushing them out. Suddenly, imagining him in cowboy boots isn't as funny. I can see him wearing a cowboy hat, and I can't completely dismiss the ripple it causes in my core.

That's it. I'm losing my mind.

Audrey hops off the bed and joins Gianna in front of my closet. It takes her just a minute to pull out a teal T-shirt that Gianna bought me for my birthday last year. The fabric is thicker than a standard tee, and the V-neck stops a hair above the tops of my boobs. It's not too revealing and never dips low enough to show off my chest … but it feels like it might. And, according to Gianna, there's an allure that comes along with that.

"What about this?" Audrey asks. "Pair those with your gold stars that have the little diamonds in the center. It's comfortable enough for a road trip, conservative enough for an attorney's office, and fun enough for a ranch." She glances into my closet again. "You're only going for the afternoon, right?"

"Yeah. I think we're just going to the attorney's office, and then he wants to see his brother. Maybe he'll visit his brother while I'm talking to the attorney. I don't know."

Gianna pulls out my favorite pair of jeans. "Your ass looks amazing in these."

"Where are your white sneakers with the tan detailing?" Audrey asks.

"They're in the shoe rack by the door."

"Wear those," Audrey says. "It'll keep it looking fun and fresh, and if you do wind up on a ranch, your toes will be covered."

I wouldn't have thought about that. Good call.

I take the items they chose and hang them on the back of my bedroom door. Having this decision be over quells a bit of the nerves blooming in my stomach. At least now I can worry and overthink about something else.

"Now that's done, how about we order pizza and do your nails? They look like trash," Gianna says, shrugging. "You can't go to all the trouble of having us pick out an outfit and not do your nails."

"I'll order the pizza," Audrey says, heading toward the living room. "You figure out the nails."

Gianna wraps her arm around my shoulders and smiles at me. "How are you feeling?"

"Honestly? Better."

I smile sheepishly. Gray and I are barely on cordial terms these days, and our relationship is strictly professional. I don't even really like the man, and I know he feels the same about me. So what I wear on this trip doesn't matter. It's not like I'm trying to draw his attention—or anyone else's, for that matter. I deal with enough men in my work life. I sure as heck don't need one in my private life, too.

"I don't know why I got all weird about this," I say. "I'm sorry."

She laughs. "You don't have to understand. I do. And we got you, friend. One of these days, you're going to believe that."

My heart swells as she leads me to the bathroom to retrieve my manicure kit.

Thank God for good friends.

CHAPTER
EIGHTEEN

"That's probably the last book I've read," Gray says, stepping on the gas pedal and passing the slow-moving tractor we've followed for more than a couple of miles. "What about you?"

I gaze out the passenger side window, taking in the beauty of rural Tennessee. I've always loved getting out of the city. Gianna's family would visit Kentucky every summer, and I tagged along a few times. Even as a child, I appreciated the peace and quiet, probably because my home life had neither.

Today has been a lot easier than I expected. I spent the morning ordering supplies for Blakely's party and communicating with Wayside about Gray's deliverables for the sports drink campaign scheduled to run this fall. It was just enough to keep me from stressing over Gray picking me up at one thirty for our trip to Sugar Creek.

"The last book I read was probably *Romeo and Juliet* or *The Great Gatsby* in high school," I say.

Gray makes a face, looking offended.

"What?" I ask, laughing.

"I just ... expected more from you. That's all."

"Don't judge me." I shake my head, amused. "I haven't had a lot of free time since high school. Some of us weren't rugby stars with leisure time."

"Oh yeah. *Right*. Should've seen all the leisure time that I've had to play with." He looks at me over the top of his sunglasses. "What kind of overachieving bullshit were you up to after high school, anyway?"

I chuckle, wrapping my arms around my middle, and shrug. "Let's see. I graduated at seventeen and took on my second job. Worked both of those for a full year until I started community college." I glance over at him. "Then I added a third job for shits and giggles."

He flinches. "Third job? What are you? Wonder Woman?"

"That sounds better than saying that I refuse to die."

His brows pull together atop his sunglasses. "What's that mean?"

The sun is warm on my face as I watch the greenery slide past my window. I've already said more to him than I usually tell people—and verbalized it in a more genuine way, to boot. For some reason, I don't feel the squish of my stomach, warning me to stop talking, though. It's probably because I don't care what he thinks of me. It's actually nice just talking without hyperfocusing on every single word leaving my lips.

"I mean that I moved out of my father's house at seventeen," I say, sagging into the seat. "Found a studio apartment that I could afford in the Pliny Building and finished the last couple of months of high school."

"Your dad let you move out at seventeen?"

"*Let me* is a creative way to say it. Hey," I say, sitting up, "is that a covered bridge?"

I lean forward as we approach the red structure with a black roof. It's wide enough for two lanes of traffic to pass each other and not much more. Beneath the bridge is a slow-moving creek bubbling and meandering through the landscape.

"Yeah," Gray says, slowing the truck. "Welcome to Sugar Creek."

The tires rumble across the wooden boards of the bridge as we travel over it, the sound echoing, bouncing off the graffiti-stained walls on either side. Black birds line the rafters and watch us like little silent inspectors deciding whether we're worthy to visit the town or not.

"This is like a movie," I say, squinting against the sun as we pull out of the tunnel.

"Or a book for those of us with imaginations."

I smack his shoulder playfully. He chuckles, his dimples dotting his cheeks. Those little dents trigger a wave of warmth throughout my body, and I look away before he can see the heat in my face.

We pull into the village with neat homes and manicured lawns spaced out perfectly from one another. Some of them have white fences, others have window boxes filled with beautiful flowers. Nearly every house that we pass has a porch swing, and all of them are adorable.

Gray rolls down our windows, stretching his arm out of his to wave at a middle-aged woman sweeping the sidewalk. The fresh air filling the cab is sweetly scented. It's a balm to my perpetually overstimulated nervous system.

"That was Amanda LaRoche," Gray says, pulling his arm back inside the truck. "I went to school with her daughter." He points at a small brick building with black shutters. "That's Doc Buckley's office. He's delivered most of the people in Sugar County at this point. He used to come to the elementary school every winter dressed up like Santa Claus." Gray starts laughing, looking at me with a sparkle in his eye. "My buddy, Brooks, ended that when we were in fifth grade. He fished his keys out of his pocket. Then when the staff was looking for them later, he held them up and said, 'I found these, but they can't be Santa's because they have a tag on it for Doc's office.'"

"What a little shit," I say, laughing, too.

He turns the truck down a road to our right, and I can't help but notice how relaxed Gray seems. The pinch that usually lives between his eyes has magically disappeared, and the muscle connecting his neck to his shoulders isn't flexed. His lips press together as if he's holding back a grin. He's less devil, more devilishly handsome. I can't decide whether I like it or hate it.

"What is *that*?" I scoot to the edge of my seat and try to focus on a blur racing from the post office to the fire department. "Is that …" I narrow my eyes. "A cat with three legs?"

"Yup. That's Blooper. He had an unfortunate accident with Biscuit Jones's lawnmower probably twenty or thirty years ago."

"Um, I don't think cats live that long."

"Maybe not average cats, but Blooper isn't average."

"Oh, of course not," I say, giggling.

"I mean it." He stops at a sign and then turns left. "Half of the houses in Sugar Creek have a cat house outside for him in case he stays the night. Everyone keeps food and water out for the little guy. When the weather is bad, he holes up with the fire-fighters."

"Why doesn't someone just take him in?"

"Someone tried once upon a time, but legend has it that Blooper fought a ghost, tore down all the family's curtains, and pissed on everything they owned. No one else has been ballsy enough to try to capture him again."

I huff. "I'd try it, the poor thing."

"You would, huh?" He smiles. "I'd like to see that. One feral animal against the other."

"You're such a jackass," I say, turning away so he doesn't see my grin.

Gray slows the truck and stops at another sign. It's more of a roll-stop since no one else is around, and we turn onto a street on a slight slope. Hanging baskets hold flowers cascading down the streetlamps with whiskey barrels sitting below. There's a flower shop, Piper's Pizza, and a small building on the end with a sign reading Brew Ha Ha.

"Is that a coffee shop?" I ask, laughing.

"Cheesy, huh?"

"No way. It's clever."

"Whatever you say," Gray says.

He stops the truck in the middle of the road and throws it in reverse. His arm extends along the back of my seat with his large hand gripping my headrest. My heart thunders in my chest as he glances casually over his shoulder and pilots the truck perfectly into the center of a spot.

Damn.

"We're here," he says, fishing his wallet and keys out of the console.

I clear my throat and gather my things while shoving away the photographs my brain snapped of Gray only moments ago. The competence. The confidence. His body language screams that he knows what he's doing, and he's damn good at it.

I'm really losing my effing mind.

Clutching my purse, I hop out of the truck without breaking my neck. Gray meets me on the sidewalk but avoids eye contact by dipping his head to slide a black hat low on his forehead. "Ready?" he asks.

I pat my purse. "Ready as I'll ever be."

Gray leads me to an oversized window with green-and-gold sign lettering on the glass. *Jewell Law.* He opens the door and waits for me to enter first.

The room is straight out of another era—green carpet, a standing ashtray, and a giant framed map of Sugar County that I'm sure was once white and not faded yellow. There's a desk in the center, but no one's staffing it.

"Hey, Joe," Gray calls out.

"Come on back."

Gray's hand brushes against the small of my back as he guides me forward, and the contact catches me off guard. The heat of his touch in such a vulnerable, intimate spot has me shivering. My instinct is to pull away and distance myself from him, but I appreciate knowing Gray's there as I walk into the unknown. *I can't believe I just thought that.*

"Betty's working at the mayor's office today," a man I presume is Joe says behind a dark wooden desk as we round the corner. He's older than I imagined—probably in his late sixties, early seventies—and has shiny black hair that's slicked back. The mole on his chin somehow softens his otherwise severe persona. He smirks at Gray. "Didn't know I was gonna get to see your ugly face, too."

"Consider it a bonus." Gray laughs. "Joe, this is Astrid Lawsen. Astrid, this is Joe Jewell." He leans over and whispers loud enough for Joe to hear. "He looks like a dipshit, but he's a pretty damn good lawyer."

"Yeah, well, that's better than being a pretty-boy dipshit," Joe cracks back, his big belly vibrating with his chuckle. He turns his attention to me. "You're too pretty for this guy."

"Oh," I say, my cheeks flushing. "We're not together. Not like that."

Gray shifts at my side.

Joe holds out a hand. "What do you have for me?"

"I brought the letter with me," I say, digging in my purse and handing it over to the attorney. My palms are damp, and I glance at the envelope, hoping there's no sweat stains on the paper.

"Hey, Gray," Joe says, opening the envelope. "My lunch is ready at Piper's. Will you go get it for me?"

Gray's gaze drops to mine, and immediately, I sense his concern about leaving me. I fight the urge to reach out and touch his hand ... as that would make things awkward for sure.

"I'll be here when you get back," I say, nodding.

He nods, steals a look at Joe, then ducks out. When I turn back to Joe, he's reading through the letter with a sour look on his face.

"What's this about?" he asks, his voice full of gravel. "Ex-boyfriend, I'm guessing."

"How'd you know?"

He looks at me over the top of the paper. "This isn't my first rodeo. Grab a seat."

I settle into a brown pleather chair that smells faintly of cigar smoke. My jeans squeak against the material like new sneakers down a corridor. I'm not comfortable, but I don't dare move another inch lest I sound like a child.

"Were you ever on this lease?" Joe asks.

"No. Never. Trace already lived there when I moved in. I did pay rent a couple of times, but I never signed anything." A cold knot forms in my stomach. "And Trace kicked me out and had another woman living there for I don't know how long after I left."

Joe places the paper on top of the envelope and grabs a pen. "Do you have the dates of when you moved in and out?"

"Um, I moved in about six years ago in October and moved out in March four years ago. If you want exact dates, I can get them."

He scribbles notes on a legal pad. "No, that's fine." He motions toward a smaller pad of paper and a pencil on the corner of his desk. "Write down your contact information there for me. Name, phone, address, and email."

I take it and jot down my details.

"I'll take care of this," he says, watching me as I put his things back on his desk. "You'll get a copy of all communications either by mail or email."

The door opens behind me and footsteps sound through Betty's office.

I lick my lips. "Before we get the ball rolling, how much do you charge? Because I might have to make payments, if you can do that. If not, I have a credit card, but I'd rather not pay that way if I can help it."

"Don't worry about it."

"But—"

"Piper said if it's cold, it's your fault," Gray says, plopping a bag on Joe's desktop. "You were supposed to pick it up an hour ago."

Joe rolls his eyes. "Piper can settle the hell down. I paid for it, so what's it to her?" He peers into the bag with chunky fingers. "Looks like they got it right, for once."

Gray winks at me.

"I'm gonna eat," Joe says. "You two get the hell out of here. It was nice to meet you, Astrid."

"But we didn't get a chance to discuss payments," I say, my heart pattering.

Joe looks at Gray. "Get her outta here, will ya?"

"Let's go," Gray says, motioning with his head to follow him.

"But …"

"Come on." Gray's tone has a warning embedded in the notes. "See ya, Joe."

"Goodbye."

I stand, feeling an urgency to settle the payment terms, because I'm not sure what Joe expects. It complicates it more that he's Gray's friend. So if I can't pay, that could hurt my relationship with Gray, which, in turn, could hurt my relationship with Renn. Before I can start a protest, Joe takes a bite of his sandwich and turns his attention to his computer.

"Thank you, Joe," I say, my voice wobbling.

If he hears me, he doesn't show it. *What the hell?*

I run various scenarios through my head as we walk back to the truck. The taillights blink as Gray unlocks the door, and I climb into the cab, having decided that I'll send a couple of hundred dollars to Joe when I get home. At least that'll be something, and we can go from there.

"I grabbed us lunch," Gray says as we get our buckles fastened. "Didn't know what you wanted, but you got a ham and cheese. Piper's daughter is also allergic to nuts, so they're safe for you to eat."

My throat is thick with emotion as I look at his expressive brown eyes.

It's hard to accept that this Gray exists in the same body as the Gray that I met at the gas station. I never would've thought that asshole could be this considerate—about my allergy, Joe, and bringing me to Sugar Creek. I keep looking for the catch but come up empty.

The engine roars to life, and we start back the way we came.

"Ready to head to my brother's for a little bit?" Gray asks.

I smirk. "Do you mean the ranch?"

He fires me a playful, dirty look. "Don't start."

I laugh. "Of course, I don't mind. You brought me here, after all. Thank you again."

"Thank me by getting my sandwich out, please."

"Oh. Sure."

I pull out two sandwiches and decide they're the same. So I unwrap one of them, leaving the wrapper gathered at the bottom, and offer it to Gray. He reaches for it, his knuckles grazing mine as he takes it from me.

My eyes dart away from his. *Think of something to say.* "Joe and I didn't discuss the price of his services, and I'm worried about it."

Gray chews slowly. "Well, don't."

"That's easy for you to say."

"Joe had a daughter my mom's age," he says after swallowing. "Her name was Grace, I think, and she was friends with Mom. Grace had a boyfriend who … hurt her." He glances at me out of the corner of his eye. "Let's put it like that. So you could say that Joe has a soft spot for women who are getting fucked over by men."

I frown, imagining Joe as a father to a young girl. He's hard and brusque, but something tells me he's a great father. *One who heals rather than destroys young souls.*

"It's his way of helping settle the score or something," Gray says. "If you feel like you must do something, just write him a note. Nothing too mushy. That'll be all he needs."

Gray stops at a sign and takes a deep breath, then he turns to me. Our gazes connect. When I look at him this time, it doesn't quite feel like we're just coworkers. It doesn't seem like we're two people who secretly hate each other anymore, either. Maybe it's the start of a tolerance or an understanding. Either way, I like this much better than wanting to suffocate him in his sleep.

He gives me a half grin and takes off again. "Can I ask you a question?"

"Sure."

"The ex—the one who that letter was over—is he the reason you love chess?"

The question is simple, but I hear the layers in it. He's not just asking about Trace, nor is he asking about chess. The words I used at his apartment when I told him about my driveway chess habit echo through my head.

"Because the habit started when I was avoiding going in the house."

This isn't the first time he's remembered something I've said —something important. Things that matter. It's slightly terrifying to know that he paid attention because he could use the information against me. But, so far, he's only used it to get to know me better. And if I'm being honest, it's been so long since anyone outside of Gianna and Audrey gave a shit about me that it feels nice. Especially while I'm in the middle of this Trace crap.

I give him a small smile and a shrug. "I guess one good thing came out of my relationship with Trace, huh?"

I can't read the look he gives me, but my heart swells, anyway. I'm thankful when my phone buzzes in my lap and gives me a reason to look away.

Audrey: Just checking in. Are you okay, Astrid?

I sneak a peek at Gray again. He's chewing on his bottom lip, and the wind coming in from his partially lowered window feathers his hair. He's not relaxed like before, but he's not angry like usual, either.

And I must wonder … *why?*

He looks over his shoulder at me, and we exchange the softest smile.

Not once did I ever expect to be so grateful to Gray Adler. He intervened and set this up with Joe—which just might result in a no-pay situation—and let me tag along on his trip. I hate to admit it but having him with me today did make it a smidgen easier. I'll never tell him that, though.

Me: I'm pretty good, actually.

Gianna: Ride that fine-ass man like a horse.

Oh, Gianna. I laugh and settle into my seat.

What a mindfuck of a day this has been. At least the hard part is over.

CHAPTER
NINETEEN

GRAY

Gravel crunches beneath my tires as I turn onto the long driveway leading to Blackbird Ranch. The sign Grandpa proudly hung when he was about my age shines above the gate. The stone pillars that Mom hated stand tall on either side with solar lanterns on top of them.

The thought of Hartley using solar *anything* makes me smile.

A wooden fence borders the driveway, separating our private road from the forest on either side. The trees are thick, and the vegetation is dense and dark. Despite not being in those woods for a decade or more, I have no doubt I could find my way through them blindfolded.

I peek at Astrid, finding her taking it all in.

The feeling of being home settles over my soul. It's been too long since I was here—so long, in fact, that I forgot how the world ends at the start of the gate. Back here, it's a world all its own and ruled by hard work, loyalty, and family.

My chest grows heavy as nostalgia for a time long gone takes up residence between my pecs.

"You grew up here?" Astrid asks, unbuckling herself.

"Yeah. I grew up here with my parents, my dad's dad—my pap—and my brother, Hartley, who you'll meet in a second."

Her gaze settles on the main house coming into view. "I know you love rugby and all, but I don't think I could ever leave a place like this. It's so … peaceful."

The way she says it hits me in the heart.

"Some things run in the family, I see," she says, laughing.

What? I spy Hartley's giant white pickup truck parked just outside the garage. He comes out of the garage with a shit-eating smile and waits for us to pull up.

"Look at you," he says, grabbing me for a hug as soon as my feet hit the ground. "How the hell are you? Still a shrimp, I see."

I chuckle, taking in his six-foot-one, solid two-hundred-thirty-pound frame. "We both couldn't be great looking, so God gave you height."

"You're full of shit," he says, grinning from ear to ear. He takes a step back, and his attention is drawn to movement at the front of my truck.

I follow his gaze to Astrid. Her arms are folded across her middle. Gone is the easygoing girl I had in the truck with me. Astrid with the clipboard is back—minus the actual clipboard.

"Come here," I say, smiling gently at her. "Astrid, this is my brother, Hartley. Hart, this is my assistant, Astrid."

His eyes light up. "*This* is the assistant?"

"Yes." I hide a grin. "This is the assistant."

"Whatever he's said about me comes from a place of ego and stubbornness that I fear you know all too well." Astrid holds out a hand. "It's nice to meet you, Hartley."

"It's very nice to meet you. I can tell we have a lot in common," Hartley says as they shake hands.

A small smile touches her lips.

"I gotta run a couple of keys to the guys at the south gate." Hartley turns to me. "You guys can ride with me or head on in and grab a drink."

Astrid is more relaxed than she was a few moments ago, but I think introducing her to the crew might be more than she's ready to handle today. *Those guys are a rowdy bunch.*

"We'll stay here," I say.

The relief is evident on Astrid's face.

"I'll be about thirty minutes," Hartley says, getting into his truck. "The keys are in the side-by-side if you want to take it for a spin."

"You're good with staying here, right?" I ask her as Hartley starts the truck.

"I was hoping you'd choose that option because I need to pee."

"All right. Let's head inside."

The steps creak as we climb onto the porch and find the screen door closed. It pulls open with the same hitch it's had my entire life, and something about that makes me smile.

"The bathroom is down the hallway," I say, pointing to my right. "First door on your left."

"Thanks."

I take a deep breath, filling my nostrils with the scent of cinnamon apples. I can't help but wonder if Hartley burns the same candles Mom did or if the scent has leached into the walls. It's the smell of *home.*

I mosey around the living room, taking in the similarities and differences since I was here last. A new mounted deer head, a size bigger than Pap's, hangs on the back wall. We never thought anyone would break that record, but it looks like someone did.

Pictures line the built-in cabinets surrounding the television. I take them in one by one, many of them sitting in the same spot they have for years. Miniature rocking chairs that Hart and I used as kids are next to the fireplace. The television, though, is new and much bigger—a flat-screen that looks like a picture frame. Mom would've hated it. I find that amusing.

"There you are." Astrid comes into the room. "Your brother has the best hand soap that I've ever smelled." She sniffs her fingers. "It's vanilla, I think. Maybe with blueberries."

"You'll have to ask Cathy. I'm sure Hartley has no idea."

She moves to the window overlooking the backyard. "Who's Cathy?"

"She's worked here since I was nine or ten years old. She takes care of the house and took care of Pap. Mom was an ER nurse and worked long shifts, and Dad was busy with the ranch, so Cathy came in and took care of things while everyone was busy."

"I love that you all lived here together."

I join her at the window. "Yeah, I loved it, too. Pap had a *Playboy* subscription and a cigar habit. When you're a teenage boy, those are great things to have at your disposal."

"You were a handful as a kid, weren't you?"

"You could say that."

She grins softly. "How much of this do you own?"

"Me? I don't own shit, but Hart has over a thousand acres."

"*Oh.* Wow."

I slide a hand in my pocket. "It's pretty impressive. He has … I don't know how many head of cattle. Horses. Chickens. Goats." I study her before I speak again. "Want to take a ride around the property?"

She smiles. "Yeah. Sure. I'd like that."

We exit the house and head outside. She grabs one of the water bottles from my truck that I bought at Piper's, so I hop in the side-by-side and pick her up.

Astrid giggles as we whip around the side of the house, leaving tracks in the yard that I'm sure Hartley will yell at me about later. I hate to tell my brother, but it's worth it. Hearing Astrid enjoy herself is worth all the shit he'll undoubtedly give me, because I sense this doesn't happen often with her.

The more I see Astrid without her trusty clipboard, the more I kind of like her. I find myself wanting to know more about her, wondering what makes this confusing woman tick. She handles herself with complete confidence in some moments. In others, she seems almost fearful. *Why?*

"Look at that," she says, pointing at a little spring trickling out of the side of a rock ledge. "That's the cutest thing I've ever seen."

I wheel us over to it and slow down. "Want to get out and take a drink?"

"No, thanks. I don't want to die of dysentery."

"Dysentery?" I snort. "Really?"

She wrinkles her button nose. "Fine. I don't want a parasite. Better?"

"You won't get a parasite."

She looks at me like I'm full of shit.

"I mean it," I say, entertained by her reaction. "Mom used to bring jugs out here and fill them up a few times a week. She swore it was healthier than tap water because we got minerals and shit from it. Hartley and I turned out fine."

She makes a face. "That's debatable."

I laugh, bumping her shoulder with mine as I press the gas once again, and we ride along quietly for a while. Astrid points out the buzzards circling a clearing in the trees, and two deer jumping the fence before darting into the forest. Her eyes twinkle as she takes everything in, and I wish we had more time for me to show her the barns and fields.

"Your mom seems pretty cool," she says out of nowhere.

"I don't know about cool, but she was a great mom."

Astrid leans back in the seat and turns her head to me. "Did you have a good relationship with her?"

"Yeah. We all had a good relationship, really. Mom and Dad were strict with us, but we had a lot of fun, too. We'd play euchre together, we had fun traditions for every holiday, and they never missed our games or school shit." I pilot the machine down the hill on a path that's only faintly still visible. "What about your parents? Did you get along with them?"

It's a touchy topic. She's told me enough to paint a clear picture of her upbringing—specifically with her father—but I don't want to dig and ask the pointed questions I'd like to have answered.

Where was her mother? Was Astrid neglected? Abused?

My jaw clenches at the thought of a baby Astrid being in pain and having no one give a shit.

"My mom died in childbirth," she says just loud enough to be heard over the motor.

Fuck. "I'm sorry."

She shrugs helplessly. "You didn't know." She takes a breath. "My grandma lived next door to my dad and me until I was eight, but then she had a heart attack in the front yard while she was taking her trash to the road. I found her after school."

My God. My heart aches for her. My fingers itch to grasp her shoulder and pull her into my side—to offer comfort that I doubt she got from her father.

"My dad was a sonofabitch." She bristles, tensing again. "And that's all I have to say about that."

I should keep my mouth shut. It's not my place to say anything more, or to inject myself into her private world, but I can't help it. I have to say something.

"As much as you've annoyed me over the past couple of weeks, you've also been impressive," I say, swallowing through a constriction in my throat. "I hate to think that your strength comes from necessity, especially at such a young age."

The corner of her mouth lifts. "I'm glad it did. Otherwise, I would've been a statistic in one way or another." She side-eyes me. "Instead, I'm just a heartless bitch."

I blow out a breath, embarrassed. "I'm really sorry I said that to you. It was wholly unfair."

She shrugs like it doesn't matter. "Where are we headed?"

I don't want to change the subject. I want to apologize until she hears it and believes it, because the locker room ordeal now makes perfect sense. Before, I was sorry for being mean. Now I'm sorry for being unknowingly cruel. But as I start to speak again, I remember something my therapist once told me: an apology is for whoever I hurt, not for me.

If I'm truly remorseful for what I said, then I must prioritize what she needs over what I feel like I need.

So I have to let it go for now.

"I thought you might like to see Sugar Creek," I say, ducking as a strand of thorns whips at me from the side.

"It runs through your property?"

"There's a joke that the creek touches everyone's property somehow. But, yeah, it runs just a little way down this path."

She shifts in her seat. "There was a time not long ago when this would've been dangerous."

"Really? Why?"

"Because I would've wanted to drown you in the creek."

I laugh. "You mean you don't anymore?"

"Maybe not today," she says, fighting a grin.

We round a large pine tree, and the water comes into view. It's a bit wider and deeper here than in most places. A handful of trees have fallen in the vicinity, and by the looks of the rope swing hanging off a limb and the leaf litter covering the picnic table we hauled down here as teenagers, it doesn't look like Hartley comes back here anymore.

"This is beautiful," she says, hopping out with her water bottle in hand. "*Wow, Gray.* Look at this place."

I shut the engine off and climb out, too. "Do you like it?"

"What's not to like?"

"We used to hang out here all summer. Mom or Cathy would pack us a picnic basket and a cooler full of lemonade, and we'd bring a little radio that I got one Christmas. We'd swim and shoot the shit. It was a good time." *No, it was the best time.*

I let my gaze roam around the land, chastising myself for not truly appreciating life here. Sure, I have great memories with my family, and Brooks and I had a ball, but I had one foot out the door from as far back as I can remember. I was convinced the small-town life wasn't for me.

But I've seen the world now and all it has to offer. And, while I've had a lot of experiences—both good and bad—I realize it's not for me, either. I've pondered whether coming back home would make me feel like a failure or inadequate in some way, or if Hartley would have feelings about me coming and going as I see fit. But being here? It's the most contentment I've had in a long fucking time.

Astrid peers off the edge of the embankment into the water. "It sounds magical."

"They write about this in books. I could suggest some, if you'd like."

She glares at me playfully before turning back to the water again. "There are little fishes. Look at that."

"There's a heron on your right just upstream."

"I can't get over this," she says, looking toward the bird. "Is that a rope swing?"

I nod. "Yeah. This is one of the only places in the area where it's deep enough for that kind of thing. The water pools here and gets lazy instead of flowing steadily."

"One of my childhood dreams was to use a rope swing. I saw one on—*ah!*"

Astrid's foot catches on an exposed tree root and slips out from beneath her. In slow motion, she falls forward, eyes wide, hair trailing behind her, and water bottle pressed to her chest.

She lands with a thud.

"Are you okay?" I ask, racing to her side and kneeling beside her. "Does anything hurt?"

"I don't think so." She groans, turning onto her side and looking up to me with gold-flecked eyes. The crushed plastic water bottle squeaks as she moves off it. "Nothing besides my pride, anyway."

I brush a lock of hair off her cheek, my knuckles swiping against her smooth skin, and a zing of heat rips through me. It doesn't stop until it reaches my toes. Her gaze pierces mine as her lips part, and I can't help but wonder if she felt that, too.

"Are you sure you're okay?" I ask as she sits up.

"Yeah." She glances down at the front of her shirt. It's soaked from the water that was in her hand, and a dark smudge streaks down the right side of her chest. She groans again. "Oh, great. What is that? Mud?"

I shove my tongue in my cheek and decide if I should tell her that the streak isn't from mud.

Astrid pulls the fabric away from her body, giving me a clear view of the tops of her round tits.

Heat creeps up my neck as I try to look away. Suddenly, she's not a shrew, and she's not the woman I work with. She's a verifiable fox. I can't stop myself from imagining my hands on her body, her nipples in my mouth, and the sound of her voice as she moans.

"What is that?" she asks with a shrillness to her tone that snaps me right out of my daydream.

"What's what?"

She points. *"That."*

I try my absolute hardest not to laugh. "That? That's rabbit poop."

She scoots back like it's a pile of poison with the ability to reach out and bite her. The color in her face drains. Her fingers lose their grip on her shirt, and it falls against her again. She squeals, pulling it away from her skin.

It's fucking adorable.

"Can I get rabies from this?" she asks.

"No, you cannot get rabies from this." I twist my lips together, but the laughter comes anyway. "You'll be fine."

She hops up and backward, putting more distance between herself and the small pile of shit. "Seriously? I might throw up."

"Hey, at least it's not dysentery," I joke.

"This isn't funny, jackass."

I clear my throat, trying to be serious. "You're right. We'll head back to the house, and you can get cleaned up."

"I can't wait that long. I have ... *poop* on me." She shivers.

"What am I going to do?" she whines. "If I had a sports bra on, I'd just take my shirt off."

"Not a bad idea."

She cocks her head to the side and glares at me.

"Hey, leave it on and risk rabies," I say, holding my hands at my chest. "It's up to you."

"Remember when I said I hated you less? I didn't mean it."

I grin smugly at her as I reach for the hem of my T-shirt. "I'm pretty sure you clarified that then."

Her eyes drop to my waist. It feels like trails of lava are left on my skin as she drags her gaze up my body along with my shirt. *Over my abs, up my torso, and across my shoulders.* Her lips are parted when I ball it in my hands and smirk at her.

"Take your shirt off and you can wear mine," I say, holding it out to her.

She swallows. "Then what are you going to wear?"

"Are you offended by me being shirtless?"

She rolls her eyes but takes my offering without touching me. "Turn around."

Sure. Take the fun out of it. I twist on my heel. *Taking the fun out of things really is her forte.*

I watch the afternoon sun shine through the trees, casting shadows on the forest floor—and try to forget that Astrid is topless just feet behind me. I'm only a man, after all. One who just realized today that his assistant is fucking hot.

"Okay," she says. "You can turn around."

I do and find her shirt *and bra* hanging off her fingers. My tee is tied in a knot at her belly button, the fabric drawn to her middle, showcasing the natural shape of her tits. They're rounded and hang in a sexy drop. Her nipples strain against the cotton.

Thank God I wore gray and not black today.

"Don't make this weird," she says, trudging by me to the side-by-side.

"There's not a damn thing weird about this."

"You're making it weird."

I bite my bottom lip to keep from smiling and climb into the seat beside her. She places a hand over her chest and lifts a brow at me.

"Try not to Indy 500 it back to the house, please," she says. "As you're well aware, I don't have a bra on."

"Who said I was aware of that?"

I look at her over my shoulder and find her fighting a grin, too.

"Thanks for telling me." I shift the transmission into drive. "That's good to know."

"Gray!" she squeals, breaking into a fit of laughter as I stomp on the gas.

The sound of her laughter follows us all the way home. And despite thoroughly enjoying that Astrid can laugh at the situation, it also causes a knot to form in the bottom of my gut.

My assistant is not only a smoke show, but she's also really fucking funny. *Fuck me.*

CHAPTER
TWENTY

Astrid

"I'll learn to play euchre, but I want to be on your team," I say to Hartley.

"Fine by me," Gray says, sitting back in the kitchen chair. Still shirtless. "I don't want to be your partner anyway. You can't even walk and talk without falling into a pile of rabbit shit."

I gasp, but it quickly turns into a giggle. "How rude."

Hartley winks at me.

"I'll study up," I say, standing up and taking my bowl to the sink on the other side of the room. "I'll be the best damn euchre player Tennessee has ever seen."

The brothers share stories from their childhood and how their pap would cheat at cards. I listen as I knock the crumbs from my party mix into the trash and then rinse the bowl before putting it in the dishwasher.

Hartley's kitchen is as cute as a button. The decor is stuck in the nineties with geese in bonnets with dusty blue bows around their necks on the wall border. The cabinets have a distinct orange hue. Blue-and-white checkered curtains hang on either side of the window overlooking the sink, and containers labeled sugar, flour, and coffee are displayed beneath the microwave. It's oddly charming.

I ensure the lid is fastened to the plastic ice cream container that housed the party mix before returning to the table.

"We probably should be going," Gray says as I reach my chair. "Are you about ready?"

"Yeah. Sure. Can I get my shirt out of the dryer?"

"If you want to take them with you, then you better," Gray says.

I roll my eyes at him and head to the laundry room.

We inadvertently spent the whole afternoon and evening with Hartley. Hart took us on another ride in the side-by-side to look at different fields. We stopped to check on the goats, which was my favorite part of the day aside from witnessing this version of Gray—a relaxed, happy Gray.

More than once today, I've thought about the picture that I saw at his apartment. This must be the man that woman loved. I can easily see Gray making her laugh like she was in the image, tossing a ball back and forth on the beach, and earning the look of adoration that was so heavy in her eyes.

My stomach squeezes as I shove it out of my mind again.

"You have to be kidding me," I say, pulling my damp shirt out of the dryer. "How can it not be dry? It was in there for two cycles."

I shouldn't have washed it and my bra in the sink, but I didn't have a choice. Now I don't really have a choice—I'll have to wear Gray's shirt home. Thankfully, my bra is dry enough to wear, so I put it on beneath the shirt.

The feeling of Gray's fabric against my skin sends a small thrill through my body. I lift the neckline for the hundredth time and breathe in the scent of his cologne mixed with laundry soap. It feels forbidden to have something of his touch me like this, and it also gives big red flags that I like it. *God, I like it.* And I wish I didn't.

Every time our eyes have met, I've wondered what he thinks

about me wearing his shirt. *Does he like the idea of it? Does he hate it? Does he not have any feelings about it whatsoever?*

I sag against the dryer when my phone buzzes.

Gianna: Still doing okay, babe?

Me: Yup.

Audrey: Are you home yet? Need us to come over?

I frown in anticipation of their reaction.

Me: I'm still in Sugar Creek.

Audrey: Still?

Gianna:

Audrey:

I snort.

Me: We're at his brother's house and are heading home now. Settle down.

Gianna: This is what I've been working on today ...

A picture of a urinal fashioned into what I think is a bird bath fills the screen. I narrow my eyes, taking it in from every angle. I'm not sure how to respond to this, so I wait for Audrey to take the lead.

Audrey: So creative!

Me: Just what I was thinking.

Gianna: It's a fountain, but I don't have the
water flowing correctly yet. Anyway, see my
vision now?

Me: Totally.

Audrey: Absolutely.

My fingers hover over the keyboard when the sound of a male's voice that I don't know cracks through the house. *Who is that?*

Me: Gotta go. Xo

I shove my phone in my pocket and tiptoe into the living room.

Oh. A man who's a little taller than Gray, with light hair and a shit-eating smile stands next to Hartley. His face is washed in mischief. He screams trouble in a way that would make Gianna very, very happy.

I lift my chin, clear my throat, and then enter the room with a confidence I don't quite feel.

Gray's brows pull together. "Still not dry?"

I hold my shirt in front of me. "Nope. You really need to get your dryer repaired, Hartley."

"Cathy's been saying that," he says, sighing. "I—"

"Well, excuse the hell outta me," the other man says, his

sights set on me. "But I don't think we've met. I'm Brooks Dempsey, and who might you be?"

Gray elbows him in the ribs. "Brooks, this is my assistant, Astrid. Astrid, meet my friend Brooks."

"Astrid, it's nice to meet you," Brooks says.

I steal a look at Gray, who's watching me closely. I'm not sure what to make of it, but if he's wondering where my loyalties lie, I'll make it clear. "Well, Brooks, I don't know if it's nice to meet you yet or not. But hello, regardless."

"Ah, hell," he says, making everyone laugh.

"We were just heading out," Gray says. "We—"

"The hell you are." Brooks looks offended. "It's Sugar Days, brother. You gotta stay."

Gray's face falls. "Nah, man, we can't. Astrid rode with me, and I told her this would just be an afternoon thing."

"I can call an Uber back to Nashville," I say, tucking a strand of hair behind my ear. Riding in a car with a stranger for the next hour and a half sounds like absolute misery, but it's better than robbing Gray of a fun night with his friend.

"Why?" Brooks asks. "You're coming with us."

My shoulders sink as I turn frantically to Gray. "Don't worry. I'll call a car." I take my phone out of my pocket and step a few paces toward the laundry room, but Gray's voice stops me in my tracks.

"Wait." His hands are shoved in his pockets with no attention paid to the others in the room. Just me. "If you go back tonight, I'm taking you. There's zero chance you're getting in the car with a random person."

Something flutters deep inside me next to my heart. The ache in my chest is soft and gentle, unlike the painful pulls I'm used to. The fact that he would go out of his way, prioritizing me above his friend and his family, knocks the wind right out of me. *Who does that?*

His smile, dimples deep in his cheeks, is just for me.

"Or you could stay and have fun tonight," Brooks says. "I'll be your personal Sugar Creek tour guide."

"The hell you will." Gray shoots him a look over his shoulder. "You mind your own damn business."

Brooks and Hartley exchange a grin.

My mouth is dry as I try to read the room. I can't decide whether I'm really wanted here or not. They're probably just tolerating me—Gray does seem to have manners here, after all. The last thing I want to be is an inconvenience.

"I could just hang out here," I offer. "I don't want to put anyone out."

Gray lifts a brow. "Aren't you the one who told me you needed A. Fucking. Break?"

"I didn't mean in this context," I say, laughing.

"Stay," Hartley urges. "It'll be fun."

"Don't say that," Gray says. "She definitely won't stay if she thinks she'll have fun."

I mock him. "Shut up."

"I'll buy you a funnel cake," Hartley offers.

"Fine. I'll dance with you at the bandstand," Brooks says, grimacing. "You'll endure many glares from the other women salivating for their chance with me. That's on you."

Gray licks his lips. "You don't have to worry about that."

All three men watch me with careful anticipation, waiting for my response. I shift from foot to foot, still uncertain how I should proceed. This is something I've never done and, if Gianna would do this, I'd tell her she was asking for trouble.

Going with three men I just met to a festival at night in a place I don't know? These types of situations are how podcasters make a living.

But standing in this room with Gray, Hartley, and Brooks, I don't feel fearful. I don't doubt their intentions for a second. I don't sense danger. As a matter of fact, I haven't once gotten an indication that something was amiss with any of them.

Dare I say that I feel … safe?

I shrug. "We don't have shirts."

"Your closet is full of stuff," Hartley says to Gray. "You'd probably be able to scrounge something up for the two of you."

Gray lifts a brow at me.

The thought of going home feels like a wet blanket being thrown on top of me. It's heavy, and lonely, and suffocating. Besides, if I stay, I'll have a story to tell my friends, for once. *And Gianna will die.*

"Okay," I say. "If you want to go, Gray, let's go."

"Atta girl." Brooks claps his hands like he's cheering on a sports play. "The Fish Fry ends in about an hour, and I've waited all week for that. Can we put this into high gear?"

Gray bends his finger at me. "Come on."

My chest feels like someone's holding a sparkler too close to me, and bits of hot ash are pinging my skin. I can barely think a cohesive thought. A part of me cheers my bold, brave decision, and the other part of me laments my recklessness. It's hell to be me.

Gray opens a door and pops on the light. "After you."

I pass him, careful not to touch him, and take in what must be his old bedroom. Posters on the walls. Trophies on shelves. A stack of books by the bed.

"This room gives Gray vibes," I say, sitting on the edge of the mattress while he rummages in the closet. "And it looks like you really did read books."

"Did you think I was lying?"

"Eh, kind of."

He slides some hangers to the side. "Gee, thanks. I'm more than a handsome face, you know."

His back muscles ripple as he moves. They're thick and dense, with ridges and lines that I didn't know existed in the real world. The taper from his shoulders to his waist is ridiculous.

"Yeah, I know," I say, blushing. "Thanks for bringing me

here, by the way. Not just *here*, but to Sugar Creek and to see Joe. You've gone out of your way to be kind to me today, and I appreciate that."

He stills but doesn't turn around. "You make it sound like that surprises you."

"Well, in my experience, if people do choose kindness, there are usually limitations. It's human nature, I guess." I laugh nervously. "I've made this weird, haven't I?"

Gray pulls two shirts out of the closet and turns to me with them in his hand.

In the dim light from the ceiling fan, he looks mysterious. Shadows hide the sharpness of his features and exaggerate the ridges and valleys of his body. He's the kind of guy who people stop and stare at. I can't help but wonder what our relationship could've been like had we not gotten off on the wrong foot.

My breath hitches as he comes closer with a twinkle in his eye.

"Have you had fun?" he asks, his voice low and controlled.

"Honestly? Yeah. I have."

"Good. Me, too."

"Bet you didn't think I had *fun* in me, did you?" I grin and get to my feet.

He stops just inches in front of me, close enough where I could easily reach out and touch him—something my fingers itch to do.

I can hear my heart pounding and feel the rush of hot blood circulating through my veins. The intensity and warmth of his gaze draws me in, and suddenly, I'm not sure where this is going.

This is Gray Adler, my coworker. The giver of migraines. *The man I … loathe.* But, at this moment, he's something else, too, and I'm afraid to put a name to it.

His dimples shine. "Believe it or not, I did think you had it in you."

"Oh really?"

"Really."

The room shrinks and the temperature rises so high that I'm sweating. Everything around us blurs into oblivion. It's only Gray and me here.

My heart flutters as he offers me one of the shirts, and I reach for it, tentatively at first. But when my knuckles graze his, I melt into the contact.

The backs of my knees hit the edge of the bed, and if I rock even a bit, I'll fall onto my back. I'm held up by a prayer and Gray's dark, hooded eyes.

"If you didn't hate me, I might kiss you right now," he whispers.

He's close enough to feel the heat of his breath. I pant, working hard to remember how to perform basic bodily functions.

I lift my chin, my inhale shaky. "If you didn't hate me, I might let you."

His grin sears its way right through me, melting me into a puddle at his feet. He searches my face as if he's wondering if I'm just playing with him or if I mean it. I give him the slightest nod.

Slowly, he lowers his lips to mine.

I can nearly taste the sweet anticipation hanging in the air between us. Goose bumps break out across my heated skin, and I feel both vulnerable and acutely aware of it. But, instead of being freaked out and desperate to run, the only place I want to go is in his arms.

I part my lips, my eyes fluttering closed. *He's so close.*

"Hurry the fuck up in there!" Brooks shouts from the other room.

I gasp, filling my lungs with the oxygen I've been depriving them. I'm stunned ... by all of it. *I almost kissed Gray Adler.*

His lips form a thin, tight line as he shrugs on a shirt. The vein in his temple throbs as he tosses me one of my own. "I'll wait out here."

"O-kay," I say, watching him walk out of the room.

I sit on the bed again and bury my head in my hands.

What the hell just happened here?

CHAPTER
TWENTY-ONE

"Did he feel bad about it?" I ask, taking a sip of my third beer. It's supposedly a fan-favorite concoction that only comes out during the spring fair. It's so popular, in fact, that it's the only alcoholic beverage served at the festival. All I can figure is that it's a local delicacy because it tastes like trash to me.

Brooks snorts, telling me without telling me that my question was ill-informed. "No, sunshine. He was in the gym to prove a point."

Sunshine? I lift a brow, and he winks with a cockiness that has me rolling my eyes.

"I thought you were training, which by definition would mean that you were trying to help each other improve," I say.

Brooks shakes his head. "Gray, get your girl."

Our group of Gray's family and friends who are hanging outside of Patsy's laughs.

Although I know that no one is laughing at me—because they truly are some of the nicest people I've ever met in my life —I still blush … and refuse to sneak a glimpse at Gray. The heat of his gaze warms the side of my face.

We've not spoken about our *almost* kiss in his bedroom, mainly because Hartley rode to the fair with us. We've not had a moment alone, but his leg did rest against mine in the truck. His palm has lain in the small of my back multiple times this evening. And he wiped cotton candy stuck to my bottom lip with his thumb, nearly killing me in the process.

I'm buzzed. I'd blame it on the beer, but it started well before Hartley bought the first round at Patsy's a couple of hours ago. This is so foreign to me, and I wish I had Gianna here to explain it since she seems to know everything when it comes to attraction. Because I *am* attracted to Gray.

God, help me.

I snap a picture of the group and send it to Audrey and Gianna. It takes Gianna point-one seconds to reply.

Gianna: How does it feel to be God's favorite?

I giggle, sitting at an empty picnic table to the right of Gray and the guys.

Me: Wish you were here.

Gianna: Not as much as I do, I promise you that. Who are those people? Specifically, the three guys who are not Gray.

Me: Gray's brother, Hartley, is in the flannel shirt. His best friend Brooks is in the navy T-shirt. Their friend Jasper is wearing the cowboy hat, and the girl with him is Meadow. I haven't decided whether they're dating or if she just wants to date him.

Gianna: She wants to fuck him. He's not into it. Look at their body language.

I lift my sights to the two of them standing next to Gray. Meadow's hand is casually placed on Jasper's shoulder, but he's leaning slightly away from her. If that means anything, then Gianna is right. *Wonder what she would have to say about my body language with Gray?*

He catches my attention and mouths, "Are you good?"

I grin and nod.

The sky is an art piece as the sun dips just above the brick buildings lining Sugar Street. Vivid oranges and pinks, with flashes of electric purple, paint a spectacular background for the Sugar County Fair. Lights flash from food trucks offering grease-soaked and sprinkle-covered snacks. Children's joyous shouts ring out as they risk their lives on various rides, especially the one that tips them upside down. Chimes ring somewhere in the distance as someone wins a cheap prize that took twenty bucks to win—and it's wonderful. Blissful, even. Things hit different in this small town.

Even the people.

Me: Sometimes I wish I was as bold as you.

Gianna: *pops collar* Thank you for that compliment.

Audrey: You don't have to be bold, Astrid. Just be you. That's enough.

Gianna: *gags self with spoon*

Audrey:

Gianna:

Me: I'll keep you posted on the events of the evening.

Gianna: Feel free to send pics. Nudes (not of you), preferably.

I snort and darken my screen.

"Here you go," Hartley says, holding a funnel cake in his hand. "Beer and funnel cake go together like beans and cornbread."

"Really?"

"Nope. Not even a little bit." He laughs. "But the line for lemon shakeups was outrageous, so you get what you get."

"You'll hear no complaints from me," I say, taking it. "Thank you."

"Yeah, of course."

I rip a corner off the confection, getting powdered sugar all over my fingers, and pop it into my mouth. The dough is sweet and slightly crispy. I haven't had one of these in forever.

Hartley sits beside me, watching his brother and friends trade stories. He folds his hands on the table. "I'm glad you came by with Gray today. It was nice meeting someone from his life."

I take another bite. "Does that not happen often?"

"Nah, Gray keeps his work life and home life separate. Always has. But once Mom and Dad died, he definitely pulled away."

My throat tightens right along with my stomach. I set the funnel cake on the table and dust my hands off to the side. I knew they had passed, but I didn't expect anyone to bring it up, and I surely wasn't going to poke around about it.

"How long have they been gone?" I ask carefully, unsure how alike he is to his brother. *Will he flip-flop from hot to cold? Clam up? Or speak freely?* I have no clue.

"It'll be eight years this fall." He exhales, and the heaviness of the topic is written in the lines around his mouth and eyes. "I worry a lot about Gray, and I try to keep in contact with him as much as he'll let me. But, if you haven't recognized, he's a pain in the ass."

I grin at Hartley. "I have recognized that, believe it or not."

He chuckles. "He's happy with you around."

I flinch, pulling away from him to get a better look at his face. Surely, he's joking. "I think he's just happy to be home."

"No, I think it's you." He smiles at me. "You're good for him. And you must have the patience of a saint to put up with his shit, so thank you for that."

"He's not that bad." *Now that we've stopped fighting all the time, anyway.* The thought makes me curious, and I take a swallow of beer to help make me bold. "Can I ask you something, Hartley?"

"Sure."

"Before Gray came to Nashville, he had a reputation for being … difficult. I'm sure you've seen some of the headlines written about him."

He nods, staring off into the distance.

"I'm having a hard time making sense of the fact that the Gray in those reports is the Gray I see in Nashville, who is the same Gray that's here tonight. So what gives?"

Hartley leans back, stretching his legs out in front of him. His palms scratch down his thighs like I've seen Gray do a million times. All the while, I pray silently that I haven't overstepped my bounds and put my nose where it doesn't belong.

"My dad always said two things when it came to other people," Hartley says, drawing his attention back to me. "The first was to always give people the benefit of the doubt. Think the best of them, if at all possible. The second was that the way someone treats you is who they are. You judge them based on what you see and not what you hear."

There's a depth to his gaze, drawing me into the moment, making me contemplate his words. It's a steady, gentle look that still holds a magnificent amount of weight. He thinks what he's said is important and clearly wants me to understand that.

Point received.

The band begins to play on the stage, which is just the bed of a semi-truck with a few plants and advertisements from local businesses hanging from it. The song they start with is an oldie but a goodie. I recall it playing at my grandma's house when I was a little girl.

I sigh, swaying softly to the music and contemplating Hartley's words. There's more to it than meets the eye, but I can't sort through the beer-induced fog well enough to get to the nugget of truth.

"Astrid, do you want another beer? Bottle of water? Anything?" Gray asks, suddenly appearing at my side.

I smile up at him. "The ground is already a little wobbly, so I think I've had enough."

"I'm going to go grab another one. Be right back."

Hartley stands. "I'll go with you."

Couples begin to dance on the closed road in front of the stage, their arms draped around each other. Everyone in Sugar Creek seems so … happy. No one is rushed or busy. Even the children who speed by—all hyped up on candy—seem to be living their best life. It's a relief—better than I could've imagined.

A long, deep breath fills my lungs, going deeper than any breath has managed in a long time. It slows my heartbeat in a way that yoga, medication, and a caffeine-free lifestyle all failed to accomplish. *How is that possible?*

"You." Brooks's smile is full of mischief as he sets his sights on me. "Come on."

"Excuse me?"

"Dance with me."

Dance with him? I glance over my shoulder and spot Gray watching us. "I think I'll wait here."

Brooks leans closer, giving me a wicked grin. "Look, as Gray's best friend and the only person who probably knows him better than he knows himself, you need to dance with me. Sometimes it takes a little competition to spur men into action."

I laugh, leaning forward on my elbows. "You see, Brooks, for that to be true, you must assume that Gray hasn't already sprung into action or that I want him to."

"You see, Astrid, I know he hasn't *sprung into action* because I've been talking to you for three minutes and I can still chew my food properly." He chuckles. "And I know damn good and well you want him to because if there's anyone that I can read better than Gray, it's women."

"Oh, please," I say, laughing. "You don't have a confidence problem, do you?"

He leans back and holds out his hand. "What's not to be confident about? Now, are you going to dance with me or not?"

I glance at Gray again. He has a marker in his hand, signing a shirt for a little boy. An older woman is standing entirely too close to Gray to be comfortable, and Gray's clearly not happy about it—the tension in his body proves that—but he's occupied.

"Fine," I say, getting to my feet. "I hope you know what you're doing."

"Honestly? I never know what I'm doing, but it always works out."

"I love that for me," I say, not sure what I'm doing either, but *here we are.*

Brooks leads me through the small groups of people to the street. He slides an arm around my waist, careful not to grip me too tightly or make too much contact, and I nod at him in appreciation.

"So what do you do for a living?" I ask.

He scoffs. "Not a fight fan, huh?"

"When you look at me, do you see *fight fan*? Do I give off that impression?"

"I'm not sure what impression you make. You're quite an enigma."

I snort-laugh. "An enigma? Really?"

"Yeah. If I had to put it into words, I'd say you're a lady in the streets, although you're currently wearing Gray's high school rugby shirt, and possibly a freak in the sheets."

He thinks *I* fit *that* vibe? Whether he means that or not, I don't know. His smirk makes me think he's just screwing with me, but that doesn't take away from the heat scorching my face as I try not to die in embarrassment.

"So you're a fighter," I say, firmly redirecting this conversation to more neutral territory. "My friend's brother is a fighter."

"Oh, really? What gym does he fight out of?"

I wince. "Boston?"

"That's not a gym. It's a city."

"It's the best I can do."

Brooks opens his mouth, but before anything can come out, a set of large hands perch on his shoulders, and he's yanked backward. He twists, raring back with a fist—ready to pound someone into the asphalt. Once he realizes it's Gray, he drops his arm and bursts out laughing.

"You about met your maker, buddy," Brooks says as Gray stands him upright. "And, no, you may not cut in."

Gray wraps an arm around my waist and pulls me into his

side. I gasp, going wide-eyed at the contact, but melting into him all the same.

Gray lifts a brow at Brooks. "It's a good thing I didn't fucking ask, then, isn't it?"

My God.

Brooks smirks, walking backward and pointing at me. "You are very welcome. I take thank-you gifts in the form of gift cards and cash."

"You are trouble!" I call after him, giggling.

Gray's fingertips press into my side as he guides me in front of him. My skin sizzles beneath his touch, responding to him well before my brain can catch up. His gaze is rich and warm as he bites his lip to keep from smiling.

"Your friend is a character," I say, trying to keep my words even as Gray connects his hands in the small of my back.

"Oh, he's the main character in his own mind." Gray grins. "What did that fool have to say, anyway?"

My palms skim his chest and over his shoulders, committing every layer of muscle to memory. "Nothing much. He was offended that I didn't know who he was. Speaking of that, I saw you giving an autograph up there."

"It's no big deal."

"I think his mom wanted a different kind of signature, if you know what I mean."

He snorts. "That wasn't his mom. His mom was my third-grade teacher. That woman runs the farmers' market just outside of town."

"She's very ... hands-on."

"That's what Brooks tells me," Gray says.

"Oh really?"

He chuckles. "It's obvious that you don't know Brooks. Nothing is surprising about that guy. However, he's fucked half ... or more, of Sugar County."

The band shifts gears, starting a popular nineties country

ballad. More couples join us on the street. I notice many eyes, mostly women but some men, too, checking out Gray. *But his?* They're solely on me.

I toy with the hairs on the back of his neck, enjoying the ease I feel in his arms. I'm aware that putting my guard down is probably a major mistake—lowering it has never *not* bitten me in the ass. But the beer and possibly the town's tranquil, unhurried vibe have chipped away at some of my restraint, and lowering the shield—if only for a moment—is incredible.

"So nothing's surprising about Brooks," I say. "Tell me something that would surprise me about you."

"What do you want to know?"

"What are my parameters?"

The corner of his lips pulls to the sky. "Are you going to stay within them?"

"It depends on what they are," I say, giggling.

He adjusts his hands, pulling me even closer to him. "What do you want to know?"

Gray has never been this open with me or this willing to talk. He's never had me in his arms in the middle of a fair either, but that's not the point. The point is that he's trying to let me get to know him better—and I appreciate that. More than he'll ever know.

I force a swallow, knowing that asking the one question I've wondered about a hundred times could shatter our newfound peace. But I do it, anyway. "Who was the woman in the picture in your apartment?"

He takes a deep breath, averting his eyes to something over my head. My heart pounds, wishing I could take the question back. I shouldn't have asked it. It was the beer talking.

"I—"

"Caroline," he says.

I cup the back of his neck with my palm. "Thank you for answering that."

"She's no longer in the picture, if you're curious. No pun intended."

"May I ask why not?"

He looks briefly at the sky and sighs. "I have this way of … that is, my life's complicated." He settles his gaze on me. His eyes are clear and unguarded, and it takes my breath away. "I make a lot of shitty choices sometimes, Astrid."

"So Caroline is out of your life by your choice or hers?"

"Mine."

The shirt I'm wearing bunches up in the back, and his fingers dust against the sensitive skin just above my ass as we turn in a half circle. Our gazes lock on contact, and he touches me again, slowly, seeking approval.

I hitch a breath. My body doesn't ask, *it demands* to be touched by him again. I lace my fingers through the back of his hair, bringing our bodies so close that even a raindrop couldn't come between us.

"What about you?" he asks, his voice rougher than before. "Is there a man out there who thinks he's your guy?"

Does Caroline still believe she's your girl? The question is on the tip of my tongue, but I don't ask it. It matters, but maybe not enough for this conversation. Or perhaps I'm scared to know the answer.

"I think the idea of being my guy would strike fear in most men's hearts," I joke.

His brows pinch together.

"No," I say, hyperaware of the small designs he's drawing on my back. My throat is as dry as a bone, so I swallow to wet it again. "There's not been a man in the picture since Trace."

"The guy the letter was over, right?"

I nod.

His eyes narrow, and he laughs softly. "How in the hell is that even possible?"

"What do you mean?"

He starts to speak but sighs instead.

The song comes to an end, and I expect him to let me go, but he doesn't even loosen his grip on me in the slightest. Our dance fades into the next tune chosen by the band, and our gentle, lazy side-to-side sway never ceases.

"I'm going to say something," Gray says. "And I hope it doesn't … make things weird."

I grin despite my heart palpitations.

"Astrid, you're fucking gorgeous."

What? My hands move to his chest to push away, but he stops me with the sweetest smile.

"You're brilliant. Talented. Strong as hell." He chuckles as if he's remembering our disagreements. "How do you not have a line of men fighting for you?"

"Probably because I'd fight them back." It's a joke designed to segue the conversation elsewhere, but one look at Gray and I know that's not going to happen. Resigned, I dangle my arms over his shoulders again. "I don't have men fighting for me, as you say, because I don't want one."

"Why not?"

"I don't know," I say with a shrug. But that's a lie. I do know. Although I could leave it there, Gray was honest with me, so the least I can do is be honest with him, too. "I have trust issues. I guess that's probably the crux of it. Every time I'm in a relationship, I have to defend myself."

"Defend yourself from what?"

"Lies. Unreliability. *For daring to breathe.*"

I've never put this into words before, so getting it out in the open is so freeing. Sure, there's a chance that Gray will feed this back to me at some point and make me feel small over it, but most men never share anything real with me, yet Gray has tonight. So maybe it'll be okay.

"For the record," he says, a tease in his tone. "I like it when you breathe."

My shoulders sag, and I giggle. "Thank you. I appreciate that."

"Do you know what else?"

"What's that?"

He pulls back and looks me in the eye. "That shirt you're wearing? It has my last name on the back in big, bold letters."

"I know."

"And everyone here who sees us together with you wearing my shirt will think we're together."

Oh God. My cheeks flush. "I'm sorry. I didn't think about—"

"I think that's *so* sexy." He bends forward, his breath hot against my skin. "I've never been prouder for a woman to wear my name."

"Really?"

"Are you kidding me? Look at you. If you're with me, I'm batting way outta my league."

My knees wobble. I clutch his shoulders to steady myself, gasping a quick breath. Whatever's happening is happening out of left field and at full throttle … and I desperately don't want it to stop.

No one has ever said anything like that to me. I'm not sure that anyone aside from Audrey has said they were proud of me for anything. So for Gray Adler to say he's proud to have me wear his shirt with his name in big, block letters on it in his hometown? That's so, *so* wild.

His eyes sparkle as he peers into mine. "There's only one part of today that I'll always remember as a mistake."

"Which one?"

"The moment I didn't kiss you."

I don't know where the courage comes from, or if the years of Gianna's stories have sunk in, but I find an ounce of bravery and use it.

"You could fix that, you know," I say, sounding far more confident than I really am. Because, on the inside, my brain is screaming that this is a bad idea. *You don't do vulnerable, Astrid.*

There's a reason you're cautious. Hell, you're here because you were vulnerable with the wrong man—Trace. But my body? It's entirely on board. Gray has shown enough kindness and protectiveness today to sway it to the dark side.

I'm always so controlled, so particular that I don't have fun, and consequently, I never truly enjoy myself. If I'm going to dive into the fun puddle, what better way than to do it here? *With him?*

Gianna will be so proud.

We stop swaying to the music, and every voice, body, and sound fades into the background. At this moment, only two people exist: Gray and me.

He releases me from his grasp. But, before any distance is put between us, he cups my cheeks with both palms and studies me with a soft intensity that makes me whimper.

A fire blazes in my core, spilling out and flooding my veins with piercing-hot flames. I lick my lips as my hands find his waist, and I feel his carved obliques. I could overthink this. I could find a million reasons to stop this in its tracks and walk away with my head held high.

But I don't want to. I really don't want to, and for once in my life, I'm just going to do what feels good. If it hurts later, hopefully the ecstasy was worth it.

His hardened cock presses against my stomach. I hold my breath, awaiting his next move. His grin is salacious, and I choke back a moan.

"Fuck it," he whispers, dipping his lips to mine.

Yes!

I lift on my toes to meet him in the middle, when I'm bumped from the side. *Oof.*

"Sorry about that," Brooks says, but I can tell he's not sorry at all.

"I'm going to fucking kill you," Gray says through gritted teeth. He takes my hand and laces our fingers together.

Blood pours past my eardrums as adrenaline washes through

me. I'm too worked up to fully understand what just happened, but I'm annoyed enough to attempt to fight Brooks myself.

"Let's go, Astrid," Gray says, tugging my hand.

Brooks leans toward me as I'm being led away. "Steakhouses are good choices for the gift card."

I roll my eyes and turn, trying to keep up with Gray.

CHAPTER
TWENTY-TWO

"So do you still think Brooks has main-character energy?" Astrid asks. "Because I'm starting to think it might be main-*villain* energy."

I sling open the passenger's side door of my truck with a bit more force than necessary. "Yes. Main character. But he's the main character who wants to die in this chapter."

She bursts out laughing as she climbs into the cab and gets settled. I swing the door shut and move around the front to the driver's side.

I almost kissed Astrid Lawsen. Fuck.

Her soft cheeks were in my hands. Her gorgeous body was pressed close to mine. I've never seen a set of eyes that were so clearly saying *yes*. And then Brooks had to act like he was twelve years old. *What the actual fuck?*

This is the first exchange we've shared since I led her away from the bandstand. My emotions were running high, and I didn't want to fuck up and inadvertently snap at her. So I chose to say nothing at all—at least until I could talk myself off the ledge.

I don't know what the hell Brooks was up to tonight. He wasn't being malicious; there's no chance of that. But whatever sideways thing that sprang to life inside his head was born from a brain that's been punched too many times.

My hands ball into fists at my side as I slow my pace and take a long, deep breath.

I also don't know where Astrid and I go from here. I'm not even sure where she wants to go from this point. Desires and intentions have been put into the universe, and now they must be dealt with. But it's not like Astrid is just another girl who I nearly kissed. It's her. She's my coworker and practically my boss.

Although I'd never admit that thought to her.

I climb into my seat and start the engine. Stretching my arm along the back of her seat and getting a whiff of her perfume in the process, I back out into the street. She sits quietly, not saying a word until I put the truck in drive.

"Is this a good time to bring up the fact that we brought Hartley?" she asks.

"Are you always in work mode?" I grin at her. "Sometimes you can let other people figure their shit out, you know."

"Oh no. Not me. If I see a situation unfolding and it looks like chaos, I need to clean it up. Put things in order. And the fact that we just left your brother miles from his house without even letting him know really disturbs me in the greatest way."

I chuckle. "Well, let me clue you in on a little fact. Hartley knows every person at the fair, so I have the utmost confidence that my little brother can figure out how to get home. Further, I wouldn't be surprised if Hartley's already home, in bed, with his eyes closed."

Astrid eyes me skeptically.

"Hartley staying out late is like you letting someone else be in control."

She scoffs. "While I understand that analogy, I'm sort of offended by it."

"Good for you." I stop at a sign and wait for a family to cross the street with their dog in tow. "So did you have fun at the fair?"

"That's what you want to talk about?"

I shrug, looking at her puzzled. "What do you mean? I feel like that's a reasonable, polite question to ask."

"Okay. Fine." She cocks her head to the side, mocking me. "Yes, Gray. I had such a lovely time at the Sugar County Fair. Your friends are so kind, except for Brooks, and I feel blessed to have experienced the local brew even though it tasted like warm kangaroo piss."

"Did you just say warm kangaroo piss?"

She sits back as I press the gas again but doesn't answer me.

"How in the hell do you know what warm kangaroo piss tastes like?" I ask, laughing. "And you were worried about rabbit shit giving you rabies. It sounds like you need to worry about something else."

Astrid sighs. "It was an expression. You know what I mean. But in all seriousness, yes. I did have a nice time at the fair. It was … cozy. I'm not a hug lover by any stretch of the imagination, but it felt like a warm hug in an unobnoxious way."

I bite my lip to keep from laughing and flip on my turn signal.

I'd love to know what's causing Astrid to be so talkative tonight. I was afraid she'd clam up at the fair and not want to talk to anyone, but that wasn't the case at all. She and Hartley spoke for quite a while. Brooks obviously engaged with her, the fucking dickhead. And I saw her laughing with Jasper and Meadow earlier in the evening.

Is it the alcohol? The fresh air? Is she just nervous?

Does she want fucked?

"Did you know that I've been to three festival-type situations in my life?" she asks.

"No, I didn't know that. And while I don't know the average

number of fairs that people visit, I feel like that's on the low end."

"I went to one when I was six. I still have the glass bottle I filled with colored sand. Then I went with Gianna's family when I was thirteen or fourteen to a fair in Kentucky. Audrey and I went to the state fair here a couple of years ago for a concert."

"I've been to more than I care to remember," I say, turning onto a gravel road. I discreetly reach down and adjust myself without her knowing. "Sugar County has this one in the spring, and then the town of Sugar Creek has one in the fall. We'd go to a few other local ones around, too. Dad loved nothing more than a good corn dog and throwing darts at balloons."

She grins. "This sounds like a celebratory community."

"You could say that."

"I wish I could," she says, a taunt thinly veiled in her tone. "I was hoping to have a firsthand account of fireworks tonight, if you catch my drift."

My body tenses, every muscle growing so tight that I nearly wince. *Is she serious right now? Because I can make that happen.* I groan. *God, I'd love to make that happen.*

I've only gotten a glimpse of her body through her clothes and the top of her tits in her shirt, and that's enough to make me want to blow my load. Creamy skin that looks soft and smooth. Deep curves from her waist to her hips that would fit my hands perfectly. I can imagine her juicy ass bouncing on my dick while my name kisses her pouty lips.

Fucking hell.

I ease the accelerator and take a quick look at her to decipher her intentions. There's a chance, a decent one, that I'm reading too much into this—that I'm seeing things how I want to see them and not how they really are. If that's true, the last thing I want to do is put her in an uncomfortable position.

I just need to be sure.

On the one hand, her forwardness fits her personality perfectly. Astrid loves to be in control. In her words, she needs it.

By being the aggressor in this situation, she maintains her grip on the ship, so that makes absolute sense. But she also seems to have an aversion to personal connections with people. While sex can be impersonal, I'm not a random guy she picked up at the bar and will never see again.

Does she mean what she's insinuating, or is she just playing me?

"What do you think would've happened if I had kissed you back there?" I ask, gripping the steering wheel.

"Is that the question you want to ask me?"

"What do you mean?"

She sighs. "I mean, do you want to know what I think would have happened if you kissed me? Or are you really wanting to know what I *hoped* would happen after that? Because there could potentially be two completely different answers to that, and I want to know which one you're looking for."

This woman. I take a deep breath, ignoring the ache in my balls. "Are we taking the blanket off the baby?"

"I was hoping we'd be taking more than that off by now, but you seem to be avoiding the topic."

Easy, Adler. Easy.

Few times in my life have I been given the green light by a gorgeous woman and not jumped on the opportunity. It's happened, but the instances are few and far between, so I need to make damn sure Astrid has thought this through. I know she has trust issues. I know how important her job is, and if she hasn't given this enough thought and weighed the potential outcomes, the last thing I'd want is for it to hurt her or her position with Renn.

I can't let that happen. I won't.

"Look, Gray, I'm not good at this," she says, her confidence slipping. "I'm not good at flirting. I'm not good with dealing with men at all unless I work with them."

"You can say that again," I say. But so that she knows I'm joking, I reach out and give her thigh a quick squeeze.

Unfortunately, I don't think about touching her before I do, and forcing myself to release her leg takes an effort worth a gold medal. The feeling of her in my palm sends a shot of heat directly to my cock. I have to sort this situation or get the hell away from her. *Stat.* I have ninety minutes with her in this truck, and right now, there's no way out.

"All joking aside, you're doing a fine job dealing with men," I say. "Jasper couldn't take his eyes off you. Brooks would've fucked you tonight if he could've gotten away with it." *Fucker.* "And I'm at your mercy right now. I just want to make sure you're not making a decision you'll regret later."

"These conversations are hard for me. I'm so awkward about things that have nothing to do with spreadsheets and emails. Basically, I'm socially inept, I think. I can order people around if I have my clipboard in hand, but without it, I never feel brave enough to go after what I want. No one would take me seriously if they knew that."

"I think you're being too hard on yourself."

"It seems like it's the only way to experience something hard tonight."

I lick my lips, chuckling at her joke—mostly because I don't think she's joking.

The road forms a Y, and I take the right arm. My tires hit gravel, sending a plume of dust around both sides of the truck. The headlights bounce as we hit potholes that have formed due to a lack of attention from the county. She sits quietly, but I can feel her energy bleeding off her. Nerves. Anticipation. *Hope.*

She nibbles a fingernail and looks straight ahead.

"I can't risk messing this up," I say, choosing my words carefully. "So I need you to tell me what you want. No jokes, no insinuations. Tell me what you want from me."

Her cheeks flush.

"I'm not trying to embarrass you," I insist. "If anything, I want to empower you. Ask me for what you want. Order me around like it's your job. You're exceptional at that."

She grins. "Is that really what you want me to do?"

"You're results-driven, and it would definitely get the results you're after."

I smirk as her gaze drops to my lap, and she realizes just how prepared I am to make good on my promise. Her eyes widen at the sight of my cock straining against my pants. Each breath causes her chest to rise and fall dramatically, and it's all I have in me to keep the truck on the fucking road.

Parted lips. Dilated pupils. Touching her collarbone with her fingers.

Motherfucker.

I hold the steering wheel tightly so that I don't accidentally reach for her. Knowing that she wants me even a fraction of how badly I want her is enough to drive me crazy. But like the saint I am not, I wait.

"Okay," she says, sitting taller in the seat. She tucks a strand of hair behind her ear. "You grew up here. You must know a spot we can go right now to fuck."

She doesn't have to tell me twice.

I slow down and turn the traction control off while piloting the truck to the side of the road. Then I crank the wheel and smash the gas, sending a rooster tail of gravel through the air as we spin in a one-eighty.

Astrid grips the door handle with one hand and my bicep with the other. Her squeals turn into a fit of giggles as I let out of it a little bit, and the truck straightens out on the road.

"Oh my God," she says, laughing as she drags her hand away from my arm. "What the hell are you doing?"

"Taking you to get fucked."

She falls back in her seat and exhales. "I can't hear you say that."

"Why not?"

"It's been a long time. I'm in a bit of a drought, and you're … you."

I hook a right onto a dirt road with branches hanging over it. "I'm going to take that as a compliment."

"Good. Because I meant it as one."

We travel into the pitch-black, far away from any streetlamps or porch lights. The lane gets bumpier the farther we get from the road, and the sky grows inkier and the stars more twinkly.

Astrid grabs the door handle once again as I steer us off the road and onto the soft earth.

"I'm taking a big risk here," she says. "You could just as easily take me into the middle of nowhere and kill me for all I know."

"You must really trust me, huh?"

She smiles. "Or I'm desperate. One or the other."

The fact that it's been a long time since she's been with someone is mind-blowing, almost as mind-blowing as seeing her walk around town all night with my name splashed across her back. Astrid, the classy, intelligent, sexy-as-hell spitfire, garnered looks from every man in Sugar Creek and didn't give one of them the time of day ... except me. *Kill me now.* It's been months since I've had sex. If she wants to talk about desperate, *I'm desperate.*

The truck's engine roars as we reach our destination—the top of the highest hill around with a view for miles. Thanks to the bright moon hanging overhead, the view isn't totally lost on Astrid.

"Oh wow," she says, unbuckling herself. "Look at this. It's the country version of the view from Renn's office."

I turn off the truck and smile at her sense of awe.

"Are you sure that no one will call the police on us for being up here?" she asks.

"Can't you live on the dark side and not follow the rules just once?"

She frowns, her lips pressing together in the cutest little pout.

"I'm kidding," I say. "No one's going to call the police. I promise."

"How do you know?"

I shake my head and climb out of the truck. "I know because

the only person who'd call the cops is probably at home and in bed right now. But even that's a mile or a mile and a quarter away from here." I point across the treetops before opening the back door. "So I think we're safe."

"This is a part of Hartley's property, isn't it?"

"Yup."

"You could've led with that," she says, watching me rummage through a bin in my back seat.

"Where's the fun in that?" I tug the quilt Mom gave me when I turned sixteen from the bottom of the container. Along with our first set of keys, she gave Hartley and me quilts, first-aid kits, and an emergency whistle *"just in case."* We either kept it all in our vehicles, or we didn't drive. It's a habit that I have never broken.

Astrid gets out of the truck as I'm opening the tailgate.

The weather is warm with just a hint of crispness in the air now that the sun has gone down, and I hop into the bed and spread the quilt over the bottom.

"This view is amazing," she says, staring up at the sky. "Look at how many stars there are. It's so pretty." When she turns back at me, she stills.

"I can guarantee that my view right now is even prettier." I hold out my hand. "Come up here with me."

She lays her hand in mine and places a foot on the small step by the tailgate, and I then hoist her up.

We're eye to eye, chest to chest. Breaths ragged. Expectations high.

Things just got very, *very* real.

CHAPTER
TWENTY-THREE

Things just got *so* freaking real.

I listen to Gray's breath cut through the silence of the night, the tempo quick and hurried—matching mine. A gentle breeze ruffles the ends of his hair beneath his hat, lifting his woodsy cologne and taunting me with it. *Like I need to be teased anymore.*

Five minutes ago, I knew exactly what I was doing. I weighed the pros and cons of having sex with Gray and decided the risk was worth the potential reward. My logical brain deduced that. But here we are, precisely where I asked to be, and the alarm bells are ringing in my head.

"So," I say, forcing a smile, "here's the thing. It's not my favorite thing about myself, but it is a part of who I am." I heave a breath. "I overthink things."

"You don't say?"

My smile is wide … and real. "I know that I just spent the truck ride telling you that this is what I want—*and it is,*" I add quickly. "But I talk a good game, and I know that I seem like the kind of woman who knows what she wants. You'd be surprised to learn that I'm a lot more nervous than you might think."

"About what, Astrid?"

"Oh, life. Relationships. Sex." I pause. "You."

He brushes a lock of hair off my shoulder with the gentlest touch. "Do you want my honest take?"

"On what?"

He grins. "You."

"Um, I don't know. That depends on what you have to say."

His chuckle rumbles through me. "I think your tough-girl act is a mask that you hide behind to protect yourself." He searches my eyes for a reaction—one I struggle to keep from him, mostly because I'm not sure how I feel about him nailing me so easily. *Although, I'd love for him to nail me in other ways right now.* "And believe it or not, I can relate in a lot of ways."

I take in a shaky breath and exhale it with my whole body.

"If I were a betting man," he says, "I'd guess that you protect yourself because you've never been safe enough to relax."

His words are a shot to my heart. They're a key that unlocks a lockbox filled with my truths. *How does he know this about me?*

I'm not prepared for the hot tears that fog my vision, or the ferocious kindness swimming in his dark brown pools. I feel seen in a way that's brand new to me. Understood without saying a word.

He runs a thumb across my cheek while sharing the sincerest, sweetest smile ever bestowed upon me.

"Regardless of what happens tonight, or when we go back to Nashville—whether you hate me or not—you're safe with me," he says softly.

I sniffle back a heap of emotion, but then it hits me that I came here to get fucked and, instead, I'm crying. And for once, I'm not crying because someone's being an asshole. I'm crying because he's … not.

"There you go," I say, laughing through the feelings clogging my throat. "You had to go and ruin everything."

His chin tilts to the sky as he laughs, too.

I dry my face of any errant tears with the bottom of my shirt.

The cord that's been wound around my chest for as long as I can remember is slightly looser. I consider momentarily that he could be lying to me, just telling me what he thinks I want to hear—but I dismiss it almost immediately.

Because that's not true. That's not what he's doing, and I know it in the depths of my soul.

My heartbeat quickens as I wrestle with his promise that I'm safe with him. The sentiment that I've yearned for my entire life, for someone to see me and care for me enough to protect me, has surprisingly been shared ... by Gray Adler.

How the hell is this happening?

It's a mind fuck, a case of mental vertigo. The man who I've sparred with, fought against, and loathed is offering me shelter. It's a dizzying realization, one that makes both no sense and all the sense in the world.

But the more I think about it, and the longer I stand in front of Gray with my truth bared for him to see, I'm not panicked. *I'm at ease.* The bubble of loneliness, my constant shadow, deflates and my lungs fill to their full capacity.

This has never happened before, and it may never happen again. And I have a feeling he understands what it's like to have your trust broken. Even if I don't know by whom.

If I'm going out on limbs tonight and taking big risks, I might as well go all the way.

"Will you do me a favor, Gray?"

"Anything."

This has to be the most complicated, overthought moment before sex that has ever existed. *Who talks this much when on a bed of a truck with someone like Gray Adler?*

Me. That's who. And it's exactly why I can't have any fun in my life.

I gather my courage along with the deepest breath. "Just for one night, I want to know what it feels like not *to* be in control."

His pupils dilate, and his eyes widen in surprise.

"Take control," I plead. *"Please."*

I barely get the words out of my mouth before his lips crash against mine. I gasp, frozen in shock, before giving way to the sensation of being enveloped in his strong arms. I'm pulled so tightly against him that I can barely breathe, or think, or do anything other than kiss him back.

He wraps my hair around his fist and tugs my head to the side. I whimper as he kisses the corner of my mouth, then along my jaw before dragging his mouth down my neck.

"Look at that," I say, as he draws his tongue over the top of my shoulder, leaving me quivering against his chest. "You can follow orders after all."

He nips my earlobe, making me squeal, before releasing his hand from my hair. Our gazes collide, brown against green, as we pull apart, panting. Anticipating. *Needing.*

There's a hint of a smile in the curve of his lips. "Let's see if you can."

Oh. Shit.

Heat blossoms in my belly at the intense deliciousness of his gaze. It slides down my body, grazing my skin through my clothes and nearly setting them on fire. The weight of his attention is so heavy that it leaves me scattered and breathless.

"Arms up."

It's not a request. *It's an order.*

A breeze kicks up as my hands inch toward the dark sky. Gray licks his lips and reaches for the hem of his shirt. I gasp as his fingertips dust across my stomach and up my sides as he draws the fabric up and off me.

He balls it in his hand and then tosses it deeper into the truck bed. His eyes never leave me.

"You have no clue how gorgeous you are, do you?" he asks, as if he can't quite believe it himself.

"I know that I lost my shirt and you're still wearing yours."

He grins. "You've seen me shirtless before."

"Yeah, but I hated you then."

His laughter makes me smile, too.

"Turn around," he says.

"But your shirt—*ah*."

He captures my words with his mouth, his lips commanding mine to open. His tongue slides past them with authority. There's no rush, no urgency … like we have all night.

"There," he whispers as he pulls away, nipping my bottom lip in the process. "I finally figured out how to shut you up."

I yelp, touching the center of my mouth.

"Let's remember something," he says, taking a step back. *"I'm in control."*

"Okay, I did say that. But—"

"No buts. Now turn around."

I shiver against the wind as I turn my back to Gray. His reflection in the back glass of the truck grows closer to me. Still, I'm not ready for the feeling of his hands against my bare skin, gathering my hair and laying it over my right shoulder.

"Relax, sweetheart," he whispers against the shell of my ear.

He works the snaps of my bra deftly and lets it fall forward. I catch it at my chest, pressing it against my thundering heart. I'm aware of every breath, every groan of the truck, every flicker of the stars. It's all too much yet not enough.

Gray moves away from me, pulling my bra from my hands. "Let me see you."

My nipples are hard against the cooling temperature. I cup my breasts in my hands, pulling them up and toward my sternum. They're full and heavy in my palms as I pivot to face him.

"Drop your hands," he says.

I look up at him through my lashes while my arms drop to my sides.

His tongue swipes along his bottom lip. "You're un-*fucking*-believable."

"And you still have your shirt on."

He grins. "Shoes off."

I comply, willing to do whatever it takes to speed this along. The ache in my core is overwhelming, and my panties are soaked. I need him inside me like I need my next breath, and this joker seems to think we have all the time in the world.

"Good girl," he says, teasing me. "Now let's work on getting you out of these jeans."

"Yes. Let's."

He chuckles, reaching for my button and zipper. "I have to figure out a way to keep you this cooperative."

"Well, depending on how tonight goes, I might be able to give you some tips by morning."

"Pretty sure I'll have it worked out shortly." Gray kneels in front of me, hooking his fingers in my waistband. Slowly, he drags the denim down my legs. "I could come in my pants from this."

"Don't you dare," I say, stepping out of my jeans. "If you come without shoving your cock in me, I'll spread vicious lies about you to your teammates."

He laughs, tossing them to the side. Then he rocks back on his heels.

"And your shirt is still on," I say, sighing with all the dramatics that I can muster. I scoot my panties to my feet and then kick them at Gray's face. "There. I helped again."

He catches the lace in the same motion as he sits on the side rail of his truck. "Get over here."

"Yes, sir."

"I could get used to this," he says, holding my boobs in his hands. "You have the nicest tits I've ever seen."

"Aren't you just a gentleman?"

He shakes his head at me, his eyes hooding, as he sucks a nipple into his mouth.

Finally. Motherfucking fireworks.

My back arches, shoving my chest closer to him.

One of his hands massages one breast, while his hot, wet mouth lavishes attention on the other. I straddle his knee, heat pouring from my pussy as my juices coat my inner thighs. I need friction. I need relief. But all I can do is tip my head back and moan into the night.

"Do you like that?" he asks, moving his mouth to the other side.

The breeze picks up again, the cool air dancing across my naked body, my hair billowing around me with each gust. The chill touches me in places that have never been exposed to the elements, and somehow, *I love it.*

No one's around. There are no houses, no security lights, no cameras. But the possibility of it, the idea that I'm completely naked in the bed of a truck with a man sucking my tits—and readying to do a whole lot more—is exhilarating. Thrilling. *Addictive.*

Gray slides a hand down my stomach and slips it between my legs.

I widen my stance, tipping my head back and moaning again.

He rubs my clit in slow, sensuous circles. "I fucking love how wet you are," he says, his voice husky. "This is such a turn-on."

"I concur. Now make me come."

He lowers both hands, denying me.

My eyes fly open. "What are you doing?"

"You aren't coming yet." He moves me back gently before he stands. A wicked smile graces his lips. "We just got started."

CHAPTER
TWENTY-FOUR

Gray

Who knew I had this much self-restraint?

I glance down at the quilt that I spread out earlier. It's not terribly soft, but it will keep dirt and debris from scratching her skin. And, right now, that'll have to be good enough.

"Lie down," I say, hopping off the tailgate.

"Where are you going?"

I look up at her and grin. The moonlight catches the moisture coating her legs. Her tits are perfectly shaped in subtle teardrops, and her mouth puckers like she wants my cock in it.

What more can a man ask for?

"Lie. The fuck. Down."

She rolls her eyes but eases herself onto the quilt. As soon as she's settled, I grab her ankles and jerk her to the edge of the tailgate. The material acts like a sled, delivering her to me like a gift I'm about to devour.

My cock strains against my pants. It's so hard it *hurts*. The ache in my balls radiates to my abs and groin, begging for relief.

But before I can get to that, I have to satisfy her. I may never get this chance again.

"Oh God," she gasps as she realizes my intentions.

I spread her legs, laying her pussy out for me to take in whatever way I want it. Her flesh is pink and absolutely drenched with her need for me. It's more than I could've imagined. I could never, in my wildest, most feverish dreams, have envisioned that I would have Miss Manners naked and splayed out in the back of my truck. *Fuck me.*

My hands slide beneath her ass, tilting her pelvis toward my mouth.

"Gray ..."

I blow across her swollen bud, and she squirms in my hands.

"Your scent makes me crazy," I say, breathing in the sweet smell of sex. "I bet you taste amazing, too."

"Gray, please—*oh!*"

Her knees fall to the sides as I drag my tongue through her pulsing slit. She quivers, shaking around my mouth as if she's ready to explode. Her hands dig into the quilt and ball it into her fists as she groans her pleasure into the air.

"Do you feel that?" I ask, flattening my tongue against her clit, thereby stealing her ability to speak. I chuckle as she squirms, giving the bud another flick. "Oh, I'm definitely using this in the future to shut you up."

She moans, louder this time, as she flexes her hips against my face. I smile into her pussy, learning the rhythm of her body.

Her reaction to me—hungry and reckless—has my cock screaming in protest.

I bury my face into her pussy, fucking her with my tongue. Kissing her with my lips. Nipping her with my teeth. Her taste is an aphrodisiac. I want—*I need* more. I add a finger, slipping it through her folds, and groan as she grips it tightly. I curl my finger, stroking her G-spot as she starts grinding against my hand.

"*Gray!*"

Her legs begin to shake, a telltale sign that she's about to come, so I give her clit a final kiss and then blow on it as I pull away slowly.

She struggles to prop herself up on her elbows. Her eyes are wild as she peers down at me. "Why did you stop?"

"Because you were about to come."

"Precisely."

I grin. "Maybe I'm greedy, but the first time you come tonight, I want it to be on my cock."

Her eyes are hooded. "Yes, please."

Over her protests, I go back to the side of my truck. I make quick work of shedding my clothes, wiping my face off on my shirt, and digging a condom out of my middle console. By the time I return to Astrid, she's sitting on the tailgate, miffed.

"I didn't even get to watch you undress," she says, pouting. "What kind of bullshit is this?"

I laugh at her adorableness. "I promise you can watch me undress later, okay? But right now, I want to bury myself inside your pretty little cunt."

"*Oh.*"

She lets me lift her off the tailgate and then wraps her legs around my waist. Her chest is plastered against mine, and the heat of her pussy is hot against my stomach.

Her pillowy-soft lips find mine as her hands drag through my hair. She tugs my head back, sucking my tongue into her mouth—lighting the match to my gasoline-soaked fuse. Her nails dig into my scalp. I can feel her wetness sliding against my stomach, sides, and the top of my overly sensitive cock.

I have half a notion to put her in the truck and give her some privacy as I rail her, but something tells me she's enjoying the freedom of the great outdoors. I don't give a shit. I just want to be inside her.

"You get a choice," I say, as she pulls my lip between her teeth.

"What?"

"Would you be more comfortable inside the truck, or do you want to be fucked out here?"

She pulls back, her eyes glistening. Her grin is mischievous. "Out here. *Definitely out here.*"

"Oh," I say, teasing her. "Okay. I have an exhibitionist on my hands?"

"I don't think that's the only thing on your hands right now." She snorts. "Bad joke."

"Yeah, not one of your best." I set her on the tailgate again. "Give me a second."

She groans. "For what?"

I dangle the condom in the air.

To my surprise, she hops off the back of the truck. Her tits bounce as she lands, and the sight of that makes my cock harden even more. She drops to her knees on the ground.

"What the hell are you doing?" I ask. "Get up."

She palms my cock, earning a groan from me. A bead of precum glistens on the head, and she swipes it off with the tip of her tongue. I watch, fighting a full-body shiver, as she spreads the liquid along her bottom lip before sucking it off.

Fuck.

Who would've thought she'd be on her knees, asking me to let her suck my dick? My cum was just on her tongue. I had no clue the queen of the clipboard could also be a sexy-as-fuck vixen.

"Have it your way," I say, holding the sides of her head in my hands. I position her directly over my shaft. "Put me in your mouth."

Her eyes blaze as she watches me watch her slide her mouth over my cock.

I can't combat the shiver this time. It starts at the back of my neck and winds down my spine, sending a flurry of goose bumps over my skin. It's too hot, too wet, too tight. She's too fucking gorgeous.

Now I'm the one at her mercy.

She flattens her tongue and runs it along my dick, up and down in a wonderfully slow, torturous tempo. Her small hand grips me perfectly, pumping my cock as she watches me through those thick lashes. I'll come to the picture of this for the rest of my fucking life.

Her spit drips down my shaft and over my balls. The sound of her slurping on my cock and the occasional moan are the hottest things I've ever heard. Sexy. Intimate.

I clench my jaw, holding her skull tighter. Each stroke feels better. Each lick, flick, and suck is a step toward the ultimate payoff.

Moving her head with my hands, I pump myself deeper into her mouth.

"There you go," I groan, flexing my hips. "You're making me feel so good."

She jacks me off tighter with her fist covered in saliva.

"Your mouth was made for this cock," I say. "You're doing such a good job."

My eyes squeeze shut, tears forming in the corners for the intensity of the sensation. I'm ready to come. *I'm so fucking close.* My balls swell, threatening to spew my load down Astrid's throat. As if she senses it, she braces herself and takes all of me she can manage.

No. The word barrels through my head, and I force myself to pull away. She fights me, sucking harder in refusal to let me go. It feels so fucking amazing that I almost give in.

Almost.

I whoosh a breath, nearly doubling over. She falls back, catching herself with her hand, and smiles up at me.

"You just about fucked up," I say, chuckling.

"I was trying to." She giggles. "I wanted to feel you blow it in my mouth."

My blood runs hot. "Keep talking like that, and you might get your wish."

I rip open the condom and roll it down my length, then I grab the quilt and throw it on the ground. Quickly, I double it to give it a bit of extra padding.

"Hands and knees," I say, motioning to the ground. "I don't think either of us can last much longer."

"We are finally on the same page."

"Glad to hear it."

She gets on all fours with her round ass stuck up in the air. It's perfectly peach-shaped, and I wish I had more restraint tonight because I'd love to eat her out with her bent over like this. But that'll have to wait until another night.

Please, let there be another night of this. This will never be enough.

"Let's go," she says, looking at me over her shoulder.

I kneel behind her and line myself up with her opening. She pushes back against me, shimmying her pussy on the head of my cock. I grin, cracking my palm against the curve of her ass at the same time as I push in one rough motion until I hit the back of her pussy.

"*Oh fuck,*" she squeals, sucking in a breath.

"I wish I could see those tits bounce," I say, sinking inside her tight cunt again. "This is heaven, Astrid. Fucking heaven."

"Harder."

I grit my teeth, unable to keep pacing myself to make it last as long as possible. "Like this?"

My fingers bite into her waist hard enough that I worry about bruising her.

I pull her back while I thrust forward, pounding into her. She shrieks but continues to meet me thrust for thrust. She rocks back, greedy for more, and I'm all too willing to give it to her. I'm not sure if I'm fucking her or if she's fucking me, but either way, it's mind-blowing.

I'm one lucky motherfucker any way you look at it.

"Fuck!" Astrid screams, moaning as her pussy quivers around me. A sheen of sweat coats her pale skin as her arms begin to give out. Her entire body vibrates as she's wracked by wave after wave of her orgasm.

"Stay with me," I grunt, palming her ass with both hands. The feeling of her globes jiggling with each movement sends me to another level of euphoria. "Give me all of it."

I bite down as my own climax smashes into me.

It's an intense explosion, ripping through me like a gunshot. My muscles tighten everywhere. Contractions ripple repeatedly in my stomach, and I fight to keep my eyes open, to appreciate the beautiful woman under me, but the power of the orgasm is too much.

Still, the pictures in my mind's eye are of Astrid's ass up in the air and the silky pink flesh of her pussy. The images flash through my head and deliver with them the final jolts of pleasure. I sigh, shaking off the rest of the energy, and open my eyes to find Astrid watching me over her shoulder.

"That was hot," she says, grinning.

I return her smile and pull out slowly. Then I get to my feet and tug her up along with me.

Her eyes are happy, but a bit weary, and I'm not sure what to do about it. So I do what I want—what feels *right*—and pull her into a hug. She collapses against my chest with a soft sigh.

"Are you okay?" I ask, kissing the top of her head.

She nods. "Tired."

"You should be tired." I kiss her gently again and then lean away. "It's probably getting late, too."

"I guess we're not going back to Nashville tonight, huh?"

My chest tightens. "We can, if you want. Or we can stay at Hart's. Your choice."

She studies me for a few seconds before she smiles. "Let's stay at Hart's, as long as he won't care."

I grab her some tissues to clean up and get myself sorted, too. All the while, I'm flooded with thoughts about how right this could be ... but also how bad this could go.

God, please don't let me fuck this up.

CHAPTER
TWENTY-FIVE

The ceiling fan whirls softly, sending a gentle flutter of air around Gray's childhood bedroom. His bed is soft, much softer than mine at home, and his pillows are like puffed marshmallows spun into cotton. I curl up next to the wall, beneath a poster of a sports star that I can't name, and scroll around on Social.

I can't wipe the smile off my face. Naturally, I'll overthink everything eventually because I always do. But the idea of spoiling my pure bliss tonight is unfathomable, and I'm too realistic to not know that something will ruin it for me soon enough.

That's life, baby.

My ears perk up as Gray's footsteps pad down the carpeted hallway. My core tightens, already associating Gray's presence with pleasure. It's a wild concept, one so far from the migraine I associated with him when we first met. Will this change once we're back in Nashville? The thought worries me, and the fact that I'm worried about it, that a part of me openly acknowledges that I want more of this, concerns me more.

"You have two choices," Gray says, knocking the door closed with his hip. "I found a Rice Krispies treat and a chocolate bar.

Can you eat either of these?" He hops on the bed next to me. "Neither says they have peanuts in them, but … how do you know? Do we trust these companies?"

I laugh.

"What?" He turns his face to mine with his brows pinched together. "Are you laughing at me?"

"No. I'm not laughing at you. I just think it's so nice of you to be so cognizant of my allergies."

He drops the snacks onto his bare chest. "I can't kill you yet because, if I recall correctly, *and I do*, you insinuated that you wanted me to nut in your mouth." He grins mischievously. "I'm not going to let a nut steal *that nut*, if you follow me."

I giggle. "Oh, I follow you now. But I'll *swallow you* later."

My phone chimes as a text message alert pops on the screen. I roll onto my back and hold my phone up in the air, opening my app.

Gianna: So there's this guy …

Audrey: I don't know how you keep finding them. Haven't you exhausted the supply in this city?

Gray unwraps the Rice Krispies treat. "Which one of your friends has the taser?"

"Gianna."

He offers me a bite of the bar, and I nibble the corner.

> Me: Thoughts about this one?

Audrey: Wait. Do we know this guy?

Gianna: It was the guy from the email. The one who banged his coworker's wife.

Audrey: I have a bad feeling about this one.

Gianna: You would be right, my sweet little Auddie. The sex could've been an email.

Gray takes a bite, then snuggles up to my side. "What is she talking about?"

"God only knows." I chuckle.

> Me: The sex could've been an email. I'm struggling with that one, G.

Gianna: I mean, he was a great emailer. His delivery was smooth, his points intriguing yet satisfying. I craved more. But sex with this buster? It would've been better if he had typed it out and hit Send.

Audrey: Sorry. 😞 Are you home yet, Astrid?

I whoosh a breath as my stomach turns to knots.

Obviously, I'll tell my friends about tonight in vivid detail. It's sort of fun to be the one with a story to tell for a change. But I haven't had time to process the events of the evening, and I really don't know how to explain it to Gianna and Audrey with Gray peering over my shoulder.

He offers me another bite. "You gonna answer them, or what?"

"Yeah. Just trying to figure out how." I bite off the edge of the bar, then chew slowly. "They'll take this the wrong way."

"What way would that be?"

I glance over my shoulder at him.

Gray studies my reaction to his question, watching my every blink and sigh. He's freshly washed from our shower a little while ago. His torso is bare, showcasing his ridiculously crafted muscles and tanned skin, and a pair of blue running shorts sits low on his hips. If I didn't already know what he was packing beneath them, I'd be dying to find out.

"My friends are both dramatic, but in opposite ways," I say.

Gianna: Shall I get my hopes up?

Audrey: Take a breath.

Gianna: Out of the three of us, one of us should be having great sex. It isn't you. It's not me. But it could be Astrid.

Gianna: Thick thighs and rugby guys. I'm here for it.

"Me, too," Gray says, chuckling. "Let's send them a selfie."

"*What?*"

He shrugs, running a hand along my inner thigh. My legs open for him ... just in case.

"You want to send them a selfie?" I ask, my jaw slack. "Are you serious? You don't care that we're half naked in bed?"

"I'm the lucky fuck in bed with you," he says, nuzzling his face in the crook of my neck. "Why do I care who knows it?"

Oh. I feather my fingers through his hair. My head leans against his as he presses kisses against my throat. The gesture is tender and sweet, rich yet subtle, and flames the slow burn simmering in my chest.

I forget about my friends and ignore their incoming text

messages. Instead, I close my eyes and just live in this moment with Gray. A blanket of peace settles over the two of us. *Does he feel it, too? Does he notice the sprinkle of magic in the room—the shift in temperature that feels like possibility is blooming?*

I might be crazy. The facts lean that way. It's not like me to go out of town with a guy, let alone stay all night with him at his brother's house after getting fucked in a field out in the middle of nowhere.

Who am I right now? I grin. *I don't know, but I think I like her.*

"Look up," I say, positioning my phone over our heads.

Just before I press the button to take a picture, he sucks on the spot where my shoulder meets my neck. I squeal, pulling away as my finger triggers the red circle. The light flashes, capturing the two of us in a playful moment that I have a hard time believing includes me.

But it *is* me. It's my face pulled together in a carefree laugh. It's Gray's arm extended across my chest, keeping me close to him. It's our heads sharing a pillow with a rugby team logo stamped on it, and it's his dimple sunk in his cheek as he laughs at my reaction.

Before I can think about it and talk myself out of sending the image, I fire it off to the group chat.

Their responses come immediately.

Gianna: OMG YOU ARE MY HERO.

Audrey: Oh, wow!

Gianna: And I thought you didn't listen to a thing I said. I stand corrected.

Audrey: How do you feel, Astrid?

Gianna: Hopefully, she feels sore and used. What kind of a question is that?

Audrey: 😊 I'm trying to check on her emotions.

Gianna: Don't ruin this for her, Auddie.

I giggle as Gray settles next to me on his side, reading their messages. "I don't know what to say about them."

"They're a good balance, I think. Good and bad."

"You can say that again."

Gianna: Ignore us. Go get you some dick, babe.

Audrey: Enjoy yourself. Call me when you get home.

Gianna: I'M SO PROUD OF YOU.

I click the button on the side of my phone and drop it beside me.

Gray's fingers skim beneath my shirt, drifting across my stomach and over my hips. It's as relaxing as it is intoxicating. I listen to him breathe and let my eyes flutter closed.

"Tell me something about you that I don't know," he says.

I hum, trying to determine what kind of fact he wants to know. *A historical fact, like my birth year? Does he want to know how*

I voted in the last election? Or does he want to know something random and pointless?

"Okay," I say, choosing the latter. "I don't have any tattoos."

"Is there a reason, or you just haven't gotten one?"

"There's never been something that I feel strongly enough about to want it on my skin forever. It feels like a commitment." I grin. "Tell me about yours."

He lies back and bends his knee, pulling his shorts so I can see the intricate art on his thigh. It's more delicate than I realized. Each line is so intentional, so precise, that I can tell there are multiple pieces blended instead of one large design.

"Well, each one of these means something to me," he says, tracing the dark ink. "The first one I got was this rosary. I got it the weekend after my parents died. I was struggling and just having a really hard time accepting that they were gone, and I was drawn to the pain of the needle more than anything."

I press a kiss to his shoulder. "May I ask what happened to them?"

"Sure." He clears his throat without looking at me. "Dad had to go to Kansas to pick up a horse a buddy of his was training, and Mom decided to tag along for once. A tornado ripped through the little town they were staying in during the night. The storm came out of nowhere. Mom died instantly, but Dad pulled through for a few days. We were able to talk to him and tell him goodbye. So I guess that's good."

My heart splinters at the pain on his face. *How tragic.* I kiss his shoulder again before placing my hand on his stomach, just letting him know I'm here.

"So that's the rosary," he says, heaving a breath. "This is the number nine in roman numerals since I'm number nine in rugby. The cigar is for Pap, and the blackbird for the Blackbird Ranch, obviously. The cowboy hat is for Hartley."

"I would think a heart would've been the logical choice," I say, hoping my joke will ease the tension in his voice.

He chuckles. "I was a little inebriated and not thinking clearly when I chose that."

"I guess that's a reason not to drink and ink."

His chuckle turns to laughter, and the light is back in his eyes. My shoulders fall in relief.

My attention falls on a snowflake at the bottom of the design. It's tiny, barely noticeable, but its daintiness is beautiful, and I can't help but wonder what it represents.

"So if you had to get a tattoo for the things that mean something to you," he says, putting his leg down, "what would you get?"

"Gosh, I don't know."

He grabs the chocolate bar and unwraps it. "It's not like you're really getting them. You don't have to overthink it."

"Come on. You know me. I overthink everything." I laugh, taking a piece of chocolate from him. "Okay, I'd get a star for my grandmother. It was our thing. And I'd choose something for my mother, but I have no idea what."

"Do you know anything about her?"

"Honestly? No." I break the candy into two pieces and eat one. "My father never talked about her. He just pretended she never existed. I only have one picture of her that I hid in a Bible growing up because it was the one place my dad wouldn't look."

Gray takes a deep breath, choosing his words carefully. "You told me once that your father was a sonofabitch."

"I must've felt nice that day."

The only sound filling the pregnant pause between us is the whirling of the ceiling fan.

I lie still, focusing on my heart rate. It rocks against my ribs as if it's gearing up to fight or flee—because that's what thoughts of John Lawsen do to me. They put me in survival mode.

Gianna knows some of the things I experienced with my father, although not all. It wasn't something we liked to spend our time chatting about in high school. And I've shared some things with Audrey, but not a lot—probably not even enough to paint an accurate picture of my life on Hemlock Street.

The only person in the world that I have told more to than anyone else is Trace.

Acid fills my stomach as memories of Trace weaponizing my experiences against me. The name-calling. The belittling. He used my wounds as a target and shot arrows into them until they wept.

"I'm not prodding you for information," Gray says, wrapping his arm around me and pulling me close to his side. "But I want you to know that I meant it when I said that you're safe with me. I've gone through my share of shit, and when you have no one to talk to about it, it just festers."

Thinking about my father usually feels like a scab being picked off an old wound. I brace myself against Gray's body, waiting for the discomfort and pain to streak through me. Yet … it doesn't. I monitor my breath, feeling the air enter and exit my lungs, and the panic doesn't come.

"He was an alcoholic," I say softly, the words flowing out of my mouth. "My grandmother said it started when Mom died. When I was born. A fact he never let me forget."

Gray kisses the side of my head, nuzzling his face in my hair.

"He always said that I was selfish from the start," I say. "That I killed my mother and would do anything to get what I want. He'd punish me for everything and nothing—withholding food, refusing to let me use hot water for showers, and making me wear dirty clothes to school."

Gray's body stiffens, and his grip on me tightens. He doesn't speak, but I can feel his jaw tense against my skull. And his reaction, as if he cares about the pain that little Astrid went through, has tears pooling in the corners of my eyes.

"I wasn't allowed to play sports," I say, blinking back the tears. Sand fills my chest just like it did when I lived with him. "I wanted to be in the band in junior high and found a guitar at a yard sale. The woman ended up giving it to me for free." I sniffle against the burn across the bridge of my nose. "Dad smashed it against the wood stove the first night I had it."

"*God,*" Gray bites out, squeezing me.

"He stole my journals and teased me relentlessly about what was inside them. His friends would come over and make comments about my body and say wholly inappropriate things to a preteen girl. Dad didn't care. If I got upset, I was being an emotional bitch, and he'd make me clean the house or he'd smack me with an open hand because if his hand was open, it wasn't abuse."

I take a breath, feeling like I'm being suffocated. I can sense the sting in my cheek, the bruise on my arm, and the pain searing my scalp from being dragged around the house by my ponytail.

"He refused to buy me tampons when I got my period and called me a little whore for having the audacity to menstruate," I say hurriedly. "So I got a job at fourteen. But he just bullied me into giving him my paychecks so he could buy lottery tickets and vodka because he had to pay for the utilities and whatnot."

A tear rolls down my cheek.

"Fuck, Astrid." He exhales slowly. "I'm so sorry."

I clutch his arm as something inside me cracks open. It's a flood of emotion, a wave of memories that I haven't thought about in a long time. But unlike past moments when I've faced these things myself, they don't take me out with them. I don't get washed away with the tide.

That's progress. That's empowering. It's freeing.

"Where is your dad now?" Gray asks, his tone frigid.

"He's dead."

His chest rises and then falls, as if this information is a relief to him, too. "Have you ever shared this with anyone?" Gray asks softly. "Or have you kept this to yourself for all of these years?"

Dad's voice, followed by Trace's, echoes through my brain, making it hard to swallow. It's devastating to remember such moments, but it's also heartbreaking that I chose to deal with this sort of man a second time. I survived them both, but I'll never, ever deal with it again.

"You want me to spend my money on tampons? Fuck no. That's not my fuckin' problem."

"You're a selfish little bitch. It's no wonder your father had to knock you around."

"How about this? Don't turn a light on, use any hot water, or eat any of my fuckin' food. Then maybe you'll realize how much I do for you around here!"

"I'm either going through your phone or you're getting the fuck out. I can't help you grew up like a piece of trash and don't know how to act. I have to protect myself here, Astrid."

My inhale shakes. I slip my foot over Gray's legs, craving his proximity. "I told Trace. He just used it to pick up pointers on how to hurt me."

"Where's *he* now?" Gray's body tenses again. "Just curious."

His tone sends a ripple of energy through me, like there's a buffer between me and my trauma. It offers me the space to breathe, to recalibrate from the memories, in a way I've never experienced before. It's as if I can set down my sword and rest. "I don't know. But now you know why I have trust issues."

"And that's why you jumped to the conclusion that I was a bully at the gas station."

"No, you *were* a bully at the gas station." I extricate myself from his grip and sit up, facing him. "You could've picked any other pump. There was no reason for you to growl and beep your horn at me."

He smiles, amused. "I couldn't pull up to another pump without backing up and making a whole production out of it. Some of us don't drive little cars that can spin on a dime."

"Because some of us are confident in our manhood."

Before I know what's happening, I'm being tossed on my back. Gray hovers over me with a decadent smirk. I giggle, squirming unsuccessfully to get away—not that I *really* want to get out from under him. I really want to see what that smirk is all about.

"Are you sore?" he asks, kissing me on the tip of the nose.

"Yes."

"*Oh*." He frowns. "Well, then …"

He starts to roll off me, but I wrap my legs around his waist. Placing my hands on his face, I peer into his eyes, and what I see startles me.

Kindness. Concern. Safety.

And, most of all, *attraction*.

That's a plethora of conditions that, together, are a little too much to take at once. But I do know what I can take instead …

"Hey, Truck Boy," I say, smiling at him. "Will you shut up for once and fuck me?"

He growls before capturing my lips with his own and making me forget about everything except him.

CHAPTER
TWENTY-SIX

ASTRID

I yawn, rolling from my stomach onto my back. Sunlight streams into the room, filling it with the promise of a new day. Birds chirp outside the window, and something pings in the distance.

Where the heck am I?

My eyes struggle to open. My brain takes even longer to process my whereabouts. Once it all comes together and forms an accurate picture of my location, I sink into the mattress and release a satisfied sigh.

Gray's bedroom.

I stretch, and a delicious ache emanates from my groin. I'm naked, covered only by a navy blue blanket ... except my breasts. The skin on my chest is marred by various light bruises from Gray's mouth.

I shiver as memories from last night stream through my brain.

The truck. Gray's face framed by my legs. His lips covered in my cum.

The length and thickness of his cock, and the salty bead sitting at the top waiting for me.

My knees throb, and I jerk the blanket away to see red marks from the hard ground. *"Stay with me. Give me all of it."*

I can see his face as he utters the commands, a mixture of strength and tenderness that makes it hard to breathe even now. I told him that I wanted him to take control—and it still blows my mind that I could verbalize my need to him, of all people. But the way he handled it, as if he understood what I was really asking and delivered in such a thoughtful way, leaves me reeling.

What else is this complicated man capable of?

I fall back into the pillows and giggle. "Who knew I had a praise kink?"

Ping! Ping! Ping!

I stand, wobbling for a moment on my exhausted legs, and make my way to the window. Squinting, I focus on the bodies standing around a fence post—four of them, to be exact. As they come into focus, I bite back a moan.

Hartley stands between Jasper and Brooks as Gray pounds a tool against a stake. *Shirtless … in cowboy boots.* Sweat coats his skin, and his muscles ripple in the light as if the sun's whole purpose is to highlight the perfection of his body. Movies are built around this scene, and I would be remiss not to capture it for posterity … and my personal use later.

I rustle through the blankets until I find my phone. Then I snap a picture and post it in the group chat.

Me: Yeehaw!

Gianna: And the gifts keep on giving.

Me: I'm not mad about it.

Audrey: I'm not seeing anything to be mad
about. 😊

Gianna: Saturday. I'm tired of Stupey's, so how
about Rhubarb at 7:00 p.m.?

Me: Sounds good. It's my turn to pay. My raise
hit my bank account on Friday, so here's to
having a bit of money (if Joe comes through for
me). 🙏

Audrey: I can make it. Sending you and Joe all
the good juju!

Gianna: Prepare a monologue, Astrid. I want
EVERY detail.

Me: 🤭

I perform a quick check of my email, then succumb to my growling stomach. A glance out the window shows the guys still working hard. So I get dressed sans panties—*where did they go?*—and freshen up in the bathroom. My finger makes a decent toothbrush in the absence of the real thing.

I head to the kitchen, following the scent of bacon and coffee. I'm greeted by a robust woman in a red-and-white checkered apron with the makings of a pie crust in front of her. She smiles as if she's been expecting me and asks if I'd like a cup of coffee.

"Yes, please," I say, feeling slightly awkward.

"It's a beautiful morning out there, isn't it?" She offers me creamer, but I shake my head. "I'm Cathy, by the way. The boys said you were sleeping. I saved you some breakfast, if you're hungry. Do you like bacon and eggs?"

She made me breakfast? "Who doesn't like bacon and eggs?"

"Vegetarians." She laughs, motioning toward the table. "Sit. Relax. I'll fix you a plate. Do you prefer white or wheat toast?"

I take a seat, puzzled. *What is happening here?* Gray mentioned Cathy yesterday—I vaguely remember him saying her name. *But why is she acting like my personal chef?*

"You don't have to do that," I say, fidgeting in the chair. "I'm sure you have other things to do."

She pauses, her hand stretched midair for a spatula. The grin she gives me is the warmest, sweetest thing that washes away any hesitation I have about letting her wait on me.

"Darlin', my job is to do whatever the boys tell me to do," she says. "And I was given strict instructions this morning to make sure you're comfortable and fed. *With no peanuts.*"

Of course, Gray mentioned my allergy. Even when he's not here, he manages to hold space for me. He was obviously thinking of me before I was awake today, considering my needs and comfort. What a wild concept.

What a complicated, enigmatic man.

I take a cup of coffee from Cathy and settle back in my seat, a little thrown off and struggling to regroup.

"The boys are fixing a fence this morning," she says with her back to me. "Well, they're supposed to be doing that. But Brooks and Jasper showed up a little while ago with some papers from town for Gray, so God knows what they'll get done with those two heathens here."

I chuckle. "I met them both yesterday. Jasper seemed pretty calm and rational. Brooks, though? He was … not."

She snort-laughs. "You have them pegged already. Brooks Dempsey is more than a handful. I'll tell you that for certain. I've known that boy since he was knee high, and he's been a rascal since day one." She shakes her head, turning to me with a plate in her hand. "He's a good boy, though. They all are." She places my breakfast in front of me. "I gave you wheat toast since you didn't specify. Let me know if you want jelly or jam."

"Thank you, Cathy. This is very nice of you."

"I hope you enjoy it," she says warmly.

"It looks wonderful."

Cathy goes back to her pie crust, leaving me alone with my bacon and thoughts. I've not known Hartley for twenty-four hours, but I'm sitting in his home getting served breakfast by his house manager. Under no circumstances should I find this comfortable or inviting, but I do. Everything about this place—about the ranch, the people, and the town—feels natural to me. I'm not sure what to make of it. *Am I still in an orgasm high? Will I go to bed tonight, relive this Sugar Creek experience, and cringe myself to sleep?*

It's a solid possibility. But I might as well lean into it anyway. I'm already this far in.

"Gray said that the two of you work together," Cathy says, rolling out a round of dough.

My cheeks flush. "Yes. I'm his assistant—and I know how this must look, considering ..." I stumble over my words. "You know, I just came out of his bedroom looking like this ..."

I smile sheepishly at her.

"Honey," she says, laughing. "Don't look at me that way. I might be old, and I might've helped raise that boy, but that doesn't mean I can't see." She shakes her head, still amused. "He's a good-looking little devil. Charming as all get-out. This is a judgment-free zone because, heck, if I were your age and had the opportunity, I can't say I wouldn't be in your shoes."

I shrug, grinning at her reaction. "I appreciate your open-mindedness."

"Of course. I've lived long enough to know that you must risk it for the biscuit sometimes. You'll never get much out of life if you don't. Trust me on that." She scoffs, flopping her dough into a pie plate. "I've been married and divorced three times—twice to the same man. Lordy, I should've learned the first time, but my daddy always told me I had a hard head. Guess he was right."

"At least you've lived your life. You've followed your heart."

"Maybe a little too recklessly, at times."

I take a bite of bacon.

"What about you, Miss Astrid? Do you follow your heart?"

"I thought this was breakfast, not an inquisition," I joke.

She laughs. "Oh, I don't mean to put you on the spot or anything. I'm just chatty. My mom didn't name me Cathy for nothing." She glances at me over her shoulder. "Chatty Cathy. Get it?"

"Yes, I get it." I laugh, too. "And you're not putting me on the spot. I'm just at a point in my life where I'm concerned that my heart is a broken compass, if that makes sense."

"*Three divorces, Miss Astrid*. Of course, that makes sense." She pinches the edges of the crust quickly, creating the most beautiful crimps around the top of the pie plate. "But here's the thing. I've come to believe that your heart compass can't be broken. It keeps trying to lead you north. What messes you up is when you let your brain and hormones into the mix. They can sabotage even the strongest of hearts."

I take a bite of eggs and then sit back with my coffee. I watch Cathy fill the pie shell with an apple filling, letting my mind massage the lesson she shared with me. She's not wrong. It makes perfect sense that we'd naturally be led to our person because the universe has a way of pulling things together with some mystical, magnetic power that I don't understand. I see it all the time. Cottage cheese and peaches, assholes and politics, cats and laptops. Take one look at a small child and a mud puddle, and the point is proven.

If her theory is correct and my heart compass works just fine, *where would it lead me if I could take my brain and hormones out of it?*

"What can you tell me about Gray?" I ask, placing my mug back on the table. "Do you have any insights you want to share with me?"

Cathy laughs. "How much time do you have?" She opens the

oven and sets her pie on the middle rack. "I think the biggest thing is to remember that he might look like some kind of Greek god, but he's just a mortal being like the rest of us. That kid has such a good heart in him—sometimes to his own detriment."

She grabs a towel from beside the sink and starts cleaning up her mess.

I take a bite of toast, pondering her observation. She seems to know Gray on an organic, personal level, so her opinions of him hold water. If she thinks he has a good heart, that means something. *But what does she mean when she says it's sometimes to his own detriment?* I can't help but wonder if that doesn't factor into his time at Denver. I've failed to understand why that version of Gray—the version who showed up in Nashville—is so different from the one I've come to know. And I also can't help but wonder if it's tied to his relationship with Caroline.

My stomach tightens at the thought of the woman in the picture.

I hate not knowing anything about her, mostly because she doesn't seem like just another ex who broke his heart. She seems to hold a chunk of Gray's past that he's not ready to share … or give up. He doesn't owe me anything, least of all the insight into his previous relationships, but it does make me feel a certain way to know that I found it so easy to talk about my painful moments with Trace, and Gray keeps his past with Caroline on lockdown.

If I knew what happened between them, I believe I'd understand the inner workings of Gray Adler a lot better. I don't know why it matters because it's not like Gray and I are an item. We just fucked a few times this weekend, and I'm certain he'll want to go back to his normal life when we get back to the city. *But what if …*

What if I dared to believe there could be a world where Gray and I had a real connection? What if I were brave enough to take my head and hormones out of the equation and see where things led? Would it lead to Gray, or am I just so desperate for a man to be kind to me that I'm being unrealistic?

"Gray hasn't brought a woman around the ranch since high school," Cathy says. "You can imagine my surprise when I saw him this morning and then discovered he brought you along."

I pick up my fork again. "That was probably a shock, huh?"

She smiles over her shoulder. "Yes, but now that we've chatted for a few minutes and I've gotten a pretty good read on you, it's also a delight. His momma would've loved you, Astrid. And that just makes this old woman's heart so full."

Huh? I shake my head, certain that I've misheard her. I put down my utensil before I drop it and it clatters to the floor.

"That's ... really nice of you to say," I tell her, wondering if I should share that Gray and I aren't together-together.

"I assume you know what happened to their parents," she says, somber.

"Yes. Gray told me they died in a tornado."

She nods, turning around and facing me. Crow's feet pinch the corners of her eyes, and lines curve around her mouth. But her eyes, bright and blue, are as clear as the Caribbean waters. "When I told you that Gray's heart can be to his detriment, what I meant was that he puts a lot of pressure on himself. Sometimes that leads to him carrying unnecessary guilt. That's an important part of understanding who he is."

I tune out the faint pinging from outside and the hum of the oven. My breaths deepen, pushing through the constriction in my throat. The air has shifted from light and fun to something heavier, something much more real. My gut tells me to listen ... and take notes.

"Why do you say that?" I ask, my voice controlled.

"Well," she says, drying her hands on a towel. "Gray was supposed to meet his dad in Omaha the weekend the tornado hit. Ronnie, Gray's dad, had to pick up a horse from a friend that Sunday. At the last minute, Gray canceled, so Anne, his mom, went with Ronnie."

No. I lay a hand on my chest, feeling it shake with every breath.

"That guilt isn't his to carry around," Cathy says. "And I know if Ronnie and Anne were here, they'd be so upset with him for feeling the way he does. It's stolen a lot of joy from his life." A slow smile touches her lips. "But that's why I know they'd love you. This morning, Gray was the happiest that I've seen him since before they passed away."

I grip the edge of the table as her words slam into my heart. This woman knows Gray through and through, and she believes that he's happier than she's seen him in years … *because of me?*

Before I can begin to process her observation, the door opens to the laundry room, and the guys tromp in. They chatter back and forth like old friends. Seeing Gray so relaxed makes me smile. It also makes me question whether Cathy is right. Maybe it's being home that makes him happy and not me.

"There's a gaggle of trouble," Cathy says.

"We learned from the best." Jasper kisses Cathy on the cheek. "Is that an apple pie?"

She bops him on the nose. "It is. And if you come back for supper, you can have a slice."

"He'd better still be here helping me with this fence," Hartley says, opening the fridge and tossing the guys each a bottle of water. "Especially since Gray has to leave."

My gaze drifts to him. His shirt is thrown over his shoulder, and dirt spatters across his sweaty skin. He's a real-life ad for pickup trucks or construction equipment, and I suddenly understand the attraction to a blue-collar man.

"Are you about ready to head back to Nashville?" he asks me.

"Yeah, sure." I smile at him. "I'm ready when you are."

"I'm going to grab a shower and then we can hit the road."

"I'll be ready."

He walks behind me on the way to the shower, trailing his finger across the back of my neck. I avoid eye contact with anyone in the room as I fight a flurry of goose bumps breaking across my skin. Whether I'm addicted to his touch or have already been conditioned to associate it with earth-shattering orgasms, I don't know. But as I watch him walk down the hallway, all I can think is I'm fucked—and not the way I want to be right now.

CHAPTER
TWENTY-SEVEN

Astrid

"We haven't been here in forever," Audrey says as Chessie, our server, escorts us to a round table in the corner of the restaurant. "I can't even remember what I order."

"They have great salads," Gianna says, taking a seat between me and Audrey.

Rhubarb, the little place we serendipitously found a few years ago, is one of our favorites. It used to be in our constant rotation but fell out for some reason last fall. None of us can remember why.

I place my purse on the empty chair at my side, taking in the warm, welcoming ambiance. The owners, Marcie and Geoff, told us that the name Rhubarb came from the paint color they chose for the interior. Marcie had her heart set on the pinkish-red hue titled rhubarb, and it became the whole theme for the place. Then Geoff went into a scientific study about why they chose mustard as an accent color, and how restaurants routinely brand themselves with an orange scheme because it triggers something in your brain and makes you hungry.

I could've lived the rest of my life and not known that.

Chessie sets three menus on the table. "Can I get you started with drinks and an appetizer?"

"Sangria for me," Gianna says.

"Do you know what? I'll take a strawberry lemonade," I say.

"Ooh. I'll take a strawberry lemonade, too," Audrey says. "And no appetizer, thank you."

Chessie scribbles on a notepad and promises to return with our drinks shortly.

"I didn't get the memo that we weren't ordering alcohol," Gianna says, handing us each a menu. "I thought we were celebrating tonight."

Audrey takes the laminated sheet from Gianna. "Well, since we haven't gotten many details so far, maybe it was gross and there's nothing to celebrate."

"Come on." Gianna snorts. "You've seen the man. If there's anything gross about him, I'll stop using blue on my nails—and you know how I feel about that."

The menu is familiar, hosting the same dishes as it did last year, and I scan the lists for my favorites. As I check out the pulled pork sandwich and try to recall whether it's peanut-free, a smirk slips across my face.

"You have two choices. I found a Rice Krispies treat and a chocolate bar. Neither says they have peanuts in them, but ... how do you know? Do we trust these companies?"

"See what I mean?" Gianna sighs. "We're celebrating for sure."

I pull down my menu and realize that my friends were watching me. Very little gets by them, and my grin certainly didn't. Gianna's brow is quirked, and Audrey bites her bottom lip, looking like she's ready to leap from her chair and dance out of happiness.

God, I love them.

"It was a total ten out of ten," I say, unable to stop from smiling. "Highly recommend."

Gianna and Audrey giggle, clearly happy for me.

"I know you want details, but I don't even know where to start," I say. "It's the most unexpected thing to ever happen to me … repeatedly."

My thighs clench together at the thought of all those repeated moments. The truck bed, the ground, the shower. The bed. And since we've been back to town, we can add Gray's kitchen counter and sofa, and my bed and on top of my washing machine in the spin cycle.

What a time to be alive.

"Repeatedly," Gianna says, eyes twinkling. "Attaboy, Gray."

Chessie brings our drinks to us, and we place our orders quickly. Audrey, of course, orders what one of us gets instead of making her own decision. Chessie is barely out of earshot before Gianna's throwing questions my way.

"So where do things stand?" Gianna asks. "Are we friends with benefits? Enemies with bennies?" She wags a finger my way. "I've done that before, and let me tell you, it was some of the best sex of my life."

I sip my lemonade, using the action to buy me some time. I knew this question would come up, and I've contemplated how to answer it over the past few days. Unfortunately for me, I didn't find an answer, and that's left me in a place of uncertainty. *And uncertainty?* It's something I don't do well.

"Honestly, I don't know where things stand between me and Gray, and I'm afraid to think about it too much," I say. "It's just crazy to think I'm in this position with him, considering I hated him when we first met. And now, a few weeks later, and I'm trying to decide whether our week of having sex on every surface I can think of means anything more than we like to fuck."

I pull my phone from my purse and find a number I don't recognize on the screen. Whoever it is gets sent to my voicemail.

"Where do you hope they stand?" Audrey asks much more gently than Gianna.

I shrug. "Again, I don't know. It's not like I set out to date this guy. I didn't match with him on an app or meet him in a bar and decide that I was, in fact, going to engage in a relationship with him. It just happened. It's fun for now—a lot of fun, really. But I have no clue how he sees things. Does he think there could be something between us? Is he just playing around with me while he's stuck in Nashville and expecting me to understand that?" I frown. "I don't want to get my hopes up."

Audrey plays with the pearl on her necklace. "It's okay to be hopeful. If you don't have hope in life, you have nothing at all."

Gianna rolls her eyes. "As sweet as this is, let me be the voice of reason and point out that this has transformed pretty quickly."

Audrey holds up a hand. "I will admit that I'm not as experienced as either of you—especially our friend Gianna here—but I do feel like I have a valid point." She clears her throat, sitting a bit taller in her chair. "I think it speaks for itself that you were able to take this relationship, albeit quickly, from hating his guts to letting him up in yours."

My jaw drops.

"Audrey Maria Van!" Gianna gasps. "What just came out of your mouth?"

I cover my mouth, giggling at them. Audrey's face is as red as the walls of Rhubarb, and Gianna's expression is a hilarious mix of shock and pride. I can't believe she said something borderline crude. But, considering she's around Gianna a lot, it's surprising that it's taken this long for her to shed some of her good-girl tendencies.

"Can we go back to the point you were trying to make, Auddie?" I ask, giving her an out.

"Yes," she says quickly. "I was trying to say that it's been a natural progression from enemies to semi-friends to lovers, and there's something beautiful and organic about that. It's not like you met him, gave in to lust, and then had to backtrack and figure out all the bad parts of the guy so you could fall in love with him. You started at the bad and then worked your way to the good."

"I'm not in love with him," I say, lifting a brow.

"And let's nix lovers from our vocabulary," Gianna says. "It sounds so two-minute missionary to me, and I can guarantee you that Gray Adler isn't that."

I smirk. "No, no, he isn't."

Audrey sighs, frustrated with us—but that's par for the course. "All I'm saying is that you trust him, Astrid, because you wouldn't have let it get this far if you didn't. And coming from you, I think that speaks volumes."

Chessie approaches us with our meals. The salads are beautiful with fresh lettuce and spinach, perfectly grilled chicken, and homemade croutons. We dig in as soon as she leaves.

"What do you want to happen with Gray, Astrid?" Audrey asks. "In a perfect world, where do you see this going?"

I stab a piece of chicken and then shove it in my mouth. It's rude to talk with your mouth full.

Her question assumes that I have a say in what happens between me and Gray. And, to some extent, I do. But if he wants to shut things down and walk away, then I don't. I'm wary of having a door shut in my face. Again.

But this is the thing that's kept me up every night this week. It's impossible not to wonder if us seeing each other nearly every night and texting on and off all day means we're headed in a certain direction. The selfies and quick check-ins between errands or practices feel like more than two friends. I don't text Gianna and Audrey like I've been communicating with Gray.

My phone lights up, and I glance down and see Gray's name and the little cowboy boot emoji beside it. I pick it up, opening the app with butterflies in my stomach.

Gray 😬: We won. 😊 A bunch of guys got banged up, so we get Sunday and Monday off to rest.

Me: Is everyone okay? Are YOU okay?

Gray 😬: I'm fine. No one's seriously injured. It's just the last leg of the season and everyone's tired and the damage is starting to accumulate.

Me: Need a massage? 😏

Gray 😬: I need something, but I don't know if a massage is it. 😉

My fingers fly across the keys.

Me: I volunteer as tribute. 🙋

Gray 😬: LOL We're on our way home, but it'll be late as hell when we get in. Want to come over tomorrow?

Me: I have to scope out a venue for Renn tomorrow morning at ten o'clock. It shouldn't take more than an hour or so because I've already reviewed the catering options and security protocol. I can be out of there and across town to you by one.

Gray 😬: Can't wait.

Me: Ditto.

I drag my gaze up to my friends. They're watching me,

amused. "What?"

"I know that look," Gianna says, tossing a crouton in her mouth. "You were just setting up a fuck date."

"You don't get bonus points for knowing that because even I could decipher that one," Audrey says.

Good to know I'm broadcasting my business all over my face.

Gianna sighs, picking up her fork. "It's just strange that it's you and not me. Don't get me wrong, I'm happy for you. Thrilled, really. I want you to be the happiest little redhead in all the land, but my life is boring right now, and I'm jealous."

"What's happening at work?" Audrey asks her. "I'm sure that's not boring."

"No, not boring," Gianna says. "But not exciting in a good way. Remember the guy I saw last weekend?"

"The guy screwing the other guy's wife?" I ask, pouring my vinaigrette on my salad.

She nods. "Yes. Him. Well, I made it clear that we weren't a match and told him—nicely, of course—to be on his merry way. He's called, texted, and emailed me daily. I've blocked him on everything I can block him on, but he's now making fake Social accounts to message me."

"Are you safe?" Audrey asks, concerned.

"Yeah, I don't like the sound of this," I say, exchanging a worried glance with Audrey.

"It's fine. I threatened him with a restraining order yesterday and haven't heard from him since. Speaking of emails," Gianna says, "did you get mine about the extension for your column response, Astrid?"

I nod, trying to spear a crouton. "Yeah. I've been working on it, but I won't rush until you tell me when you need it."

"Perfect."

Chessie swings by and drops off our check. I slide it next to my plate so I can ensure my friends let me pay the tab. Not only is it my turn but I'm now making double my income thanks to

Renn. If Joe comes through for me, my financial life just might be salvageable.

And, if the stars align, my personal life might be salvageable, too.

"Guess who I met in Sugar Creek, Audrey?" I ask.

She lifts her brow, taking a drink of her lemonade.

"A fighter. He's one of Gray's friends. Brooks something."

"I'll have to ask Drew if he knows him," she says. "Speaking of which, I've decided that I don't want to wait until the Cape to make my move on Seth. I'm going to pop up in Boston and ask him to dinner and make a go at it. Do you think that's a bad plan?"

Gianna leans forward and laughs. "No, it's not a bad idea. It's a great one."

"And we're here for you every step of the way," I say. "Tell us when you need us, and we'll help you pick outfits, go with you to get your nails done—whatever you need."

Audrey sits taller, her smile touching the corners of her eyes. "Thank you, guys. I love you so much."

"Love you, too, Auddie," Gianna and I say.

I sit back with my lemonade and listen to my friends debate whether Audrey needs to go shopping before her big Cape Cod weekend. It brings a smile to my lips. We have been there for each other through thick and thin. We've cheered each other on, held each other when we've cried, and shared more laughs than I could ever count. They're a cheat code for life.

For a long while, I truly believed that if I had to survive the rest of my life with only Gianna and Audrey, I could be happy. And I still firmly believe that. They're the greatest friends.

But if this weekend has shown me something, it's that I love being with someone who is there for me in ways that they can't —ways that I didn't realize were so important. Someone who can shield me from the world when I need it, even if I won't admit it. Someone with the biggest heart who cares for me in the smallest, most intimate ways, and gives incredible orgasms. *Let's never underestimate the power of the big O.* I didn't realize I needed that until Gray.

Gray's presence in my life brings a whole new level of fulfillment. I didn't understand how it felt to have someone want to know you, to ask questions, and to be patient enough to hear the answers. Being in his arms, in his sphere, colors my world differently … and sometimes my knees and breasts and lips.

I blush and turn back to my salad as Gianna starts one of her famous work stories.

Maybe Audrey is right. Perhaps it's okay to hope for something more. And if it's not, I might be screwed.

CHAPTER
TWENTY-EIGHT

GRAY

"Not too bad, Adler. Not too bad," I say, turning a full circle between my living room and kitchen.

It took me a while this morning to get up and moving. My body is sore everywhere from the game yesterday, a barn burner against our division rivals. Ridge came through for us in the end and led us to a win, but we're all paying the price for the physicality of the match today.

That has not, however, stopped Nico and Ridge from blowing up the group chat. It's so obnoxious that even I've had enough. I left it last night but had been added back by the time I woke up this morning. *Fools.*

I gather the wad of charging cords off the kitchen island and tuck them into a drawer. It's not exactly as organized as Astrid would have it, but at least they're out of sight. If I leave them out, or have anything out of place, she'll stress about it when she gets here and start trying to fix it—and that's not why she's here.

She's here to relax with me.

Just thinking about her is like taking a shot of happiness,

which is funny, considering she was so *not* happy when I met her. But now that I've gotten to know her better, I can't hear her name without smiling. She's a powerhouse, capable of anything, and I'm in awe of the things she can manage and accomplish in one day. I could never come close.

But, somehow, she lets me get close to her.

"Astrid, what are we doing?" I run a hand over my head as the rhythm of my heart changes. It beats harder and faster, each pulse both a warning and a wish. I don't know which is a bigger problem.

There's no way of knowing where this thing with Astrid will go. Hell, I'm not even sure how she feels about me. But the more time we spend together, the more I know I want this to go somewhere, and the fewer fucks I give about how fast this is going. There isn't a scenario I can conjure up where she doesn't fit into my life. It feels like she's supposed to be in my arms, business deals, and hometown.

It's terrifying. But it's also right. And if that's true, whether it be now or later, I must be prepared in every way to be the man she deserves.

No matter how much it hurts.

Knock! Knock!

"Come in," I say, my voice raspy as I face the door.

Astrid steps through the threshold, rewarding me with a big, bright smile as she swings the door shut behind her.

"How was your morning?" I ask, wrapping her up in my arms. She nuzzles her face against my chest and sags against me. "Did you check out the venue?"

She nods, making no effort to pull away. So I stand in place and hold her until she's damn good and ready.

"It was perfect." She kisses my chest and then leans back. "Renn wanted to find the perfect place for Blakely's birthday party, and I found it today. It's beautiful and intimate but can fit all the people he wants to invite. I think. I hope." She winces. "It's perfect. I have to stop overthinking it."

"Well, you look beautiful even if you are an overthinker."

She smiles. "How do you feel today? What can I do for you? How can I help?"

"You can come to the couch and watch a movie with me."

"I don't see how that's going to help you," she says skeptically.

"How about this. How can *I* help *you* today?"

Her hands go to her hips. "I'm your assistant. It's *my* job to help *you*."

I chuckle, knowing it won't do a damn bit of good to argue with her—not when she has this look in her eye. But I try, anyway.

"You realize that every time we're together doesn't mean we're working, right?" I ask, taking her hand and leading her into the living room. "I didn't ask you to come here as my coworker. I mean, if you want to dress in a secretary's skirt or a nurse's outfit, then that's a different story. That I'll accept."

Astrid smacks me, laughing, as I sit and pull her down onto my lap. She shifts around, getting comfortable against my chest. Her ass grinds on my cock, but I don't think it's intentional. It doesn't stop it from getting hard, though.

"Your game went well yesterday, right?" she asks, holding our laced fingers in the air. "Look at this. You have so many bruises."

"Comes with the territory."

"Do you ever worry that you'll be permanently damaged?"

I take a deep breath. "No. Not really. Rugby is relatively safe."

"In my professional opinion, I disagree."

Laughing, I wrap my arms around her and pull her to me. "Your professional opinion, huh?"

"When you add the number of years I worked for Renn and now you, I've been in this industry for a long damn time. I think I qualify as a pro, thank you very much."

"Whatever you say, sweetheart."

She giggles. "I'll pretend you meant that as a term of endearment, so I don't have to kick your ass."

Good. Because that's how I meant it.

We sit together in the quiet, her head lying between my collar and jaw, and our fingers tangling lazily like neither of us wants to hold on tight or let go.

As I watch our fingers move, I realize it's a metaphor for the two of us. We aren't really together. But we aren't exactly single, either. And maybe it doesn't matter what our official status is because it doesn't change anything for me. I'm riding this fucker out to see where it goes. We may not have known each other for that long, but I've lost too many years to being unhappy. *And this?* This is motherfucking happiness.

Astrid drops her hand from mine and lets it fall to the couch. I watch it drift to the cushion and feel my heart go right along with it. Then it hits me.

If I have any chance of holding her hand, I have to make sure mine is empty first.

There's no way around it.

"I got a letter from Joe today," she says. "Well, it was a copy of the one that he sent to the landlord's attorney."

"Oh yeah? What did it say?"

"Well, I can't read legalese, but I think it said fuck around and find out."

I laugh, my chest shaking. "Yeah, that sounds like a Joe letter."

"I pray to God that I never get one. I'd pee my pants." She leans her head up and looks toward the kitchen. "Your phone has been buzzing since I got here. Do you hear it, or am I hearing things?"

"It's the fucking team chat," I say, sitting up, too, and groaning. "The last time I looked, they—meaning Nico and Ridge—were trying to put together the top fifty sports movies of all time. And you'd think they were arguing about something that fucking matters because these assholes take it to the next level."

She shakes her head, amused. Then she climbs off the couch and sets up my chessboard. Each piece gives a soft thud as it takes its square. There's a cadence to it, like a heartbeat, that adds to the peace in the room around us.

"What are you thinking?" she asks.

I rest my elbows on my knees. "I was thinking about how I could get used to this. I'm not saying anything crazy, just that I enjoy having you here. Playing chess with you. Going out to eat." I pause, smirking. "Fucking."

She laughs, scooting to the other side of the coffee table. "I'm glad you added that on the end because I was starting to think you didn't want me anymore."

"Impossible."

Her gaze flickers to the ground before she looks at me through her thick lashes. The vulnerability in them slices through my heart. "I could get used to this, too, you know."

The air around us crackles as neither of us says a word. Instead of speaking, we sit with our admissions, searching each other's gaze. There's a slight nervousness in her eyes, but I can't blame her for that. This scares the shit out of me, too.

"Chess?" she asks.

"Sure."

"Good. I was afraid you'd chicken out since I beat you last time."

"Oh really?" I make a face, mocking her. "That's not how I remember it."

"Of course, you don't. No one likes to remember getting whipped."

She hops up on her knees, her arms pressing her big tits together. Thanks to her low-cut top, I have a clear view of her cleavage, and it sends a shot of energy straight to my cock.

"Want to make a wager?" I ask, wiggling my brows.

She snorts. "Careful, buddy. You're going to lose."

"Strip chess. You lose a chess piece, then you lose an article of clothing. First one of us to disrobe gives the other oral."

"I don't know if I want to win or lose," she says, laughing. "This is a terrible game."

"Well, I guess that's the good part of our wager. We both win no matter how it ends."

She licks her lips, her eyes heated. "Losers first."

I study the board, trying to remember how she played last time. Nothing comes to mind other than what she's going to look like riding my cock in a few minutes. I grimace, adjusting myself and then moving out a knight.

Fuck it.

Astrid immediately pushes a pawn forward. I move mine so it's face-to-face with hers.

"Interesting choice," she says, moving her knight to protect her pawn.

"I like to keep things fun." I use my bishop to attack her knight. "Your move."

She takes a moment to interpret the board, ultimately deciding not to address my move. Instead, she mirrors my position and moves her bishop.

"Ah," I say, taking her knight with gusto. "Lose the shirt, sweetheart."

She peels the fabric away from her body and over her head, leaving her tits overflowing in a black bra that's so sheer that I can make out her peaked nipples and dark areolas.

Motherfucker. I suck in a breath, catching her shirt as she tosses it my way. My blood is so hot that it singes my veins. All I can think about is getting my mouth on her and burying myself into her little body.

"Lose the shirt, Adler." She takes my bishop with an outside pawn, snapping it off the board and humming as I toss my shirt on the floor. "Good lord. There should be a rule that you aren't allowed to wear a shirt when we're alone."

"I'd prefer you naked when we're alone, so arrangements can be made."

"We might be able to work out a deal."

I move a pawn to attack her bishop, but I see my mistake as soon as my hand is off the piece.

"Pants," she says, taking my knight with her bishop. "Get them off."

I slide my shorts down my legs and kick them near my shirt. My cock springs free, already hard and swollen in anticipation of her tight pussy. I fist myself at the base, jacking myself from root to tip while watching her eyes widen.

"Damn," she says, sucking in a breath. "You could charge for that."

"For what?" I ask, laughing.

"Just to watch you jack yourself off. Remember, I did a lot of research into alternative ways to make money. You can make bank if you have a big cock and some time on your hands. *Or* said big cock *in* your hands."

This woman. "I guess that's a viable income stream once I retire from rugby."

"Yeah, I don't know how I feel about that. I'm afraid I'd see someone make a comment on a thread somewhere online and I'd have to fight them." She shrugs helplessly. "Can't help it. I am who I am."

"I'm honored that you'd fight someone over me."

She winks. "I didn't say over you. I said over your cock."

"Thanks for the clarification." I shake my head. Glancing down at the board, I see my next move. "Your bra is mine," I say, taking her bishop with a middle pawn.

"Oh no. How terrible," she says in faux horror. "Whatever will I do?"

She stands slowly, her eyes glued to mine, and removes the thin piece of fabric stretched across her chest. What little support the bra gave her is now gone, and her teardrop-shaped tits hang perfectly. She's a sight to behold, the sexiest woman I've ever seen.

"How invested are you in this game?" I ask her, pulling a condom from the pocket of my shorts.

"Depends on my other options. Do you want to go for a jog? I'll play chess." She smirks as I rip the condom wrapper open. "Want me to ride you?" She takes her hands and levels the rest of the chess pieces, and the sound echoes through the apartment. "Game over."

Thank God. I roll the rubber over myself, wishing I had the self-restraint to wait. But I don't. I need to be inside her *now.*

She slips her shorts and panties over her hips, then steps out of them. "I'm literally soaked. My thighs are sticking together."

"Get over here."

She steps over her garments and straddles me on the couch. I slip my fingers between us, coating my hand with her arousal.

"Damn," I hiss, so hard I think I might explode.

Her gaze is hungry as she hovers over my tip. Her breasts are in my face, close enough for me to suck. That earns me a sweet, wanton moan as she slides herself onto my cock, burying me to the hilt.

"I need a second," she says, swallowing hard. Her lashes flutter as she sucks in a breath and moans again.

My thighs flex, shaking at the intensity of her pussy wrapped around me. She's so tight that I'm barely able to breathe. So beautiful that I can't think. So flawless that … I'm fucked.

"You're a dream, Astrid," I whisper, running my palms over her tits. "Every piece of you is perfect."

Her muscles tighten, and her pussy constricts even more. I growl, lowering my hands to her hips and urging her to move.

Slowly, like she's trying to torture me, she begins to rock her hips against mine.

"This is my favorite," she says softly. "Do you want to know why?"

"Why?"

"Because I like watching you fall apart. I love knowing that I have the power to make you feel like this."

Her gaze is wide and clear, her honesty pure and vulnerable. How did I ever think this woman was only a shrew?

The weekend, siding with me rather than falling for Brooks's charm. The way she looked at me at the ranch … as if she had always been a part of it. Her easy banter with Hart.

Cathy's whispered words as we left. *"She's it, Gray. Your mama and daddy would've loved her. Don't let her go, my boy."*

Cathy is right.

She's it.

I'm just not sure what I did to deserve her.

I press kisses over her chest, shoulder, and run them along her jaw. Holding her face in my hands, I take her mouth in mine. We kiss slowly, deliberately, each movement, every flick of our tongues bringing us closer to our climax … but closer together, too.

She pulls back, grinding harder on my cock. The tempo increases. It's urgent. Needy. *Desperate.* Her hands find my shoulders, and her nails dig into them, clutching on to me as she bounces on my dick.

Her tits jiggle in my face, while her ass cheeks jiggle in my hands.

Astrid rolls her hips, lifting and then crashing down in a smooth, quick succession that drives me wild.

"You are so fucking sexy," I say, meeting her thrust for thrust.

"I can't take it much longer. I'm so close," she says, gasping for air. Her motions come faster. "I'm going to come."

I grit my teeth, holding back as long as I can. Her pussy grips my cock as the muscles begin to spasm around it. "Look at me when you come. Eyes on me."

She squeals again, this time the sound ending in a moan. Her gaze finds mine just before she falls apart.

"Fuck!" she shouts.

I groan, my body shaking as it gives in and releases its load. My teeth grind together, the vein in my temple pulses … I can barely hold myself together.

My hands find her hips again, and I guide her back and forth. "Don't stop yet. *Fuuuuuck.*"

Astrid trembles as she milks the rest of her orgasm on my dick, and I shiver violently as the last waves of mine crash through me. I blow out a breath as she collapses onto my shoulder, her breaths heaving right alongside mine.

I wrap my arms around her and drop my head into the crook of her neck, feeling things in places that have been dead for a long time.

"That was so good," she says, giggling. "But I need to get up and use the bathroom."

"That wasn't good," I say, helping her off me. "That was amazing."

She beams, laughing again as she makes a quick escape to the bathroom.

I sigh, leaning back on the couch for a moment and letting myself regroup. But as my gaze sweeps the apartment, it settles on the bag I brought home from Hartley's—and the envelope tucked into the front pocket.

I know what I have to do … and that I have to do *it now.*

"She's it, Gray. Your mama and daddy would've loved her. Don't let her go, my boy."

"I won't, Cathy," I whisper. "I won't."

What I have to do first is not for Caroline and me.

It's for Astrid and me.

CHAPTER
TWENTY-NINE

ASTRID

I belt out the last lyrics of a song about Jack and Diane, letting the wind whip through my hair as I head to Gray's. The Swill is ahead on my right, and I slow down to make the turn into the neighborhood.

The late morning is beyond beautiful. The air is warm but not sweaty, and the sun is bright but not burning. Everyone on the road seems to be in a great mood, letting each other merge in traffic and not running red lights. I didn't need all of that to perk me up today. I have a whole day with Gray to look forward to since he has the day off.

"Auddie, no," I say, laughing through the Bluetooth. "Don't panic. I'm sure Seth hasn't answered your message because he's busy. A lot of athletes don't even check their messages on Social because they get such weird ones."

"Are you sure? Because I'm worried that I've made it awkward between us and now I can never set foot near my brother again."

"I promise you haven't made it awkward. Gianna and I both proofread your message last night. It was friendly, slightly flirty, and made you sound like *the doctor that you are.*" I pause to let that sink in. "You are a catch, girlfriend. Seth will probably see that message and panic himself because guys don't score girls like you without trying."

She sighs. "Okay. Not sure I believe you, but thanks for lying to me anyway."

"Anytime, anytime." I pull off my sunglasses and toss them onto the passenger seat. "I'm pulling up to Gray's, so I'm going to go. If you need me to talk you off a ledge later, call me. I'll keep my phone close."

"You're the greatest, Astrid. Love you."

"Bye, Auddie."

"Bye."

I end the call, park at the curb, and gather my things. I'm on the sidewalk walking toward Gray's in two seconds flat.

It feels like I'm floating to his apartment, and the shit that usually weighs me down and has me trudging through the day is gone. Well, it's probably still there, but I hardly notice it. It's hard to think about your problems and what could go wrong and how many goofy things you said that day when someone's telling you how amazing you are. Talk about *lie to me anyway.*

The older man on the porch who I see every time I'm here, practically every day, takes his cigar out of his mouth and waves with two fingers. I smile, waving back.

I round the side of the building and start up his porch but quickly stop. This morning's groceries are stacked all over the porch. *What the hell?* I step over the bag of fruit and ring Gray's doorbell. While I wait for him to answer, I sort through the bags and find that the milk's warm.

My stomach tightens as I ring the bell again. I listen closely, but don't hear any footsteps. He never makes me wait this long.

I slide my phone from my pocket and press his name. He answers on the fourth ring.

"Hey," he says, his voice eerily low.

"Hey. Are you okay?"

He hesitates. "Yeah. Why?"

"Well, I'm standing on your porch to hang out with you today—not wearing panties, as you prefer—and your groceries are piled out here." I laugh. "I was afraid you were dead in there."

This pause is two moments long enough to trigger a sense of dread in my gut.

I force a swallow, shifting my weight from one foot to the other. "Gray?"

"So I guess you didn't get my text this morning, huh?"

I pull the phone away from my face and open my texts. There's nothing since last night. *What is he talking about?* "The last text you sent me was at nine o'clock when you asked me if I made it home, and I said yes."

He groans. "Fucking Wi-Fi." His sigh is filled with frustration, and the sound of it tells me I'm going to be feeling similarly soon. "I didn't want to panic you, but I had to leave town late last night. There was an emergency."

"Oh my God. I'm sorry." My eyes dart around the porch. "Is everything okay? What can I do to help?"

"It'll be fine. I promise. I just need to be … here to make a couple of decisions, and then I'll be home late tonight."

My brain sorts through what could possibly be wrong. *Is it Hartley? Brooks? Jasper? Did something happen to Cathy?* I press a hand to my heart as if the pressure can keep it from beating out of my chest.

"Okay," I say, my thoughts scrambled. "Um, is everyone okay? Hartley? Cathy?"

"Yeah, Astrid. Everyone's okay." He sighs again, and I can hear exhaustion in his tone. "My flight gets in late. I'll come by and see you when I get home, all right?"

Flight? I stand a bit taller, adding that information to the mix. It's not like I know his whole family, but I thought they were all in Sugar Creek. *So where the hell is he flying?*

"I'll explain everything tonight, sweetheart," he says. "But I have to go now."

"What about the groceries?"

"The code to the lock is four-seven-eight-six-two. I hate to ask you to take them in, but I didn't realize you ordered me stuff."

I frown. "Yeah, I just thought since we were going to hang out all day that I could restock you while I was there. But don't worry. I'll sort them. Four-seven-eight-six-two?"

"Yeah. I'll see you tonight, okay?"

"Okay," I say.

"And Astrid?"

"Yeah?"

He takes a breath. "You're the only thing that will get me through this day. Remember that. See you soon."

And the line goes dead.

"What the fuck was that?" I pull the phone from my face and look at the screen. *Call ended.*

Oof.

I shove the device in my pocket and punch the code in the lock before I forget it. I'm operating in a haze, my brain preoccupied with making sense of Gray's emergency.

The door clicks open, and I step inside the apartment, propping it ajar with a bag of rice. Nothing about what he just said makes sense. But he did sound frazzled, and he doesn't get frazzled often. So whatever is going on must've blindsided him.

Poor guy.

I cart the bags into the kitchen and then close the door securely. The apartment feels different without Gray here, but I still love it. Maybe it's because I can see *us* all over the place. At the coffee table playing chess, having tacos on the kitchen bar … Gray carrying me down the hall to the shower after our fun got a little messy on the couch.

That was such a great night.

I turn to grab a carton of eggs when I notice a letter lying open on the counter. A strange calm washes over me as I peer at the letter like it's going to leap across the room and bite me. Something tells me it can … and it will.

An envelope is on top of the sheet of crisp white paper. I flip it over in my hand and see a Denver return address. It's made out to Gray specifically, but there's no last name on the return address.

My hands shake as I toss the envelope on the bar and pick up the paper. It's a single sheet with no letterhead or logo, and the words are handwritten in a woman's penmanship.

I lean against the counter for support, knowing I shouldn't read this, but I'm unable *not* to.

> *Dear Gray,*
> *I've started this several times over the past couple of months, but I can't seem to get it right. There's a lot to say, but it's all so complicated and laced with pain and grief, and the last thing I wish to do is to bring you any more suffering.*

The paper trembles as I hold it, fighting the lump in my throat so I can continue to breathe. I don't know what I expected, but it sure as hell wasn't this. *What is going on?*

> *First, and most importantly, I want to thank you for paying for my rehabilitation services over the past two years. I know it was you. I just put it together over the past few months. I can't fathom how you found the money, Gray, and the sacrifices you've had to make to do this for me. There aren't enough words to thank you*

enough. You are an amazing man. But we knew that before this happened.

I swallow, the action hot and nearly painful. It feels like I'm peeking into a room that I haven't been invited into, but I can't stop reading.

I was so angry with you for a long time. Blaming you was easier than blaming my sister, and it was easier than blaming the weather or the other driver. You were still living and breathing and hating you for the accident gave me a place to put my grief. But I saw you on television late one night doing an interview, and I saw the pain in your eyes. It was the kind of grief that those who have experienced can identify. I lay in my hospital room and bawled my eyes out, praying for you. You were hurting this whole time, too. And instead of being angry at Caroline, you were figuring out how to take care of me, her baby sister. I've never felt so low and like such a bad person.

Tears stream down my cheeks, staining my shirt, mixing with the snot running out of my nose. I can barely make out the words anymore. My heart aches for Gray, for whoever is writing this letter—for whatever has happened. Something horrible and tragic. *But what?*

Caroline loved you, Gray. I don't know how you feel

about her now, and I hope this letter isn't bringing up unwanted memories, but I want you to know that none of this was your fault. I hope you don't carry around guilt for something you didn't cause. You are a good man, Gray Adler. And I will always root for you and will be here if you ever want to talk.

Again, thank you. You've given me another shot at life, and I can never repay you. I had what I hope to be my final surgery, and I'm leaving the rehabilitation facility next week. I want to leave this behind me, and to do that, I had to clear the air.

Love,

Liza

I hiccup a sob, and the paper falls from my fingers, joining the rest of the mess on the floor.

CHAPTER
THIRTY

GRAY

"Sir, you can go back to Ms. Winter's room," the lady perched behind the reception desk says.

I stand, wiping my hands down my jeans, and nod. "Thank you."

"Of course. Have a good day."

I put one foot in front of the other and follow the signs to room 656. Each step gets harder, and every breath is more difficult. I may as well have been tackled on the pitch because every muscle in my body aches. *I might die here, and no one will know where to look for me.*

Until I walked inside the building, I was certain that I had to do this. Moving on with Astrid meant finding closure for the sins of my past. If not, I'd carry this weight into our relationship, and that would be the epitome of ruining her. I won't ruin anyone else except maybe myself.

I take a deep breath and blow it out. Shoving all thoughts of Astrid out of my mind, I knock on the door to room 656.

"Come in," Liza calls out.

God, please be with me. I tap the handle and let myself in.

Liza looks up from a book and smiles as if she expects me to be a staff person. But when her eyes land on mine, everything changes. "Oh, Gray."

"Hey."

She drops the book, tears streaming down her face, and sobs into her hands.

My heart breaks, knowing I did this—that I'm responsible for this woman's agony all this time later. I sit on the edge of the bed and wrap my arm around her, pulling her into my shoulder. Her dark hair bounces as she cries. It's the same color as Caroline's. I freeze, staring at the black strands, and feel my heart go from breaking to shattering.

I shouldn't be here. *Why did I do this?*

You're a fucking fool, Adler.

Liza pulls back, her cheeks streaked with mascara. She wipes her face with the backs of her hands and looks at me like I'm an apparition. I wish that were true. I'd happily disappear from this room and never come back.

"I can't believe you're here," she says, reaching for a tissue.

"That makes two of us."

She chuckles sadly, drying her face. She looks older than I remember. There are scars down her arms and one on the top of her forehead. I can only imagine the others on her back and stomach … and on her soul.

The worst scars are always hidden.

"How are you?" she asks softly. "Are you okay? You look great."

I lick my lips and look at the ceiling as shame and guilt threaten to knock me off the damn bed. It's not fair that I'm here and *looking great*, when Liza is sitting in a rehab bed after God knows how many surgeries, and Caroline is in a wooden box six feet below the ground. I'd love for someone to explain that bullshit.

"If it makes a difference, I want you to be great," she whispers.

Hot liquid pools in the corners of my eyes, and I blink as furiously as I can. I don't risk looking at her. I don't even try to speak. I stare at the wall like a fucking pussy and try not to cry.

"The accident wasn't your fault, and I hope you know that, Gray. We had no business coming to Denver, and you told us as much. But Caroline was too hardheaded to listen and …" Her shoulders rise and fall. "And God had another plan for my big sister."

"Do you believe that?" I ask, pulling my gaze to hers. "Do you believe she died because God had other plans for Caroline? Or do you think that the whole thing could've been avoided if I had driven my ass to the airport and picked the two of you up during a fucking snowstorm? Because one of those things seems more plausible than the other."

She shifts in her bed, wincing at the movement. "So you've decided that you're smarter than God now? That wasn't on my bingo card for this year."

"Liza …" I sigh, standing up. I need some space—some air. The windows never open in these places, but I stand by it and stare across the courtyard. "I'm sorry."

"For what, Gray?"

When I don't answer her, she releases a breath that sounds like it's been held in her chest since the accident. It's long and cold, frustrated and angry—and ready to move on. I get that. That's why I'm here, too.

If it weren't for Astrid, I wouldn't have had this conversation with Liza. I would've lived with the unknown and guilt for the rest of my life and been satisfied with the punishment. But Astrid makes me want more for myself so I can give it to her.

When I look into her beautiful green eyes and see the pain buried in them, I know I can help. *I want to.* Sometimes it feels like it's my reason for being on this earth. But I can't do that if this part of my life still feels like it's seeping puss out of an infected wound.

"Will you clear up something for me?" she asks. "Not that it matters now, but it's something that I've always wondered."

I look over my shoulder at her.

"Were you and Caroline dating when we flew in that night?"

"It doesn't matter."

She plants both hands on the white blanket and stares at me. "It matters to me."

"No," I say, wandering around the room. "We'd broken up. I'd broken up with her, to be exact. But you know Caroline—she'd fight tooth and nail to get what she wanted, and she claimed to want me." But that wasn't true. Maybe at one point it was, but it wasn't at the end. "I told her not to come, and when she called from the airport, I sent her to voicemail. I had no idea you two flew in or that you were going to drive through a snowstorm to get to my house."

Liza nods, as if she's waiting for me to drop a bomb that she suspects is lurking behind the scenes. I look up at her, and our gazes connect. I don't have to say anything.

Her face falls. "I knew it."

"She was stealing money from me to buy her drugs," I say, my voice hollow. "And if I didn't keep cash around and kept my cards on me, she'd pawn my shit. She stole my teammate's cash once when he came over to work out. She was out of control." *And nearly ruined my career after rumors started swirling that I was an addict, too.*

"Dear God."

"I got her to go to a rehab. Remember that trip she took to Florida?"

"Yeah. I knew it."

"I did everything I fucking could, Liza … except I didn't tell you." *Which just might be my greatest failure of all.* "When I finally broke up with her for good, I told her that I was going to call you. She promised me she was breaking the news to you because she was moving into your house. Was that a lie? Half the shit she said was a lie at the end. Was it easier to believe her?" I shrug. "Probably."

She lifts her chin, tears clouding her eyes again. "And should I have trusted my intuition and prodded her about it? Absolutely. But I didn't. Caroline was so good at making you believe things, and I fell for it."

Yeah, I know. That's how I fell for her.

"I should've handled things better," I say, swallowing past a lump in my throat. "I could've helped her more. I could've answered that fucking call. But I was being selfish like I always am and—"

"Don't." She glares at me. "Don't act like you're selfish, Gray Adler. How much money have you paid for my bed in this rehab center?"

I look away, the band wrapped around my chest threatening to snap.

"You say you're selfish," she says. "But you somehow found out that my insurance denied rehab after my first surgery, and you set up a blind trust and paid for it anonymously. *For two years.*" She shakes her head in disbelief. "I never could have afforded the care if it hadn't been for you. I might not have walked again, or fed myself, or brushed my teeth. But you, Mr. Selfish, made that happen for me without wanting any credit for it."

She weeps again, tears forming streams down her cheeks. I cough, sniffling back emotions that I don't want to handle right now.

I had no idea this would be her response. I was sure Liza hated me *because* of the accident. I came to see her in the hospital a week after the wreck, and she screamed at me to leave and never come back. So I didn't. But maybe I should have.

"Why did you decide to come here and see me?" Liza asks.

I shove my hands in my pockets. "You asked me to, and I thought it was the least that I could do for you." I pause, nibbling my bottom lip. "And I was hoping I could find some closure. I'm … I'm tired, Liza."

I'm tired of fighting for myself. I'm tired of feeling so hollow, feeling so bound … yet so utterly alone.

She holds her arms wide, and I hesitate before sitting on her bed again and letting her hug me. The contact breaks me. I cover my face with my hand and cry quietly, relieved to have found some relief from the guilt that's crushed me for so long.

I may never be able to get closure from my parents' death, but it is easier to internalize. If my father couldn't make it, I sure as hell wouldn't have done him any good. I just would've died beside him. That might've saved Mom, but she would've never been okay again without Dad. I know, in the deepest part of my heart, that Mom would've chosen to go out just like she did—in the middle of the night in Dad's arms.

"I'm sorry," I say, sniffling as I sit upright. Liza offers me a tissue, and I take it from her. "I feel like I let you and Caroline both down, and I'm sorry."

She pats my shoulder. "I'm sorry for not talking to you about this before now. It wasn't fair of me to let this pain fester in your soul for this long."

"You were kind of busy getting your body screwed back together," I say, grinning sheepishly.

"Hey, it should be fun going through a metal detector if I ever fly again. Can you imagine how that thing will light up?"

Her smile makes me chuckle—and it might be the first real, true, free laugh since the wreck.

"So tell me, what's your life like?" she asks. "Do you have a wife? Children? I see you're still quite the rugby star."

I roll my eyes, making her laugh. "No kids, no wife. But there is a woman who I'm serious about, and that's one of the reasons I came here, if I'm being honest with you."

"Why?"

"I needed to be able to make peace with this. This woman,

her name is Astrid, she deserves the best of me. And I think I stopped being the best of me the night Caroline died."

It wasn't just that Caroline died, but also because it created a Caroline-sized hole in Liza's life … who also lost her dreams. And I haven't been able to let go of that guilt. But I need to.

It's time.

She leans back against her pillows, wincing. "From here on out, let's agree not to assign blame for the accident. I'll say it was God, and you can say it was snow or whatever makes you happy. But it wasn't my fault, your fault, or her fault. Okay?"

"Okay," I say, wobbling forward. It's as if a weight has been pulled from my back suddenly, and I'm struggling to find my balance. A world without blaming myself for Caroline's death— *what kind of world will that be?*

I grin softly. *It'll be a world with Astrid.*

"You've given me my life back," I say earnestly, searching Liza's eyes. "I can't thank you enough for that."

"And you saved mine quite literally."

I stand, a hundred pounds lighter, and smile down at Liza. "If you need anything, call me."

"You are officially banned from helping me ever again," she says, laughing. "Go take care of your woman. Send me a Christmas card, if you must, but that's it."

I turn toward the door with my chin tucked to my chest.

"Gray?"

My hand on the knob, I turn to Liza. She's smiling at me.

"Thank you for coming," she says. "I needed this as much as you."

I nod, giving her a final look, and then slip out the door.

CHAPTER
THIRTY-ONE

GRAY

My headlights light up the dark, dead-end street as I creep my way toward Astrid's house. It takes every ounce of self-restraint not to slam on the gas and race the last few yards to her. But it's late, and people are probably sleeping, and I can't make my problem anyone else's … any more than I already have.

Astrid's car is in the driveway alongside a small blue coupe that I haven't seen before. *Who the hell is that?*

I park beside the curb and am practically out of the truck before I turn off the engine. I jog across the lawn, vaguely aware of the exhaustion settling in my bones, and rap my knuckles lightly against the door. There's too much energy coursing through me to stand still—too much anticipation of the upcoming conversation with Astrid, so I try to peek in the windows for any signs of life. I should've called her and warned her that I was close by, but figured I'd let her sleep as long as I can.

"Come on, sweetheart," I mutter, knocking again—a little louder this time. "Please answer the door."

Finally, a light turns on in the hallway, and the door handle turns.

I start to step forward, my heart in my throat and words touch my tongue, but I recoil when I realize it's not Astrid greeting me. It's taser girl.

"What are you doing here?" she asks, dressed in pajama pants and a tank top. Her hair is wild, and her eyes are groggy like she's been asleep.

"Is Astrid home?" I narrow my eyes, stopping myself. "I'm sorry. What's your name again?"

She sighs. "I'm Gianna, and you aren't seeing Astrid tonight, so fuck off." She starts to close the door, but I catch the edge with my hand.

"Excuse me?" I ask, flinching. "What do you mean that I'm not seeing Astrid tonight? She's expecting me. I told her that I was going to come by when I got back to town."

"Cool story, bro."

"Gianna, *please*," I say, unnerved by the look in her eyes. I've been through far too much today to deal with her. "I need to talk to Astrid."

She glances over her shoulder, then turns to me. The icicles she throws my way would kill a lesser man. "I'll tell you what you need, Gray, and that's to get in your truck and go home. I just got Astrid to fall asleep, which was no small feat tonight since you left her a fucking mess. She's finally resting, and you aren't waking her up. Period."

I left her a fucking mess? I lick my lips, as my mind spins. Yes, I talked fast on the phone, and it probably could've been construed to be suspicious, but she should know I'd come back and explain … *right?* "Is she mad that I left town?"

"The fact that you're asking that question is indicative of the problem." She lifts a brow. "Is she mad that you left town? Theoretically, I'd say no. But when you don't tell her and flee in the middle of the night, and she discovers on her own that you were not flying to an emergency like you said, but were rather meeting a woman named Liza in Colorado … yeah, Gray. It's a little suspicious." Her jaw flexes. "If you know anything about Astrid at all, you can deduce why this is a problem."

The porch drops out from under me. I blink once, then twice, trying to wrap my head around what Gianna just said.

There's no way that anyone knows where I went today. I told no one—not a single soul. *So, how does Astrid know about Liza?*

I gulp.

What else does she know?

I swallow a surge of panic and try to control my breathing. Getting frantic won't do anyone, least of all me, any good. *Oh God.* Bile creeps up my throat as the gravity of the situation lands on my head. She thinks I'm lying to her. She thinks there's another woman.

She probably thinks I've been playing her like every other man in her life has played her in the past.

I'm going to be sick.

"In order to expedite this conversation and get you out of my face, I'll throw you a bone since you seem to be … perplexed," Gianna says. "You left a letter on your kitchen counter."

"*Oh fuck.*" I hiss a breath, my heart pounding erratically.

I only read Liza's letter twice, because the first read fucked my head. It took everything in me not to throw something as the guilt ripped through me again. But the second time I read it, I saw … absolution. Even if that wasn't truly how I felt until I saw her, Liza's peace about her enormous loss snapped something in me.

She wasn't writing a letter full of blame and malice. She wrote a letter to … set me free.

And even though I can't see how Astrid could have misinterpreted those words, they were still words of warmth from another woman. I hate that Astrid believed I wasn't trustworthy, but I didn't imagine that she'd be reading something out of context, either.

"She doesn't know what she read. Please, Gianna, let me see her. Let me explain."

"If I had my taser, I'd tase you for fun."

I growl. "I'm not in the mood for your dark humor."

"Well, I'm not in the mood for you. So kick rocks, dude."

"I just need to explain … *Astrid!*"

She steps into the hallway behind her friend, looking shocked to see me. Her eyes are swollen, and her lips are puckered together. *She's been crying.*

My beautiful girl is broken because of me.

"Hey," I say, sidestepping an unhappy Gianna. "Hey, sweetheart. Let me explain."

"What is going on, Gray?" Astrid asks, the sound muffled by the emotion in her throat. Will she hear me out? Or has she already made up her mind? *Fuck. No. This woman … I can't lose her.*

"Want me to kick his ass out?" Gianna crosses her arms over her chest. "Give me the signal and I'll dropkick him to his truck."

I glare at her. "Stop it."

"You don't get to come in here and—"

Astrid clears her throat. Gianna and I both turn to her despite the tension rippling off us both. I halfway worry about turning my back on Gianna because if she stuck a knife in my back, I wouldn't be surprised. And, in some sick way, I might even respect her for it. At least one of us was standing up for Astrid tonight.

"He's already here," Astrid says, resigned. "I'll talk to him."

Gianna pushes the door closed, letting it slam on the hinges. She points at me as she walks to the guest room. "I'm not kidding. I'll slice your throat and swim in your blood if you make her cry again. Don't believe me? Try me. I know people."

"Thank you, Gianna," Astrid says, her voice raspy. But there's a glimmer of a smile that gives me hope.

"Keep this energy for people who are a real threat," I call after Gianna.

She flips me off. "Tread lightly, asshole." Then she's gone, disappearing around the corner.

I waste no time pulling Astrid into my arms, pressing kisses to the top of her head. *God, I've missed her. It's only been one day, yet being here feels like … I'm home.* She's rigid at first with her hands planted on my chest like she might push me away, but she gives in slowly and collapses against me.

Her back shakes, and I can hear faint, muffled cries. The sound slices through me like an ice pick to the heart. I don't know how to make it better—just that I must. It's my responsibility, and not just because I caused this.

Because she's my girl.

"Hey," I say, pulling back and taking her face in my hands, wiping tears away with my thumbs. "Are you okay?"

The look in her eye isn't the one I'm used to these days. It's sad but guarded … like she doesn't trust me.

"I have trust issues. I guess that's probably the crux of it. Every time I'm in a relationship, I have to defend myself."

"Astrid, sweetheart, listen to me," I plead. "I handled this all wrong. You should've never been in this position, and that's my fault. But I swear to you, it's not like you think."

"You let me walk into a situation and have to question everything I believed in about you—just like everyone else has done to me," she says, her bottom lip quivering. "No note, no conversation—well, there was a note. Unfortunately, not to me." She fake laughs before it turns into a whimper.

I want to kiss her pain away. I want to take over the conversation and make her hear me. But that's not what she needs. *She needs to be heard.* She needs to know that I value what she has to say, and that her feelings matter to me. I can't just brush them under the rug and make this about me … like everyone else has done before me.

"Your groceries were hot on your doorstep," she says,

knocking away a strand of hair stuck to the tears on her cheek. "What am I supposed to think? Where were you today that was so important that you couldn't tell me? That you lied to me?"

I take her by the hand and lead her into her bedroom. I shut the door softly, then sit next to her on the edge of the mattress. She keeps space between us, and I don't infringe on that. If she needs space, I'll give it to her. I'll give her anything she wants. She already has my heart in her hands. Everything else is a moot point.

"I flew to Denver," I say carefully.

"Why?"

I take a deep breath, reminding myself to go slow. I can't just skip over the details because I don't think they matter. They matter to Astrid.

"Gianna said you saw a letter in my apartment. That letter must have been really confusing," I say.

A solitary tear streams down her cheek. "This has to do with Caroline, doesn't it? The woman whose picture you got so angry about when I picked it up, that I quit my job."

"Yes. This has to do with Caroline."

She stares at the wall, sniffling. "What happened to her? And why were you paying for Liza to be in a hospital? I thought she was your … that you two were …" She faces me, her eyes red. "That's why the bonus money was so important to you, wasn't it?"

I nod.

And even though it's going to be hard, for the first time in forever, I need to be completely honest. I won't stay quiet like I did when rumors were flung around the world about me. No, with this woman, I can be honest. The rest doesn't matter.

"This is so confusing, Gray. I've sat with this all day, trying to put pieces of a puzzle together that I don't have the box for. I don't have any foundation for this. I can't make sense of it because I don't know who these people are, and you left me here thinking the worst." She swallows. "That letter was horrifying. It was heartbreaking, not just for Liza but also for you. When I thought about you reading that and how that must've felt, I just wanted to hold you and help you, because that couldn't have been easy. And then to realize that you didn't even bother to tell me anything ..." She smiles sadly. "It felt like you had a connection with these other people, and I had to take a back seat. Like you were just playing me."

She's right. Of course, she's right. That had to be how she interpreted it because it's the logical solution.

I run a hand over my head and try to focus. I can beat myself up about this later. Now's not the time.

"Astrid, I get why you thought that," I say, dropping my hands to my sides. "And the fact that you didn't just rage and, instead, worried about me and Liza while you dealt with your own pain says so much about you, and why you're the best person I've ever known."

Her shoulders slack, and it takes everything I can muster not to pull her into me.

"Ask me whatever you want," I say. "You're in control."

"I don't even have enough information to ask a pointed question."

"Should I start from the beginning?"

"Yeah," she says, the word barely a whisper.

Here we go ...

I take a deep breath. "I broke up with Caroline about two and a half years ago. We'd been dating for a while, a couple of years at most. I wouldn't say we were serious, really, because I never had any intention to marry her or be with her long term. But she was the closest thing to a serious girlfriend that I'd ever had."

Astrid nods slowly, taking in the information I'm sharing with her.

"At some point, Caroline became hooked on drugs," I say. "Before I realized what was happening, it got really ugly. I should've seen it earlier. There were signs, and I missed them."

She shifts on the bed, squaring her shoulders with mine. It's a good sign, I think, so I keep going.

"We fought a lot about it, and I ended up breaking up with her. She'd gotten kicked out of her apartment and had been staying with me. But when we broke up, she went to live with Liza, her sister. A part of me thought that if she changed environments and was with her family that she'd be better off. Maybe something about me or the traveling for the team or ... something was making her problem worse. Maybe she could get help somewhere else."

I sigh, the words sounding like they're coming from someone else—and I wish that were true.

"What happened to her, Gray?"

"It was a few days before New Year's, and Caroline insisted on flying up to Denver from Texas where their family was spending the holidays. I told her no, created a firm boundary, and held to it. I made sure she was safe and then stopped answering her calls. But she and Liza flew up anyway, and rented a car, and tried to drive to my apartment in a snowstorm." My stomach twists, squeezing so hard that I grimace. "A semitruck lost control and crashed into them, killing Caroline and almost Liza."

Astrid gasps, covering her mouth.

"I blamed myself," I say, wiping my nose. "Because I could've just answered the phone when she called that night. I should've. I was unfairly cold to Caroline, and I didn't have to be. If I hadn't, then maybe she'd still be with her family."

She touches my arm as if she's in shock. "I am so sorry. That's ... horrible." *It wasn't fun.*

"The last time I talked to her family before today was when her father threw me out of Caroline's funeral. He punched me in the face, and I just stood there and cried like a baby."

I felt so damn guilty, and it was like being back at my parents' funeral. The guilt had been crushing—devastating. I couldn't hold myself together. It was just too much.

"Oh, Gray …" She presses a quick kiss to my shoulder. "When did you get the letter?"

"Brooks gave it to me before we left Sugar Creek. Joe saw Brooks at the gas station and gave it to him to bring to me."

Her brows pull together. "Why did Joe have it?"

"Because he ran the blind trust I set up to pay for Liza's rehab care. I wanted it to be anonymous. I didn't know if she'd accept my help, and I had to do something."

Astrid gets up, pacing around her room. I sit and wait, because there's nothing else I can do. I'm at her mercy. My heart is in her hands.

Finally, after a few minutes, she stops.

"Why did you lie to me about where you were going?" she asks, the pain I haven't seen in a long time back in her eyes.

What did I tell her this morning? An emergency? I panicked and was overwhelmed, plucking a reason out of the air and figuring I'd explain later.

"If you'd shared this with me, I would've supported you, Gray. I would've wanted to be there for you. Instead, I'm fighting this internal battle between kicking you out and kissing you, and it's fucking with my head."

"I'm sorry."

"You lied to me. You told me I was safe with you, and then you made me question that."

She takes a deep breath, and I can practically see the way she collects herself playing across her features. Even hurt, she's beautiful. Everything I've ever wanted.

"You're right. I lied to you," I say. "I was impulsive and terrified, if I'm being honest. I didn't know what I was walking into, only that I had to do it. Because when Caroline died, Liza blamed me. They all did. That destroyed me in a way that I can't describe. It reminded me that they were the third and fourth people I've hurt while putting my career first." I gulp, squeezing my eyes closed as images of my parents flash to the forefront. "I had to find closure, Astrid." I open my eyes and find her gaze.

"Being with you lately? It's fucked with my head. Maybe this isn't the right time or place to tell you this, but when we're together, I can see us together. Like *really together*."

She swallows, otherwise not moving a muscle.

"And I couldn't think about that—I couldn't get my hopes up about being with you—when I know that I still held too much space for Caroline. Hell, I've been paying for Liza's rehabilitation bills for two years. How can I be with you if I have such enormous secrets?"

"You can't." She shrugs as if she can't decide whether she's resigned or angry. "Gray, I understand why you needed to see Liza. I respect that, and I'm glad you did it. It sounds like you both needed it to heal, and I'd never deprive someone of healing from their trauma."

"Because you're an angel."

"But I have to be honest, too. I'm hurt you didn't tell me about this. I told you *everything*," she says. "I was vulnerable. I shared things that humiliated me, and all the while, I explained to you that the things that hurt me the most were feeling invisible and being neglected emotionally. And then you withhold such important things—*things that matter*, and lie to me. That fucking hurts."

"*No, no, Astrid.* Don't you understand? I never would've gone to see Liza if it weren't for you. I would've just lived with the guilt and been miserable for the rest of my life. But you—*you* made me face it because *you* deserve more." I take her hands and pull her in front of me. "Did I just botch this whole thing? Probably. Did I make an impulsive decision? Yes. I absolutely didn't handle it the right way. But you matter to me so much that I got on an airplane today to get this behind me so I can be with you. I like who I am when I'm with you, Astrid. You've given me … purpose. And I like seeing you smile, and hearing you laugh— and I want more of both. *For you.* Let me be your person. Let me be the man you can depend on."

She laces our fingers together, watching them tangle. It

reminds me of being on my couch with her—the moment I realized that I'm falling in love with this woman. I can't tell her that tonight because it'll feel like I'm just saying it. But I can show her. And I will.

"I wish you would've told me. I would've wanted to be there for you," she says softly.

"And I appreciate that more than you can imagine." I take a shaky breath as my bones begin to ache from exhaustion. "Astrid, sweetheart, I'm sorry that I hurt you today. You're the only thing I care about. I've been fucked up in the head for two years, unable to pull my head out of my ass—nearly lost my reputation and my career over it. And I didn't give a fuck." I fight the burn in my chest and keep going. I have to get this all out in the open. "You gave me the courage to face my fear and find peace, to put the past where it belongs. Because you? You're my future."

Please, please believe me. Please don't push me away.

"What are you saying?" she asks, her eyes widening, tears filling them again.

"I'm saying that I'm probably going to mess up because I tend to do that. But I give you my word that I will never make choices without including you in them. I want us to be a team from here on out."

The corners of her lips tilt to the ceiling, and it's like a light shining in my soul.

"I'm giving you my heart because I know it's safe in your hands. And I want you to know that yours is safe in mine." I lean toward her. "Always."

She launches herself at me, letting me envelop her in my arms.

CHAPTER
THIRTY-TWO

"I really wish you had told me about this before now." Hartley sighs through the phone. "That was a lot to go through on your own."

Telling Hartley about Caroline and Liza wasn't something I ever planned on doing. But I've thought a lot about my relationships with the people in my life over the past few days. I got the idea, from my pap, probably, that being a good friend, or brother, or son, meant not sharing the hard parts of your life with them. The goal was not to be a burden.

But I've come to realize, or theorize, anyway, that I might have been wrong. Because sharing the darkest part of my life with Astrid has only brought us closer together. It freed up a part of me that had been … trapped. Sharing the dark weakens it, allowing more light to shine through.

"Yeah, I know," I say. "I should've said something. But I've put it behind me now and we're all good."

He chuckles. "I like this version of you."

"What version might that be?"

"You're a mortal, just like the rest of us."

My laughter joins his, and it feels good.

"So you're on the back end of the season," Hartley says. "Any plans for the offseason?"

I pace the kitchen as my stomach winds into a knot.

In a perfect scenario, I'd go back to Sugar Creek for the offseason. Find a little place back there to fix up and spend more time on the ranch. But that feels like a dickhead thing to do to Hartley—just come back when I want to and leave when I need to. All the while, he's stuck there every day.

"We have that cabin behind Baker's Pasture," he says. "It's been empty for five or six years now. I let Jasper crash in it from time to time, but it's yours if you want it."

I swallow hard. "Really?"

"Hell yeah, really. Why do you sound surprised?"

"Well, you know, I mean that I don't want to just waltz onto your ranch because I have a few months."

"I don't know why not." He sighs again. "Look, Gray, this ranch is mine because it's Alder land. Which means it's yours, too. It's my workplace, and will continue to be, but this place has been in our family for generations, and that will never change."

He's so much better of a man than I am.

"Don't get me wrong," he says, laughing. "Stay the hell off the equipment. You already lost one piece in the creek."

I smile. "Oh, come on. That was fifteen years ago."

"Again, you've already lost one in the creek. But this is your home, too. Or I want it to be if that makes you happy."

I rub my chest, massaging the tightness behind my ribs. It's a good pain. It's only there because I never expected to have this relationship with my brother again. I'd convinced myself he was pissed at me. Now, I realize that I made that up because it was easier for me to justify being gone.

"Maybe one day our kids will cause mayhem in these fields like we did," he says.

"We gotta have kids first, Hart."

"Yeah, and I gotta find a mama for my kids before that. Anyway …"

I frown, knowing that he's thinking about Mia right now. But he'll never bring her up. He hasn't for years.

"Speaking of women, where's Astrid?" he asks.

A smile stretches across my face as I look at the clock on the microwave. I've checked the time every twenty minutes for the past three hours, wondering what she's up to and if she's liking her surprise spa day. I had to form a truce with Gianna to figure out where she'd like to go and what treatments she might like best, and we got through it without me being threatened with a taser. That's progress.

"Astrid is at the spa getting pampered," I say.

"That's nice."

"She never does anything for herself. Her friend Gianna picked her up today for lunch, but she dropped her off at the spa instead." I look over my shoulder as the door unlocks from the keypad. "Hey, she's home. Can I talk to you later?"

"Anytime. Don't forget about that cabin, Gray."

I grin. "I won't. Thanks, Hart."

"Later."

I set my phone down as Astrid comes in wearing the softest yellow sundress. It causes her freckles to pop and her hair to shine. She's feminine and relaxed … and sexy as hell.

She tosses her keys and purse on the couch and then makes a beeline for me.

"You," she says, leaping into my arms. "You're tricky."

I pick her up as she wraps her legs around my waist. "You're gorgeous."

"Thanks to you." She dangles her arms off my shoulders and kisses me lazily. "Today was such a nice surprise. Thank you."

"You mentioned never having a massage the other night, so I thought you'd enjoy one." I kiss her again. "Because when I give them to you, I always wind up naked, and we forget about the massage."

She giggles.

"You enjoyed it, then?" I ask.

"Oh my gosh. I loved it. Like, *loved it.* I fell asleep twice, which was crazy. I feel like a brand-new person."

"Good," I say, setting her on the counter. "Because I bought three day passes for you and your friends to go this weekend. Gianna said she and Audrey were available, so I thought it would be fun for you to have a girls' day."

She smacks my shoulder. "You did not."

I nod, grinning at how happy she looks.

"You don't have to do this, you know. Spas are so expensive."

"I'm going to spoil the shit out of you," I say, planting kisses across her jaw and down her throat. "You've entered your spoiled era."

She giggles again, turning her head to give me more access. "God, that feels good."

"Dinner is being delivered in about an hour," I say, nibbling on her earlobe. "Do you want to take a walk or something?"

"Just because I said I missed my walking pad while I work doesn't mean I want to take walks with you." She pulls away and grins mischievously. "But I love that you listen."

"Want to tell me anything else?"

She takes my hand and scoots to the edge of the counter. Her legs spread wide.

I swallow, my body temperature rising as she lowers my hand between her thighs.

"Yes, Mr. Adler, I would," she says, guiding my fingers through her slit. She's hot and wet and so fucking soft. "I'd like you to know how much I'd love to be on my hands and knees while you pound me from behind." She leans back, pushing my fingers into her. "I've thought about you all afternoon."

"I can tell."

She bats her lashes as I sink another finger into her, twisting them to hit the spot she loves so much. Instantly, she moans.

"I had to jack off in the shower after work," I say, rubbing her clit.

She sucks in a hasty breath. "What did you think about?"

"Your mouth sucking me off, and how your pussy clenches around my cock just before it explodes."

"If you keep doing that," she says, groaning, "I'll explode on your hand."

I pull one strap of her dress down, and then the other. The fabric pools at her waist. I lift one of her tits out of her bra, appreciating how it hangs over the edge in the most perfect teardrop.

As soon as my mouth hits her nipple, her moan grows louder. Every octave it rises, so does my cock.

Her hips flex, grinding against my hand as I work my fingers into her.

"Do you want to fuck my fingers?" I ask, supporting her back with my free hand. "Grind on me. Use me to make yourself feel good."

"I'd rather it be your cock," she says, her eyes fluttering shut.

I flick her nipple with my tongue. "It will be. But I want to watch my girl come right here."

Her legs begin to shake, and she reaches for my shoulders to brace herself.

"Dammit, Gray," she says through clenched teeth, her nails digging into my skin. "*Fuck!*"

"You're so beautiful," I say, whispering in her ear. "It makes me so hard watching you get off like this. You have no idea how perfect you are."

Taking her cues, I ease my motions and let her fall gently back to reality. She sags against me, blowing her hair out of her face.

"That was so good," she says, wincing as I remove my hand from her thighs.

"Do you still want to be fucked doggy style?"

She licks her lips, her eyes darkening. "Blow job or doggy style. Your turn to pick."

"If you think I'll ever pick anything over your pussy, you're wrong."

She laughs as I toss her over my shoulder and carry her into the bedroom.

Someday, she'll learn that she'll always get what she wants from me. And, until then, I'll have fun proving it.

CHAPTER
THIRTY-THREE

ASTRID

What a week.

I knock on Renn's door, balancing my bag on my shoulder. I've run around this morning like a chicken with its head cut off. Renn's mom, Rory, is in town and needed help with a few things, and I offered my services. I always jump in if any of the Brewers need assistance—except Tate, if I can help it—and Rory's errands weren't hard. Just time-consuming.

But it's Friday. And I'm in love.

Gray and I haven't said that we love each other, but ever since he returned from seeing Liza a few weeks ago, I know it's true. I can feel it. We've had many talks about our past, and he's been an open book in the best way. He's taken me back to Sugar Creek to visit his family and friends and showed me around the little town and all his childhood haunts. We keep saying that we're taking things slow, but I don't know what that means anymore. I can't think of the last night I spent alone.

"Come in," Renn says.

I push my way into his office and close the door behind me. "Hey."

"Hey to you." He sits up in his chair. "Thanks for your help with Mom today. She's usually so on top of her shit, but this new boyfriend of hers has scrambled her brain."

I laugh, biting my lip because what's going through my head —that more than Rory's brain is probably getting scrambled— wouldn't be a welcome response to my boss.

Renn lifts a brow. *Yup. I was right. Not welcomed.*

Setting my bag on the floor, I take the seat I always choose and grab my clipboard for notes. "So what do you have for me?"

"How are you, Astrid?"

I balk. "I'm fine," I say slowly. "Why are you being weird?"

He chuckles.

"You're freaking me out," I say, chuckling too.

"First things first," he says, fiddling with a pen. "Where do we stand on my wife's party?"

I glance down at my list. "The only thing we're waiting on is a playlist that Ripley is putting together. I still don't know why you let him take control of that," I mumble, much to Renn's amusement. "Gannon has literally doubled the security at his own expense. He said that if his kids are there with a bunch of strangers ..." I look at Renn and shrug. "I just let him have it. You can't tell Gannon no and survive to tell the tale."

"Hey, as long as he's paying for it."

I laugh. "Jason is making sure we have a plane to bring the Carmichael family up from Florida. There was a slight issue because they're bringing so many people, but Jason's working it out. And that's it." I smile brightly. "You're good to go."

"Where did we wind up on the attendee count?"

"Two hundred and twelve, give or take. You know a lot of people, my guy."

"The problem is that everyone loves my wife." He winks at me. "You and Gray are coming, right?"

I sit back in my chair and sigh.

Renn was so great when he found out that Gray and I were together. I worried about telling him—afraid that he'd find it a conflict of interest or think that I was unprofessional for getting involved with a coworker. His response? He laughed and said that it was about time. Apparently, he suspected this was going to happen when he learned that Gray defended me in the locker room back when we still hated each other.

I'm glad he suspected it because I sure as hell didn't.

"We actually can't make it," I say. "Thank you for the invitation, though."

"What better thing do you have to do than come to a huge party that the best party organizer in the world organized?"

I snort. "Calling me a party organizer is a reach itself, but I'll accept your compliment." I grin at him. "Gray and I are going to the ranch. It's Cathy's birthday. She's a woman who has worked there for years and is like family to them. Gray and Hartley are throwing her a surprise party. I planned that one, too."

"That's fair. Just know you're welcome to show up. You're like family to us."

Renn throws that line out there like it's not a big deal, but it literally stops me in my tracks. *"You're like family to us."* I look away, batting back tears, because at some point over the past few weeks, I've turned into a person with feelings.

It's so gross, as Gianna would say.

A knock raps on the door behind me. My gaze lands on a set of broody and familiar deep brown eyes.

"What are you doing here?" I ask, gripping the armrests so I don't spring off this chair and rip his clothes off right here. *I told him not to leave the house in gray sweatpants.*

A slow smirk settles against his lips.

"Bastard," I whisper as he sits next to me.

He laughs. "Hey, Renn."

"Hey, Gray. Good to see you. Ready for the game this weekend?"

"If you're asking me if I'm ready to bring a title home to Nashville, then the answer is yes."

"Glad to hear it." He pulls out a drawer and then flops a

stack of papers onto the center of his desk. "I have something to show you."

Gray's brows pull together as he scoots to the edge of his chair and takes the papers. He scans them, not bothering to give me any indication as to what it's about, and then pulls his gaze to Renn's.

"Are you joking?" he asks, jaw slack.

"Nope."

"But I thought this wouldn't be decided yet," Gray asks slowly.

Renn smirks. "I'm the boss. It's a perk of the job to be able to do what you want, when you want to do it—if it fits within the league rules, of course."

"It's super rude to have a conversation with me sitting here and not tell me what you're talking about," I say.

Gray turns the papers so I can see the front page. Contract extension is written in bold letters at the top.

I cover my mouth to hide my gasp, my eyes growing as big as saucers.

"You deserve it, Adler," Renn says. "I've seen the change in you that I hoped to see. As I believe I said to Astrid not long ago, you're one of the best players in your position in the league. Something was holding you back, and I knew that once you worked through that, I'd be the luckiest CEO in the league. You showed up for the team, but you really showed up for yourself. And that's the most important thing." He smiles. "I'm really proud of you."

Gray slowly puts the papers back on Renn's desk. It's clear he's shocked and a bit stupefied, but over the moon at the same time.

I grab his bicep and squeeze. My sleeve pulls back just far enough to show the new tattoo on my wrist, a queen chess piece. Gray beams, running his hands down his face, giving me a clear shot of his king chess piece tattoo on his wrist in the same spot. He offered to cover the snowflake on his thigh, the one he got after Caroline's accident, but I told him to keep it. She's a part of his story, and covering a tattoo wouldn't make that go away. Besides, your history—the people, places, and experiences—make you who you are. And I happen to quite like the man he's become.

"That means a lot to me, Renn," Gray says, blowing out a breath. "Thank you for everything. You saved my life in a lot of ways."

"That's me. A lifesaver." Renn laughs. "You saved yourself. She probably didn't hurt things." He winks at me. "Your agent will get these papers later today. But I wanted you to relax going into championship week knowing that you're a Royal for the foreseeable future."

Gray stands and shakes Renn's hand. "I couldn't be prouder to represent this organization. Thank you for the opportunity to play here."

"Wait," I say, getting to my feet too. I try my best to appear sober. "Does this mean I have to work with him, too? Or am I done being this guy's assistant at the end of next week?"

They both laugh, not taking me seriously at all.

I laugh, too. "No, but seriously."

"Let's see how things go," Renn says, smoothing his tie down his chest. "But don't get any ideas, Miss Lawsen. Whether you work for him or not, you still work for me. And don't let my brothers try to poach you, either."

"Trust me," I say, picking up my bag. "The two of you are enough to keep me busy." *And satisfied.* But only one of them satisfies me in *that* way. Daily. In multiple ways.

We say our goodbyes, and I follow Gray into the hallway. The office is buzzing. We dodge the staff, Gray's hand locked in mine until we get to the elevators. Once the doors close, we sigh.

"Congrats," I say, kissing him.

"Careful." He nips my bottom lip between his teeth. "You should stop doing that."

I pull back. "Why?"

He glances down at his crotch, and I'm immediately reminded of why I told him not to wear those sweats.

"I'm done for the day," he says. "What about you?"

"Yup. I'm on my way home."

"Let's go to Stupey's for dinner—after I change, of course."

We exit the elevator and make our way through the lobby. Jory and Breaker shout at Gray from The Royal Café as we pass, but he just waves at them and keeps walking.

"I can go by the store and grab things for dinner," I say, squinting against the sun. "It'll be much cheaper than eating out, and I have to call Audrey back. She just found out that her crush got married last weekend."

Poor Audrey. She took the news—in the form of a Social post that her brother commented on—better than expected. But she's still devastated.

He groans. "I told you. I have money now. Joe called me this morning, letting me know that the trust to take care of Liza has been dissolved."

I'm not sure what to say to that, so I just nod.

From the sounds of things, Liza's body has gone through so much trauma, but she's finally healing—inside and out. The doctors tell her she doesn't need any more procedures, and she's also found an amazing therapist. She started making podcasts, from what I hear, which is bringing in some income, and it's making what was an absolutely awful event into something positive.

"Joe also told me that he forwarded you the correspondence he received from the landlord's attorney. They've assured him that they won't be coming after you. If they have anything else to say, they're to send it to him, and he'll take care of it."

I reach for Gray's hand, lacing our fingers together.

I did it. I'm free.

Now, if only they find Trace and make that sucker pay, there will be justice in the world.

The air smells prettier, and the wind feels gentler as we walk through the parking lot. Gray's ridiculous truck is parked next to my little car. The sight of them makes me smile. Who would've thought the day that I marched to his window and gave him a piece of my mind it would lead to this? That the asshole honking his horn at me to hurry would be the same man helping me clear up problems created by men before him?

"So Stupey's?" Gray asks, leaning against my car. "Let me spoil you."

"Let you? *Gray*. There's no letting you do anything. You just do what you want and hope for the best."

"I don't know what you mean," he says, smirking.

I roll my eyes. "Let's see. You sent my friends and me on a spa day last weekend. You booked a vacation to the beach after the season is over for the two of us. Hartley called a couple of days ago, asking me what color to have the guys paint the cabinets in your cabin on the ranch."

"Our cabin, but semantics."

My heart swells, filling with more love than I ever could've imagined having for anyone. I don't deserve Gray Adler—even though he says that about me. I don't know what the future holds, exactly, but I do know one thing.

It'll be with him.

Actually, I know two things. It will also be happy. Rich, because I've found a man who not only values and hears me, but makes my happiness his priority. I know he'll never weaponize my weaknesses, and he'll never do anything to crush me or my dreams. *How I found this man will never cease to amaze me.*

"Fine," I say, tossing my bag in my car. "Stupey's for dinner."

"Great."

"Great." I kiss his cheek. "I'll see you at your house?"

"Sure. See you at home." He turns away before I can correct him. "Oh, Astrid?" He grabs his cock through his pants. "No car chess. Straight inside. Got it?"

I laugh. "Bet I beat you home."

"Home, huh?"

I blush. "Yeah, home."

His smile stretches from ear to ear as he reaches for me. I fall happily into his arms—right where I'm supposed to be.

EPILOGUE

ASTRID

The crowd is *electric.*

"Roy-als! Roy-als! Roy-als!" I yell along with over half of the eleven thousand people watching the championship game between the Royals and the Bulldogs.

The stadium's packed. Even the overflow areas are filled with rugby fans, many of them wearing Adler on the back of their jerseys. It took me a moment to get my bearings this afternoon when I saw the outpouring of love for Gray. He always has fans at games, but nothing like this. I hope he takes a second to appreciate it today. *To know he deserves it.*

"Do you have any idea what's happening?" I ask Hartley, not sure if he can hear me over the roar around us. I twirl my star earring and watch the chaos below us. I have no idea what's going on. *I need to watch a movie about rugby before next season.*

He chuckles. "Yes. We're in a good spot."

I glance at the scoreboard, wondering if I should point out that it's still 21-21, and the time is winding down. It seems like a legitimate time to be nervous.

"Let's go, Adler!" Hartley shouts, but there's no way in the world Gray can hear him. I can barely hear myself think.

Gray searched the stands until he found our little posse before the game began. I will never forget the look in his eyes as they grazed over the line of bodies there to cheer him on. Audrey, Gianna, and I sit in a line in Adler jerseys that Audrey added glitter and sparkles to, so we stand out. Hartley, Jasper, and Cathy met us here. Thanks to another surgery on his shoulder, Brooks is the only one missing.

"I'm so stressed," Audrey says, chewing on a nail. "I don't know what to yell or when to cheer. I just wait for you to do it, and I join in."

I keep my eyes on number nine on the pitch. "I'm waiting on Hartley, so no judgment here." Hartley whistles, clapping and shouting as a Royals player speeds down the grass. "Yay! Go faster!"

"Did you just say *'go faster'*?" Gianna asks, laughing.

I cringe as the player gets knocked down by a huge Bulldog and is shuffled to yet another Royal. "I'm not cut out for this." I peer over the guy in front of me to try to find Gray again. "Come on, guys!"

"Go, Gray!" Cathy shouts, shaking her purple and gold pompom.

Less than a minute is left. The tension is thick in the stadium, with the crowd on their feet as if their leaning and dodging tackles from the stands will help the guys on the field. I do my part just in case there's rugby magic that I don't know about.

"Here we go." Hartley bumps my arm, his eyes glued to the pitch. "Astrid, you'd better be watching."

"Watching what?" My heart pounds as I bounce on my toes. "What are we looking at?"

Number Two from the Royals throws it into a group of players from both teams, which feels like a terrible plan, but no one else seems panicked about it. He falls to the ground, and

Gray picks up the ball and shuffles it out to another purple jersey.

I yell, clasping my hands tightly in front of me. *Ten seconds left.*

Our player bursts down the field, causing the crowd to erupt. A blue jersey finally cuts in front of him just before the tryline, forcing our guy to make a decision. I think he's going to cut it to the left. His body moves that way, as does the blue jersey. But the ball flies to the right … into the arms of Gray.

Oh my God. "Go, Gray!"

Audrey clutches my arm, her nails biting into my skin. "Go, Gray!"

He races forward, splitting two blue jerseys, before he leaps across the tryline on his stomach.

I scream, jumping up and down, as the time hits zero. Gianna and Audrey form a group hug, all of us bouncing around too much to do much but knock a beer out of a guy's hand who was sitting beside Gianna.

"Roy-als! Roy-als! Roy-als!"

We join in the chant, tears streaming down my face as I watch Gray run around the pitch in celebration with his teammates.

I glance at Hartley. He's chuckling—standing like a proud parent—practically beaming. He looks over his shoulder at me and grins.

"I wish our parents could see this," he says, biting his bottom lip and struggling to stay composed. "They were so proud of him." He smiles. "Thank you."

"For what?"

"You brought my brother back to me. I can't thank you enough."

Fucking emotions. Tears stream down my cheeks as Hartley pulls me into a hug. It's not as warm as Gray's, nor as strong, and it doesn't smell as good either since I got Gray to start using fabric softener. But this hug feels different. It feels important. It's one I won't forget.

"Miss Lawsen?" A man wearing a security suit pokes his head around the side of Jasper. "Follow me."

"Go," Hartley says. "He'll take you down to Gray."

I look over my shoulder at my friends, who shoo me away.

"Tell him we're proud of him," Hartley says as I walk by.

Jasper smiles at me as I slide by him, and Cathy pulls me into a quick hug. Rivers of mascara streak her cheeks. I hope Gray gets to see that today.

The guard says nothing as we pick our way down the stairs and through the crowd. I stick close to him through a gate and step onto the grass. Despite the mass of bodies and the pure pandemonium, my gaze immediately finds Gray's.

I run to him, ignoring the guard telling me not to run, and meet Gray in the middle of the pitch. He gathers me into his grassy, sweaty arms, hauls me into his soaked chest, and swings me around in a circle.

I feel like I'm floating in a dream.

"You're amazing," I whisper into his ear. "We're all so proud of you."

He finds the spot he loves in the crook of my neck and presses a kiss there, letting it linger a few long moments. Even though we're surrounded by players and their families, and by the media and the team staff, it feels like it's just the two of us. Maybe it is just the two of us.

"Good work today." Breaker smacks Gray on the back.

Gray pulls away and looks up at him. Something happens between the two of them, something I can't hear or understand. But Gray nods at him.

"You too, Break."

"I want to apologize to you, Astrid, for how I acted in the locker room," Breaker says. "I was an ass."

What? "Um, yeah. Thanks, Breaker. I appreciate that."

Gray clasps Breaker's hand before he walks away.

"I didn't expect that," I say, shaking the shock out of my system.

Gray grins, his dimples setting deep in his cheeks. "I did."

Yup. Something happened between them.

I stretch my arms over his shoulders and gaze up into those pools of expensive chocolate—like the kind you get on Valentine's Day. "How do you suggest we celebrate this victory, champion?"

"I suggest we celebrate by moving in together."

His response catches me off guard. Instead of answering, I just stare at him like a goof.

"If you don't want to, I understand," he says. "And there's no pressure. But I was just thinking that I can take better care of you if we officially live together." He pauses before a slow grin crosses his lips. "You know, since I love you and all."

I start to laugh in disbelief, but the sound fades into a hiccup, which turns into tears.

"Is that a yes?" he asks, his eyes shining.

"That's a yes. Because, you know, I love you, too, and all."

Gray lifts me again and spins me around, my giggle trailing behind us. He puts me down and glances back up in the stands.

"They're all here," he says like he doesn't believe it.

"Yeah. They're all here."

His attention drifts back over to me, and he drags his thumb down my cheek. "You're the best thing that ever happened to me."

"So you don't hate me anymore?" I tease.

He laughs, taking my hand and rubbing my ring finger on my left hand. I don't know if that's a hint or a subconscious gesture, but I'm glad he knows me well enough to know that I need to go slow. He's my person, and I have no doubt that I will be Mrs. Gray Adler one day.

But this day? Today, I'm happy being his number one fan.

ASTRID'S COLUMN

Dear I Need Help,

Your question has left me stumped for a few weeks. Every time I start to respond, I see another angle to consider.

Keep in mind—I'm not a professional. You should consider making an appointment with one and hearing them out.

My gut instinct is that this isn't about flirting, nor is it about boundaries. Your letter doesn't read as someone with low confidence, either. I bet you're a strong and successful woman who knows what she brings to the table. (Go, you!)

If we were sitting down for a glass of wine, I'd ask you how often you and your man have honest conversations. How vulnerable are you with one another? Do you feel safe enough in your relationship to speak freely about who you are and what you need?

Because something is amiss here, and you know it. Your lack of empathy for your boyfriend's opinion and his needs says a lot, too.

Hold off on the wedding until you can be honest enough with yourself to figure out why you need this attention, and until you feel safe enough with him to explain it and be heard.

You deserve to be happy. So does he.

Not every story has a villain. But if you don't do the work to find happiness—whatever that looks like for you—you could wind up being the villain in your own story.

I'd hate to see that happen.

A.

Renn Brewer's book, THE PROPOSAL, is live now on Amazon and Audible. Chapter One is next for your reading pleasure.

MORE FROM ADRIANA LOCKE

Chapter One
Blakely

"Could you die quietly?" Ella sighs, pulling her sunglasses down and squinting into the sunlight. "And maybe do it over there, please?"

Two quintessential frat boys, a label I'd bet my life on yet feels like a disservice to fraternities everywhere, cease their constant complaints about being hungover. Their whining is a show, a pathetic effort to gain attention, and one we're over—especially Ella.

They fire a dirty look at my best friend. She cocks a brow, challenging them right back, and waits.

Lying on the chaise next to her, I smirk. *How many seconds will it take for them to realize they're outgunned by a five-foot-three pistol with bubble-gum pink toenails?*

Eight … Nine … Ten …

They gather their things quietly, watching Ella like she might toss them into the pool if they don't act quickly enough.

I wouldn't be shocked if that happened, either.

Ella St. James doesn't surprise me much anymore. She carried a tray of freshly baked snickerdoodle cookies when she rang my doorbell three years ago. She was adorable, wearing an apron with embroidered cherries and a white silk ribbon in her hair while welcoming me to the Nashville neighborhood. It starkly contrasted with the following weekend when she took me out so I could *get acquainted with the city*. That night ended with Ella jacking some guy's jaw for trying to grope me on the dance floor and me picking her up from the police station in an Uber at three in the morning.

"Thank you," she says, sliding the glasses up her nose and returning to her book.

Las Vegas is sweltering. Blue water sparkles just inches from our feet, and I swear it only amplifies the sun's rays. We should probably get a massage or go shopping to beat the unbearable heat, but I didn't fly for almost four hours to stay inside.

I could've celebrated my new job and birthday like that in Tennessee.

"How do you think I would look with red hair?" I ask, stretching my legs in front of me. "Not bright cherry red, but a more purple-y, crimson-y red."

"No."

I furrow my brows. "That wasn't a yes or no question."

"I was cutting to the chase." Her fingertip trails along the bottom of the paperback. "That's not the question you were really asking."

It wasn't? I settle against my chair. *Yeah, it wasn't.*

It was a last-minute attempt at being young and reckless before I turn thirty tomorrow.

This whole birthday crap has been a bit of a mind fuck.

I've lived the past ten years with little abandon. I've traveled, dated, and swam with sharks. Went on a ten-city tour with a rock band. Attended a movie premiere, got engaged (and unengaged), and ate pizza at the world's oldest pizzeria in Naples. *Check that off the bucket list.* And with every year of fun, I assumed I had nothing to worry about—that I would have my shit together before I turned thirty and became a real adult.

That was an incorrect assumption.

By all accounts, I should be in a stable relationship and burdened with a mortgage and enough debt to bury my soul until Jesus returns. Appliances should excite me. I should have a baby. *I should understand life insurance.* Instead, I just broke up with *another* bad boy with commitment issues, re-upped the rental contract on my townhouse, and refilled my birth control.

But that all ends in six hours. I have to turn over a new leaf when the sun comes up. It's time.

Ella's book snaps closed. "This is not a tri-life crisis, Blakely. It's just a birthday."

"I know that."

"But do you?"

"*Yes, I do*," I say, mocking her. "I'm not in crisis mode. I'm just transitioning into this new era of buying eye cream and freezing my eggs, and it's a little … terrifying."

She sighs. "You've been buying eye cream for years."

"Yeah, as a hedge against the future. This *is* the future."

Ella rolls onto her side, brushing her dark hair off her shoulder. "While I can't relate because I have a solid two years before I'm thirty—"

"Was that necessary?"

She laughs. "You're freaking out for no reason. Tomorrow is just another day."

"I know. *I really do.* There's just this pressure to get my ducks in a row and start making serious progress, or else I'll be fifty with no husband or kids. And I want both."

"All I ask is that you be a little more selective on the husband part because the last few guys you've dated ..." She whistles. "Not good, Blakely."

Yeah, I know.

"I know you feel your biological clock ticking or whatever it is, but you *have* been doing big things," she says. "You're the new artist manager assistant at Mason Music Label. Remember, you little badass? That's impressive."

I shrug happily at the reminder. That's true—a dream come true, really. *And even more of a reason to get my shit together.* "But would I be even more impressive as a redhead?"

"The answer is still no."

I groan. "*Come on.* I want to go out on something big. Something fun. Something wild that I'll remember while I'm taking vitamins and going to bed before ten."

Ella reaches for her water. "Fine. But let's find something else. Red doesn't suit your skin tone."

"Like what? I'm not getting anything pierced, and I don't think I'm ready to commit to a tattoo."

"You've been wanting a tattoo since the day I met you. As a matter of fact, weren't you looking at tattoos when I brought over those cookies?"

I laugh. "Yes. But it's so permanent. What if I don't want it next week?"

She rolls her eyes.

"What else is there?" I ask. "Let's think."

"Well, you could find a man with money and get a quickie wedding on the Strip."

I laugh again, turning over onto my stomach. "At this point, that's the only way I'll get married—inebriated and to a stranger." *The guys I date aren't marriage material. I'll probably be alone forever at this rate.*

"Hey, people find love in all sorts of ways."

"True, but the odds that I'll find a marry-able man in the next few hours is incredibly low." I fold my arms under my head. "In lieu of sexy strangers with an engagement ring in their pocket, what else do you suggest?"

She taps a finger to her lips. "We could go to a show tonight. A male striptease or something like that. It might be a way to get your juices flowing—"

"*Ew!*"

"*While lacking permanence.* Then just see where the night takes us. Be free-spirited."

"You just want to go because it's one more way to needle Brock."

Her grin is full of mischief. "So? What's your point?"

Ella and my brother have been *a thing* for almost two years. *What kind of thing?* I'm afraid to label it, although I'm fairly certain they're exclusive without declaring exclusivity.

On the one hand, Ella is a lot to handle. She's smart, opinionated, and doesn't need a man—and she knows it. She also has a propensity to make decisions and weigh the risks after. That drives Brock nuts.

On the other hand, dating Brock would be a nightmare. Women throw themselves at him wherever he goes. Men stop him for autographs and to *man-swoon* over him. And during the season, he's focused and mostly unavailable. That doesn't always work for Ella.

I watch this back-and-forth and vow never to get into a relationship with a player—an athlete or otherwise. *Again.* I've done that before, and it didn't end well.

"I'm taking it you two are still fighting," I say.

"We aren't fighting. There's nothing to fight about." She lifts her chin to the sky. "I'm right, and he's wrong. That's all there is to it."

"I agree. You're right this time."

Her eyes widen. *"You're damn right I'm right.* I'm not putting up with him taking off to Miami with his friends and not even mentioning our anniversary."

"How can you have an anniversary if you aren't in an official relationship?" I snicker. "Isn't that what you always tell me? That you aren't in an official relationship with him?"

She waves a hand through the air, dismissing my question. "It's a prelationship, but that doesn't change anything in this circumstance."

"A *what?*"

"A *prelationship.* The formative stage where boundaries and expectations are established so you can determine if the other person is willing to abide by them." She pauses. *"Brock isn't."*

I roll my eyes and let it go. They'll settle this before Brock returns from Miami and we're home from Vegas. I've seen it too many times to count.

"Then fine," I say, sitting up. "Let's go to a show. But if my brother asks whose idea it was, I'm not taking the blame."

"Tell him it was mine. *I want him to know.* A little competition never hurt anyone."

"Competition for your non-boyfriend?" I ask, grinning.

"Precisely."

I shake my head as a bead of sweat trickles down my face. I wipe it away with the back of my hand. "I'm ready to go in and grab a shower."

"And I need to make reservations for dinner." She sits up, slipping on her flip-flops. "You owe me, you know."

"What do I owe you for?"

"For depriving me of my right as your best friend to throw you the most outrageous, amazing birthday party that Nashville has ever seen." She stuffs her water bottle in her bag. "I'm known in certain circles as the girl who throws the best bashes. I can only wonder what everyone is thinking about this."

I laugh at her ridiculousness, slipping my cover-up over my

head. "You've thrown me a huge birthday party every year I've known you. You can miss this one. It won't hurt."

She frowns. "Maybe it won't hurt *you*, but it pains *me*. I have a reputation to uphold."

"You'll survive."

I drop my phone, towel, and water bottle into my bag. I skim the area around me to ensure I have everything.

"Ready?" she asks.

"Yeah." A bubble of excitement fills me. *Let the birthday festivities commence.* "Let's go find trouble."

Ella shares my smile as we slide our bags on our sun-kissed shoulders. I spot my book under her chair and grab it. *How did it get there?*

As I stand, my gaze falls on Ella. Her wide eyes are twinkling. I've seen this look enough times to know things are about to get real.

"What?" I ask, frozen in place.

Her grin pulls wider. "I think trouble just found us."

Oh no.

This book is live now on Amazon and Audible.

ABOUT THE AUTHOR

Adriana Locke is a USA Today and Amazon Charts Bestselling author with a knack for writing swoony, unforgettable contemporary romances. At nineteen, she traded her small-town roots for big-city life, only to realize her heart beats for quiet mornings and cozy chaos. These days, she's living her happily-ever-after in Ohio with Mr. Locke—her high school sweetheart—four lively sons, and two hilariously hyper Jack Russell terriers.

When she's not penning love stories that will leave you laughing and sighing, Adriana is battling the epic quest of missing silverware, "gardening" (a.k.a. chatting with her plants), or leaving her grocery list on the counter as she heads to the store. Grab a cup of coffee, settle in, and let her books whisk you away to a world of heartwarming romance and irresistible heroes.

www.adrianalocke.com